CU00839244

The three MINDER BACK AGAIN and MINDER – YET AGAIN! are based on the popular television series created by Leon Griffiths, starring Dennis Waterman and George Cole.

Here at last in a Sphere omnibus edition.

To Gordon
Best wish
George Cole

Also by Anthony Masters in Sphere Books:

BOON

LEAVE IT OUT ARTHUR!

The MINDER series:
MINDER
MINDER – BACK AGAIN
MINDER – YET AGAIN!

Anthony Masters

SPHERE BOOKS LIMITED

SPHERE BOOKS LTD

Published by the Penguin Group
27 Wrights Lane, London W8 5TZ, England
Viking Penguin Inc., 40 West 23rd Street, New York, New York 10010, USA
Penguin Books Australia Ltd, Ringwood, Victoria, Australia
Penguin Books Canada Ltd, 2801 John Street, Markham, Ontario, Canada L3R 1B4
Penguin Books (NZ) Ltd, 182–190 Wairau Road, Auckland 10, New Zealand

Penguin Books Ltd, Registered Offices: Harmondsworth, Middlesex, England

MINDER First published in Great Britain
by Sphere Books Ltd 1984
MINDER – BACK AGAIN First published in Great Britain
by Sphere Books Ltd 1984
MINDER – YET AGAIN! First published in Great Britain
by Sphere Books Ltd 1985

MINDER © Leon Griffiths Limited 1984
MINDER – BACK AGAIN © Leon Griffiths Limited 1984
MINDER – YET AGAIN! © Leon Griffiths Limited 1985

1 3 5 7 9 10 8 6 4 2

Printed and bound in Great Britain by
Richard Clay Ltd, Bungay, Suffolk

Publisher's Note

Minder

PART ONE

The occasion was not distinguished.

'It's a fight for the undiscerning fan,' said Arthur as he disconsolately watched the two fighters limping round the ring. It was a heavyweight bout and looked as if the two veterans were boxing from memory – from a distant memory. The punches were hard when they came but the gaps in between them seemed endless.

'Fair fight, eh?' commented Harry.

Arthur lit up a cigar and looked bleakly round at the grimy walls of the tatty hall. Then he turned back to watch the two boxers, one black, one white, as they clumsily slugged it out.

'They're not exactly class, are they?'

Harry grinned and pulled up the collar of his grubby raincoat. It was cold in the hall and he felt chilled to the bone.

'That's not the point, Arthur,' said Harry. 'Those guys are giving good value, aren't they? They like fighting – they don't like each other. That's how all Eric's bills score.'

'Yeah,' said Arthur. 'I'm sure you're right.'

'Here comes the action,' said Harry, sucking in his breath. 'I like it.'

The black fighter had just landed a haymaker on the white fighter who was even now reeling across the ring on legs like jelly. He landed on the bottom rope and stayed there, swaying. He didn't fall down but neither did he have the energy to get up. The black fighter closed in for the kill and it was all over.

Arthur winced as the final blows rained in.

'Do you reckon he'll get up?' Harry asked with mild curiosity.

'He shouldn't have come in the first place,' said Arthur, relighting a sodden cigar.

Harry watched the final body-blow, and then said:

'How's Terry?'

'In the pink.'

'Terry would have loved this.'

'Would he?'

'Yeah – great fighter was Tel. You know –'

'What?'

'Eric would give him a chance.'

3

'What at?'

'The fight game, Arthur. You're not concentrating, are you?'

'What on earth would Terry want here?'

'Eric would give him a bash. He'll take on anybody – bouncers, minders, old fighters, has-beens –'

'Has-beens?' asked Arthur quickly. There was an edge to his voice.

'Oh – I don't mean that about Terry. What I'm trying to tell you is that Eric likes a guy with heart. Heart and bottle.'

Arthur laughed angrily. 'Do you really think Terry would degrade himself by joining a blood and snot circus like this?'

'Just asking, Arthur. That's all – just asking.'

'Well, don't ask.'

'But he still does a bit, doesn't he?'

'Well – he takes care of people from time to time. Then again he might supervise some premises. But most of the time he improves himself.'

'What at, Arthur?'

'Evening classes, or something.'

'Blimey.'

'You see, Harry, you got my Terence all wrong. Haven't you?'

'If you say so, Arthur.'

The white fighter was now lying on the floor of the boxing ring, whilst the scattered crowd gave vent to tepid applause. The black fighter, meanwhile, had retired to his corner and was going through a ritual of clumsy jubilation.

'My boy's not for this,' insisted Arthur. 'He's in a different league.'

Harry kept quiet. He knew when Arthur was making up his mind.

'Get out and shut up!'

Terry dragged the two young hooligans towards the door of the pub.

'All I did was to play the juke box,' protested one of them.

'With your Doc Martins? You're out.'

'I left a pint of lager on the bar.'

4

'You threw it at the barman. Remember? That's why you're leaving.'

'Yeah?'

They were at the open doorway now and Terry suddenly released his hold.

'It's bye-bye time.'

'We'll get you.'

'Naughty.'

But at that moment one of the yobboes twisted round in a highly acrobatic manner, aiming a back kick at Terry as he did so.

'Blimey,' said Terry, as he caught the blow on his elbow. He hadn't been expecting that – not from a kid. At once they ran off and for a moment Terry wondered if he should go after them. Then he decided against it. His elbow hurt too much, and, besides, he was knackered. Those lousy yobs were getting him down and there was no doubt that a combination of small-time bouncing and minding for Arthur was driving him spare. There must be more to life than this, he mused, rubbing his elbow as he walked back into the garish din of the pub.

'Had a bit of trouble?' asked the barman.

'Nothing I couldn't sort out.'

'Oh yes – looks as if someone's upset you.'

'It's the job that gets me down,' said Terry.

'This job – or the other one?'

'All the jobs get me down.'

'Why not go to the Job Centre, then?'

'Eh?'

'The Job Centre – you know – where you get jobs.'

'I just might give it a try.'

Arthur and Harry sat and waited for the next attraction as the dazed and bloodied white boxer was led past them by his seconds.

'I thought you'd like the bill,' said Harry hopefully, but Arthur was not to be drawn into an optimistic conversation.

'I don't know why they didn't have the fight in the gutter – it's where it belonged.'

5

'Or in the road,' returned Harry. 'Like in the old days.'

Arthur relit his cigar gloomily. 'What old days?'

'The 'thirties – when blokes fought it out on the street corner for a few pennies.'

'Very nice.'

'"Think of the nostalgia –'

'I am.'

'Now, why don't you have a chat with Eric? You're a man who likes to make the odd pound – and Eric likes spending it. You two should get on like a pair of love-birds. You'll soon be billing and cooing at each other like nobody's business.'

'Will we?'

'By the way,' said Harry, changing the subject hastily, 'you still into property?'

'I dabble, Harry. I sometimes dabble.'

'Well – I got a very nice modernised flat – clean as a whistle with a lovely postal code.'

'Why do you want to sell?' asked Arthur with just a hint of suspicion in his voice.

Harry cleared his throat.

'My Marge has pushed off with a double-glazing sales-man.'

'No!'

'She was as loyal as a spaniel.'

'That's a charming picture.'

'Thank God I've got the lease in my name, but I couldn't live there.'

'Why ever not? Thought you liked it there?'

'Be sensitive, Arthur – there's too many memories – and the new double glazing! I'm going back to me little bed-sit.'

For the first time that evening, Arthur began to look interested.

'How much money are we talking about?'

'Search me, Arthur. I'm out of touch. Of course – it's not been an easy life, particularly with that little stretch in Hull. Everyone knew I was innocent.'

'Yes,' said Arthur, 'any decent liberal Judge would have ignored all that evidence about the shotgun in the car boot.'

'I even had a brace of grouse in there and all.'

'Pity they were out of season, Harry. Now – this flat –'

But Harry was already looking at the next two boxers who were climbing into the ring. Flabby and overweight, they looked finished before they had started.

'Give 'em a bus pass each – and some supplementary benefits. That's what they really need,' remarked Arthur, still thinking about the flat.

'Don't knock it, Arthur. There's plenty of loot in this game.'

The two boxers lumbered clumsily towards each other.

Has he bitten? Harry wondered. If so – it could be a bite at two cherries.

Arthur Daley sat in the back of a taxi, wondering about Harry's flat. There could be something in it – something worth following up. He was feeling the pinch at the moment and needed something to happen. In fact, life had been so slow that it had hardly been worthwhile Terry minding him over the last few weeks. Gazing vacantly from the taxi window, Arthur's mind ran over a dozen potential money-making schemes, but they were all schemes he had tried before – schemes that had failed and were not likely to respond to the kiss of life. Gloomily he continued to stare out into the street – until he saw Terry. For a moment, Arthur could hardly believe his own eyes. Terry was standing outside a Job Centre, studying the notices in the window. Then, to Arthur's horror, he went inside.

'Oi!' yelled Arthur, but to no avail. The street was empty. Then he turned to the cabbie and excitedly asked him to stop. Grudgingly, the cabbie pulled up and Arthur tumbled out in a highly ruffled state.

'I'll be back in a minute.'

'Hold on.'

'Eh?'

'Now look – our destination was Berkeley Square and now you're going into a Job Centre.'

'I'll be back in a minute, I tell you.'

'I'll have the fare now.'

Arthur turned on him indignantly, panting slightly with his hat askew, as he stood agitatedly by the side of the cab.

7

'You think I'm going to do a runner?'

'*I* don't know, do I?'

'A man of my calibre. I'm an employ*er* – not an employ*ee*.'

'I don't care if you're the Chairman of the Board – I want the fare.'

Arthur dug reluctantly into his pocket and produced some loose coins.

'You don't expect a tip for this, do you?'

The cabbie pocketed the money and grinned.

'I don't expect you'll get a job, either.'

Arthur came quietly up behind Terry, who was examining the cards inside the Job Centre with grave interest.

'I can't believe I'd ever see you in such a humiliating position – I really can't, Terry. So, it's dossing under the arches next, is it?'

Terry went on looking at the cards, without the slightest reaction to Arthur's tirade.

'The idea of you – you of all people – being *here*. My friend, my associate – the boy I brought in from the gutter, nursed, trained and taught.'

Still Terry said nothing.

'I mean – look at that lot. Maggie's millions.'

Terry turned on Arthur with a patient smile. 'Look, Arthur – all I'm doing is sussing out the job market.'

Arthur gave him an outraged look, as if he was committing a sacrilege. Then he turned to the notice-board with contempt.

'Look at 'em – motor cycle messengers and audio-typists. My God, Terry, is this the end of your ambitions? These aren't for you – these are for *workers, civilians*, the *hoi polloi*. This is *work*.' Arthur made the word '*work*' sound like an obscenity.

But Arthur did not succeed with his attempt to inspire Terry. He merely succeeded in annoying him.

'Look, Arthur – just button it, will you?' said Terry. 'I've had enough of being on the door in the Acton khazi, facing up to lippy hooligans and getting Kung Fu kicks on the shoulder. I've just got myself a season ticket to the casualty

8

unit – and it's not something I wanted. I'm also broke.'

Arthur smiled bravely, anxious to placate Terry and knowing how to do it.

'Now, why didn't you say, Tel. Look at this,' he bent over one of the cards, lighting his cigar and dropping ash on it, 'look at this – handyman for a block of flats. That's not so bad, is it?'

Terry ignored his sarcasm and moved over to another card. It read:

> PLAYLEADER
> ARE YOU GOOD WITH CHILDREN?
> A NEW ADVENTURE PLAYGROUND
> NEEDS A PLAYLEADER. RELIABLE,
> RESPONSIBLE, PATIENT. WOULD
> SUIT AN ACTIVE YOUNG MAN AND/
> OR PHYSICAL EDUCATION INSTRUCTOR.
> ASK FOR DETAILS AT DESK.

Without comment, Terry walked straight over to the desk, where an attractive young woman had just finished dealing with another client. Arthur watched him go uneasily. Just as he was about to follow him, he felt a hand on his shoulder and turned quickly.

'Hallo, Arthur. Long time no see.' The middle-aged man seemed highly amused to see Arthur in such unlikely surroundings. 'Now, what chance have the likes of us got if you're down here after a job as an audio-typist?'

Arthur frowned, unwilling to see any humour in the situation. He felt insecure in this place, where offers of work – the wrong kind of work – surrounded him. 'Do I look like a man after a job? I've got two employment agencies of me own – what would I want a job for?'

'Well, Arthur –'

'Now, if you register at my office and give me a pony – you could be a Marketing Director in Milton Keynes.'

'You must be joking.'

Arthur pulled out a business card and gave it to him grandly. 'It's only up-market jobs with me. Not like all this rubbish here.'

9

Reading from the card, the man slowly intoned:

'The Boardroom Sauna Club.'

Arthur looked slightly confused. 'Eh? Oh. I see. You'd better keep that one – never know when it might come in useful.' He quickly produced another card, gave it to the man and then walked towards the counter, where Terry was engaged in earnest conversation with the girl. Terry was explaining that he didn't have any qualifications, but he had been a boxer – and had helped to teach self-defence in a youth club.

Arthur listened in silence for a while, but suddenly could bear it no longer. 'Never mind that,' he said brusquely 'he's got a job.'

'Ignore him,' said Terry.

'And as for youth activities – ask him why he beat up a couple of juveniles last night.'

'I'll chin you,' put in Terry menacingly.

But Arthur ploughed on: 'See how aggressive he is, miss. Now, this boy's had a very deprived childhood and no way could he be a playleader. Besides – as I say – he's got a job.'

Terry turned to Arthur reluctantly. 'What job?' he said blankly.

But Arthur was determined to sustain the moment of interest. Arthur still addressed the girl. 'You see, miss – he gets two grand for fifteen minutes.'

Terry smiled understandingly and turned back to the girl. 'The man's a nutter,' he said.

'So, forget about audio-typing and climbing up ropes. Put it this way – this man thought the Job Centre was a new boutique. Look at his schmutter – not my style, but he likes it. All Pierre Amies and Yves Lawrence Corner.'

The girl looked fascinated but Terry raised his eyebrows and Arthur continued.

'You see, lovey, I'm his guvnor and I pay his stamps.'

'Why do you do that?' asked Terry.

'You see,' Arthur continued to address himself to the girl, 'he's not one of three million unemployed – he's a fraud. Don't be misled by the way he looks.'

'Shut up, Arthur.'

'And now, Terence, I bring you tidings of great joy.' Arthur gave Terry a beatific and beguiling smile. He paused and there was a long, awkward silence. Finally Terry broke it:

'I'll have to have a word with him,' he said reluctantly to the girl.

'I would,' she said enthusiastically, 'it sounds – intriguing.'

'You don't know him like I do.'

'Why don't you come back and tell me what happens?'

Terry paused whilst Arthur's smile froze.

'Don't mind if I do. How about six o'clock?'

'Fine.'

'I'll even buy you a drink.'

'I'd like that.'

Arthur put his arm protectively round Terry's shoulders. He turned to the girl like a king. 'You see – I come in and you get a result.' He gently turned Terry away from the counter and began to lead him towards the door.

'Why does an intelligent kid like her work in a place like this?'

Ten minutes later, Arthur and Terry were sitting in the back of a cab in the heart of dockland. Arthur gave the impression of being full of largesse, but it was at times like this that Terry was at his most wary.

'Well?'

Arthur lit a new cigar, taking his time about it. Then he said: 'You're fit, aren't you?'

'I'm fit.'

'Course, some fighters are a bit like good claret. They mature. Now, just cast your mind back to good old Archie Moore. Almost fifty – and he was still slugging.'

'Pity he didn't knock anyone down.'

'Then there was Jersey Joe Walcott. What a punch.'

'He was punch-drunk.'

'I went along to one of those pirate shows last night. You know, unlicensed.'

'That figures.'

'The wife could have knocked out most of 'em.'

11

'Arthur – no!' Realism dawned and it made Terry want to throw up.

'They were bums, Tel. Walk-ons.'

'And I'm one of them?'

'No – you had class. You wouldn't even sweat – and you know I love you like a son.'

'Let your son do it.'

'They're giving money away. Now – don't you owe me a favour?'

'I done a favour seven years ago. Remember?'

'For some very influential people, Tel.'

'They were great. This ain't your night, they said. I had to hold the guy up for seven rounds.'

'The price was good.'

'You should 'ave taken care of me.'

'I didn't know you then.'

'But I could have been somebody then. I could have been a contender.'

'You're not with me. You *were* the contender – that was the whole point, son.'

'Oh, yeah.'

'You were to lose to whats-is-name Wilson. Then he'd be a contender with a quick return bout. You could have murdered him. But what did you do instead? Went in like a dying swan!'

'I got resin in me eye.'

'Yeah? You was like Sir John Gielgud on a bad night. They should have nicked you for over-acting instead of just taking your licence away.'

'So, what happened?' said Terry bitterly, 'Wilson becomes a champ.'

'An ageing rabbit.' Arthur paused reflectively. 'You got your money, didn't you?'

'Did I, hell? They took the purse away. Your mate said the bookies wouldn't pay out.'

Arthur winced. 'I forgot that, Tel. But now I remember I lost more than you. Much more. No wonder you owe me a favour.'

'Blimey – you do come it, don't you?'

'Look – the motor's in dock and I've got problems.'

'Problems?'

'Like forty videos of *E.T.* with no ending.'

'Yeah?'

'And what about forty gross of denim shirts?'

'What's wrong with 'em?'

'What's right? They've got nine-inch collars and thirty-six inch sleeves. Do for a midget with extra-long arms.'

'That's your problem, Arthur.'

'I should be taking that playleader job. Not you.'

'I'd love to see you on a rope.'

Arthur paused reflectively. 'Alf was champion of the world when he was older than you, Terry.'

'Great.'

'And there's always Sylvia.'

'Sylvia?'

'Sylvia what's-it. Rocky. I mean – I know it was only a film. But where are your dreams, Tel? In audio-typing? In swinging on ropes? You should have a dog, like Rocky's'.

'Look, Arthur. I've got plenty of friends. I don't need you to look after me. Not like this anyway. Me friends can.'

'Oh, Terry. But tell me one thing?'

'What?'

'Where are your friends now?' Arthur rapped on the cab's partition. 'I'll pick up my own motor now,' he said grandly.

When Arthur had collected the souped up Jaguar that he drove so erratically through the London traffic, he headed for Harry's flat. Once in there, he was almost asphyxiated by the unwashed smell of the place. Dirty shirts and socks littered the main room and the furniture was both tatty and broken. Harry was in a vest and old grey trousers with greasy looking slippers on his bare feet.

'You look a real picture,' said Arthur.

'I was going to tidy up –'

'So this is why they call you Dirty Harry.' Arthur looked round and sniffed, wrinkling up his nose in distaste.

'I used to be a ringer for Clint Eastwood,' volunteered Harry. 'Mind you – he's a bit taller, isn't he?'

Arthur smiled. 'The man wouldn't hang his poncho in this gaff – any chance of opening a window?'

Harry moved obligingly to the window and began to struggle with the frame. But it would not budge and he retreated hopelessly.

'I don't like draughts,' he said.

'It's a nice flat,' said Arthur looking gloomily at the window. 'Tight?'

'Since she left, I've let the place go. I don't even do much hoovering.'

'I had noticed. Ever thought of a dustpan?'

'She took it with her.'

'Now, Harry,' Arthur laid a fatherly hand on Harry's grubby shoulder, then quickly took it away – 'you can buy dustpans nowadays.' Arthur looked around him again, with a grimace. 'So this is the flat that's on the market?'

'Lease and fittings.'

'Fittings?'

Harry looked unhappy. 'Furniture too.'

'So you call this furniture? How would you describe it? Middle-period Hilda Ogden?'

'It's all good stuff.'

'It's not worth a penny.'

'Arthur –'

'It's drek, Harry. All drek!'

'It's a nice address.' Harry waved to a newspaper laden sofa. 'Why don't you sit down?' He began to push the newspapers on to the floor. Beneath them was an old pair of underpants. Arthur remained standing.

'I haven't seen the cat for a week,' muttered Harry.

'Probably suffocated somewhere,' suggested Arthur. 'Or gone down the Welfare.'

'What about the Arabs then?' asked Harry, clearing away some dirty plates and a lethal-looking can of half-opened sardines. 'They're always looking for flats.'

'They wouldn't stable their camels in here.' Arthur sighed and sat down on the sofa. He quickly rose again as there was a snapping sound from the springs. 'What about the rent? Is it controlled?'

14

'Oh, yes,' said Harry, a little too quickly.

'And the lease?'

'My solicitor's drawing it up.'

'How much?'

'Ten grand.'

'Three – it's all it's worth.'

'It's only ten minutes from the West End.'

'It's a doss-house. Three and a half.'

'I was thinking of six.'

'When even the cat's left?'

'I can't accept that, Arthur.'

'Look – I'll give you three thousand seven hundred and fifty. How about that, Harry?'

'That's unacceptable, Arthur.'

'I'll never be a rich man with this kind of generosity.'

'It's not enough, Arthur.'

'But it's a deal, isn't it, Harry?'

That night Terry took the girl from the Job Centre down to the Winchester Club for a drink. Her name was Nicky and Terry hoped he was on to a winner.

'Do you want a table – or shall we sit at the bar?' he asked her, hoping that he would not have to introduce her to the all-knowing barman, Dave. Luckily she suggested a table and Terry was able to face Dave alone.

'You've just missed Arthur.'

'Good. Gin and tonic for the lady – and I'll have a pint of lager.'

'You won't.'

'Eh?'

'The lady can have what she likes. But you're on orange juice.'

'What the hell for?'

'Arthur says.'

A blind fury seized Terry and he immediately wanted to do something violent – preferably to Arthur.

'You've gotta lose at least twelve pounds,' said Dave.

'What's all this about?'

'Your comeback. Arthur reckons you're about ready.'

15

'I'll kill him.'

'It's the other guy you've gotta kill.'

'He's got no damn right to –'

'Arthur's very keen.'

'Arthur – bloody Arthur is on the make. Again.'

'How can you misunderstand him so?' Dave grinned and started polishing glasses. Something in his confident movements made Terry feel he was arguing a lost cause.

'I am *not* boxing,' said Terry very slowly and clearly. 'I've retired.'

'That's what I said to Arthur.'

'Licensed *or* unlicensed.'

'You know what Arthur said?'

'I don't *want* to know what Arthur said.'

'He said: "We'll win." That's what he said.'

'We?'

'He's afraid you'll lose your bottle. Now – what was it? ' Vera and Harmonic for the lady – and an orange juice for you.'

Terry glanced at Dave. Then a strange feeling of familiarity flooded over him.

'I've been here before,' he muttered to himself.

Arthur's alarm went off at ten to six and he woke blearily, knowing there was something important to do. He slept alone, his wife having elected years ago to move into the next bedroom. This suited Arthur for various reasons, an important one being that he was free to use the phone at any time of the night without interference.

Gradually, Arthur began to wake, remembering with an exhilaration that he had not felt for months, that he had a new job for Terry. He dialled his number.

'Yeah?' Terry's voice was sleepy and churlish.

'You alone?'

There was silence. Then Terry said ungraciously: 'What the hell do you want?'

'It's six o'clock and the air is clean. No traffic, no carbon monoxide –'

'You gone crazy?'

16

'No – I'm very comfortable here, snuggled up in my pit.'

'Why not get some more kip? I could do with some.'

'But you should be up.'

'What?'

'In a track suit with a woolly hat.'

'You *are* crazy.'

'And heavy boots.'

'Arthur –'

'You should be pounding the streets, my son.'

'I'm not going back into it.'

'Five miles good run and then a nice cuppa tea.'

'Get off the phone, Arthur.'

'Quick half-hour of breakfast TV and into the gym.'

'Push off!'

'Punish yourself, Terence. And get up this second!'

With a smile Arthur replaced the receiver on a string of expletives from an enraged Terry.

Terry buried his face in the pillow and pulled the eiderdown over his head. He was determined to resist Arthur's pressure. He remembered the humiliation of his last time in the ring – and thought again of the unhappy way that all Arthur's plans had of backfiring with himself as victim. This time he was determined that Arthur would not succeed in persuading him into disaster.

Arthur and Harry were standing opposite a shabby door between two shops. On the door was a small, grubby notice. It read:

NATIONAL ASSOCIATION OF FAIR FIGHTING

'There you are,' said Harry in a proprietorial manner.

'Very nice too,' replied Arthur.

'That's Eric all over.'

'What's Eric all over?'

'Fair,' said Harry. 'You won't regret getting into this, Arthur.'

Arthur clapped his hand on Harry's shoulder, ' *You* might, Harry boy. *You* might.'

Eric Morgan's appearance cheered Arthur up when they met him in his tiny, cluttered office at the top of a long flight of narrow stairs. He was in his early thirties and had a pink, freshly scrubbed look that went well with his lilting Welsh accent and stockbroker style. A slightly ageing whiz-kid, he certainly knew how to chat up Arthur. Shaking hands with him vigorously, Eric said, 'Arthur Daley – a legend in your own life-time. Do you know – my Da even used to talk about you?'

'Did he now?' Arthur smiled horribly. 'I knew quite a few Taffs in those days.' He winced as the handshake continued and was then mercifully terminated.

'Still,' said Eric with his too easy smile, 'count your fingers, though,' he said.

'I'm an open book. How is your old fella?'

'Still in Broadmoor.' Eric turned grandiosely to Harry. 'Be a good boy and go and get a cup of tea somewhere.'

'If you insist,' replied Harry and made a slow and reluctant exit.

When he had gone, Eric said to Arthur: 'I want to be a millionaire before I'm thirty-five.'

'We all wanted to be that when we were young,' said Arthur in a fatherly tone.

'Didn't you miss out?' replied Eric sweetly.

Arthur suddenly itched to wipe the smile off Eric's face, but he was not a man of violence. He considered that to be Terry's province. 'I get by. Quite well.'

Eric smiled. Arthur knew he was going to find this rather superior aloof smile very irritating in future.

'You see, Arthur,' said Eric, 'I'm a radical. I'm for alternative boxing and I'm against the establishment.'

'You one of the militant tendency then?'

'Power to the people.'

'That's what I say.'

'My Da had some strange ideas.'

'He would have – being in Broadmoor and all that. No disrespect, mind you.'

'My Da thought of boxing as folk art.'

'Oh yeah?'

18

'All those after-dinner shows they have now. It's elitist crap. What I want – what the people want – is legalised street corner scraps! Are we speaking the same language, Arthur?'

'Well – I like a bit of skill, you know.'

'Skill?' Eric looked outraged. 'Skill's for snooker. I want blood. Blood, Arthur.' He thumped on the desk to underline his words.

Arthur nodded uneasily. 'I like a bit of claret myself. Talking of drinking –'

'Don't touch it. Tell you what – I'll give you a grand for your boy.'

Arthur laughed lightly as if Eric had made a tiny joke. 'Terry wouldn't demean himself.'

'Not for a grand?'

'Not a chance.'

'You know Jackie Wilson –' Eric's voice was a little on edge and Arthur felt a warm glow creeping over him.

'Wilson? Terry would have to prop him up for seven rounds.'

'But would it be an attraction?'

Arthur considered, 'I'd sell a couple of hundred tickets myself.'

'Then, you've got two grand!'

'And a half?'

'The fight's not at the Albert Hall.'

'What do you want?' asked Arthur slowly. 'Blood or "Beethoven's Fifth"?'

Eric stared hard at him and Arthur knew the vital moment had come.

'OK,' said Eric reluctantly, 'you've got yourself a deal.'

With a squeal of tyres Arthur pulled up the Jag outside Terry's flat, and climbed out. For a moment he stood, wide-eyed with sheer astonishment, at the extraordinary sight that greeted him.

'What the hell are you doing?'

'Grafting,' said Terry. He was sitting on the first floor sill, cleaning the windows.

'You'll do yourself a mischief.'

'I never knew you cared.'

'Oh, but I do care, Tel. I do care very much.' Arthur came and stood below him, looking up in great, slightly flushed, concern. 'Get down,' he said, 'now.'

'Why?'

'As your manager – I insist you get down!'

'As my what?'

'You heard.' Arthur lit a cigar. 'We got money in the bank – and Jackie Wilson to fight.'

'Who?'

'Yeah – that'll make you drop your chammy.'

'Arthur –'

'Now be friendly, Tel. Don't tell me to go away.'

'Go away, Arthur.'

Terry swung himself back over the sill and into his flat. Arthur hurried inside and up the stairs. Puffing slightly, he let himself in. Terry was sitting on the bed, looking suspicious. 'What are you on about, Arthur?'

'Wait till I get my breath.'

'You're not fit, Arthur.'

'Window cleaning?' Arthur sat heavily down in a chair. 'Yesterday it was audio-typing and swinging on ropes. Today it's window cleaning.'

'They're my windows.'

'So it's a pirate show.' Arthur stretched out his legs and puffed out cigar smoke in a luxuriant cloud. 'But you're top of the bill.'

'No.'

'Had a better offer?'

'No.'

'What have you got? One night stand on the door of the disco?'

Terry said nothing.

'Diary full?'

Terry said nothing.

'I'm offering you dignity –'

Still Terry said nothing.

'Respect.'

'Are you kidding?'

20

'Money.'

Terry was silent again but Arthur could see that he was thinking.

'You don't have any money right now. Do you, Terry?'

Terry was still thinking.

'You've got your old dressing gown, haven't you? With your name on the back? I'll even take it to the cleaners. Personally, Hey –' The light of inspiration came into Arthur's eyes. 'How about sponsorship? Nick the cleaner would love that. I can see the wording now – Two hour service . . . Alterations our speciality . . . Try our new luxury shirt service . . .'

'There's no space across the shoulders,' said Terry.

'Then let's shove it on your backside! Blimey, Tel – you could be a walking industry.'

Glumly, Terry moved to the kitchen area, where two used tea-bags sat equally glumly on the draining board.

'Do you want some second-hand tea?'

'You're top of the bill, Tel.' Arthur rose to his feet, pushing home his advantage.

'You're with Jackie Wilson.'

Silence.

'He's ex-champion of Britain. Ex-champion of the Commonwealth.' Arthur paused dramatically.

'Why's he doing it?' asked Terry, for the first time showing a flicker of interest.

'Because like many good men before him he frittered his wealth away.'

'Oh yeah.'

'Boozing all night. Badly advised business ventures. Fair-weather friends who didn't have an umbrella between them.'

'I've heard it all before,' said Terry, putting on the kettle.

'Of course you have, Tel,' replied Arthur, laying a fatherly hand on his arm. 'It's the old, old story. In the immortal words of Willie Pep – "First you lose your legs and then you lose your friends." ' Arthur paused for that to sink in. Then he spoke quickly and decisively. 'You've got a month.'

Terry was silent again. Then he said:

21

'This guy, Wilson –'

'Yes Tel?'

'He owes me, doesn't he?'

'Course he does. You made him.'

'I mean – I could've been a champ.'

'Course you could, boy. But you can have your chance again.'

'I don't –'

'Be positive, Tel. *Think* positive.'

'I can't help remembering what happened the first time around.'

'Forget it. I'm gonna look after you. And besides –'

'Besides what?'

'Think of the money.'

'How much, Arthur?'

'Enough to buy you some new tea-bags, Tel.'

Gradually, if reluctantly, Terry began to accept Arthur's idea. It was at least a better idea than earning lousy money doing lousy jobs and getting kicked in the elbow for his trouble.

'You've got a month.' Arthur's voice echoed in Terry's mind as he prepared for his first training work-out. It was early – horribly, unaccustomedly early as Terry pounded the dew-fresh streets of Fulham. He wore a track suit, a towel round his neck and a pair of the heaviest boots he could find. The streets were empty and although he began to sweat very quickly, Terry felt a sense of exhilaration as he thundered over the pavements. He was breathing hard and the exhilaration was beginning to leave him as the car slowly passed him. This was getting too much like hard work, thought Terry, and the memory of other similar mornings filtered gloomily into his mind.

Twenty-five yards ahead, Terry noticed that the car had stopped. As he drew abreast of it, a familiar face gazed up at him.

'I trust we are not fleeing from the scene of the crime.'

'With these boots?' Terry came to a relieved halt.

Detective Constable Rycott smiled sadly. 'Why not? If I see someone in unusual garb at six o'clock in the morning in a residential area – it is my duty to take note.'

'I'm training.'

'Quite. But what for?'

'I'm making me come back.'

'Oh yeah.'

'I've got a fight in a month.' As he said the words Terry felt a sense of pride.

'Didn't you have a fight last week?'

'This is different. It's boxing – the fight game.'

'Where is your venue, young man?'

'I dunno. Ilford maybe.'

'A couple of "briefs" for your local custodians of law and order might be a nice idea.'

'That's Arthur's department.'

'In that case it'll cost me the Royal box!'

Terry grinned. 'It's going to cost a bleeding orange box for you, Mr Rycott.'

'Isn't that nice? Do you know – if I wasn't on me way home – I could nick you.'

'What for?'

'Anything really. Loitering with intent. Parking on a double yellow line. It hasn't been much of a week for me.'

'No?'

'It's been slow. What I could have done with was a nice bank robbery and a couple of transvestites kidnapping the Mayor.'

'So sorry.'

'I haven't been in the local paper for months.'

'I'll put the whisper round for you.'

'I'd be grateful. Now, on your way, Terry. I'd like to see you work up a good sweat.'

With a groan Terry pounded into action again and for a few minutes, Detective Constable Rycott kerb-crawled beside him.

'Go it, Tel!'

'You're a right sod, you are.'

'Now, now – insulting language to a police officer.'

After a while Rycott drove away, leaving Terry to his solitary sweating.

Three quarters of an hour later, Terry arrived back at his flat. He felt terrible, light-headed with exhaustion. In fact he was so shattered that he did not see Arthur's Jag parked in the entrance.

'Gawd help us,' said a familiar voice.

Terry lay back in his chair, too exhausted to even unlace his boots.

'Make some tea,' he gasped.

'I've had tea,' said Arthur cheerfully. 'Couple of rashers, scrambled eggs – and a slice of toast.'

'Tea,' moaned Terry.

'What a two and eight. Do you know – I've got more of a chance of beating Jackie Wilson than you. Look at the state you're in.'

'I'm out of practice.' Giving up Arthur's potential tea-making abilities as a lost cause, Terry stumbled to the kettle.

'I'll have coffee,' said Arthur.

Terry said something unintelligible.

'What was that, son?'

'Nothing, Arthur.' Silence.

'What you need is a trainer.'

'I'm training meself. I do know a bit more about boxing than you do, Arthur.'

'You reckon?'

'Yes, Arthur.'

'I know more about everything than you do, Terry. History, current affairs, motors, politics, hang-gliding, the fine arts – but particularly about the noble art. Now you tell me – who was the only man who won the World Heavyweight title when he was on the canvas?'

Terry said nothing.

'Got yer, haven't I? Max Schmeling won the title from Jack Sharkey on a foul. You didn't know that, did you? Now give me another one.'

24

Terry handed Arthur a cup of instant coffee.

'I'll find you a trainer.'

'I said I can train meself, Arthur.'

'Look, son – as your manager *I* call the shots. So I chose Soldier Atkins.'

Terry laughed mockingly. 'Not old Soldier?'

'He's the best.'

'Three score and ten and plus.'

'Don't you knock the old-uns. They know what's what.'

'So here we are down memory lane,' began Terry.

But Arthur frowned over his coffee.

'Terence – you want to win this fight?'

'Yes. That's why I don't want Soldier Atkins.'

'If you want to win you have to trust your manager, and Soldier Atkins it's gonna be.'

Terence began to mimic Soldier: 'Old Tommy Farr said to me . . . and Len Harvey, what a gentleman . . .'

'Old Tommy Farr, now he could have a fight. Nobody could take liberties with Tommy. And then Len Harvey – what a gentleman – in and out of the ring – and with the sweetest straight left in the world.'

Terry glanced ironically at Arthur as Soldier went into his familiar anecdotes but Arthur stolidly ignored him. Around them the gym was full of action, with the heavy bags being thumped and with the staccato fire of the speed-ball pummelling their ear-drums.

Arthur turned to Terry and beamed at him.

'See he knows it all. Don't you Soldier?'

Soldier, an upright, elderly man with a military air replied: 'It's in me bones, Arthur.'

'And the family – eh Soldier?' Arthur sounded like the benevolent superintendent of an old people's home.

Soldier beamed happily. 'My dear old Mum weighed in at eleven stone seven pounds – your kind of stamp, Terry, and a very similar style – a real walk-in fighter was the old lady. She was the undisputed champion of the Co-op queue during the war.'

Terry looked at Arthur, and then at Soldier. He seemed

restless. 'No disrespect, Soldier. But what exactly are you gonna do for me?'

'I'm going to make you a winner, son.'

'But –'

'People say the last fight was hooky.'

'You can say that again.'

'You were on a hiding to nothing,' said Soldier in a derisive tone.

'It was a set-up,' replied Terry.

'A bit of villainy.' Soldier cleared his throat. 'Maybe they wanted to be sure.'

'I had him all over the place.'

'You simple-minded?' said Soldier with sudden contempt.

Terry turned to Arthur, 'You tell him.'

But Arthur merely looked uncomfortable 'Well – he was the favourite. Er – Wilson, I mean.'

'Odds on, was he?'

'As I remember it.'

'What are you saying?' Terry asked slowly. 'He was going to win anyway.'

Arthur shrugged. 'So they reckoned.'

But Soldier was more positive. 'He *was* going to win. They just wanted some insurance. Isn't that right, Arthur?'

'That's about it, Soldier.'

Terry stared unbelievingly at them both. 'They thought I couldn't win?'

Arthur looked away unhappily. 'Yeah.'

'Now he tells me.'

'I didn't want to tell you, Tel. I tried to protect you from the knowledge.'

'Thanks, Arthur.'

'Wilson was in on it – of course.' Soldier's voice was bland.

'This gets better all the time.' The bitterness was in his voice now. 'You mean – he wasn't even trying?'

'Look, Tel –' Arthur snapped. 'What the hell does it matter either way? You buggered it up. Then you had your close encounter with the law. It's all history. Who cares now?'

'I bloody care,' said Terry.

'And I reckon Wilson cares,' said Soldier.

'Isn't this great? A couple of has-beens trying to even up a score.'

Terry turned his back on them and began to walk angrily towards the door. En route he took a wild and vicious swipe at the speed-ball.

'He's got the hump,' said Arthur.

'Good,' replied Soldier. 'There's nothing like creating a little adrenalin to make a man fighting mad.'

Terry went straight to the Winchester Club. He was in a blind fury and when Dave suggested an orange juice he told him what to do with it. Quickly Dave poured a pint of lager and put it on the bar in front of Terry.

'So you knew about it as well?' Terry began aggressively.

'Everybody knew – except you. I mean – be fair, Tel. He *was* a bit tasty.'

'Was he?' said Terry, almost to himself.

'Very. Clever, talented, a bit flash – you can't take away his record.'

'And what does that make me – a mug?'

'No. I wouldn't say that, Tel.'

'Then what?'

'Do you really want to know?'

'Might as well.' Terry affected not to care – but it was all too obvious that he cared very deeply indeed.

'It makes you a natural fighter.'

'*What?*'

'That's why they wanted insurance all them years ago. That's the thing about natural fighters – you knock them down and they gets up again. But who needs all that, eh? It's the hell of a way to make a living.'

'I see.' Terry looked abstracted. Then he felt a familiar hand on his shoulder.

'You left without saying goodbye, Terence.' Arthur sounded sure of himself and Terry now knew why. He was accompanied by Soldier, who appeared equally cheerful.

'I'll have the usual, Tel. How about you, Soldier?'

'Just a large brandy.'

'I'll need another four tickets,' said Dave to Arthur. He

turned back to Terry with a grin. 'Some of your fans need 'em. They reckon you'll knock him out.'

'I'm in the chair then?' asked Terry mildly.

'Training expenses,' muttered Arthur.

'Terry,' said Soldier in an admonishing tone, 'that's your last drink until the victory party. Tomorrow we start work – and boy – I do mean work.'

'Sounds great,' said Terry, searching for his wallet.

The training programme nearly killed Terry. Skipping, press-ups, the punch-bag, the speed-ball – Soldier took him through his paces with a punishing determination. There was no let up to the programme and Arthur, watching it, saw Terry gradually and painfully come into a shape and form that was beginning to look promising. His sparring became more positive, more aggressive – and Soldier's well-worn but sound advice was with him all the time. He even began to enjoy the road running and Terry was well ahead of Arthur and Soldier when they followed him in the kerb crawling Jag. Local people began to acknowledge his public progress and stall-holders in the market would cheer him on, occasionally throwing him an apple. Indeed, local interest in Terry's challenge was becoming so great that Arthur, predictably, decided to turn it to his own advantage.

Terry, wearing a new track suit that Arthur had somewhat grudgingly bought him, was standing outside a Greek butcher's in the Fulham Road. Arthur was trying to persuade him to accompany him inside.

'Look, Arthur – leave me out of the sponsorship wheeler-dealing.'

'I need you, Terry. You gotta show yourself.'

'Arthur – I'll show myself in the ring.'

'You have to meet the *people*. You're the local boy. And show a little gratitude – look what I'm doing for you while you're enjoying your training. I'm working on contracts, tickets – getting GBH of the earhole from Soldier.'

'You're the manager, Arthur.'

'And *you're* the product. So come inside the butcher's *now*.'

Reluctantly, Terry followed Arthur inside to find Chris Christodoulides, the butcher, in a state of mild euphoria. He flung his arms round Terry and, having caught him in a warm embrace, said:

'You gotta win, Terry – you really gotta win. For you – I give you the best Scotch sirloin.'

'Great,' said Terry, trying to extricate himself.

Chris let go and rushed over to the counter to cut an enormous steak.

'He can eat two of them,' said Arthur.

'Then two it will be,' he continued to cut. Then he said: 'You get the tickets?'

'Four – that'll be a score each. The best in the house.'

He handed Chris the tickets. He looked at them and exclaimed: 'A score? These say fifteen pounds.'

'Yes,' said Arthur slowly. 'That was a funny business.'

'It was?'

'Arthur's full of jokes,' said Terry. 'Keep us rolling.'

Arthur frowned. 'You ain't gonna believe this Chris, but I had to buy them from a tout. On my landlord's life – it's a sell out.'

'Fancy that,' said Terry.

'It's really caught the public imagination.'

'Of course,' put in Chris naively. 'I want to see my old pal.' He went to the till and took out a few notes. Meanwhile Arthur made good his opportunity.

'You know, Chris – if you had a side of beef, we could have a good picture for the local rag. Terry punching the beef. Remember Rocky?'

'The beef is all cut up,' said Chris. 'How about spring lamb?'

'That'll be fine,' said Arthur.

'You mean I'm gonna punch a little English spring lamb?' complained Terry. 'No way.'

'See – that's your problem, Tel,' Arthur explained patiently.

'What's my problem?'

'You ain't got no killer instinct.'

*

29

Outside the shop, Arthur decided to part company with Terry. 'You run back to your flat.'

'Thanks. You wouldn't be offering me a lift in the Jag.'

'Training, Terence. What would Soldier say?'

'A lot.'

'Incidentally – I'll have one of those steaks.'

Terry hugged the plastic bag to him.

'They're for me. Training. What would Soldier say?'

'Don't I eat?' Arthur looked stunned.

'As you're selling tickets over the odds – you can buy a turkey and some chippolatas.'

Arthur gave him a wolfish grin. 'You hit 'em on the chin – and I'll hit 'em in the pockets.'

'That's an established tradition,' replied Terry.

'And now I'll trouble you for that steak.'

Reluctantly Terry dipped into the bag.

Brenda was thirty, had seen a bit of life and wear – but she could still turn a few heads. Cool and well preserved, she was sitting at the top of the stairs just outside Terry's flat. Her blonde hair looked as if it had just been styled, and her complexion was as immaculate as ever.

Terry, running up the stairs to the flat and taking pleasure in not being out of breath, paused mid-flight and stared up at her as if he had seen a ghost. For Brenda was not only extremely attractive – she was also the wife of Jackie Wilson and was the very last person he would have expected to see outside the flat.

'Blimey,' was all Terry could think of saying.

'Ain't you gonna invite me in, Tel?'

'I'm – I don't think I should.'

'Scared of what Arthur would say?'

'I was thinking of Jackie.'

'Well, if you're scared of him – God help you!'

'I'm not scared of Jackie.'

'Then – invite me in.'

Slowly Terry walked up the last few steps, unlocked the door and Brenda followed him in.

'I thought you'd be helping out your old man,' said Terry.

'You were always good for a photo at the weigh-in.'

'He doesn't do much training these days.' Brenda gave Terry the benefit of a little pout. 'Don't I get a kiss?'

Terry gave her a perfunctory kiss. Then he said:

'Now, let me guess, Bren. Jackie's got the flu – or is there a deal? Someone fancy a nice big bet?'

'Those days have gone.' She sat down heavily on the sofa. 'Don't I get a drink?'

Terry opened the door of the fridge with a flourish. 'Orange juice, grapefruit juice – or a couple of tea-bags?'

'You really are serious, aren't you?'

'Yeah.'

'He ain't.'

'Oh?'

'He reckons he can lick you anytime. I used to think that too.'

'Did you?'

'Not now.'

'Should be a good fight, then.'

'He could lose an eye.' She was looking at Terry very intently.

'So whose idea is this?' Terry's voice was utterly sceptical. 'Yours or his?'

But she was not to be thrown and Terry tried to avoid her intense look.

'The doctor says he's got a detached retina.'

'Then he shouldn't fight – it's as simple as that.'

'It's not as simple as that –he's got his pride, you know.'

'Don't tell me – tell him.'

'The fight doesn't mean anything – does it? No headlines – just a bit in the local rag.'

'Listen, Brenda, try to get this through you. He doesn't have to fight. Let's call it off. I can fight somebody else.'

'And what's Jackie gonna do?' She sounded indignant. 'He's skint – we've got two kids, a mortgage, debts up to here . . . it's a joke fight.'

'A joke?'

'All I'm saying is – let it *be* a joke fight.' Suddenly the indignation was gone, replaced by a note of fear.

31

'That makes me an all-in wrestler?'

'Well – old ladies like it.'

'Don't be bloody silly, Bren.'

'I'm not *being* bloody silly.'

'You're really serious, aren't you?'

'I'm serious.'

'You want me – to go easy on him.'

'That's all – it's his pride, Tel. That's all I'm asking.'

Terry looked steadily across at Brenda. 'Put it like this, love – I'll consider it.'

Brenda got up. 'I appreciate that, Terry. How about coming out for a quick one?'

'No thanks.'

'Why not?'

'Because I'm training.'

'But –'

'And whether or not I go easy on Jackie – I'm still in training. Get it, Bren?'

'I get it,' she said, walking to the door of the flat. 'No fun till after the fight, then.' Brenda gave a little pout again and Terry said, 'Not ever, love.'

The solicitor's office was tatty – to say the least. Mr Darrow sat at a battlefield of a desk, its top strewn with dog-eared papers, overflowing ashtrays and half-empty coffee cups that looked as if they had been there for days. Darrow himself was almost corpse like – with a deathly pallor and round shoulders that were spotted with dandruff. A rickety looking vintage typewriter stood on a bamboo table and the shelves around the cramped office were overloaded with dusty ledgers and documents.

Arthur and Harry sat themselves down upon two extremely fragile chairs and Arthur gloomily lit up a cigar. Immediately Darrow further depressed him:

'May I trouble you for one of your fine cigars? I seem to have mislaid my own cigar case.'

Arthur silently handed over a cigar.

'How kind. Now – this is the document, Mr Daley?'

In front of him, stagnating in the mess on his desk, were

two pieces of paper. Darrow leant back, drawing reflectively on his cigar. Arthur noticed that he was smoking it as if it was the first cigar he had smoked in years.

'I had suberb chambers in Lincoln's Inn – but I wanted to get back to the people. The grass roots, you understand?'

'The grass roots do the typing?' Arthur looked down censoriously at the ill-typed documents that were littered with mistakes.

'Dear Miss Penrose. Her nimble fingers aren't what they used to be.'

'No – poor dear,' said Harry.

Arthur contented himself with raising his eyebrows.

'I'm bringing in a new word processor next week, gentlemen. I think it will obviate the problem.'

'Does Miss Penrose know how to work one?' asked Arthur.

Mr Darrow smiled sadly. 'I shall be facilitating her work with an assistant, Mr Daley.'

'How kind – isn't the document you've drawn up rather short?'

'Economic, Mr Daley. Economic. I have dispensed with any ramifications with the ground landlord. This is what I call a simple transfer from tenant to tenant –'

'Yes, but – I don't know how to put this, Mr Darrow,' said Arthur.

'Please feel free, Mr Daley.'

'Is it legal, Mr Darrow?'

Darrow looked suitably affronted. 'Well really, Mr Daley – I've worked for some of the largest property companies in the country. I mean – the Duke of Westminster –'

'The *who*?'

'I mean, of course, the *old* Duke.'

'I see.'

'Anyway – you can take this simple lease to your own solicitor . . .'

'That's a laugh,' said Arthur. 'I saw him on the street the other day and asked him how things were. Two days later I get a bill from him.'

Arthur waited in vain for the humorous response, but all Darrow could say was:

'I think I've heard that remark before, Mr Daley.'

'Go on,' said Arthur. 'You can't have done.'

A few minutes later Mr Darrow clearly had nothing else to say and so Arthur and Harry prepared to take their leave.

'You might get that re-typed, Mr Darrow,' said Arthur. 'Just so other people can read it.'

'I don't think I can trespass on any more of Miss Penrose's time,' began Mr Darrow.

Arthur leant on his desk and smiled very sweetly. 'Give Miss Penrose my compliments,' he said, the smile changing to a leer. 'And tell her, I'll make it worth her while.'

'Now lads – I want everything painted white – including the cat – if you can find him. I want brilliant white – and the job finished in a couple of days. How about it?'

There was a mumbled, unenthusiastic response from the three young blacks who were standing in the tatty gloom of Harry's flat. All the furniture had been stacked up against one wall and pots of (bargain) paint had been acquired by Arthur. He had also hired buckets, step ladders and some tarpaulins that looked as if they had come from a butcher.

'A couple of days?' queried one of his newly hired workers. 'That's a bit strong, isn't it?'

Arthur turned on him impatiently. 'We're not talking about David Hicks. Splash it on – white, white and more white. You've got to work like bleeding niggers.'

'Thanks,' said one of the young blacks.

'No disrespect,' said Arthur hastily. 'That's a figure of speech, innit?'

'Is it?' the youngster asked, unappeased.

'You work like three sweaty Irish navvies, all right?'

'That's even worse.'

'Two days anyway,' snapped Arthur, 'wherever you come from.'

Terry's jogging was now a real physical joy to him. He felt tremendously fit and could take most of the exercise in his stride. But to make his training even more interesting, he was now joined by Nicky, from the Job Centre, wearing a very fetching track suit and inevitably trying to match Terry's stride.

'You're not sweating,' she said as they ran laughing up the stairs to Terry's flat.

'That was fun – not running.'

'You must be fit.'

'I *am* fit.'

'Well – I'm not,' Nicky collapsed puffing into an armchair.

'Want to use the shower?'

Nicky looked at him for a moment. Then she said:

'Why not?'

She got up and Terry, with a gracious bow, showed her where the shower was.

'Tea?'

'Great.'

Nicky showered as Terry busied himself with his tea-bags. Then, through the gushing water, Nicky shouted:

'You haven't asked me to come to the fight.'

'Didn't think you'd want to.'

'I've never been to a boxing match.'

'Eh?'

'I said – I've never been to a boxing match.'

Terry filled the kettle. 'There won't be a lot of boxing. It'll be easy for the punters.'

'Why?' Nicky sounded bewildered.

'Because old pros slow down. You can see the punches – and the misses. It's not really for the connoisseur.'

'I'm not exactly a connoisseur.'

'No – but this is memory lane.'

'Then why are you fighting?'

'I don't know,' said Terry. 'It's pathetic!'

'And painful?'

Terry began to make the tea. As he did so, he considered his reply. 'The body punches can be bad, but the blood – well it looks worse than it is. As for the pain – it all depends on whether you lose or win.'

'I see,' said Nicky. 'So – why didn't you ask me to the fight?'

'I just don't think you'd like it. They're – they're special birds who go to fights.'

'Thanks.'

'Look – I don't mean to put you down, Nicky.'

'It's all right.'

'Sure?'

'Yeah – it's all right, Terry.'

Nicky turned the shower on harder. Why wasn't she one of Terry's special birds? Conscious of being clumsy, Terry poured the tea into cups. There was a knock on the door and Terry had a nasty premonition. When he opened the door he found he was right – it was Arthur.

'Relaxing, eh?'

'Well –'

But Arthur pounded on, sounding very elated.

'I woke up this morning and I thought – this is it. 'Er indoors had a dream.'

'Oh yeah?'

'You won.'

'That's nice.'

'Oh – she's well into the premonition game. When I had that unfortunate little business at the Crown Court – 'er indoors had a –'

Just then Nicky entered the room in Terry's dressing gown.

'Oh my Gawd,' said Arthur.

She looked fantastic, glowing with health and her hair still wet from the shower. Arthur rounded on Terry.

'You haven't?'

'Look Arthur –'

'In broad daylight. A few hours before a fight.'

'She's had a shower,' said Terry in a voice that was meant to reassure.

'We were jogging,' said Nicky.

'Is that what they call it now?' said Arthur aghast. He turned back to Terry again. 'You know you've drained your vital fluids, don't you?'

'This is my day off,' said Nicky reasonably.

'*And* giving out your supplementary benefit,' wailed Arthur.

Terry grinned at Nicky.

'I forgot to tell you about Arthur.'

'I don't like his innuendoes,' began Nicky.

'Get yourself covered up,' stuttered Arthur, noticing that her dressing gown had opened slightly. 'I'm as liberal as the next man.'

'You're *not*,' replied Nicky.

'But I walk into a well-known bird-bandit's lair and find a comely Richard flaunting her Arris around the gaff –'

'We were just about to have tea,' said Terry.

'Tea? You're supposed to be at a medical check.'

'All right. No sweat.'

'I'm the one whose sweating,' said Arthur.

Terry turned to Nicky. 'Sorry love. I've got to go.'

'Who is he?' asked Nicky.

'My manager,' said Terry. 'His word is law.'

Terry's medical check-up, with background supervision from Arthur, was straightforward. The elderly medical officer began by fumblingly placing a tight band around Terry's arm. He then proceeded to attach it to a blood pressure machine.

'Any illnesses recently?' he quavered.

'No,' replied Terry.

'Eh?' The medical officer was clearly slightly deaf.

'I've been OK,' yelled Terry.

'Anything wrong with your eyes?'

'You tell *me*.'

He stared blearily into Terry's eyes and Terry could smell stale alcohol on his breath.

'They're fine.'

Terry turned to Arthur. 'He's mutton.'

'That doesn't mean to say he's not a good doctor, Terence,' admonished Arthur in a penetrating stage whisper. As he spoke, the M.O. was reading off Terry's blood pressure.

'Well?' asked Terry. 'Am I normal?'

'Excellent – yes, excellent.'

'I say – I'll have a go at that,' said Arthur.

'Eh?'

'Can you take my blood pressure as well?' shouted Arthur.

37

'If you like,' said the M.O.

'Might as well have a go,' Arthur said to Terry, 'Mine might be higher than yours.' So saying, Arthur took off his jacket and rolled up his sleeves.

'Will you be at the ringside?' Terry asked the M.O. doubtfully.

'Ringside?'

'The role square,' said Terry patiently.

'I'm sorry?'

'The boxing ring,' he yelled.

'I'll be there.' The M.O. turned to Arthur. 'Open your mouth, please.'

Looking worried, Arthur did as he was told.

'Couple of nasty cavities at the back.'

'He's a bleeding dentist,' whispered Terry. 'Now we've got problems.'

'He'll be fine if you get your teeth knocked out – How are mine, mate – are they bad?'

'You should see your dentist.' He took a look at Arthur's blood pressure. 'And your doctor as well.'

Arthur, always a hypochondriac, was instantly alarmed. 'Why?'

'Eh?'

'I said – *why*?' shouted Arthur a shade hysterically.

'I don't want to worry you,' began the M.O.

'But you are,' yelled Arthur. 'I haven't been sleeping that well.'

'Eh?'

'How high is it?'

'High enough.'

'There you are,' said Arthur, turning to Terry. 'I've got it.'

'Got what?'

'The entrepreneur's disease. They drop like flies in Throgmorton Street.'

'You're not under that kind of pressure, Arthur,' said Terry soothingly.

'No? Look at you – lovely and fit. You know why that is?'

'Why is it Arthur?' asked Terry humbly.

'It's because you don't work.'

'I see. And what am I doing tonight?'

'Manual work doesn't count. Churchill had what I've got.'
He turned to the M.O. 'Can't you give me some tablets?'

'Eh?'

'Some *tablets*,' Arthur shrieked, but the M.O. merely
nodded and smiled for he still could not hear what Arthur
was saying.

'Have your usual twelve vodkas instead,' suggested Terry.

'I suppose you think my medical problems are funny?'

'Don't worry, Mr Daley,' said the M.O. 'Nobody ever died
from cavities and I'm sure you realise the importance of oral
hygiene.'

'What's he on about?' asked Arthur impatiently.

'I think he's saying you'll get by.'

'But it's not my teeth I'm worried about –'

Terry spoke quickly over Arthur's mounting tirade: 'Did
you examine Wilson, Doc?'

'Yes – he's fine.'

'Anything wrong with his eyes?'

'They're A1.'

'You sure?'

'Are you questioning my competence, young man?'

'Not at all, sir.' Terry smiled obsequiously and turned back
to Arthur. 'If he's the doc – then what's the referee gonna be
like?'

'Eric's got everything under control, Terry.'

'I'm sure he has.'

Arthur buttoned up his jacket slowly and went to the door.

'Where are you off to – the Winchester?'

'I'm going for a lie-down.'

'Blimey.'

'In my state of health, Terence, you can't be too careful.'

'I see.'

'And I hope you don't expect too much help in the corner
tonight, Tel – not in my state of health.'

Arthur went slowly out, breathing heavily. A few seconds
later Terry followed him into the corridor, but Arthur was
nowhere to be seen. He must have legged it, thought Terry.
But he soon forgot about Arthur – it was bloody weird about

the doc not spotting the detached retina in Jackie Wilson's eye. Still, thought Terry, the doc was no good, was he?

Terry lay face down on the table in the tatty dressing room. Soldier, whilst gently massaging his shoulders, was giving him a long, nostalgic lecture on tactics. He was wearing a snappy white tunic with the name TERRY McCANN on the back. With Soldier was an assistant who was clutching a miscellany of Vaseline, swabs and water-bottles, whilst Arthur paced nervously about, his cigar smoke swirling, rather like an expectant father.

'Hot innit?' said Arthur. He looked at Terry's inert form. 'Why isn't he saying anything?' Arthur asked Soldier with a quaver in his voice.

'He's edgy, Arthur – under pressure.'

'Don't say anything about pressure to me,' replied Arthur. 'No one knows how ill I am.' He turned to Terry. 'Is he confident, then?'

'Course he is. I've seen 'em like this before. Mean!'

Terry could stand it no longer and he looked up. Rather than feeling mean, he was both tense and nervous – and the conversation being held over his head was not helping.

'I'm here, you know,' he said. 'I can talk.'

'Len Harvey was the same,' Soldier said to Arthur. 'Calm, but edgy.'

'How the hell can you be calm and edgy at the same time?' asked Terry.

'You see, Arthur,' continued Soldier, 'he's got inner confidence – and he's ready to go out there and do business.'

'Is he?' asked Arthur doubtfully. At that moment one of the stick-on letters that Arthur had supplied for Soldier's tunic fell off, leaving the name 'ERRY McCANN'. Arthur did not consider this was a good omen. Meanwhile, mentally, Terry was going over and over the business of Wilson's eye. Brenda had seemed genuine enough, yet how had the doc missed it? But then the doc was not exactly with it.

'O.K., chaps? I have a capacity crowd for you.'

Eric was standing at the door, beaming and looking hopeful.

'Yeah,' said Arthur sourly. 'I sold most of the tickets, didn't I?'

'I still haven't had the money yet,' returned Eric, his Welsh accent making his voice sound deeply wounded.

'Haven't you?' asked Arthur, fumbling in a number of pockets.

'How's your boy?'

'Fantastic. Let's talk business outside, shall we? I wouldn't want to interrupt Terry's train of thought.'

'What's that?' asked Eric.

'He's thinking mean, aren't you, Terry?'

'Yes, Harry.' Terry had his head down again and Soldier had returned to massaging his shoulders.

Out in the corridor, Arthur somewhat reluctantly handed over the money.

'Any betting around?'

'Plenty. Even Steven. You going to back Terry?'

'I'm not a betting man, but I know he's fit. I also know that Wilson hasn't done much work and he likes a drink.'

'He's got class, though.'

'Has he?'

'But you want to back Terry?'

'Who do I see?'

'Me,' said Eric with a smile.

'I should have known!'

'You're due a monkey on the purse. Why don't you double it?'

'But if Tel loses – I lose everything.'

'Quick, aren't you?'

Arthur stared with active dislike at Eric.

'You've got yourself a bet,' he said.

The atmosphere in the hall was a mixture of cigarette smoke, sweat and stale beer. The audience was predominantly male and Nicky looked around her, feeling self-conscious and jumpy. Then the crowd noise was broken by a tinny fanfare on the P.A. system and Terry jogged into the arena, wearing a hooded dressing gown and accompanied by Soldier and his assistant. Arthur walked regally a few paces behind them,

41

rather as if he were the star attraction himself.

As Terry ran towards the ring he could make out a number of familiar faces – Detective Constable Rycott, Chris the Greek butcher, Dave and others. But rather than reassuring him, they merely made him feel uneasy. As Terry climbed into the ring he saw Brenda sitting in the front row and his uneasiness increased. That eye – that bloody eye. Wilson was already there when he arrived and as Terry stripped off his gown and began to limber up, a buxom girl in the ring was strutting around with a placard indicating the number of rounds in the fight.

'Who's the bird?' Terry asked.

'Eric's cousin – she goes to the loser,' Arthur replied seriously.

'What's up, Arthur?'

'I'm ill.'

'You're so reassuring, aren't you?'

'You don't know what kind of strain I'm under, Tel.'

'Anyone would think you were going into the ring.'

'I feel as if I am.'

Then the M.C. stepped into the middle of the ring and began to announce the fight.

'Ladies and Gentlemen. We now come to the main event in tonight's programme. A middleweight bout of ten rounds introducing the popular Fulham Typhoon – Terry McCann.'

There was a burst of applause and through it Terry said to Arthur: 'That was your idea, wasn't it?'

'What?'

'Typhoon – The Fulham Typhoon.'

'It's an image, isn't it?' Arthur replied vaguely, his hand shaking on his cigar.

'Pull yourself together, Arthur.'

'I'm ill, Tel. Very ill.'

'You'll be all right.'

'And one of the greats,' continued the M.C. 'Ex-middleweight Champion of Britain and the Commonwealth – Jackie Wilson. And your referee, Ladies and Gentlemen, is Bernie Sandilands.' There was full applause, the M.C. left the ring and the referee called Terry and Jackie to the middle. In the audience, Detective Constable Rycott turned to a plain-clothed colleague and whispered:

'I hope you've got your notebook, my son. There's plenty of faces on the wanted list, here.' He stared round the audience. 'I mean – look over there – that's Archie Harris – he should be in Parkhurst, shouldn't he?'

Meanwhile, Soldier was saying to Terry, 'We've got time, Terry. Plenty of time – so feel him out.'

But Arthur was not having any. 'Knock him out, Terry. Soon as you can – then we can go home early.'

Terry attempting to ignore Arthur, suddenly caught Nicky's eye and grinned. She smiled hesitantly back and then the bell went for the first round. Immediately, Terry was up on his toes and moving well. Wilson gave him a few tentative jabs, but they were well out of reach. Then, Wilson tried a right, but Terry was ducking and moving away, easily avoiding the blow. The audience were bored and began to catcall, suspecting they were going to witness a tame fight. But they were cheered by a flurry of punches from Terry and the sight of Wilson retreating fast. Terry pursued him to the corner where Wilson clinched and held on desperately.

'Go on, my son,' shouted Arthur, his eyes bulging and his cigar dead in his mouth.

Getting out of the clinch, Wilson also managed to evade Terry. Over-anxious, Terry tried to get in with a badly-calculated punch, but he failed to make contact. The fans groaned and the bell resounded.

'Don't let him sit down,' said Arthur scrambling into the ring. 'He'll go to sleep.'

'All right, Arthur,' said Soldier, looking disappointed.

'Get out,' said Terry.

'But what's going on?' asked Arthur as Terry sat down on his stool.

'He don't want to fight.'

'That's no reason for you not to. Come on – I've got money on this.'

'On who?'

'I've got a monkey on the Fulham Typhoon. So let's get busy.' Arthur turned desperately to Soldier. 'Go on – tell him about Tommy Farr and Len Harvey again.'

'Relax, Arthur. Now Tel, just settle down. You've got nothing to beat.'

The girl with the placard bounced into the ring and announced Round Two as Soldier said, 'Be first, son.'

'Yeah,' said Arthur. 'Get in there. And be quick.'

'Arthur,' Terry said as the bell went, 'Why don't you drop off?'

Terry was jabbing away until Wilson forced him into a clinch. Leaning on Terry's shoulder, he whispered:

'Take it easy – I'm knackered. I've got a dodgy eye.'

'Lie down, then.'

'No talking there,' shouted the referee.

Wilson twisted round Terry – and went on whispering, out of the referee's earshot.

'Don't hit me eye.'

'Then what?'

'Body shots – they're O.K.'

'Lie down – I've told you once.'

'Make it good then.'

The referee broke them apart and as he did so, Terry glanced towards Brenda. She seemed very anxious. Looking hard, Terry moved in with a series of body jabs and Wilson winced. But as he did so, Terry suddenly, instinctively knew he had been conned. Terry's face was open and Wilson was suddenly raining punches to his head. They were good – and Wilson was showing all the form and pace of a former champion. The crowd began to roar and with a right cross Terry was thrown back on the canvas. The referee began to count as blood gushed from Terry's eye but, somehow, he managed to heave himself off the ropes.

Wilson then came in for the kill with a fierce combination of punches and the crowd roared again. Nicky buried her face in her hands – and so did Arthur. Soldier stared woodenly at Terry as he pawed at the ropes again.

'Blimey,' muttered Terry as he just beat the count. For a moment he mistily caught Brenda's expression. There was a mixture of triumph and pain on her face. Terry then found himself being led to his corner by the referee and Wilson continued to prance around the middle of the ring, giving a victory salute to the cheering crowd. His two corner-men were already embracing him.

'He conned me,' said Terry muzzily to Arthur and Soldier. 'What round is it?'

'It's over, son,' replied Soldier.

'What?'

'I said, it's –'

But Terry was away from him, rushing at Wilson, whose arm the referee had not yet raised.

'My Gawd,' said Arthur, putting his hands over his eyes again.

Wiping the blood from his face, Terry pushed the referee away and was on to Wilson. His two corner-men tried to whisk him away, but Terry knocked one of them over. The other tried to swing a punch but to no avail, for Terry gave him a backhander and he went sprawling onto the canvas. Wilson squared up to Terry and in a second they were at it, toe to toe, trading punch for punch. The referee tried ineffectively to stop them as Eric shouted at him:

'Don't bloody stop 'em, Bernie. This is the last fight of the night!'

As Terry and Wilson slugged it out, the crowd were on their feet and Arthur gradually took his hands away from his eyes. He could see Dave, Chris and even Detective Constable Rycott shouting for Terry. Nicky stared ahead, her eyes glazed and, in another part of the hall, Brenda watched transfixed.

Gradually, Terry's right-hand blows and his passionate anger told on Wilson, who began to go down under the massive attack. Then, after a beautiful right and left from Terry, he hit the deck, with the crowd going crazy and Soldier yelling to Arthur: 'It's a classic fight, Arthur. A fight for history!'

But Terry did not acknowledge the adulation of the cheering. Instead, he turned away, climbed out of the ring and shouldered his way through the crowd to the dressing room. Arthur, meanwhile, having recovered his composure, went after an exultant Eric.

'Oh Taff –'

'Yes, Arthur?'

'You owe me money.'

'You reckon?'

'He won, didn't he?'

'That's a debatable point. The ref stopped it.'

'You can tell that to Jackie Wilson. We ain't exactly talking about the Queensberry Rules, are we?'

'You know what I'm going to do, Arthur?' said Eric triumphantly.

'No,' said Arthur suspiciously.

'That fight was like one of the fights my Da used to talk about. You've got a result, Arthur – and I don't want you ever to say that I'm not generous.'

'You mean –' Arthur's smile was beginning.

'You won.'

'You're a gentleman, Eric,' said Arthur, pumping his hand.

Soldier was swabbing at Terry's eye in the dressing room.

'I'm proud of you, son.'

'It was a street fight,' said Terry.

'Most fights start there.'

Arthur, clutching a wad of notes, entered cheerfully with the deaf M.O. in tow.

'Good on yer, Terry.'

'Thanks, Arthur.'

'We're on next month.'

'No, we're not.'

'Eh?' Arthur looked flabbergasted. 'Look Tel – don't you understand? You punch-drunk or something? You've got a new career. You're the people's champion.'

'Shut up, Arthur.'

'I beg your pardon, Terence. I hope all this hasn't gone to your head.'

'I had a career,' said Terry firmly, 'seven years ago. So forget it.' He looked up at the M.O. vaguely advancing towards him. 'And get him out before he has my teeth.'

'I was terrified,' said Nicky when Terry had showered and changed.

'I wasn't too happy at one point,' said Terry.

'I don't like boxing.'

'I didn't think you would.'

'You going on with it?'

'Arthur wants me to.'

'But –'

'I'm not going to do it.'

She smiled with relief. 'What are you going to do instead? Come back to the Job Centre.'

'I've got a job.'

'What's that?'

'Looking after Arthur.'

'Is that a job?'

'Not much of one.'

'Then, why not change it?'

'I've got used to it.'

'You're in a rut.'

'I know. Tell you what – let's go somewhere.'

'Where to?'

'How about my place?'

Next day, Arthur parked his car outside Harry's flat. Terry, wearing dark glasses, was sitting with Nicky in the back. Arthur got out, went round to the boot and pulled out an awful framed reproduction of 'The Stag at Bay'.

'Nice, isn't it?' he said as he showed it to Terry through the car window.

'I thought you was taking us out to lunch?'

'I will in a minute. Just hang about – I'm refurbishing one of my properties.'

Holding the picture, Arthur walked towards the flats whilst Nicky took off Terry's dark glasses and examined the bruise round his eye.

'If you had a real job – you could claim industrial compensation.'

'From Arthur?'

'Why not?'

47

'You don't know Arthur,' said Terry.

Nicky sighed, 'I think I'm beginning to,' she said.

Once on the landing, Arthur was surprised to find the door of Harry's flat open. Inside, he could see that the flat had been painted but he could also see three suitcases in the middle of the floor. Stepping inside, Arthur gazed incredulously at them until a shrewish-looking woman in her mid-forties came out of the bedroom. She stared indignantly at Arthur.

'Who the hell are you?'

'I might ask you the same, madam,' said Arthur pompously. 'I happen to own this apartment.'

'Do you now! So you're a squatter, are you?'

'Certainly not.'

'*I* live here.'

Light dawned in Arthur's eyes. 'I see – you're Harry's wife.'

'What if I am?'

'You've been blown out, love.'

'And what's that meant to mean?'

'If you will go off with double-glazing men and desert the domestic home. No wonder Harry's sold the gaff.'

'Sold? This is a council flat.'

'You must realise, madam, that I'm the legal tenant of this – what did you say?'

'I said – this is a council flat.'

'My Gawd.'

'Now – get out.'

But Arthur did not move. Instead he simply stood there, his mouth opening and shutting without a sound emerging.

'Are you going – or shall I call the police?'

In a trance, Arthur went.

Very slowly, as if he was an old man, Arthur opened the car door.

'What's the matter?' asked Terry.

'I'm ill.'

'Yeah – but aren't you still taking us out for lunch – to celebrate?'

'Celebrate what?'
'And you're gonna pick up the tab?'
'You're taking advantage of a sick man.'
'You can be sick after lunch, Arthur,' said Terry.

PART TWO

Arthur took a long time getting over Harry's con. He talked about it incessantly and both Terry and Dave took a pasting as they tried to commiserate with him.

'You're too trusting, Arthur,' said Dave one night at the Winchester and Terry agreed.

'You should have sussed it out more, Arthur.'

'You're a couple of Jim's comforters, aren't you?'

'Eh?'

'Who is Jim?'

'You don't seem to understand – either of you – that I'm a decent kind of bloke. I don't *expect* to be conned. I'm a respectable businessman.'

'You're a schmuck,' said Terry.

'Thank you, Terence. After all I've done for you – rescuing you from the audio-typists and swinging ropes, giving you a career – and then having you throw it all up. And now you call me a schmuck!'

'You should have grabbed your opportunity, Arthur,' said Dave.

'What opportunity?'

'The one Harry's wife gave you,' continued Dave. 'You should have given her a little something to remember you with. After all – you were alone in the flat?'

'You seem to forget I have 'er indoors.'

'That's never stopped you,' put in Terry.

'To decorate a council flat,' said Arthur. 'All that paint, that stripper, those brushes –'

'What stripper?' asked Terry. 'You didn't say you laid on one for the boys. I'd have given you a hand if you'd said.'

'Another vodka,' cried Arthur piteously.

'I can't put much more on the slate, Arthur. You're well over the limit.'

'Then buy me a vodka,' cried Arthur. 'Help me in my hour of need.'

'We've all been done,' said Terry. 'Lay off it for a bit, Arthur.'

'Been done? When've you been done?'

'I was done when I met you, Arthur,' replied Terry quietly.

Dave grinned. 'Cheer up, Arthur. Just think how lucky you are.'

'Lucky?'

'Yeah – Harry could've sold you the whole block.'

To cheer himself up, Arthur went to a masonic dinner the next night. Returning home by mini-cab and in a highly drunken condition, Arthur bumped into an old friend. He limped out of the shadows, a man in his late thirties who was handsome in a brutish sort of way.

'Hallo, Arthur.'

'Who the hell –' Arthur blundered about on the pavement, basically trying to stand up.

'It's Billy.'

'Blimey – what are you doing lurking?' Arthur swayed in front of him. 'You all right, Billy – oh dear, oh dear – what have you done?'

Arthur had finally noticed that there was a very nasty swelling on Billy's face.

'I need some help, Arthur.'

You look as if you could use some.'

'Like now.'

'Come and have a nice drink.'

'I need a lift – can you drive me somewhere?' Billy's voice was hoarse with fatigue.

'Can't in my state, old son,' replied Arthur shakily. 'I'm plastered – been to a function – can't cope with a car.'

'Know anyone who can?'

'Come in and tell me all about it.'

'I need a ride *now*, Arthur. I've done me leg in.'

Arthur grasped Billy's shoulder in a drunken embrace. 'Are we friends, Billy?'

'We certainly are, Arthur.'

'Really good mates?'

'You can bet your life on it.'

'Then I will get you a ride, my son – if necessary to the very ends of the earth.' He began to guide Billy erratically down the street.

'Where are we going, Arthur?'

'We? Where are *we* going?'

'Yes Arthur – where are we going?' There was a dangerous edge to Billy's voice, but Arthur was too drunk to detect it.

'We're goin' to an ole friend. A very ole friend.'

'And he'll help me?'

'He helps everyone,' said Arthur, 'even me.'

Terry was in bed with Nicky when Arthur called. He sat bolt upright in bed as Arthur lurched around on the landing. Then Terry heard the penetrating stage whisper.

'Terry – open up.'

'I'm asleep.'

Nicky clapped a hand over her mouth as she felt an overpowering urge to giggle.

'It's important, Terry.'

Terry climbed out of bed, opened the front door and pushed Arthur back onto the landing.

'Yeah.'

'You know Billy Gilpin?'

'You wake me up for introductions?'

'Billy needs a favour.'

'Does he?'

'You gonna let us in?'

'I'd rather we talked here.'

'That's not very social, Tel.'

'I'm not a very social person.'

'Look – Terry – I've said this is important.' The drink in Arthur made him slightly belligerent and Terry raised his eyebrows. Then, suddenly, he gave in and reluctantly led them into the kitchen.

'Well?'

'Any coffee, Tel?'

'Not at this time of night, Arthur. Come on – spill.it.'

'I said to Billy that there's one bloke I know who wouldn't let anyone down –' Arthur began conversationally.

'Look,' said Terry, finally coming clean. 'I've got a bird in there.'

'Nicky?'

'It doesn't matter who she is.'

'She's a girl after me own heart.'

'Let's get on with it, Arthur,' said Billy, the edge returning to his voice.

'I'll explain it all to Nicky,' Arthur lurched towards the bedroom door and Terry grabbed him just in time.

'Please, Arthur.'

'I'm sorry, Terry,' said Billy. 'I'm desperate for this favour.'

Then the interruption came.

'Coffee anyone?' Nicky appeared from the bedroom.

'Don't mind if I do, Nicky,' said Arthur. 'You really are the sweetest little –'

'Hang on,' said Terry.

'What's up?' she asked.

'I'm going out,' said Terry.

'Thanks, pal,' put in Billy.

'For a while.'

'You are, are you?' Nicky's good humour vanished.

'I won't be long.'

'It's always the same – when that man comes –' She pointed angrily at Arthur. 'That awful man.'

'Nicky,' began Arthur. 'Darling girl –'

'Shut up, Arthur,' said Terry.

'You stay out of this,' replied Arthur. 'I can –'

'The only person who's staying out is me,' snapped Nicky.

'Wait a minute –' pleaded Terry.

'No. I'm always waiting. I'm going to dress.'

'Do you want some help?' sniggered Arthur as she slammed the kitchen door.

'Your charm,' said Terry slowly. 'It always wins through in the end, doesn't it?'

Terry drove Billy in his elderly Ford. For a while they said nothing and Terry pulled out onto the Brighton road and began to drive at a considerable rate of knots.

'Not so fast,' said Billy. 'We don't want to get a pull.'

Terry slowed down. 'You're right – this motor ain't been MOT'd for two years.'

Billy was uneasily silent again. Then he said: 'No music?'

'No music.'

'I like a number called Friends.'

'Don't know it.' Terry sounded as if he wanted to make as little social contact with Billy as possible.

'It's true though.'

'What is?'

'Friends – I won't forget this, Terry.'

'No?'

'A friend is a guy you can go to in the middle of the night – and he'll help you. No questions – nothin'.'

'You went to Arthur.'

'He took me to you.'

'That's Arthur's friendship all over.'

There was a long pause. Then Billy said: 'You haven't asked, have you?'

'Asked what?'

'What happened to Billy's pretty face.'

'I don't want to know.'

'And his leg?'

'I told you – I don't want to know.'

'Arthur's got an address – I'll see you're looked after.'

'I thought it was all down to friendship.'

'And it is. But there's no harm in giving your friends a drink, is there? People don't understand that – people I've known for years. And the filth – no way would they believe my story.'

'I don't want to hear it, Billy.'

He speeded up the Ford, but Billy said quickly: 'For Christ's sake Terry – slow down.'

Terry slowed down and Billy relaxed again. 'It's a beautiful night, isn't it?'

'Mm.'

'We turn off before Brighton.'

'O.K.'

'I've forgotten me tablets.'

'Well, I ain't going back for 'em.'

'They put me on tablets, you know. Me – a champagne man. I love the bubbly – I can dance on it all night. But I get down, depressed like – that's why they put me on the tablets. They thought I might top meself.'

Terry shot Billy an appraising glance but Billy was

vacantly staring at the countryside around them. Then he said, 'Take the next turning.'

Terry did as he was told.

'Sorry about that bird of yours.'

'That's all right – it was coming.'

'What does she do?'

'Works in a Job Centre.'

'Useful.'

'Maybe.'

'I used to pull little girls like that. Moved on now, you know.'

'Oh yeah.'

'You gotta move on – I only go for the class. Strictly jet set now.'

'Well I'm still hanging around with the off-peak stand-by lot.'

But Billy was not listening. 'I was in the papers three times last month. They made me a celebrity in the gossip columns and just because of the company I was keeping.'

'I hope you're not in them tomorrow.'

'O.K.' said Billy with a sudden brusqueness. 'Next right and you'll find a little hotel at the top of the hill.'

A few minutes later, they stopped outside a shuttered building standing on top of a small hill. The night was clear and still.

'You're gonna check in at this time of night with no bags?' queried Terry. He leant across Billy to open the door for him.

'Without friends,' said Billy, 'it's not worth living.'

'You got friends here?'

'Another mate.'

'You're a lucky man.'

'That's something I always remember, Tel. How lucky I am.'

Billy got out of the car and walked over to the door of the hotel. He knocked at it gently and as Terry drove away, he could see a light switched on at an upstairs window.

The roads were empty on the way back to London and Terry drove slowly, mulling over the events of the night. There was something about his own involvement in Billy's journey that made Terry uneasy. Obviously his very appearance had underlined he had been up to no good – but it wasn't just that. It was something else that Terry could not pin down.

Arriving back at his flat, Terry climbed wearily out of the car and yawningly struggled up the stairs. He searched in his pockets for the key to the front door, cursing as he did so. What he wanted was not just a kip, but Nicky as well – two important parts of his life that Arthur had deprived him of. At last Terry found his key and he opened the door of the flat slowly. As he crossed the threshold, he had a premonition that something unpleasant was about to happen – and when he opened the sitting room door, he discovered what it was. Two young men were sitting there, one examining Terry's record collection, the other flicking through a magazine. Without asking, Terry knew they were plain clothed policemen.

'Terence McCann?' said the man on the sofa, flicking out a warrant card.

'I'd never have guessed who you were without seeing that.'

'You must have seen quite a few in your time,' said the other detective, putting down a record.

'You've no right breaking in here.'

'Breaking in? We were kindly allowed access to the premises by your associate.'

One word lit itself angrily in Terry's mind – Arthur.

'Where is he?'

'Here I am, Tel.'

Arthur came in from the bathroom, looking pale and ill. His collar was open and his black tie dangled hopelessly. He flopped into a chair and groaned.

'I don't think your friend's very well,' said one of the detectives.

'I was having a kip, Terry,' said Arthur, 'when the front door –'

'All right, Arthur,' said Terry quietly.

'Shall we take a ride?' The detective smiled up at Terry.

'What happens if I say no?'

'Well,' the detective looked at his colleague, 'Steve here

will jump on you and I'll say you assaulted him and you'll be remanded in custody . . . which would be rather silly really because all we want to do is to have a talk with you. So what's it going to be?'

'Since you put it so nicely – I'd love to come.'

'Say bye-bye to your obliging friend.'

'Yes,' said Terry reflectively. 'You've got to have friends, haven't you? Bye-bye, Arthur.'

At the police station, Terry was interviewed by an old acquaintance – the middle-aged, patient and cynical Detective Inspector Barrett. He sat opposite Terry, flanked by another, younger detective.

'You see, Terry,' said Barrett, 'everywhere I go I see dirt – everywhere I listen I hear lies. But I've always had a kind of faith in you. No trouble for five years now.'

'That's right.'

'I thought you were a walking testimony to the reformative powers of the British penal system. And then – just like that – you're running a mini-cab service for nasty villains like Billy Gilpin.'

'I gave him a lift. That's no crime – is it?'

'It all depends, Terry. I mean – two villains walk out of a shop with a string of pearls that don't belong to 'em – and someone gives 'em a lift. That's a crime, isn't it?'

Terry said nothing.

'Eh?'

'It's a crime.'

'And what about attempted murder, then? That a crime in your book?'

'Yeah.'

'And aiding and abetting the escape of a man wanted for murder?'

'I dunno what he did,' said Terry defensively.

'But I just told you what he did.'

Terry stared down at the table.

'Then he didn't mention it.'

'What did he talk about?'

'He didn't say much. He talked about friends.'

'Which friends?'

'He didn't say. He said he was lucky to have 'em.'

'What about Lord Ingram?'

'Who?'

'Did he mention that name?'

'No – what is it – a boozer?'

'He's the feller Billy tried to murder.'

'Well – if he did, he never mentioned it.'

Barrett leant across the table and spoke softly to Terry. 'Listen Terry. I'm not asking you to be a super-grass. But I *am* advising you to have a slightly more co-operative attitude. You see – if there's attempted murder on my patch I get something – see. I either get the guy who did it – or the guy who helped him get away.' He paused, sat back and spoke in a louder voice: 'Am I coming through to you loud and clear?'

'I'm with you,' said Terry.

'So, I'd like you to go and have a little think.'

'At home?'

'No, Terry – in a cell. On your ownio.'

Terry lay miserably on the lower bunk of the cell. He looked around, registering again the claustrophobia of a place that he had hoped he would never see again. A feeling of desolation swept over him. He would never be allowed to put it all behind him – not in the end.

Suddenly the door opened and a thick-set man was shown in to the confined space. He glanced round the cell quickly and then his eyes rested on Terry. When he spoke it was with a Northern accent and a very ingratiating manner, but beneath all this, Terry detected a basic toughness.

'The name's Whaley. Colin Whaley.'

'Terry McCann.'

'I've got the top one, then.'

'Looks like it.'

'That's O.K. by me.' He gave Terry a quick, insincere smile. 'I've had plenty of practice anyway.' Whaley hauled himself up to the top bunk. 'Just done a five in Durham,' he continued. 'Only out two weeks, when the bastards grabbed me. They don't give you a chance down here.' He paused as if to allow Terry to reply, but received no response. Terry was playing it cool, determined to give nothing away. 'Attempted robbery, they say. And they gave me a right kicking on the way down. Stuff the bastards – that's what I say. Stuff 'em.' He leant over the bunk to take a good look at Terry. 'What you in for, then?'

'Not a lot.'

Whaley continued, undeterred by Terry's reticence. 'I've been everywhere you know. Maidenhead, Hull – I was even up in Peterhead. I did pottery and carpet weaving up there.'

'They nicked you for it?'

'I did that inside. Occupational therapy, they called it.' He leant over again to take another look at Terry. 'Don't say much, do yer.'

'I don't stand much of a chance with you up there.'

'Don't mind me. I'm just the outgoing type. I like getting on with people.'

'I've already sussed that out.'

'Straight I am.' He swung down off the bunk. 'You seem a bit worried. Depressed like.'

Terry gave him a cynical glance. 'Don't worry about it.'

'Why not?'

'Because you might become me best pal.'

'So –'

'In a fit of depression and remorse I tell you my life story.'

'Yeah. If it helps.'

'And what I done and how I did it and the first I learn of it is when you're in the box swearing my life away.'

'You got it all wrong. I'm just trying to be a friend.'

'I've had enough friends for one day.'

'But –'

'OK?'

Terry turned over and attempted, with difficulty, to find himself a comfortable sleeping position. Disappointed, Whaley stared down at him and then, with a shrug, levered himself up onto the top bunk again.

'You don't talk in your sleep an' all do you?' Terry said.

*

The next morning, they let Terry go. He felt relieved but also exhausted and somehow institutionalised again – despite the shortness of his stay. As he walked angrily down the corridor of the police station, Barrett passed him.

'Ah, Terry – you won't go nipping off to Majorca, will you? We may want you to come in again.'

Not trusting himself to say anything, Terry simply scowled and walked on. His mood was not improved by meeting Arthur as he left the police station. Arthur was still wearing his dinner-suit, was unshaved and looked distinctly seedy.

'You've got me to thank for getting you out of there,' said Arthur.

'I got you to thank for getting me *in* there.'

'Nice innit – me walking about at this time of day looking like this. Think of my position.'

'They'll think you've been in for a fitting.'

'Fit up more like it. Think of the dinners I've been to with some of these people. I mean – a D.I., who shall be nameless, has me to thank for giving him a deep-freeze at a give-away price. A real steal!'

'I'm sure that was just what it was, Arthur.'

'That's beside the point, Terry.'

Arthur tried to hail a cab but was swiftly beaten by an Arab.

'They're as bad, an' all. If you ain't got a kaftan – you ain't got no chance. I'll tell you –'

But Terry cut firmly across Arthur's flow. 'What about Billy?'

'You never know with him. Could be doing a bit of cross-channel swimming.'

'He talked about topping himself when I was driving him.'

'Well, I hope he made a phone call about our loot before he done it.'

'You're a real friend to Billy, aren't you, Arthur? No wonder he values his friends so highly.'

'So, I'll cry a little,' returned Arthur truculently. 'But I still want the loot.'

'I'm going home.'

'No, you're not, Terry.'

'Arthur – I'm knackered.'

'You'll feel much better after a quiet sauna and a change of attire.'

'Why?'

'Because we have to visit Lady Ingram.'

'Who?'

'Lady Anne Clare Ingram. Who is –'

'– the missus of the feller Billy tried to murder.'

'That's their own personal affair, Terence.'

'So – what's ours?'

'Our wages. That's something else – innit?'

'Is it?'

'Since when have you grown cold on loot – specially after all the aggravation you've had?'

'I'm going home.'

'And then?'

'I'll meet yer.'

'Well done, Terry. That's my boy.'

'But Arthur –'

'Yes?'

'If I ever go back inside, I'm holding you personally responsible.'

'You – inside?'

'Yeah. I caught the smell of it again. Know what I mean?'

'Sorry, Tel. I wouldn't.'

'You will, Arthur. One day – you will.'

The traffic in Terry's flat was getting very heavy. Last night he had met the filth in his front room. Now he met the heavies on the landing.

A young well-dressed man was leaning against the door and another, equally well-dressed, but bigger and harder-looking, was standing a few feet away.

'Terence McCann?'

'Why am I so popular?'

'I don't know, Terry. P'raps you aren't. Not doing a runner, are you?'

'Who the hell *are* you?'

'We're not the old Bill.'

'Hard to tell, these days.'

'We only want to have a talk.'

'That's what the old Bill said. Last time it lasted too long.'

'But Bobby Altman gets to the point so much more quickly than the filth.'

'Who's Altman?'

'Friend of Billy Gilpin's.'

'Another *friend*?'

'Yeah – a big one.'

'That word's always cropping up.'

'Eh?'

'Friend. Billy was really into friends, wasn't he?'

But they were both advancing down the stairs.

'Come on, Terry,' said the well-built one. Terry turned wearily back down the stairs.

Bobby Altman believed in keeping himself fit and today was no exception. For his normal jog across Hampstead Heath Bobby, who was touching fifty and had dragged himself from the East End to the Heights, wore a well-cut track suit and highly expensive running shoes. As he came into view, a Ford Granada pulled up, disgorging Terry and his two new-found friends. On the pavement was another young man, who was standing opposite a neo-Georgian mansion that screamed money from every well turned brick.

'How much has he done?' asked one of Terry's captors.

'On his fourth mile.'

Terry noticed there was a Rolls Royce parked outside the garage and as Altman came jogging up, one of his underlings passed him a towel. As he wiped away the sweat, Altman gave Terry a shrewd, slightly patronising look. Then he draped the towel round his neck, took his own pulse and said casually to Terry:

'Do a bit of jogging?'

'Now and again.'

'Tennis, squash, badminton?'

'No.'

'Work out at the gym?'

'Sometimes.'

'I remember you, Terry McCann.'

'Oh?'

'Saw your fight.'

'Against Wilson?'

'No – first time round.'

'Oh – I see.'

'You were badly handled.'

'Yeah.'

'But you've gone a long way since then.'

'Maybe.'

'Now you're an even bigger mug.'

The other three men came very close to Terry as Altman said: 'Do come in.' He indicated the house with the Rolls outside. Terry hesitated. 'Please,' said Altman. 'Any friend of Billy's is a friend of mine.'

'You work for Arthur Daley?'

'Sort of.'

Altman was in the shower and Terry was standing in a room that had been expertly converted into a gym. New, gleaming equipment invited maximum exertion and a statue of Adonis suggested the ideal.

'You know what he is?'

Terry thought hard. To Altman, none of the things that Arthur was could be considered complimentary. But Altman did not wait for an answer.

'Arthur is a financial midget.'

Terry did not reply and Altman, still in the shower, shouted out, 'Try the speed-ball, Terry.'

'I'm O.K., thanks.'

'He said to try it,' put in one of Altman's heavies. Terry slowly crossed to the speed-ball and began to hammer it. The heavies watched, impressed despite themselves for Terry was both fast and accurate. He went into a very fancy two-handed tattoo on the ball and Altman emerged from the shower to watch him, wrapping himself in a bath-robe, handed to him by one of his acolytes. Terry concluded his work out with a hefty right hander that almost parted the

66

ball from its moorings. He then turned to face Altman who was drinking a large tumblerful of orange juice. He then sat himself down on a swivel chair and grandiosely motioned to Terry to sit down on one opposite him.

Altman took his own pulse again. 'I run for miles. I take a shower. I sit down and my pulse is normal again.'

'Lucky you,' said Terry.

'I have a very slow heart-beat – fifty-six a minute. Athletes half my age would give anything for a pulse rate like that. Now, Terry, all this means that I'm a very calm and rational man. The only time that my pulse rate quickens is when I talk about money. And the only time it starts to race is when I talk about money that's been stolen from me.'

'What money?'

'Billy Gilpin stole my money and you helped him get away.'

'I didn't know what he'd been doing.'

'And now they tell me he's dead.'

'Dead?' Terry's voice registered sudden alarm.

'Or so I hear. But I don't know whether to believe it or not.'

'Did the buzz say how he died?'

'They say he walked into the water.'

'And you reckon it's not true?'

'I say it's bullshit. With seventy grand Billy Gilpin could walk *on* the water.'

'Look – all I did was to give him a lift.'

'So what does that make you?' asked Altman menacingly.

'It makes me the guy who gave him a lift – that's all.'

'No, Terry. It makes you an accomplice. It makes you the man who helped steal money from *me*.'

'Look –'

Altman jumped up, the anger etched hard on his face.

'I'm excited now, Terry. I'm angry too – and what happens when I'm angry? My heart starts racing.'

He began to walk round Terry. 'Heard of the Ayatollah?'

'Yeah.'

'I'm a fan of his.'

'He needs a few.'

'What happens? You steal in his country and he cuts your

67

hand off. So, if you steal from *me* – then don't worry about referendums, don't worry about free votes in the House of Commons, don't worry about anything like that.' He continued to pace around Terry and then he stopped, leaning over to within an inch of his face. 'If you steal from me – I bring back capital punishment.'

'I could plead diminished responsibility.'

'And what's that supposed to mean?' asked Altman, looking sarcastically round at his three heavies.

'That I don't know nothing.'

'I see. You didn't even wonder what was in his little Gucci briefcase?'

'He didn't have a case.'

Terry sounded so positive that Altman paused for a minute and Terry knew that he was wondering, for the first time, whether or not he was on the level.

'So his pockets were bulging?' asked Altman.

'No – but his eye was bulging. And he had a dodgy leg.'

'You're St John's Ambulance, are you? An overgrown boy scout? Anybody's a bit out of sorts and you're the first to give them a helping hand. He's a pal, is he?'

'I never met him before.'

Altman seemed genuinely surprised as he once more turned to his acolytes. 'You believe that, chaps? This guy's terrific. He's the last of the English gents.'

'I just did a favour.'

'That's nice, isn't it? A nice favour – and maybe I'll even believe you.' Altman stared very hard at Terry. 'Now you're in my house and you've seen the bricks and mortar. Right?'

Terry nodded.

'You've seen this gym and you've probably noticed it's bigger and better than your living room. I've got a lot of staff and I spend a lot of money. Look at my lads – well dressed with a nice wedge in their pockets. Look at Stuart now. When he came down from Scotland he had 50p in his sporran. Now he's got a gold Dupont lighter and the guy doesn't even smoke.'

Terry watched Altman's face. He seemed to be calming down slightly and maybe he was going to be ready to strike some kind of deal. But *what* kind of deal?

'You know what a bearer bond is?'

'No.'

'Course you don't – they're like money. You take 'em to a bank and they pay you out – face value. We've been doing that, see, France, Germany, Switzerland . . . Never mind how we got 'em. We've been selling 'em, right?'

Again Terry nodded, his mind furiously trying to get one ahead of Altman – and failing.

'You need a bit of front for what I'm doing – that's why pretty Billy was on the firm. Then – temptation falls in the lad's path.'

'You sure?'

'I'm sure. And if he didn't have the money on him when he was with you – somebody's looking after it for him. That's logical.'

'Yeah.'

'How did he come to you, Tel?'

Terry hesitated.

'Come on.'

He glanced at the three heavies who looked as if they might like to see some action at any minute.

'Arthur brought him.'

'Now that figures. You don't need a pocket calculator for that.' He poured himself out some more orange juice and almost drained the glass. 'Terry – I want you to go and tell Arthur that I want my money.'

'I'm not sure he can help you – any more than I can.'

'Tell him if I don't get it – he's a dead man.'

Altman wrapped a towel round his neck and walked over to the door. En route he paused – and thumped hard at the speed-ball. Then he turned back to Terry. 'I could still punch holes in you, Tel. You know that, don't you?'

Terry said nothing.

'Know why?'

Terry still made no response.

'Because my lads would be holding you down. So you'll be telling Arthur about our little chat, won't you?'

'Yeah.'

'And you'll also tell him that if he doesn't help me – I'll kill him.'

'Kill me? Don't make me laugh.'

'He's serious, Arthur.'

'Bobby Altman? I knew him years ago in the East End. He used to thieve off thieves.'

'That ain't all that easy.'

Arthur was silent as he considered the logic of Terry's comment. 'How's he gonna kill me then?'

'He'd have a number of different ways,' said Terry quietly. 'He'd have ways other people hadn't even heard of.' He watched the first dawnings of fear in Arthur's eyes with a grim despair – for he knew what he was going to be asked to do.

'You'd better stick close, Terry.'

Then Arthur saw a vacant meter and just beat another driver to the space, after a cacophony of horn-blowing and some shouted exchanges.

'Where's this?'

'Lady Ingram's – where else?'

'Arthur, do you know how deep you're getting yourself?'

'I want our wages, Terry.'

'At what risk? You want to die – well, I won't say – young?'

'With you around, Terry, I feel safe.'

'I don't, Arthur.'

'You're the minder.'

'I'm not infallible.'

'No – I am.' Arthur rang the bell of a period house a few yards down the street. A dog barked and a few seconds later the door was opened by an attractive woman in her thirties, who looked as if she had just stepped out of a page from *Vogue*. In one hand she gripped the collar of a large Afghan hound.

'Lady Ingram?' said Arthur, looking surprised, as well as impressed.

'Yes?'

'The name's Arthur Daley.'

The dog yelped and Arthur took a quick step back.

'Don't mind Beluga.'

'My favourite caviar,' said Arthur. 'And this is my associate, Mr Terry McCann.'

'Beluga!' she admonished as the Afghan yelped again. 'You'd better come in, Mr Daley.'

Once inside Lady Ingram's drawing room, the Afghan continued to sniff suspiciously round Arthur and Terry's ankles.

'Beluga, sit!' said Lady Ingram, and Beluga slowly sat. Then Lady Ingram went to an elegant desk, opened a drawer and took out an envelope. She handed it to Arthur, who began to open it.

'It's all there,' she said authoritatively.

Arthur looked flushed. It was the first time Terry had ever seen him in this position and he gazed at him in fascination.

'Yeah,' said Arthur. 'Course it is.' He slid the envelope awkwardly into his pocket and then paused. There followed a long silence.

'That'll be all.' said Lady Ingram finally.

'Er – yes,' said Arthur. 'Come on, Terence. We'd better be getting along. I have that appointment at the Savoy.'

Lady Ingram opened the door with a bland smile. 'I'll see you out,' she said.

'No matter,' said Arthur. 'We can attend to that ourselves.'

'I'd *prefer* to see you out.'

Blimey, thought Terry, she reckons we're gonna lift something.

'How kind,' murmured Arthur. 'Most seemly.'

As they walked through the hall, Lady Ingram said, 'It is Terry, isn't it?'

'Yeah,' he replied, whilst Arthur frowned.

'I'd like to thank you.'

'What for – madam?'

'For what you did for Billy.'

'I didn't realise you – you were friends. Did you speak to him?'

'He called me from the hotel. He was most grateful.'

'That's nice to know,' said Terry, thinking of Altman and

losing all respect for her. 'By the way – how's your old man?'

'Terry –' hissed Arthur, but Lady Ingram replied without flinching or changing the expression on her calm aristocratic face.

'He's very ill. He may even die.'

She turned away from them once she had opened the door and walked back towards the drawing room, calling the dog to her side.

'Blimey,' said Arthur once Terry had closed the door and they were standing in the street. 'That was a bit strong, wasn't it?'

'Was it?'

'You've got no respect for the aristocracy, Terence.'

'Look Arthur – her old man might die – Billy's dead already – and you and me are in the shit.'

'I'm not worried about Bobby Altman,' said Arthur in a pale attempt at bravado.

'You should be.'

'Yeah?'

'Right now, you should be.'

'Why?'

'Because his Rolls's just coming down the street.'

'Oh my Gawd!'

Arthur raced for a doorway and took refuge in it. Terry joined him.

'Who's in the car?' asked Arthur, breathing fast.

'Altman and one of his heavies.'

'They seen us?'

'No.'

'Sure?'

'Stop panicking, Arthur. I thought you had him sussed?'

'Just checking.'

'Blimey.'

'What's up?' Arthur's voice rose to a falsetto.

'They've parked outside Lady Ingram's.'

'Yeah?'

'And they're going in.'

'What do we do now?' Arthur was huddled in the doorway as if he was trying to disappear.

72

'You'd better make yourself scarce.'

'They gone in?'

'Just.'

'What about you?'

'I think I'll hang around, and see how many other people have been invited to the party.'

'Be careful.'

'Yes, Arthur.'

Arthur emerged from the doorway and, glancing repeatedly over his shoulder, hurried off to his Jag. He drove hard into the traffic, causing other cars to brake, leaving Terry crossing the street until he was walking past Lady Ingram's house at a fairly brisk trot. As he passed, he was able to see into the ground floor windows and he could make out Altman pacing up and down, talking animatedly to Lady Ingram.

When Terry reached the end of the road he crossed it, bought an evening paper and stood on the street corner, reading it. After a while, he saw Altman leaving the house with one of his henchmen. They got into the Rolls and Terry could see that Altman was still talking excitedly, but it was impossible to make out the expression on his face. Then the Rolls drove away.

Having made sure that the coast was clear, Terry strolled back to Lady Ingram's house from the other side of the street, only to discover the lady herself leaving the house with Beluga on a lead.

'Walk your dog, lady?' asked Terry with a threat in his voice.

Lady Ingram quickened her pace. 'What do you want?'

'It's owning up time.'

'I've nothing to say to you.'

'Maybe not – but I've got a few things to say to you.'

'Leave me alone.'

'I told you – I've got things to say.'

'If you don't go – I'll call the police.'

'Go ahead. But think what you're gonna tell 'em.'

'I shall tell them you are pestering me – threatening me.'

'You can also tell 'em all about pretty Billy – and Bobby

73

Altman – and how you just paid off Arthur and me.'

The Afghan began to growl as Terry spoke and Lady Ingram stopped to control it. Then she looked up at Terry. 'What do you want?'

'I'd like a drink,' he said.

They went to an exotic bar in Mayfair where Lady Ingram ordered two drinks that contained more fruit than alcohol. In the centre of the floor was a pool in which turtles and an alligator splashed benignly. Despite their presence, Beluga sat obediently at Lady Ingram's feet as the waitress brought the drinks.

Terry frowned down at the fruit. 'Shouldn't this have custard on?' he asked.

'I thought you might be more sophisticated than that,' she said, sipping hers. She seemed a shade more relaxed now.

'I was just trying to think of a sophisticated way of saying something else. But I can't – so I'll have to ask you straight.'

'Go ahead.'

'You're Billy's mistress, aren't you?'

'That's a very old-fashioned word.'

'I must have read it in a book. Let me put it another way – were you and Billy having it off on the side?'

She lit a cigarette with a faint smile.

'Well –'

'And then Billy falls madly in love with you and wants to take you away from all the squalor you live in to the squalor he lives in. How am I doing?'

'Fair,' she replied, drawing on her cigarette.

'But being a villain at heart, he can't think of a nice way to do it – so he has a go at your old man.'

'Not quite right.'

'Why?'

'My husband tried to murder Billy.'

Terry stared at her, the statement taking a while to sink in.

'What Billy did was in self-defence,' she continued.

'You told the law that?'

'Would it help?' she asked off-handedly.

'Help me and Arthur, for a start.'

'But would they believe it? I mean – whom would you believe, Terry? A hereditary peer of the realm – or a –'

'Handsome little gangster from Canning Town?'

'You could put it that way.'

'Fancy another fruit salad?'

'I wouldn't mind.'

Terry signalled to the waitress and then continued his inquisition. 'So, while the two of them were fighting for your affections – what the hell were you doing?'

'Nothing much,' she replied blandly.

'What was the plan, then? Were you gonna run away with Billy?'

'I don't know. Maybe.' She stubbed out her cigarette.

'Was that why he nicked the money?'

'What money?' she muttered.

Terry spoke bitterly, 'Come on, duchess – don't give me all that for Christ's sake. Bobby Altman lost seventy grand. Billy had it – and Billy hid it. My guess is that pretty Billy thought that would be enough to keep you in the style to which you are accustomed.' Terry ended on a mocking note and it produced anger in Lady Ingram for the first time.

'What the hell does it matter to you anyway?' she asked viciously.

'Not a lot,' replied Terry with irony. 'It's just that Altman thinks Arthur's keeping the money and if he don't get it back he's gonna kill Arthur. And as I'm supposed to look after Arthur maybe he'll have a pop at me an' all.'

'I thought that's what you were paid for.'

Terry stared at Lady Ingram for a minute and then said, 'I wonder what Billy saw in you? Couldn't have been your heart of gold, could it?'

Lady Ingram rose to her feet. She seemed quite unruffled and her beautiful face was expressionless. 'I must go now.'

'Not so fast, duchess.' Terry grabbed her wrist.

'You're hurting me,' she said.

'Oh dear – but I won't delay you long. As everyone's so heavily into friendship and doing favours – I wonder if you would do me one?'

'Such as?'

'Get your old man to tell the law the truth.' He let her wrist go and without saying another word, Lady Ingram led the Afghan past him. For a moment the dog looked back at him.

Then she said, 'You'd better come with me.'

Terry sat alone in the reception area of Charing Cross Hospital. After some time, Lady Ingram emerged from a corridor. She crossed the floor and spoke quietly to Terry, 'They won't let anybody else see him.'

'You tell him about me?'

But before she could answer, Terry felt a sickening sensation in the pit of his stomach as a familiar face hove into view.

'What the hell are you doing here?' asked Inspector Barrett.

'Friend of the family,' replied Terry.

'Mr McCann wanted to see my husband,' explained Lady Ingram.

'Did he? How considerate.' Inspector Barrett beamed at Terry, as if giving him the aura of a minor saint. 'I believe he's making a bit of a recovery,' he said to Lady Ingram.

'He's much better, thank you.'

'That's good – in fact we've got good news all round.'

Terry looked up at Barrett but he had his attention focused on Lady Ingram.

'They just fished Billy Gilpin's body out of the sea.'

Once again Lady Ingram was expressionless as Terry's gaze flashed up at her. 'Has anyone identified the body?' she asked.

Barrett, looking as if he was really enjoying himself, said, 'Oh yes – his sister's just been down there. Tide had carried him well out. Feller thought he'd hooked a nice piece of Dover sole – and up comes Billy boy. I was just going to let Lord Ingram know, milady.'

'Thank you.'

Barrett looked at her very closely for a moment – and then walked slowly away.

Suddenly he paused, and looked back at Terry.

76

'If you will pardon the expression, Terry, this might let you off the hook.'

He walked on towards the corridor and disappeared. When he had gone, Terry took hold of Lady Ingram's arm. At once he could sense that she was rigid with shock. But to all outward appearances, she still seemed very self-composed.

'Do you believe him?' she asked.

'Why not?'

'Because Billy was such a good swimmer.'

Terry, still holding her arm, led her towards the exit.

'He was gonna fake a suicide, was he?'

She nodded and Terry's voice grew harder.

'So, all that stuff he told me about depression and tablets and topping himself – it was all a load of crap, wasn't it?'

'Yes,' she said dully.

'And that was all to set me up as a party to a big conspiracy, wasn't it?'

'I don't know.' For the first time, Lady Ingram sounded desperate.

'What *do* you know then?'

She hesitated.

'Come *on.*'

'All right then. He was going to swim out to sea for about a mile. Then a friend was going to pick him up with a motor launch and they were going to head for the Normandy coast.'

'And then?'

'Another friend was going to drive him to Paris – and then he was going on to the South to stay at a villa.'

'Who owned that?'

'A friend.'

'As I thought,' said Terry explosively.

'What's the matter?'

'Nothing really – it must be just great having all these friends.'

That night, Arthur, carrying a very elaborate executive-style overnight bag, left his flat and headed for his Jag, which was parked in the drive. He got in, revved the engine and had just edged out into the street when he was overtaken by a Granada Ghia which crowded him abruptly into the kerb with a squealing of brakes.

Two of Altman's men got out and advanced on Arthur who was trying to lock the doors of the car from the inside. But he was too late as one of the heavies threw open the front passenger door and peered inside.

'Hallo, Arthur,' he said.

Terry was on the phone in the smoky atmosphere of the Winchester Club.

'Didn't he leave a message for me then? No – it's O.K. I'll have to hang on until he shows up. Cheers.'

He put the phone down and crossed to the bar.

'Couple of G and T's, Dave.'

'No lager, Terry?'

'No lager.'

Dave poured out the drinks and winked at Terry.

'Bit of class you got over there, Terry.'

'Mm?'

'Unusual to see the likes of her in here.'

'She's slumming.'

'Thought that was it.'

Terry took the drinks over to Lady Ingram who was sitting at a table in the furthest and darkest corner of the Winchester Club.

'Slice of lemon O.K.? That's all they had in the way of fruit.'

She smiled. 'It's fine.' She looked around her. 'So this is the natural habitat of Terry McCann, is it?'

'I'm surprised Billy didn't take you to places like this.'

'He was a champagne man.'

'So he kept telling me. This is where he belonged though – I mean – what was he? Just a little thief.'

'You're the same species, are you?'

'I don't steal – and I wouldn't land a pal in trouble. That's how I treat me friends.'

'So you beat people up for a living instead?'

'Who told you that?' asked Terry indignantly. 'All I do is escort a few drunks to the door. Sometimes I look after people who can't look after themselves. I don't cause trouble – I stop it!'

'And how do you recognise trouble, Terry?' she asked innocently.

'It's not that difficult. You soon know when it's just booze that's talking. The fellers who keep telling you how many fights they've had are no threat. Then there are the ones with the bold blue eyes and the smart suits who think they've been in *The Day of the Jackal*.' Terry gave a derisive laugh. 'They're terrific at shouting at birds in the typing pool – but when it comes to the action – they're non-starters. In my game, see, you don't look for trouble: you just keep an eye out for the guys who can cause trouble.'

'So, you're always right, are you, Terry?'

'Not always. There's one lot I can never tell.'

'What are they?'

'Nutters.'

'What do they look like?'

'That's the hard bit – they look like anybody. Even you, duchess.'

'So, I could be trouble, could I?'

'Well – you've caused a fair bit so far.'

'I suppose I have.'

'How come you're involved with a burk like Altman?'

'Money.'

'How can that be? You've got a title – a fancy house.'

'Ever heard of the new poor – the impoverished aristocracy?'

'I keep seeing their houses up for sale in *Country Life*.'

'You buy it?'

'I read it at the dentist.'

Lady Ingram smiled again – but this time much more warmly. She lit a cigarette and as she did so, her hand trembled. Once again, Terry realised the strain she was going through – a strain so well covered by her outward calm. He found himself admiring her courage – and her tenacity.

'So you and your old man were the front for Altman? Poncing round Europe and flogging dodgy bearer bonds?'

'That's about it.'

'Altman must have loved that.'

'Of course he did. New money craves old respectability.'

'So why screw it up by falling for pretty Billy?'

She was quiet for a moment. Then she said, 'He was good company.'

'My mum used to say that about our old Labrador.'

'I would have liked your old Labrador.'

'What are you, duchess?'

'I don't understand –' For a moment she looked vulnerable. Then the blandness returned.

'Are you a villain's groupie?'

'No,' she paused again, 'I loved Billy.'

'Yeah, maybe you did. But he ain't coming back, is he?' The hard note had returned to Terry's voice.

'No,' she said slowly. 'He's not.'

'He doesn't need the money any more.'

'Does Altman?'

'Oh yes – he needs it all right. He needs it a lot more than the old respectability. Altman needs it enough for you to be in a twin bed beside your old man if I tell him about you and Billy.'

'And would you?'

Terry stared back at her impassively.

'Matter of fact I would.'

She started – and he saw the fear in her eyes – just as he had seen the fear in Arthur's.

'For God's sake – why?'

'Because I've got a friend too,' Terry said quietly.

'You look older, Arthur.'

Altman stood in the cellar wearing a dark lounge suit and dabbing at his mouth with a table napkin. Arthur had a cut on his cheek and looked dishevelled. But the main aura that came from him was fear. There was silence in the cellar except for the hum of the central heating boiler and the cracking knuckles of one of the two heavies that had been attending Arthur. Altman frowned at the knuckle-cracking and it stopped.

'Hallo, Bob,' said Arthur in a desperate attempt at

bonhomie. 'Bit of a misunderstanding, eh?'

'I said not to hurt him,' said Altman.

'He got a bit lippy in the motor,' said one of the heavies.

Altman caught sight of Arthur's overnight bag and he unzipped it, scattering pyjamas, shaving gear and a toothbrush. 'Well, isn't that a surprise, Arthur?'

'Eh?'

'I was expecting seventy grand.'

'You got it all wrong, Bob. All I did –'

Suddenly Altman lost his temper. 'Shut up, Arthur. I heard it all from Terry. Did he give you my message?'

'Yes,' replied Arthur hopelessly.

'You thought – a few nights in a hotel and they'll forget about it.'

'No, I –'

'Of course you did, Arthur. Then you heard Billy had been fished out and you thought – bingo – it's Christmas!'

'I haven't heard nothing.'

'Don't lie.' Altman came very close to Arthur and he backed quickly away. 'I can't stand a thief and I can't stand a liar. You don't change, do you? You were nothing in the old days, and you're nothing now.' Altman made a determined effort at self-control. 'See – you got me upset now and I don't like being upset.' He touched the cut on Arthur's cheek. 'I don't like violence and I've got to try and calm down.'

'Sorry about that,' said Arthur pathetically.

'It couldn't have happened at a worse time, Arthur. I'm entertaining a feller from the Department of the Environment, a local planning officer and a merchant banker friend. You're a great inconvenience, Arthur.'

'Bobby – all I did was to –'

'Shut up.' He turned to the heavies. 'Give him a camp bed and a lilo. We'll make an early start, Arthur.'

'Bob. It's all a mistake –' came the faint and plaintive whine from Arthur. But Altman had gone.

Arthur had a terrible night, tossing and turning, wondering what Altman was going to do to him. If only he could be at home with 'er indoors. If only Terry could rescue him. If only

– but nothing happened throughout the long, miserable night and finally, at about seven a.m. he was rudely awakened and taken to Altman's gym.

When Arthur staggered in, unshaven and looking exhausted, Altman was in his track suit and was just tying the lace of his running shoes. Arthur waited patiently until Altman finally acknowledged him.

'Bit warm in the cellar, was it, Arthur?'

'No,' said Arthur obsequiously. 'It was fine.'

'You look a mess.' There was a steely note in Altman's voice. 'Get your clothes off.'

'Eh?'

'I said – undress.'

'What for, Bob?'

'Because I said so.'

'Look,' Arthur's voice took on a pleading note, 'honest to God – you've got it all wrong. Go to my house – turn it upside down – you'll find no money. I mean – you might find a few bob there, but you won't find *your* money,' Arthur gabbled.

'I believe you. You've hidden it somewhere else.'

'On my baby's life I haven't.'

But Altman's patience was wearing thin. 'Clothes off.'

'What are you gonna do?'

Altman laughed. 'You think it's torture, don't you? Electrodes on the private parts – that kind of thing. What do you think we are – some nasty little South London mob?'

'Of course not, Bob. I've always –'

'Shut up, Arthur.'

'Sorry, Bob.'

'We're in happy Hampstead, Arthur. London's lung – that's what someone called it. Fresh air, open space, trees, squirrels, even foxes. That's why I live here – it's so healthy.' He turned to a heavy. 'Don't just stand there, Stuart. Give Arthur his gear.'

Stuart handed a mystified Arthur a track suit and running shoes.

'We're going for a run.'

'Eh?'

'One foot in front of another. Very fast.'

Arthur tried to laugh but it sounded like a sob. 'I don't run.'

'I do five miles every day. Look at me.' Altman patted his flat stomach. 'I want to do the same thing for you, Arthur.'

'No.'

'But I insist. We're about the same age, aren't we? And I'm in perfect condition. They knocked a bit off me insurance premium too. Can you believe that? They actually said, "You're in such good nick, Mister Altman. That makes you a good risk." But look at you, Arthur – flabby, too much of the old vodka. Still smoke cigars, do you?'

Arthur nodded miserably.

'Still chasing the young birds. You could lose two stone – no bother. Change your life – change your whole outlook.'

Stuart took off Arthur's jacket for him.

'Come on, Arthur,' said Altman. 'Shirt – trousers –'

Arthur tried to remove his shoes but lost his balance.

'Sit down and do it, Arthur. Your co-ordination is bad – you're not getting enough oxygen. Know what a run does?' Altman continued as Arthur struggled to undress. 'Clears the mind – business problems float away – and a clear mind helps the memory. Things come back to you – a surprising number of things.'

Arthur was now tugging on his track suit trousers.

'I don't run, Bob.'

'Don't?'

'Can't.'

'You will.'

'I'll die.'

'Now that would be a shame. But maybe your memory'll come back before you croak. Let me tell you, I had a Cartier watch – and one day I couldn't find it anywhere. I even got to the sad point where I thought one of the lads had nicked it – or the au-pair. I even shouted at my dear wife. So I went for a run and what do you think, Arthur?'

'I don't know what to think, Bob.'

'My memory came back.'

'Well –'

'I remembered I'd left my Cartier watch in my tweed jacket. How about that?'

'Very good, Bob.'

'That run found me a couple of grand's worth of watch.'
Altman smiled at Arthur, who was now wearing the track
suit which looked most out of place on him.

'There you are, you look fitter already. And now, Arthur,
I'm going to see what a good run does for your memory.'

Terry saw Arthur's Jag parked with two wheels up on the
pavement and he slowed down his old car in surprise. Arthur
would never leave his beloved vehicle in such a precarious
position. Suddenly the surety came over him – if Arthur
would never have left his car like that, then somebody made
him do it. And there was only one person who could have
done that. Without bothering to get out of his car, Terry
simply changed gear and drove off fast. Arthur was in
trouble, and he was pretty sure where the trouble was.

Altman, Arthur and Stuart crossed the road from Altman's
house to the Heath. Stuart had come along to keep an eye
out, whilst Altman was there to ensure Arthur ran.

'I'll tell you what, Arthur,' said Altman laughing. 'You
could try a runner.'

'Look, Bob,' said Arthur in a last burst of desperation.
'Jogging isn't my game.'

'It soon will be,' replied Altman mercilessly. 'Now Arthur,
on your mark, get set – go.' He set off at an easy loping pace
with Arthur alongside him. Meanwhile, Stuart got into the
car and gently coasted after them.

'Easy, isn't it?' said Altman.

Arthur gave a nervous grin. 'Yeah.'

A few minutes later, however, Arthur began to falter.
Altman slowed down and tugged at Arthur's arm.

'Come on, Arthur.'

'I can't go on.'

'Of course you can.' He grabbed Arthur's arm again and
propelled him into stumbling, struggling action. 'You've got
to understand one thing, Arthur.'

'What's that?' he puffed.

'The toughest bit comes on the second mile.'

'Oh my Gawd.'

'Lots of doctors don't approve of this if you're out of condition. They always say – never try too much, too soon.'

'Do they?'

'You could have a coronary, you see.'

'I've got a pain.'

'Indigestion, Arthur.'

'I'm having a coronary.'

'No.'

'I've got to stop.'

'I wouldn't do that. You might just find Stuart getting out of the car. And he doesn't like getting out of cars.'

'Please, Bob –' gasped Arthur.

'Now, with some fellers – it's their legs that go first,' Altman was jogging effortlessly now, 'like old fighters. Then the chest starts to get tighter.'

Arthur gave a cry of pain.

'You all right, Arthur?'

'It's bleeding McCann,' Stuart said aloud as Terry's old Ford passed the Granada. Stuart put his foot down and began to close in on Terry. He pulled out to overtake but Terry jammed on his brakes and Stuart overshot him, mounting the grass verge that ran beside the Heath. In panic, Stuart realised that the Granada was out of control as it tore over the uneven surface. He saw the steep incline coming and wrestled with the wheel, desperate to avoid it. But he was too late – and the Granada left the ground on the top of the incline and began to fly. Transfixed, Stuart screamed his guts out behind the wheel until the car began to turn over. It eventually crashed onto the track below, upended on its roof and apart from the hissing of the burst radiator, and the agitated calls of the surrounding birdlife, there was silence. Soon the birds settled down – and the radiator stopped hissing. The silence was complete.

'What the hell was that?'

'Let's – stop – find – out –' gasped Arthur as they reacted to the crash, somewhere on the Heath behind them.

'Keep going, Arthur.'

'But –'

'I said – keep going. And step it up a bit.'

Arthur nodded, gulping air, and Altman gave him a push, quickening his own pace as he did so. They entered a small woodland and Arthur stumbled. But Altman simply grabbed him and pushed him on, saying, 'Ever read the statistics?'

'What?' gasped Arthur.

'The amount of old guys who have heart attacks running.'

But Arthur was so out of breath now, that he could not reply. He barely had the strength to nod his head.

'Alarming really.' He began to increase the pace again and Arthur let out a little whine of protest. 'But that's the joy of what we're doing. You see, Arthur, if you drop dead – what do they find? Just another old jogger who's been trying too hard.'

But Arthur was in real difficulty now, gasping and grey in the face. His breath was coming in little short bursts and he staggered with his head down.

'Where's the money, Arthur?' asked Altman.

'Don't know.'

'You can stop, if you tell me.'

'Don't know.'

'Then run!' Altman increased the pace again and gave Arthur's arm another sharp tug. With great effort, Arthur looked up to the sky almost praying for help. He could see the branches of the trees as if through a mist and little red spots danced in front of his eyes.

'The money, Arthur?'

'Don't –'

'Step it up. Come on.' Altman dealt Arthur a vicious blow in the small of the back and somehow he staggered forward, his legs feeling like ton weights.

'Been abusing your body, haven't you, Arthur?'

'You're killing me.'

'The money, Arthur?'

'I don't know.'

Arthur stumbled on for a few more paces and then stopped.

'Please. I can't – go on.'

He was gulping air and his face was ashen.

'Nice, big, deep breaths,' said Altman. 'And then you can tell me.'

'I – dunno – gospel.'

'Oh dear. Naughty stories again.'

Altman began to push Arthur forward. 'One, two, three – and off we go.'

But Arthur's legs seemed to have become jelly and he staggered around like a wounded buffalo. Altman, meanwhile, ran effortlessly backwards, waiting for Arthur to collapse. He was ten yards or so ahead of Arthur when a bulky object dropped at his feet and he nearly fell over it.

'What the hell?' Altman stared unbelievingly down at his feet. Lying on the grass was a Gucci briefcase.

Terry stepped unsmilingly from behind some bushes as Altman darted at the bag, picked it up and unzipped it.

'It's great what a bit of exercise does,' said Altman gleefully. 'It brings pennies from heaven.'

'Stars is what you'll see,' said Terry and he neatly gave Altman a right-hander to the jaw. Slowly Altman went down – and stayed down. Terry then looked across to the glade to Arthur, who was leaning against a tree, eyes staring and fighting for breath.

'Look out, Tel,' Arthur managed to gasp out.

Stuart burst through the trees, a livid bruise above his left eye – and a spanner in his right hand. Stuart launched himself with a cry of hatred at Terry and then suddenly paused in mid-air as Terry's knee caught him in the stomach. He collapsed on the grass and his gasping equalled Arthur's. As Terry turned back to Altman, he saw him stir, pull the bag towards him and open it. He stared down at the money inside.

'You're never gonna count it now, are you?' asked Terry.

'No Terry. You've got an honest face.'

Terry then crossed over to the tree, where Arthur was still leaning, his breathing just a little slower. The sweat poured down over his grey features as Terry said:

'You O.K., Arthur?'

'I'm a goner.'

'Big deep breaths now.'

'I'm dying, Tel.'

'Do what I say, Arthur – just do what I say. Nice and deep.'

Arthur gave a wheezy kind of death rattle and Terry said, 'Now, come on.' He put Arthur's right arm round his shoulders and began to lead him away from the still recumbent Stuart and Altman, who was absorbed in looking at the contents of the briefcase. As they passed, he looked up.

'He'll never make a jogger,' said Altman.

'No,' said Terry.

'You – bastard –' gasped Arthur.

'But he'll always make a runner.'

'Yeah.'

Terry continued to half carry, half drag Arthur along. But soon, Arthur was leaning against a tree. 'Give me a minute – just a minute. But his greyness was lifting and Terry sighed, knowing that Arthur would milk his exhaustion to the last degree. 'I'm going, Terry.'

'Where, Arthur?'

'I'm gone. Honest to God. I need the kiss of life.'

'With your boat-race – you gotta be joking.'

'I'm a goner, Tel. You can have my watch. Take care of 'er indoors. But don't say too much – oh my Gawd.'

'Come on, Arthur.'

Terry put Arthur's arm round his shoulders again and helped him through the bushes to where the old Ford was parked on the road that ran by the Heath.

'Terry,' said Arthur, making a slight recovery.

'Yeah.'

'You know what?'

'No.'

'You're a pal. A real pal.'

'You just can't get by without them, can you?' said Terry.

PART THREE

Arthur took to his bed for a week after his jog and Terry found himself continually attending the invalid, bringing him all kinds of goodies and watched cynically by 'er indoors. But after the eighth day of bringing newspapers and whisky, looking after little deals and having to take freezers, shirts and even a new hoover to various contacts who were being done favours, Terry rebelled.

'We can't go on like this, Arthur.'

'You don't know what I've been through, Terry.'

'You don't know what I'm going through now, Arthur.'

'I was almost a goner.'

'Yeah.'

'It was a miracle I survived.'

'Yeah.'

'So the least you can do, Terry, is to help my recovery.'

'What do you want now, Arthur?'

'Look – if you could slip down to Balham and see Charlie Pierce about those radiators. Then you could nip into Bert Dingwell in Dartford –'

'Dartford!'

'And on the way back I need to see if Smiler Grey has coughed up those video recorders.'

'Where's he?'

'Chingford.'

'Christ!'

'Now, this afternoon, Terry –'

'Yeah?' Terry's voice was utterly weary.

'Nip down to the lock-up and see all's well there. And then –'

Terry stood up. 'I'm off.'

'But I haven't finished.'

'I have.'

'Terry –'

'Look, Arthur, you've given me a day's work. Let me get on with it.'

'When will you be back?' asked Arthur plaintively.

'With this lot – 'bout midnight I would reckon.'

'You can't leave me alone that long.'

'There's 'er downstairs.'

'She won't even bring me up a cup of tea.'

'I'll ask her.'

'No, don't do that.' Arthur looked terrified. 'She's in a mood. Tell you what, Tel – before you go off on your little jaunts, nip down to the off-licence and get me a bottle of whisky.'

'Oh, Arthur –'

'Now.' There was a testy note in Arthur's voice.

'Where's the money, Arthur?'

'Now, Terry, don't be selfish. How could I have got to the bank lying on my bed of suffering?'

'So what do I do?'

'Sub me, Terry. Sub me. After all – what are friends for?'

T.P. Mooney was fifty-eight – clean but not well-dressed. He stood at the corner of a busy junction, waiting for the traffic lights to go red. Then, with a pronounced limp, he hobbled up to a BMW, signalling to the driver as he made his unsteady progress. Reluctantly the driver wound down his window. T.P. Mooney, in a soft, lilting voice, said, 'Excuse me, sir.'

'Yes?' The driver's tone was not encouraging.

'I – I have to get to the hospital but there are no buses. Do you – do you think you could drop me nearby?'

Mooney was already opening the passenger door, but the driver seemed unsympathetic to his plea.

'I'm not going that way.'

'Anywhere near – that's O.K.'

'I'm sorry. I'm busy.'

'A soldier of the Queen –'

But the driver's patience was running out and as the lights changed he said, 'Get a bloody bus,' and firmly closed the passenger door. Then he drove off.

'Same to you, friend.' Mooney's soft Irish accent prevented the coldness in his heart coming into his voice. The lights changed again and, this time, Mooney walked across to Arthur's Jag which Terry was taking on his errands – without Arthur's permission. But Terry felt that if he was to drive half-way round London, then he'd make sure he drove in comfort, rather than in his own battered Ford.

'Have you got a second, sir?' asked Mooney, tapping on the window.

'I might have.'

'Oh, it's you, Terry.'

'What do you want?'

'I have to get to the hospital and –'

Terry opened the door. 'Jump in.'

Thankfully, Mooney did as he was bid. The lights changed again and as Terry drove off, he said, 'Do you really want to go to the hospital?'

Mooney settled back in his seat. 'I'm working for God's sake.'

'Sorry about that.'

'I've had enough.'

'Yeah?'

'Well – I thought I'd had a nibble with the BMW feller.' He looked around him appreciatively. 'This is a nice car.'

'It's Arthur's.'

'Haven't seen him for years. How is the old feller?'

'Bit knackered at the moment.'

'How's that?'

'Been doing a bit of jogging.'

'Arthur!' Mooney looked astounded.

'Against his will, like.'

'That's more like it. And apart from that?'

'Ducking and diving – and dreaming.'

'That's Arthur.'

'So what are you doing? Cadging lifts and putting the bite on 'em?'

'It's a living, Terry. You spin a yarn and while you're spinning it, you know you've got three or four minutes to make them feel guilty that they've got an expensive motor and a man like myself hasn't got a bus-fare. It's a knack – a flair – the hospital always gets them. Mind you – some of them like to hear you've just come out of prison. Strange, isn't it? You get a fiver sometimes, tenner if you're lucky – twenty pence for a cup of coffee if you're not. It's a living.'

Terry said nothing, concentrating on the road and feeling

touched and miserable at Mooney's account of how he was spending his life.

'T.P. Mooney,' said Terry reflectively. 'How the mighty have fallen.'

'It's hard times for us all,' replied Mooney philosophically.

'Yeah – something like that. But I used to tell stories about you, T.P. – great stories. People couldn't believe what you did. Then I heard you were ill.'

'That was a good one,' said Mooney dismissively. 'Now Terry – why don't you stop at the next betting shop? I want you to put on a bet for me.'

'What with?'

'This lot.' Mooney pulled out a crumpled wad of notes and gave him five tenners. 'I'd do it myself but I'm dead tired. It's hard work – in and out of cars all day.'

'I'm sure.'

'Banville Lad in the four o'clock at Catterick.'

'OK, T.P.'

'You know what I want to do, Terry? Retire. I'm always thinking about my old Mam sitting in her wee cottage in Donegal, gazing into a peat fire.'

'I thought she lived in Tufnell Park.'

Mooney gave a disarming smile. 'It's true – she does. But I can't think of her sitting in front of a night storage heater in a council flat, can I? We're all getting older.'

Terry grinned. 'Stuff of dreams, eh?'

'Arthur would understand.'

''Er indoors is a sight different from your old Mum. Still –'
Terry parked outside the betting shop.

'Incidentally – if you see Arthur – don't tell him how we met.'

Terry gave Mooney a compassionate and understanding glance. 'Course I won't,' he said.

'He's forgot the whisky,' Arthur muttered aloud. It was 11.30 a.m. and the hoover was making a great racket downstairs. He lay there for another ten minutes and then, with sudden decision, gingerly raised himself up in the bed. 'I'll just have to fend for myself,' he moaned as the hoover increased in volume.

Ten minutes later, Arthur was sitting in the Winchester, with a vodka and tonic and a good line in self-pity.

'Hear you've had a rough time, Arthur,' said Dave.

'Don't talk about it – it was a nightmare.'

'Are we better now?'

'No – my nerves are shot to pieces.'

'I mean – physically?'

'A slow recovery,' said Arthur.

'Do you want the ploughman's lunch?'

'I could toy with it.'

Dave passed him an enormous plate of bread, cheese and pickles. 'Very agricultural,' he said.

Just then a worried-looking, middle-aged man entered the bar and made for Arthur.

'Anthony,' said Arthur, 'good to see you.'

'Hallo, Arthur,' replied the man in a hang-dog manner.

'Dave – this is my accountant. Give him a ploughman's.'

'This on the slate, Arthur?'

'How do you think a man in my condition could get to a bank?'

'All right – all right. Just this once.'

'What'll you have, Anthony?'

'A campari and soda.'

'Dave, get the man what he wants.'

'Yes, Arthur.'

'I must see you, Arthur,' said Anthony.

'I've been ill.'

'I'm sorry.'

'I still am.'

'But we must talk.'

Arthur gave a long, drawn-out sigh.

'Bloody hell!'

'It's important.'

'All right. Dave, we'll have to leave you.'

'I'm sorry, Arthur.'

Arthur led Anthony to a corner table and said: 'Now what's

all this about? Because I've just got out of bed and I'm in a very delicate state.'

'You haven't paid any tax for five years, Arthur.'

'So?'

'They're after you.'

'*Us*, you mean,' said Arthur.

'What is it about me?' said Anthony spearing a pickled onion. 'All my clients are the same.'

'You mix with the wrong people.'

'Don't I know it! They don't hold with the system and it's getting worse. Incidentally, you haven't paid *my* bill.'

'My health –'

'For a year. Here's my statement.' He handed a piece of paper to Arthur, who pocketed it.

'I'll deal with that as soon as I'm better.'

'When will that be?'

'I'm coming on.'

'Good.'

'Slowly.'

'Ah. Anyway the man from the Inland Revenue wants to know about your expensive motor – amongst other things.'

'I've told you –'

'Yes, but you'd better tell *him*.'

'That's why I pay *you* – to tell *him*.'

'Did I hear the word *pay*?'

Arthur smiled reminiscently.

'That's a laugh, isn't it?'

'What is?'

'Money – it's like a fond memory.'

'It may be to you, Arthur, but –'

'It's like something in the dim and distant past – like Stanley Matthews and long shorts.'

'Where we going?'

'We'll nip in the Winchester for a quick one.'

'Aren't you meant to be running errands for Arthur?'

'They can wait.'

Mooney once again sat beside Terry in the Jag. He was looking down at his betting slip.

'You fancy that one then?' asked Terry.

'And if it's not him,' replied Mooney, 'it's two others.'

'Then why not bet on the other two as well?'

Mooney smiled patiently. Then he began to explain. 'There's no percentage in it. The bookies have got it sewn up. So the smart thing to do is to get other people to bet your three choices – and then take a commission from the winner.' Mooney thought for a moment. 'Is Arthur still game for a lark?'

'What – your kind of lark?' Terry said sardonically.

'See – I can't move around as much as I used to. I need a partner – someone straight, honest, hard-working, loyal – all the old-fashioned values.'

'Blimey, T.P. – you talking about Arthur?'

'Yes indeed. He's a good man, isn't he?'

'He's good as gold,' said Terry.

'Well then –'

'It'll aid his recovery, I'm sure.'

'What are you doing here, Terry?'

'I could ask you the same question, Arthur.'

'When you forgot my medicine –'

'The whisky? Sorry, Arthur.'

'I had to rise from my bed of pain and seek succour elsewhere.'

'I see.'

'And what about my little errands?'

'I'll be about them soon, Arthur.'

'How about now? How can a sick man run a business?'

'Look, Arthur, ask Dave to switch on the telly.'

'And waste more of my time?'

'Look, Arthur –'

Mooney suddenly emerged from the Winchester toilet and Arthur exclaimed, 'Blimey! Am I seeing a ghost?'

'Not quite, Arthur,' he said. 'Got the telly on?'

'Dave!' Terry said. 'Can you switch on?'

'All right – all right. Telly mad, you lot.'

'Look, Terry,' said Arthur, 'I'm a sick man – and a busy one.'

'Knock it off, Arthur.'

'Eh?'

'Just look at the telly. You may see something to your advantage.'

He did – for at the end of the race, Mooney's horse passed the post first. Arthur looked a little stunned, as if he could not credit T.P. Mooney with any kind of success at all.

'You see, Arthur, I've got a system,' Mooney explained.

'Yeah?' Arthur looked at him doubtfully, making up his mind that the win was a fluke.

'But I want a partner.'

'Yeah.'

'Someone honest, incisive, hard-headed, courageous.'

'That can't be Arthur,' said Terry.

'Shut up Terence,' replied Arthur. He turned back to Mooney. 'Do I take it that you are making me a proposition?'

'You could take it that way.'

'I'm sorry – we can't do business.'

'Why not?'

'I don't care how many winners you get – I can't strike up a relationship with you.'

'Get him!' put in Terry, but Arthur ignored the comment.

'You're famous for having more strokes than Oxford and Cambridge,' he said to Mooney.

'Hear me out, Arthur.'

'I'm listening.'

'Listen – we put an ad in *Sporting Life* and get a little office with a good address. We also put in three phones.'

'Why?'

'Just a minute, Arthur. We don't charge fees for the clients. They phone us and we give them a horse. All we ask of them is this – if you back, put ten pounds for us. And if the horse wins – please send a cheque or postal order to us.'

'They'd have to be barmy.'

'Never heard of trust, Arthur? Don't you realise that the entire commercial world is built on trust?'

'No, I hadn't got round to thinking that.' Arthur lit a cigar and Terry said:

'I wouldn't smoke, Arthur – not after you've been so ill.'

'Shut up, Tel. Go on Mooney,' he said grudgingly.

'The system is,' continued Mooney, 'you pay your debts.'

'Oh yeah?' said Arthur, thinking of Anthony and the Income Tax Inspectors.

'You work in a factory and they give you your wages at the end of the week.'

Arthur shuddered – that kind of work was obscene.

'Trust, see?'

'Yeah.'

'You win the pools – they give you the money.'

'National scandal if they didn't.'

'Exactly. Trust again. What about rent?'

'What about it?'

'That's trust, too. Of course, there are a few transgressors, like ourselves.'

'Speak for yourself, Mooney.'

'That's why they have laws.'

'And this little project will break most of them. Right?'

'Wrong, Arthur. We're only selling an advisory service.'

Arthur shook his head and got up. 'A few years ago I might have been interested. But I've been very ill and –'

'I'll even put up the money,' said Mooney quietly.

'What?' gasped Arthur, sitting down abruptly.

'And it's my shout,' said Mooney.

Whilst Mooney ordered the drinks, Arthur turned to Terry. 'Has he got any money?'

'He was very flush earlier this morning, Arthur.'

'I see.'

Mooney turned round to Arthur. 'Dave has got a bottle of Moet? Fancy some?'

'That would be very tasty.' Arthur sat bolt upright, drawing on his unlit cigar. 'So you'll put up the dough?' He sounded as if he were a man talking in a dream.

'Yes,' said Mooney blandly, 'I'll put up the dough.'

'Blimey,' replied Arthur. 'This is a turn-up for the book.'

'The Moet is seventeen pounds a bottle,' pointed out Dave from behind the bar.

'Why not?' said Mooney.

'Blimey,' interjected Arthur again.

'Enjoy your wine.'

'Now let's get this straight –' began Arthur, but Mooney was still talking to Dave.

'Can you cash me a wee cheque?'

'No disrespect, T.P.,' said Dave, 'but –'

'No matter, David,' replied Mooney. He pulled out a crumpled wad of notes and gave three fivers and two pounds to Dave. Arthur followed the transaction incredulously. As Dave opened the fridge, Mooney said, 'A drink for yourself, David?'

'Thanks – don't mind if I do.'

As Dave opened the bottle of Moet, Mooney turned back to Arthur. 'Well – are we in, or out?' he asked.

'Er –'

'Of course, you'll need some expenses.'

'Of course.' To Arthur's dumbfounded amazement, Mooney took from another pocket some clean fifty-pound notes.

'Shall we say three hundred on account?'

Arthur's right hand began to hover over the money.

'Of course, Arthur,' continued Mooney, 'you realise I'm investing in your energy and acumen.'

There was a cynical glance from Terry as Mooney gently topped up Arthur's champagne glass.

'Don't give him too much, T.P.,' said Terry. 'Remember he's a sick man.'

'Of course,' said Mooney. 'If you've been ill, Arthur, I don't know if we can –'

'Ill?' exclaimed Arthur angrily. 'I've never had a day's illness in me life.'

'Then what –'

'I've just been resting from some physical exhaustion.'

'That's all right then,' said Mooney.

'As it happens,' Arthur seemed mesmerised by the money, 'you're a very good judge of character, T.P. Isn't he Tel?'

'Absolutely.'

Arthur took the money reverently and put it into a pocket.

'The fastest hand in the West,' said Terry to Dave.

'To a fruitful partnership,' cried Mooney, clinking champagne glasses with Arthur.

'I think we should withdraw,' said Arthur.

'Sorry?'

Arthur looked conspiratorially at Mooney and then winked towards Terry and Dave. 'Walls have ears,' said Arthur.

'So I'm a wall –' murmured Terry.

'We should talk in private.' Arthur touched the notes in his pocket and smiled lovingly at T.P. Mooney. 'Excuse us,' he said, moving to a side table and beckoning Mooney to join him.

'Cheers!' said Dave to Terry.

'It's nice to see Arthur well again, isn't it?'

'Yeah – he reacts to money like other people do to antibiotics,' replied Dave.

Ten minutes later Mooney came back to the bar again. He looked flushed and triumphant. 'Sorry about that, boys, but business is business. Do you think you could call me a cab, Dave?'

But Arthur was there behind him.

'Don't worry about cabs, T.P. Terry'll drive you.' Arthur turned to Terry. 'It *was* my Jag I saw parked outside?' –

'As sure as ever was.'

'Just borrowed it, did you?'

'I thought I'd do your errands in comfort, Arthur.'

'What a good idea, Terry. Anyway – you take T.P. wherever he wants to go.'

'That's grand,' said Mooney.

'Shall I put it on the bill?'

Arthur looked shocked. 'What bill? This is a favour to a friend.'

'Be seeing you, Arthur,' said Mooney.

'The beginning,' replied Arthur, 'of a beautiful partnership.'

Terry took Mooney out while Arthur shared the last of the champagne with Dave.

'I trust you'll have a successful commercial undertaking with T.P., Arthur.'

'It's a privilege to work with him.'

'Aren't we the lucky ones?'

Arthur turned abruptly to see Detective Sergeant

Chisholm standing behind them.

'You don't half creep up on a chap,' said Arthur uneasily.

'That's my job.'

'To creep?'

'You will have your little joke, Arthur. What have we here?' he said, looking at the champagne. 'Rebate from the rates?'

'You'll have the usual half of bitter, will you, Mr Chisholm?' asked Arthur solicitously.

'Thank you – just in the line of duty. Now, as I came in – I thought I saw young Terry with the remarkable T.P. Mooney?'

'No idea. Is it a crime?' replied Arthur guardedly.

'You never know.'

'What's that meant to mean?'

'Well – T.P.'s been very active recently.'

'He's a busy man.'

'Yes, Arthur,' said Chisholm quietly. 'Busy defrauding people.'

Terry drove Mooney through the London traffic. He noticed that T.P. seemed tired, as if his conversation with Arthur had completely exhausted him.

'You O.K., T.P.?'

'I'm fine.'

'You're not ill?'

'Never.'

'What are all these rumours about your strokes an' all?'

'Strokes?' he laughed. 'I'm as healthy as Arthur.'

'That's all right, then.'

Mooney was silent for a while, then he said, 'He's a good man, Arthur.'

'All you want, is he?'

'All I want.'

'Where we heading, T.P.?'

'The Savoy.'

'Eh?'

'The Savoy.'

'You're joking.'

'Now, why should I be? I need a good night's kip.'

A few minutes later, Terry drove T.P. Mooney into the forecourt of the Savoy Hotel.

'How do you get away with it, T.P.?' asked Terry with admiration.

'It's just experience – a little bit of flair.'

'Tell me more.'

'It's nerve. You *have* to believe in it. It's a bit like insanity.'

'Yeah?'

'You've got to make up your mind who you want to be – Lord of the Realm, an international financier, a well-known theatrical impresario. Then, once you've decided, you've got to *be* that person.'

'I see.' Terry was genuinely impressed.

'You need to be a split personality – a dozen personalities.'

'I'll see you tomorrow, T.P.'

'O.K.'

Mooney slowly got out of the car. He was breathing heavily and once again Terry was tempted to ask him if he was ill. But there was something about Mooney's dignity that forbade the question.

'Cheers,' said Terry. 'Take care.'

Mooney nodded as he walked to the entrance of the Savoy. The doorman saluted him, he nodded and then walked inside. Terry smiled at the charade and swung the car round. What a man, he thought.

Mooney walked straight through the hotel and out into the gardens by the embankment. Breathing heavily, he crossed the road and stood by a bus stop. When the bus came he boarded the platform with considerable difficulty and slumped into a seat. Eventually, the bus arrived in Camden Town and Mooney managed to stagger out. Then, with pathetically halting steps he approached the entrance to a doss-house. Nodding to a couple of down and outs at the door, T.P. Mooney walked inside.

'He's just turned over the London Clinic for thirteen grand.'

'What?' croaked Arthur.

'Yeah,' continued Chisholm. 'Open heart surgery and then two and a half grand for convalescence at the Met in Brighton. He's got style, hasn't he?'

'Liz Taylor had her operation in the London Clinic,' said Dave in a voice of awe.

'No doubt,' replied Chisholm sourly. 'I expect they had Richard Burton, the Sheikh of Araby and Uncle Tom Cobley an' all.'

'Well, you can catch up with him in about ten years' time when he changes the batteries of his pace-maker.'

'They'll get him all right.'

Arthur turned on Chisholm in righteous anger. 'Is that the very best you can do?'

'What do you mean, Arthur?' asked Chisholm icily.

'You pursue a sick man when there are bank robberies every minute – there are terrorists darting around committing outrage – rape is rife in our streets –'

'You haven't been interfered with, have you, Arthur?' Chisholm gave him a wolfish grin.

'Oh, very droll.'

'We like to protect our citizens.'

'You don't realise the value of a man like T.P. Mooney.'

'He knows other people's value all right.'

'He was an 'ero during the war – an educated 'ero.'

'Oh yeah?'

'A gentleman of the old school.'

Chisholm's weary smile tightened. 'Arthur – do you owe Mooney money or something?'

'Of course not,' Arthur gulped, realising he had made a tactical error. 'I hardly even know the man.'

Mooney lay on the hard doss-house bed in a tiny cubicle whose partitioned walls were wafer-thin. He shouldn't have been allowed to lie down so early but he had managed to bribe one of the staff. He felt terrible – and the breathlessness that he had been feeling since his conversation with Arthur, would not go away. Around him, however, was blissful silence but he knew that later the night would be full of men talking in their sleep, wheezing, gasping, belching and raving in the delirium of alcohol. He remembered Terry's words: 'T.P., how are the mighty fallen.' Well – he had fallen all right and he was ill into the bargain. His only chance of rising again was the scheme he had discussed with Arthur. T.P. closed his eyes and fell into a haunted sleep in which Arthur managed to bungle the very last chance T.P. had got. When Mooney awoke he gloomily realised that his dream could very likely become reality.

Arthur looked at the long list of names outside the office door with apprehension. They read:

> MILLIGAN MAIL ORDER INC.
> VICTORY VIDEO
> INTERNATIONAL NOVELTIES LTD
> BLARNEY STONE CO
> SPECTATOR TOURS
> ANGLO-ALBANIAN WINE SHIPPERS
> HARNEY ESTATES
> BANK OF BOMBAY
> STOKE NEWINGTON CREDIT TRUST
> SMITH OF NEW YORK
> DARTMOOR GOLF CLUB
> and many, many more.

Arthur opened the door and walked into a tiny office that was crammed with people. In the middle of what appeared to be total chaos, a small, quiet, nimble man was talking to everybody. He was handing out vast bundles of envelopes, answering questions and picking up the telephone, seemingly at the same time.

'Er,' said Arthur, but the little man was too busy to notice immediately, as he threw four parcels at a giant of a man called Jason, a packet of letters to a man with a video camera at the back of the room and one mysteriously shaped parcel to someone who looked like an ageing landlady.

'I would like a minute,' interposed Arthur.

'Sure.' But he did not look up.

'I need an address.'

'Right with you.'

'Arthur!'

In some embarrassment and annoyance, Arthur saw an old acquaintance bearing down on him.

'What are you doing, Ernie?' asked Arthur reluctantly.

'Oriental carpets.'

'How do you work that?'

'Easy. I get the cheque and then I buy the carpet from a feller. No overheads, see?' He turned to the tiny man. 'Anything for British Medallions?'

'Nothing.'

Ernie turned back to Arthur. 'George Orwell, you know. It being 1984 Medallions . . . Royals, Great Battles . . . O.K. But literary things – forget it. George Orwell . . . we done a ticket there. What are you on, Arthur?'

'Er – consultancy,' Arthur replied cagily.

'You can't go wrong with that.'

'Glad to hear it.'

'We done consultancy.'

'Yeah?'

'You know – villas in Marbella. We had a Spanish waiter on the firm –'

'Now, sir,' said the tiny man, giving Arthur a fraction of his attention.

'This is the company,' said Arthur, giving him a card.

'Mayfair Course Consultants. That's nice – you can walk from here to Mayfair,' said the tiny man. 'Oi.' He looked up at a client who was rummaging through some envelopes stacked on another desk. 'Ask, don't take.'

'Bank of Bombay, sorry,' said the client.

'I'm sorry an' all. There ain't nothing there.' He turned back to Arthur's mounting impatience. 'It's fifty "lid" for a week – a long 'un for three weeks.'

'We're a very old established firm,' said Arthur. 'This could go on for years, not weeks.'

But the tiny man was on the telephone. 'So, all you've got is a letter from the Customs and Excise?' He sounded annoyed. 'Well, it ain't my bloody fault, is it?' He turned back to

Arthur again. 'He hung up. Bloody cheek.' Then his thoughts reverted to the job in hand. 'As I said – that's the rate. If you're still in business in six weeks' time we'll have another think.'

Arthur frowned – and frowned again as he saw a window cleaner gawping through the window. Was there no privacy? Then another client claimed the partial attention Arthur was receiving.

'Anything, Mo?'

'Caledonian Forests?'

'That's us last month.'

'Oh yeah. Sorry.'

'A Forest In Snowdonia Limited is what we do now, Mo.'

'Got it.' The tiny man went to a rack. 'Here we are – you got five.'

'Ta.'

'Be lucky then.'

Arthur cleared his throat loudly and the tiny man turned back to him. 'Are we in business?' he asked.

'We expect the first lot in four days,' said Arthur.

'You'll have your name on the door.'

'You need a bigger door, don't you?' He took out five ten-pound notes. 'By the way, I'll need a receipt.'

'Why?'

'Because we're a bona fide business,' Arthur snapped. 'What on earth would my accountant think?'

'OK,' said the tiny man grudgingly. 'But can you leave your own name and address and telephone number?'

'Why?' Arthur felt it was his turn to ask the questions.

The tiny man shrugged. 'Just so they can get in touch – if there are any queries.'

Arthur realised that he had been caught out and for a few seconds there was a stalemate between them.

'If we don't trust each other,' said Arthur, baring his teeth in a smile, 'where are we?'

'My own sentiments exactly,' said the tiny man. 'Arthur – is that the name?'

'That's me.'

They shook hands in mutual distrust but were interrupted again – this time by Ernie, who was brandishing an envelope.

'Mo – this isn't mine.'

'Whose is it then?'

'I dunno. It says "Do-it-Yourself – Be a Racing Tipster".'

With a grin Ernie turned to Arthur. 'They'll try anything, won't they?'

Arthur gave Ernie a sickly smile as he took his farewell.

When Terry arrived in Arthur's lock-up, he found Mooney sitting behind a table that was littered with forms, books and old copies of The *Sporting Life*.

'I've got the notepaper,' Terry said.

'What's it like?'

'Great.' He dumped it on the desk and gave a sample to Mooney.

'Not bad, eh?' said Mooney. 'West One. Mind you, it's the wrong side of Oxford Street – but who cares?'

'Just look at the directors.'

'Guy Ernest, M.B.E. – that's me. I've used that name before. But who's Lucas Herman?'

'And what about Sir John Franklin?'

'That's a boozer in the East India Dock Road,' replied Mooney. 'I reckon Arthur's done us proud. They love a title in this country – particularly the racing fraternity.'

'Where is – Sir Arthur?'

'Looking for telephones.' Mooney picked up a mug of red wine and took a sip. 'What is this?'

'Where did you find it?'

'On the shelf over there.'

'That could be red wine from Warrington. There's no labels, see.'

Mooney took another well considered sip. 'A claret – definitely a claret. A good one, too. I would say Baron Rothschild's Special Reserve.'

'You're kidding,' said Terry.

'Don't forget what I said, Terence. When you don't know – you *have* to believe.'

'Don't tell Arthur then.'

'Why not?'

'He'll certainly believe.'

'Yes,' said Mooney, 'that's why I like him.'

'Because he's a fantasy merchant?' said Terry.

'Something like that,' replied Mooney, taking another appreciative sip of the wine.

Arthur slammed on the brakes of the Jag just outside the underground station and stared, goggle-eyed, out of the window. He had been driving around for some time but now Arthur saw what seemed to him to be a near miracle. Beside the station, standing in an orderly line, were three telephone kiosks.

Bounding out of the Jag, Arthur approached the first telephone kiosk. He opened the door, sniffing at the smell of stale urine. He picked up the receiver, wrinkling his nose as he did so. He heard the dialling tone and looked in distaste at the graffiti all over the inside of the box. There were other signs of disrespect for one of the directories had been torn into small pieces (a strong man?), and part of the dialling code notice glass was broken and scattered over the floor of the box.

With a grin of satisfaction, Arthur went into the second box and experienced much the same situation. Just as he was about to pick up the receiver a middle-aged man, wearing a British Rail uniform, tapped on the box.

'Yes?'

'Excuse me, sir. I couldn't help seeing you trying the first box. Is it out of order?'

'No.'

Arthur heard the dialling tone and put the second receiver down.

'Is it broken?'

'No.'

Arthur left the second box and entered the third, watched by the mystified official.

'O.K?' he asked as Arthur emerged.

'Fine.'

'I like to keep them in good order.'

'As you should, my friend,' said Arthur pompously. 'You the Guv'nor round here?'

'I'm stationmaster.'

'You're a credit to British Rail.'

'Thank you.'

Arthur retired briskly to the first box.

'Er –' The stationmaster still looked mystified.

'What's up?'

'I hope you don't mind me asking, sir, but are you from the G.P.O.?'

'Not exactly,' said Arthur.

'Then –'

'But I am a kind of telephone expert. Know what I mean?'

'Er – yes. Yes, of course.' He looked impressed, but puzzled.

Arthur went into the box, picked up the phone, searched in his pockets and opened the door again.

'I say.'

'Yes, sir?'

'You haven't got a spare 10p on you?'

'Yes, yes of course. Here you are, sir.'

'Thank you. You're most kind.'

'It's a pleasure.'

He handed the 10p coin to Arthur who then tightly closed the door. He dialled the number of his lock-up – and Terry's voice answered.

'Daley Enterprises.'

Arthur waited for the coin to clink and then said:

'T.P. there?'

'I'll bring him on.'

'Ta.'

'Hallo – T.P. Mooney.' The soft burr of the Irish accent sounded comforting in Arthur's ears.

'I've got some good news for you.'

'Yes?'

'I've found a fabulous place.'

'An office.'

'An office with three phones. Good innit?'

'Excellent work, Arthur.'

110

'I'll be in touch soon.'

'Good – and Arthur –'

'Yeah?'

'I knew you were my man.'

Arthur rang off with a glow of pleasure. Emerging from the box, he found the curious stationmaster still on the forecourt. Arthur looked round him appreciatively.

'Lovely little station.'

'It's almost like being in the country here, sir.'

'Yeah.' Arthur turned to look at a particularly offensive slogan that was daubed on the wall. 'Not much traffic though.'

'You'd be surprised, sir.' The stationmaster looked down at his hunter watch. 'Three ten to Broad Street is due in five and a half minutes.'

'That's nice.'

'We're not dead, you know, sir.'

'Of course not. I only meant – it's not exactly Waterloo. I used to work there.'

'Yeah?'

'It's a rat race, isn't it, sir?' He smiled bitterly. 'Still, it suits me here.'

'Plenty of bunce?'

'I'm sorry, sir?'

'Fringe benefits?'

'Well –'

'Apart from having an excursion to Broad Street?'

'We've got a nice darts league.'

'So you're a bit of a sportsman?'

'I used to be.'

'I was thinking of tips, the occasional drink.' Arthur paused. 'A score in your fist every now and then. Every week?'

'For what?' He was instantly suspicious.

'Untaxed?'

'Yes sir, but –'

'As you probably realise, I'm an area manager for a large multi-national concern.'

'Really?'

'Yeah – I'm dashing around all over the place and some of my sales staff can't get hold of me sometimes. So, I suddenly thought when I passed your station – hey – three public telephones. Then I discover they're all in working order – thanks to you.'

'But –'

'I thought to myself, that's how the staff can reach me. It's all down to productivity, you see. Exports, helping the country – you know.'

'But what can I do, sir?'

Arthur squeezed the stationmaster's shoulder confidentially. 'Now if you could put a sticker on the kiosks, saying Out of Order, between – say – eleven a.m. and two p.m. and keep an eye out for vandals – you'll help the country, me and yourself.'

'But, I'm not absolutely sure I can –'

Arthur gave the stationmaster one of his special, innocent looks. 'I do hope that – I mean – you're not thinking it's illegal, are you? Would I suggest that?'

'I don't know,' said the stationmaster doubtfully.

'Of course you don't,' said Arthur reassuringly. 'But obviously I talked to our legal department.'

'You did?'

'No sweat.'

'No problem?'

'None.'

'I see.'

'Now, apart from that – my proposition is a sight more interesting than watching Jimmy Saville smiling from the train window when he passes through.'

'But, why do you need three phones?' persisted the bewildered stationmaster.

Arthur smiled patiently, immediately picking a vision which he almost believed in himself. 'New York –' he said, extravagantly pointing towards Kilburn. 'Chicago –'

'Eh?'

'Paris, Amsterdam, Hong Kong, Melbourne – there are guys trying to get hold of me internationally.'

'Are there?' The stationmaster was beginning to sound impressed again.

'There's a huge contract at stake – and a lot of jobs for British workers.'

'I see.'

'And what am I doing, you may ask? I'm on the rag and bone to San Francisco and a geezer from Milan gets the engaged tone. That's another ten thousand on the dole, see?'

'Yes. I understand,' said the stationmaster eagerly.

'But if he's got another number, we're in business. Now I'm driving from Southampton to my office in Mayfair and I stop here. Right here. This is the perfect plan – a key point, you might say. But I call it providence.'

The stationmaster was very clearly impressed. A train began to slowly roll into the station and he said:

'Do you mind if we continue this discussion on the platform, sir?'

'Not at all. You have your work – I have mine.'

Once on the platform, two passengers alighted and the train grudgingly departed.

'You see – apart from that – you've got twenty notes of folding green in the bin.'

'I understand.'

'Are you on?'

'Well – it seems very harmless, sir.'

'Harmless? This is vital work for the country.' Arthur's tone was imperial.

'And this is a most generous payment.'

'I'm a business man.'

'Yes, sir.'

'Able to strike an inventive deal that will save the country millions.'

'And help put our boys to work.'

'All part of the service.'

'Just an out of order sign?'

'A simple thing.'

'And an eye out for vandals.'

'I must have these phones working.'

'I'll see they are.'

'Good for you.' Arthur wrung his hand vigorously. 'You're a small cog in the export drive.'

'Thank you, sir.'

Arthur swept out of the station, totally encased in his own fantasy. The stationmaster stared after him, bemused and delighted.

Arthur and T.P. Mooney watched the pages spill out of the xerox machine in great anticipation. The print shop was dirty, noisy and cramped and Arthur had already noticed ink on the cuff of his white shirt. However, he was prepared to make a sacrifice for the cause.

'Caxton,' said Arthur to the printer who was studying the page, 'you do realise that's confidential, don't you?'

The printer ignored Arthur's comment. 'It's got to be a wind-up, innit?' He read out. ' "We are selling information. If you phone us on one of these telephone numbers we will give you our considered, expert opinion of three races." ' He looked at Arthur incredulously. 'I just don't believe it.' He stared at the page again, 'It gets better – listen to this –'

'We know what's in it,' protested Arthur.

But the printer continued to read: ' "When you put down your heavy wager, include a ten pound bet for us. That's our commission. You pay only when you win. We are trusting you – just as you are trusting us." '

'A most spirited rendition,' said Arthur icily. 'You should get down to the Old Vic.'

'Old Bailey – more likely,' said the printer darkly.

Arthur grabbed the page from his hand.

'Don't printers have an oath, like doctors?' he asked indignantly. 'And don't answer that. You are a privy to secret information.'

Mooney interposed soothingly: 'Don't upset yourself, Arthur – it's bad for you.' He turned to the printer. 'Are you a betting man, sir?'

'I like a punt.'

'Well – in that case – you, of all people, should know that there is good information, good connections, good sources –

that's the only way professionals earn a living.'

Mooney was so calm and persuasive that the printer suddenly began to take him seriously.

'Five thousand people,' continued Mooney, 'wrote to *us*, mister. We didn't ask them to write. Now, shall I give you a tip for tomorrow?'

'What is it?'

'Dunlop's horse in the three-thirty. John is an old friend of mine.'

'Is he?'

The printed picked up a newspaper.

'Yeah – Pancho Punch – third favourite – eleven to two, they reckon.'

'Now, obviously I can't guarantee that horse will win.'

'I bet you can't.'

'But, will you do this? Give me a tenner for the information – or will you give me fifty pounds, less tax, after it wins?'

'It's a good 'un,' said the printer, pretending to be considering the situation.

Arthur said a little too quickly: 'You're talking to T.P. – not the Scout or Captain Cola, or whatever his name is.'

'I'll give you a tenner,' said the printer after some hesitation.

'Take it off the bill,' said Mooney grandly.

'Have you got it?'

Arthur was driving the Jag round the streets near the station.

'I think so.'

'Let's rehearse.'

'I pick up the phone and I ask him for his club number. Then, I say "We've got three horses for you in different races . . . blah, blah." '

'So far so good,' said Arthur.

'Then I remind him to put our tenner on one of 'em – or even the three of 'em.'

'Then what?'

Terry sighed. 'The next guy phones and I give him three other names. Then the next guy gets three other horses and

115

then I get back to the first three when someone else phones. Simple innit?'

Arthur gave a modest smile. 'Most of the great ideas in history were simple.'

'Were they immoral as well?'

The smile left Arthur's face. 'You couldn't even spell that.'

'At least it was Mooney's idea.'

'Well – I wouldn't go as far as that, Tel.'

'Is it or isn't it?'

'T.P. came to me with a half-baked notion. I refined it and turned it into a solid concept.'

'Oh yeah?'

'And there's not the slightest hint of immorality in it.'

'Of course not, Arthur.'

'All the papers give their nap selection, don't they? Well – T.P.'s got the same form book. This is a great opportunity for you, Terence.'

'Why?' said Terry bleakly.

'You're always on about improving yourself. This is an office job, innit? You're a receptionist cum manager. You have responsibility.' Ending on that majestic note, Arthur pulled the Jag to a halt outside the station. The three telephone boxes stood beside it, each with an Out of Order sign on.

'There you are then.' Arthur gave an expansive gesture.

'What?'

'This is it.'

He indicated the kiosks.

'Where's the office?'

Arthur smiled happily at the telephone boxes and a dawning truth seared across Terry's mind.

'You mean – I'm to mind three public telephones?'

'Now, what's wrong with that?' Arthur's voice was soothing.

'Plenty, Arthur. Plenty.'

'You're always saying you like open-air jobs.'

'I'll be nicked,' said Terry hysterically.

'Course you won't.'

'Why not?'

'They're *ours*. Look at the stickers. Out of Order, they say.'

'You're out of order.' Terry's voice became threatening.

Arthur hastened to placate him. 'Terry –'

'*No*, Arthur.'

'Terence –'

'I said, *No*.'

'The stationmaster's on the firm.'

'*What*?'

'Look at him.' The stationmaster was hovering on the forecourt and Arthur gave him a cheery smile and a wave. He waved back. 'What a nice man,' he said reflectively. 'Just a simple working-class hero. The salt of the earth.'

'You pick 'em, don't you?'

'You mean, you'll do it?'

Terry gave Arthur a wry grin. In the pit of his stomach he felt a sinking sensation, but he knew once again that Arthur had somehow beaten him.

'We'll see how it goes.'

'Good for you, Tel.'

'Arthur –'

But Arthur ploughed on. 'Nothing would please me more than to accept the inaugural telephone call personally.' He brandished a buff envelope triumphantly.

'Then why don't you?'

'Because, unfortunately, I have to meet with an Inspector of the Inland Revenue.'

Terry gave an explosive laugh and Arthur frowned.

'Nothing funny there, Terry.'

'Sorry, Arthur.'

'You don't have these pressures, Tel. You're a free spirit.'

'Oh yeah?'

'I'm the one who has to fend off busybodies, the marshalled ranks of officialdom, so that you and me can get a crust.'

But Arthur's eloquence was cut off by the sound of the car door slamming. Terry had left him – and was walking woodenly towards the telephone boxes. Arthur wound down the window and said:

'I'll be giving you a bell, Terence.'

Terry nodded his head and said something that Arthur

hoped the stationmaster had not heard.

Terry stared at the telephone boxes with hostility. Then he nodded at the stationmaster, who smiled tentatively but made no effort to introduce himself. Self-consciously, Terry strolled around the kiosks – which did not take very long. Still the stationmaster smiled, as if he was hosting a particularly difficult party. When Terry had been round the kiosks at least six times a large West Indian woman came into view.

'What happen? Everything Out of Order?'

Terry shrugged and there was a pause during which neither of them said anything. It was an uncomfortable pause, which Terry finally broke. 'You want to phone somebody?' he asked.

'Not really.'

'Oh.'

The woman looked at her watch and then glanced at the stationmaster, who decided at that moment to go back inside the station. At that moment the phone began to ring in one of the kiosks and Terry smiled vaguely at the woman, as he opened the door.

'That might be for me,' she said.

'Probably me,' replied Terry.

'Well, my man phones every week. He's night porter at the Kingston Hilton – that's why he got access to the phone.'

'Kingston-on-Thames?'

'Kingston, Jamaica, man.'

'Well – I'll see.' Terry hurried into the kiosk and picked up the phone. He took a deep, embarrassed breath, cursed Arthur silently, and then said: "Mayfair Course Consultants. Can I have your name please? Thank you. Now what we have today are three good horses . . . Number One is Jones Boy, two thirty at Kempton. Number Two is Book Token in the three o'clock race at Catterick – and Number Three is Happy Days in the three-thirty at Sandown.' Terry then explained the system and eventually his caller rang off and he emerged a little shakily from the kiosk. But, as he did so, the phone began to ring in the third kiosk and the West Indian woman gave him a strange look. Terry opened the kiosk and went inside, but as he was talking, the phone rang again in the first kiosk and the woman hurried to answer it. A few seconds later she emerged in considerable confusion and went down to the kiosk that Terry was occupying. She tapped hesitantly on the door.

'Yeah?' said Terry, who was still talking.

'He wants the selections,' she replied.

Terry returned to the phone. 'Just a second, pal.' He turned back to the woman. 'Could you do me a favour?'

'Sure.'

He gave her a piece of paper. 'Just give him these names – and get his name as well.'

'Will do.'

She bustled off, whilst Terry returned to the receiver. 'Sorry about that, sir – we're rushed off our feet this morning. Now, where were we? Ah yes – the three o'clock at Kempton and we've got great hopes of this one. Great hopes? No, I'm sorry, sir – that's not the name. What I mean is that we've got great hopes of Flying Duck. Got it?' Terry was beginning to sweat, particularly as he could now hear the phone in the middle kiosk beginning to ring. Putting down the receiver, he dashed into the kiosk.

'Hallo – sorry? Where? Oh – the Kingston Hilton. Hang on.'

Terry dashed out of the middle kiosk and began to knock urgently at the first, with the sweat now pouring down his forehead. An image of Arthur crept into his mind and he mentally put Arthur's head in a noose and kicked away the chair beneath his feet. The fleeting vision made him feel much better. 'It's your old man,' he hissed for she was still on the phone. 'He's only got a couple of minutes.'

She muttered 'O.K.' at him as she gave the name of a horse at Catterick. Terry then tore back to the middle kiosk again and picked up the phone with a shaking hand.

'She's just coming. Sorry? What's going on? It's not easy to explain. Ah – here she comes.'

A few minutes later there was a slight lull. The West Indian woman was still on the phone to her husband in Jamaica, but neither of the other phones was ringing. As

119

Terry lounged against the side of one of the boxes, he spotted four kids across the road who were becoming very interested spectators to the flurried activity around the telephone boxes. They were obviously out of work and their eternal boredom had been temporarily relieved. Just as Terry was studying them – and they were studying Terry, the phone in the first kiosk began to ring again. He sprang into action and with smooth tones, he said: 'MCC – sorry? Oh yes – Mayfair Course Consultants. Can I have your name?' This was becoming automatic, thought Terry, as he grinned at the West Indian woman in the kiosk door. She grinned back and said to her husband:

'Look – I've got to go now. Why? I have to *work*. Yes work. No – I don't have to tell you everything. I do 'cos you don't tell me. O.K. you be like that. Ring me later.' She put the phone down, heard the phone ringing in the third kiosk, signalled to Terry that she would take it and hurried into the kiosk. Once in there, she picked up the phone, only to the hear the phone ringing in the middle kiosk.

'Can you hang on a minute?' she said. 'We're real busy right now.'

Leaving the phone off the hook and signalling once more to Terry, she ran to the middle kiosk, took the call, came back, took another piece of paper from Terry – and panted her way back to the third kiosk where she had left the phone off the hook. She sounded very brisk and efficient as she said:

'Here we are now. Your name please. Thank you. Now I can really tell you that we have three great winners. Ready? Jones Boy, two thirty at Kempton. Book Token – and I really fancy that one myself – that's the three o'clock at Catterick and Happy Days at Sandown in the three thirty. Sorry – oh yes, about Book Token – well, he ran last month at Windsor and came fourth, but he was coming up like an express train in the last half furlong. You're absolutely right, sweetheart – I seen it on the telly myself.' She put the phone down and turned to see that Terry had been listening to her.

'Am I any good?' she asked.

'Good – you speak like an expert.'

'I always follow the horses.'

'We'll have to come to an arrangement,' said Terry.

The four kids gathered on some waste ground behind the station and developed a battle plan.
    'They're a right pair.'
    'Couple of monkeys.'
    'What are they up to?'
    'Dunno.'
    'Must be summat good.'
    'It's bent.'
    'They're making dirty calls.'
    'Bet he's a heavy breather.'
    'What about her?'
    'She gets 'em worked up, like.'
    'So what are we gonna do?'
    'We could tell 'em they've been rumbled.'
    'The bloke – he could turn nasty.'
    'Supposin' they're doin' summat else.'
    'What could it be?'
    They stared at each other in frustrated puzzlement.
    'The phones keep ringing.'
    'They leg it from box to box.'
    'Bits of paper.'
    'Our of Order signs on the doors.'
    'Funny innit?'
    'Yeah.'
    'Tell you what?'
    'What?'
    'Let's muscle in.'
    'How?'
    'Be heavy.'
    'With him?'
    'You chicken?'
    'No.'
    'Then we could try it?'
    'And get your neck broken?'
    'If we *all* try it.'
    They looked at each other again in greater optimism. It was worth a try.

Arthur wore his most angelic expression as he and his accountant sat in the sombre offices of the Inland Revenue. The Inspector, his face set in an expression of sterile disapproval, sat opposite them.

'Employees?' Arthur was saying. 'I don't employ anybody.'

'But you've got a company,' said the Inspector relentlessly.

'Not any more,' said Arthur. 'I mean – I have *got* a company but it's not active.'

'Oh?'

'It's just a sentimental thing.'

The Inspector looked at Arthur incredulously and Anthony, Arthur's accountant, cleared his throat uneasily.

'But when this great country of ours gets on its feet,' continued Arthur, 'I'll be ready.'

'For what?' asked the Inspector, but Arthur did not reply, being well into his stride.

'The sleeping giant will wake and I'll be ready to serve her. At the moment, of course, I'm more or less semi-retired.'

The Inspector picked up a file and began to study it. Then he said: 'But you've got company assets – Jaguar car for instance.'

'That's not mine.'

'But –'

'It belongs to my Uncle Sid.'

'There's no indication of –'

'I said to him – "Sid, why do you need a car like that?" I said. "I mean you being an old age pensioner and all." So I just keep it for him. It's an old man's folly. And do you know what he said?'

'No,' said the Inspector grimly.

'He said, "You use it, Arthur. You not having wheels of your own." Wasn't that nice?'

'Charming sentiment,' muttered Anthony.

The inspector stared unbelievingly at Arthur. 'But you use the Jaguar car for work?'

'Work?'

'Yes – your company.'

'A man of my age? In semi-retirement? No. I use that

122

motor to take the old people down to the Darby and Joan Club.'

'I see.'

'Or people to hospital – or to poll. I'm into good deeds – charity.'

There was a long pause during which even Arthur looked spell-bound. The Inspector, however, remained disquietingly suspicious.

Arthur cleared his throat. 'By the way,' he asked the Inspector. 'Have you got the time?'

'Quarter past twelve.'

'Thank you.' Arthur glanced at the Inspector's watch. 'What a lovely kettle – I mean watch. I wish I could have – well, just a simple watch. But these days, well it's just an extravagance.'

Anthony gave Arthur a warning glance, knowing that he was now beginning to go over the top.

'Maybe you'll find one in your lock-up,' said the Inspector drily.

'My lock-up?' said Arthur in tones of sudden fury. 'Is that the reason for this interrogation?'

'This is merely an interview.'

'I don't care what you call it.' Arthur turned to Anthony in high dudgeon. 'Didn't you tell the man about my lock-up?'

'I said you had a few odds and ends in there,' he replied feebly.

'Did you explain about my hobbies?'

'What hobbies?' asked Anthony hopelessly.

'I make things, don't I?'

'What things?' asked the Inspector.

'Oh those things.' Anthony was not completely mystified.

'What things?' asked the Inspector.

'Toys, mainly.'

'What?'

'For deprived children.'

'Look, Mr Daley, one of my staff called at your lock-up and saw several video sets.'

'Never.'

123

'Just a few weeks ago.'

'Now wait a minute,' said Arthur pretending to think deeply, 'I can *just* mark your card on them.'

'Good.'

'They were – er – flood-damaged videos. I tinker with them. Occasionally I get a pittance for repairing 'em.'

'A pittance?'

'Certainly not enough to pay income tax on.'

'Well – how do you get by?'

'The odd crust.'

'Rent, food, clothes?'

'Bingo.'

'Bingo?'

'All down to 'er indoors. She manages well.'

'A little Metro, two children at a private school?'

'I don't know how she does it.' Arthur leant forward confidentially. 'She's an incredible woman. Of course, between you and me, I reckon she's got a few pennies stashed away in the Post Office.'

'Perhaps she has, Mr Daley.'

'Any more questions?'

The Inspector looked suddenly exhausted. 'Not for the moment.'

'I hope I've satisfied you.'

'We'll be in touch.'

Arthur rose and Anthony said:

'Thank you so much.'

'It was a pleasure,' said the Inspector.

Once outside, Arthur took his watch from his pocket and strapped it back on his wrist.

'That was a nice touch, I thought,' he said to Anthony.

'Yes,' Anthony replied doubtfully.

'So I did all right?'

'Well – I'm deeply impressed.'

'I thought you might be. You see –'

'But I'll tell you one thing, Arthur.'

'What's that, old son?'

'They're after you now.'

'What?'

'A tax-man hates a clever dick – and that's what you are, Arthur.'

'What can they do?' asked Arthur truculently.

'Who knows? That's how they got Al Capone on tax and look what happened to him.'

'Charming.'

'It's a fact, Arthur.'

'So they'll be after me. What tactics?'

'Can't tell you.'

'You're the accountant. That's what I pay –'

'Don't talk about payment, Arthur. Not unless you got it.'

'All in good time.'

'They got a thousand different ways.'

Arthur looked suddenly uneasy. Then he clapped a hearty hand on Anthony's shoulder and said:

'You're up to all the dodges, son. I trust you.'

'What's up?'

'How do you mean?'

The kid on the skateboard made a fancy pattern on the station forecourt whilst the speaker swaggered up to him. The West Indian woman was hard at work in one kiosk and Terry was having a temporary rest between calls.

'What's happening?'

'A lady's phoning somebody.'

'We live round here.'

'Nice,' said Terry looking around.

'You don't live round here.'

'So what?'

'We live round here.'

'You said that before.'

The kid was sizing Terry up and down – and he was dismayed to see how relaxed and confident he looked.

'I'm just saying it.'

'Triffic.'

'You gonna be here tomorrow?'

'We use them phones sometimes.'

'You got 10p?'

'What?'

'Then you're all right, aren't you?'

The kid turned away with a sneer and returned to his mate on the skateboard. Meanwhile, the West Indian woman emerged from one of the kiosks.

'The guy on the phone reckons he's gonna put two hundred on Jones Boy. I said to him "Take it easy man. It's only a selection – it doesn't mean it's a certainty." '

'Good on you.'

She looked back at the kiosks regretfully.

'It's gone quiet now.'

'Office shuts at two,' said Terry, looking at his watch.

'Ah.'

'What's your name, love?'

'Petal.'

'I'll tell you what, Petal – I reckon we've earned ourselves a drink. What do you say?'

'Great idea. What's your name?'

'Terry.'

'O.K., Terry – but before we go into the pub I have to run an errand.'

'What's that?'

'I just want to pop in the betting shop.'

'You ought to be out, T.P.'

'Yeah.'

'Why aren't you?'

'I'm not so good.'

The doss-house supervisor stared down at T.P.'s ashen face. 'What's up?'

'I'm sick.'

'You're breathing bad.'

'Can't catch it.'

'Catch what?'

'My breath.'

'Can I do anything?'

'I'll be O.K. if I can stay here. Want some more dough?'

'No – but if the boss comes –'

'I'll get up.'

Half an hour later, the supervisor heard T.P.'s stentorian

breathing and returned to his bed-side.

'What's up?'

'I'm fine.'

'You're not.'

'Eh?'

'Look at you.'

The supervisor stared down at the now blue-grey features on the pillow and the humped, writhing throat muscles.

'Can't you breathe?'

'Bit of asthma.'

'Rubbish.'

'I'm all right, I tell you. It'll pass.'

'I can't take the responsibility.'

'I often get these attacks.' But even as he spoke, T.P.'s breathing became worse until he could hardly draw breath at all.

'I'll call an ambulance.'

'No.'

'I must.'

'No more perks?'

'Don't be a fool, T.P. You'll die.'

With that he ran for the phone, while T.P. continued to struggle for breath. Minutes later, two ambulance men arrived with a stretcher.

'Come on, old son. You're coming with us.'

'No.'

'Look – you can hardly breathe.'

'I've business to attend to.'

'You won't be dealing with anything unless we take you to hospital.'

'I've told you, I'm staying here.'

But at that moment, T.P. began to choke.

'Come on – get the stretcher under him, Tom.'

Then the choking stopped and with it, T.P.'s breathing.

'Oh my God!'

'He's croaked.'

'Well – *do* something,' yelled the supervisor.

One of the ambulance men proceeded to give T.P. the kiss of life, but nothing happened. The other then began a cardiac massage and after thumping away for a while, T.P.'s breathing miraculously began again.

'Now – you're away with us,' said the ambulance man who had been doing the massage.

T.P. feebly grinned. 'I saw a bunch of angels,' he whispered.

'Oh yeah? Can you slide over?'

'And you know what?'

'Come *on*.'

'They were riding gee-gees.'

'That's it.'

'And they were racing at Catterick.'

'I think you should tell us what kind of operation you've had, Mr – Mr Smith.'

'With a Y and an E – Smythe rather than Smith.'

Mooney was lying in the cardiac unit of a general hospital. His bed was screened off and he was connected up to a cardiograph machine. A doctor was carefully examining Mooney and looking ominously at the livid scar on his chest.

'Well, Mr Smythe, this is obviously a recent operation. We'd like to see the report.'

'This was done by one of the finest surgeons in the country.'

'I can see that,' said the doctor. 'Which hospital was it?'

'It doesn't matter.'

'It would help us.'

'Look, if you're a doctor, you're a doctor. I feel as fit as a flea now.'

'You collapsed.'

'Morning sickness.'

'You couldn't breathe.'

'Asthma.'

A nurse bustled in and whispered to a doctor, 'We haven't got a next of kin, sir.'

Overhearing, Mooney said: 'Well – what's it to you?'

'We do need to know,' she said fussily.

'Is it a crime to die without the whole world knowing about it?'

'It's just normal.'

128

'Is it?'

'A relative – or a friend?'

'Can I phone somebody?'

But the doctor intervened: 'Look – I want you to lie very quietly. The nurse can phone someone.'

'I want to phone myself.'

'But –'

'It's a simple request –'

'You should rest.'

'For a dying man. I've even got 10p.'

The doctor smiled. 'Mr Smythe. You can phone in a few minutes.'

'I've urgent business to attend to.'

'And you've had a heart attack.'

'That can't stop me – I've had dozens.'

'Which hospital were you in?'

'I told you – it doesn't matter.'

'Come on, Mr Smythe –'

'In fact it's none of your bloody business!'

'Very well.' The doctor signalled the nurse to join him outside Mooney's screened off bed.

'A difficult patient,' he said.

'I can hear you,' yelled Mooney.

Arthur paid a short visit to a betting shop and emerged, well pleased with what he had seen. Mooney's form was good and already the winners were beginning to come up. A regular punter and an old acquaintance of Arthur's came up to him and received a surprisingly friendly welcome.

'And how are you, my old son?'

'Mustn't grumble, Arthur.'

'Picking some winners?'

'Not much luck today.'

'Oh dear.'

'You got a winner?'

'I'm always a winner.'

'You mean – your luck's changed, Arthur?'

Arthur frowned. 'I never really tried till now.'

'Oh yeah?'

'You want your luck to change?'

'What –?'

'Do you or don't you?'

'Couldn't be much worse than it is now.'

'That's bad.'

'That's usual.'

'Look – let me give you some advice.'

'I ain't got no money, Arthur.'

'Trust.'

'Eh?'

'You have to trust, old son. Let me give you this card.'

'What's this?'

'Just ring the number between office hours. My staff will advise you.'

'Blimey.'

'I'll be all right, Terry.'

'Where are you?'

'In intensive care.'

'Blimey!'

'Don't keep saying blimey, Terry.'

'What happened?'

'Had a bit of a relapse.'

'What's that supposed to mean?'

'Nothing much. But don't worry. How's the system going?'

'Triffic.'

Then T.P.'s voice disappeared protesting and a brisk nurse's voice came on instead.

'Who am I speaking to?'

'A colleague.'

'Of Mr Smythe's?'

'Of course.'

'Well, he's very ill, you know.'

'That's bad news.'

'He won't tell us which hospital he's been in before. Can you throw any light on that?'

Terry thought of the London Clinic and how much Mooney had ripped them off for.

'I'm afraid I've no idea.'

'Oh dear. You are –?'

'Mr McCann – business associate.'

'I see.'

'Will – will Mr Smythe recover?'

'He's very poorly.'

'Yes, but –'

'He's going on as well as can be expected.'

'Thank you, nurse. Perhaps I could ring back later?'

'Yes, Mr McCann, and with some information, if you can obtain it.'

'I'll try, nurse.'

Terry put down the telephone in the bar of the Winchester Club and said to Dave: 'Pint of lager.'

'Trouble?'

'Yeah – wait till happy boy hears.'

'Talk of the devil,' said Dave, pouring out Terry's lager.

Arthur came bouncing in, walking straight up to the clearly worried and depressed Terry. Arthur, predictably, did not notice.

'Haven't we had a result, eh?'

'Have we?'

'Come on, Tel. I'll have a large one,' he said to Dave. 'Haven't you seen it?'

'What?'

'Three winners,' said Arthur triumphantly. 'We've done it.'

'Great.'

'What I'm worried about now is – can we expect the right amount from the punters? Will they send their fees in, eh? You see, Tel, you've got to realise there's an awful lot of dishonesty in this world of ours.'

'You don't say, Arthur.'

'Now how many calls did you get? Oh, thanks, Dave,' Arthur accepted his large vodka and slim-line with alacrity. 'On the slate?'

'Arthur, I said –'

'David, you can hear we've done well. You'll get it – and something for yourself.'

'Thanks, Arthur.'

'Now – how many calls did you get, Terence?'

''Bout three hundred.' Terry stared down at the drink in his glass.

'Never? That's incredible. Incredible.' Arthur was very impressed.

'Say that a third of 'em put a bet on. Well – the starting prices were good, you know. Book Token at nine to two – that's forty-five pounds for us. But – will they send in the dough, eh? Are they to be trusted? I've got my doubts – but old T.P. reckons they will. He believes in trust more than I do – and I hope he's right.' Arthur drained his glass. 'Set another one up, Dave. You're quiet, Terry.'

'I wondered when you'd get round to mentioning T.P.'

'Thanks, Dave. What do you mean?'

'He's ill.'

'He's always ill.'

'He's in intensive care.'

'What?'

'You heard.'

'Oh my Gawd.' Arthur took a hefty swig. 'Who's gonna pick out the selections?'

Terry glared at him angrily. 'You really are a charmer, aren't you?'

'Why?'

'As far as you're concerned the old guy can snuff it and you're worried about his daily nap.'

'Well, it's important, Terry.'

'Is it?'

'Anyway, it's probably a false alarm.'

'How do you know?'

'Give us another, Dave.'

'I'm not putting this up, Arthur.'

'Terry, pay for it, can you? I've had a bit of a turn.' Arthur began to mop his brow with a silk handkerchief.

'Not you too.'

'Illness always affects me.'

Reluctantly Terry paid for the drink.

'Aspirin, Arthur?' asked Dave.

'I'll be O.K. in a minute.' He took his drink. 'When I've had this – when did you hear about it?'

'Few minutes ago. He phoned.'

'From intensive care? He can't be that bad.'

'He is – the nurse told me.'

'Can he sit up?'

'I dunno. Why?'

'Can he read?'

'How do I know? He might be in an oxygen tent.'

'Making calls?'

'I *told* you – the nurse said he was bad.'

'Do you reckon you could slip him a *Sporting Life*?'

'I don't believe this.'

'Look, Terry,' said Arthur, 'I can be a very sensitive man, you know. I should have known. I should never have trusted Mooney from the off.'

'Can I help you?' asked the nurse. Terry stood at the entrance to the busy ward, clutching a plastic bag and looking rather lost. In one corner he could see a screened-off area.

'Have you got a Mr Mooney?'

'Nobody with that name.'

'Ward H6?'

'Yes.'

'He came in yesterday – smallish, about fifty-five with an Irish accent.'

'Oh, you mean Sir Alfred.'

'Who?'

'Sir Alfred Smythe.'

'That must be him.'

'Well – don't you know?' she asked disapprovingly.

'Of course – Sir Alfred. Occasionally he uses another name – Mooney. I mean – that's his butler – his butler's name.' The nurse stared at him mystified as Terry got in deeper and deeper. 'He uses it when he's incognito.'

'When he's what?'

'He's a bit eccentric, you know.'

'Oh yes.'

'But he's out of intensive care now, is he?'

'Yes, but he's still very poorly.'

'Can I see him?' asked Terry giving her a hopeful smile.

'Visiting hours are two to eight.'

'Special favour?'

'Well – I'll see. There's someone with him now.' She went behind the screen. There was a short delay and then she came out with an attractive and fashionable young woman.

'I take it –'

'I'm his daughter, Fenella.'

'I see.' The nurse bustled off without speaking.

'This is what you want.'

'Eh?'

'Isn't it?' She handed him an envelope.

'What is it?'

'Your daily selections,' said Fenella in an icy voice.

'Thanks,' gulped Terry.

'I trust you won't sell them in the hospital.'

'It's not my idea, you know,' said Terry sharply. 'How is T.P. – I mean, Sir Alfred – your Dad?'

'Ill.'

'Can I see him?'

'No. I don't want you to bother him now.'

'I wasn't going to,' said Terry angrily. 'We just happen to be friends.'

'He's sleeping, anyway.'

Terry gave her a paper bag.

'What's in here – racing mags?'

They would have been in there if Arthur had had anything to do with it, thought Terry.

'Just some fruit. Anything else he needs?'

'No.' Then she relented. 'I'm sorry. I'm exhausted.'

'He's an amazing bloke.'

'Yes, tiring – even when he's ill. Would you like to buy me a cup of coffee?'

'Why not?' said Terry with a smile. The day was turning out better than he expected.

Terry brought two cups of coffee back to the table in the hospital canteen where Fenella was sitting. As Terry put down the cups he said:

'I'm sure this is a great hospital and all that – but your Dad likes a bit of luxury – like the London Clinic.'

'I know all about that – it's pathetic. I suppose you were impressed.'

Terry grinned. 'The Savoy wasn't bad, was it?'

'That's what you think?'

'What do you mean?'

'He even cons himself.' She sounded deeply angry.

'Do you know where he was living?'

'No.'

'A hostel for single men – two pounds a night.'

A look of horror passed across Terry's face.

'The humiliation was beyond him,' she continued. 'Sometimes he actually believes some of his stories. You see – he thinks he's one of nature's aristocrats. All he wants to do is to impress people. People like you – and that awful Arthur Daley.'

'I'm terribly sorry.'

'It's too late.'

'Not yet – and besides I *am* impressed, still.'

'I bet.'

'Arthur thinks T.P.'s the greatest man in the world.'

'Because he can run a tipster service from his sick-bed?'

'You don't go for your Dad.'

'Rubbish!'

'Eh?'

'You think on something. Can't you see I love him? He gave me everything – including four mothers. Don't you know the story of my education? That would be a good story for your cronies.'

'You don't have to tell me all this.'

'I want to.'

'You see – T.P. wanted me to be a success. I went to Benenden, you know.'

'What?'

'Oh yes – with Princess Anne.'

'How long for?'

'Oh, a couple of terms.' She brightened visibly. 'T.P. was flush then.'

'And then?'

135

'There was a term at Roedean, and one at Millfield. I was the gypsy of girls' boarding schools.'

'Did you know why?'

'Not at the time.' She sighed. 'I wish I'd been told T.P. couldn't pay the bills. Also – I never really knew who I was.'

'Why?'

'T.P. was always changing my name – half the crowned heads of Europe were relatives of mine – supposedly.'

Terry stared across the table at her, fascinated by this extraordinary life-style. 'What happened then?'

'I went to Switzerland – and then had a year in Paris.'

'Good times for T.P.?'

'I don't know. By the time I was eighteen I was highly educated, confident, poised, bilingual – *and* on the most wanted list in four countries.'

'I don't believe it,' said Terry.

'That's up to you.'

He was silent for a moment. 'Just a second –'

'Yes.'

'I *do* believe it.'

Fenella laughed. 'I owe him a lot.'

'Not to mention Roedean an' all.'

'Do you know the most extraordinary thing?'

'What's that?' But already Terry was beginning to realise that he was talking to an extraordinary girl.

'The thing is that sometimes he actually had the money.'

'What – you mean when he took you away from Roedean –?'

'I'm not sure *when* – but I know he had it sometimes.'

'So why did he make you assume all those names?'

'He just wanted to break the rules – that's all.'

'A rebel?'

'Not really. Life's a laugh, that was his view. What's he going to do when he grows up?' Suddenly there were tears in her eyes.

'Will he?'

'You mean – will he live? He's been ill before, and survived.'

'I'm sure he will.'

'What's gonna happen when he comes out of this place?'

'He's a very independent man.' She looked at Terry hard. 'You're not beginning to feel responsible for him, are you?'

Terry nodded.

'Well don't.'

'He's so – he gets himself into such a mess.'

'He won't come to my home – and apart from that my husband doesn't like him.'

'Husband?' said Terry in a funereal voice.

'Yes – and I don't think he trusts him either. You can understand that, can't you? He's not amused by T.P.'s stories.'

'Why not?'

'He's a merchant banker.'

'That figures.'

'So I've no idea what's going to happen to T.P.'

'Let me help.'

'What can you do?'

'I dunno. There must be something – I've got fond of the old boy. And so is Arthur.'

'Him?'

'Let me think.'

'Know what he said last night? If I do snuff it I can con my way into heaven. Then he asked me if I thought St Peter took credit cards.'

Terry laughed.

'Does he owe you any money?' Fenella asked.

'No.'

'Do you owe *him* any money?'

'No.'

'And Arthur?'

'I'm pretty sure he doesn't. But you never know with Arthur.'

'There's one thing you ought to know. It worked out for me – just.'

'So?'

'But it doesn't for other people. All T.P.'s schemes end in tears.'

'I'm used to that, from Arthur.'

'Yes, of course. I'd forgotten. They're both rather similar in a way, aren't they?'

'No,' said Terry, 'they're not.'

'But –'

'T.P. – he's got the makings of a genius.'

'The makings –'

'Yes, maybe just that. And Arthur –'

'What's he got?'

Terry rose quickly to his feet.

'Don't let's go into that just now,' he said.

Terry slept badly that night. He had a mixed, recurring dream that involved him in answering the telephone in hundreds of telephone boxes. He ran from one to the other until he began to crawl – and still the telephones rang. All Arthur could say was: 'It's expansion, Terry, it's expansion. Won't you ever understand ambition?' Then T.P. came up on a stretcher with the cardiac machine still attached to him. Arthur gave him a copy of *Sporting Life* and then ripped off the machine. T.P. died as Arthur stood over him shouting: 'Come on. It's not time to go yet. We've got a deal.'

Terry eventually awoke, sweating with anxiety, and, looking at his watch, saw that he was late for the 'office'. Cursing Arthur, he left the flat without shaving, jumped into the Ford and tore off to the station. When he arrived he found Petal with a friend.

'Hi, Terry,' she said. 'Meet Sylvia.'

She introduced him to another West Indian girl.

'Hallo.'

'She's a first class telephone operator.'

'*And* I was a receptionist as well.'

'Nice,' replied Terry.

'I brought her – just in case we get too busy.' Petal grinned. 'What's the nap selection?'

Terry produced T.P.'s envelope gloomily.

'This could be the last one.'

Petal looked disappointed. 'Why is that, man? It's all good fun.'

'Sure – but the source is drying up.'

'Why's that –?'

'Hang on – here's Arthur.'

'Who is he?'

'The boss.'

Arthur parked his Jaguar behind Terry's beaten up Ford and lit a cigar as he strolled over. He cast a suspicious look at Petal and Sylvia. Terry cut in quickly before Arthur could say anything.

'These are your new employees.'

'Eh?'

'Without Petal – I couldn't have done it.'

'You're not talking about wages, are you?'

'Yeah.'

'Look, Terry –'

'No stamps though.'

'I haven't had a penny yet,' mourned Arthur.

'That's your problem.'

'And I never asked you to sub-contract work.' Arthur turned to Petal with a hopeful smile. 'You understand that, don't you, flower?'

'Petal,' said Terry.

'Of course,' replied Arthur. 'Now –'

'So they need dough.'

'For a few minutes of answering the phone?'

'Four hours, actually,' said Terry.

Arthur turned his most ingratiating smile on Petal. 'How about a tenner? I'm well known as a generous governor.'

'Don't listen to him,' said Terry to Petal, but unfortunately, Arthur's fatal charm was working on her.

'I'd be happy to have –'

'Don't say anything,' said Terry.

'Yes, my dear?' asked Arthur solicitously, baring his teeth at her.

'Well –' All was lost – she had weakened at the worst possible moment and Arthur had triumphed.

'That's all right, Petal. You do understand, don't you?' He slipped a fiver into her hand. 'Put that in your sporran, darling.'

'You're gonna hate yourself for that,' said Terry. He turned back to Arthur. 'And what about Sylvia?'

'She ain't done anything yet,' replied Arthur sweetly. 'Now, Terry, have you seen T.P.?'

'I wondered when you were gonna ask.'

'How is he?'

'Not so good.'

'Is he going to –?'

'We don't know.'

'And the –?'

'This might be the last one, Arthur.'

'Oh my Gawd!' Then Arthur looked round and the words stuck in his throat. He tried to say something but merely made an inarticulate noise of fear and anger.

'Hallo,' said Terry. 'Where did they spring from?'

The kids had returned, but greatly strengthened in numbers. Now there were eight of them – a multi-racial gang – and three had surreptitiously occupied the phone kiosks.

'Get 'em,' yelled Arthur. "It'll be business hours soon.' He took a couple of steps towards the kiosks. 'Er – you lot – can't you read? It says Out of Order.'

'You're out of order an' all,' said one of the kids, opening and shutting the door of the kiosk.

'Cheeky lout. I'll have you.' Arthur practically gibbered with rage. At that moment, the kid on the skateboard brushed past Arthur. 'Oi – you got a licence for that?'

The boy said something very personal that made Arthur even angrier. 'Terry – get 'em out.'

'How?'

'With violence. Kick 'em up the arse!'

'They're in business if they've got 10p.'

'What's this? Betrayal?' Arthur paused dramatically. 'I left you here to mind these telephone kiosks, Terry – and now I'm threatened by Bugsy Malone and his mob.'

'You've been tumbled, Arthur,' replied Terry unsympathetically.

Arthur grimaced and one of the kids said to him: 'We live round 'ere.'

'He said that yesterday as well,' commented Terry.

'Terence!' Arthur's voice rose.

'Watch your blood-pressure, grandad,' jeered the boy on the skateboard.

Then, a younger boy, wearing sunglasses said to Arthur, 'Do you realise these telephone boxes are the only ones in the metropolitan area that haven't been vandalised.' His voice was small and menacing and it had a definite impact on Arthur, who looked uneasy. A real villain of the future, thought Terry, and smooth with it.

'That's right, Shades,' said the skateboard kid, circling round Arthur again. 'I mean – these are like gold-dust in your game.'

'What game?' said Arthur defensively.

'I don't know what game.'

'Look, sonny –' Arthur tried bravado without success.

'But it's got to be a bit iffy,' said Shades. 'I mean – it must be.'

Arthur looked as if he was being threatened by a heavy mobster. Then he saw another kid clambering over his Jag and he started to stutter:

'What – what's he doing?'

'He's an aerial freak, inne?'

'Terry,' Arthur's voice was shrill, '*do* something.'

Terry yelled: 'Oi – come 'ere!' Slowly the boy left Arthur's Jag and came across to him. 'Now, listen.'

'Yeah?'

'You can give plenty of aggravation to me and the girls messing about with the phones, but if you harm that motor, I'm gonna knock your head off.' He smiled. 'Understand?'

'Listen to what the gentleman says, like a good boy,' put in Arthur.

The boy nodded, but while he was doing so – one of the phones rang and one of the kids in the telephone kiosks picked up the receiver. Arthur rushed to the kiosk and opened the door. 'What is it?'

'Sorry,' said the kid as he replaced the phone, 'wrong number.'

'You little –' shrieked Arthur, while Shades nearby satisfied himself by saying, 'There's gonna be a lot of that.'

141

Arthur took stock of the situation, glared at Terry and approached Shades with a cagey smile. 'So you're the head-man, eh?'

'Yeah.'

'What do they call you?'

'They call me Shades.'

'Er – yes – now can I call you Shades?' Arthur draped one arm round his shoulder.

'What do you want?'

'I want a chat.'

'What about?'

'I like a young man with ambition.'

'Eh?'

'You see – what we've got here, Shades, is a rupture of communication.'

The boy tried to move away from Arthur's comradely arm but Arthur tightened his grip.

'You come here, team handed, terrorising law-abiding rate-payers who use the facilities of the GPO – to whit a public rag and boner.'

'So?'

'And you expect ransom, blackmail or even protection money. Is that the situation?'

'Could be.'

'Is it – or isn't it?'

'It is.'

Arthur smiled and steered Shades to the kerb and back. 'You see, son, I don't intend to lecture you about the ambiguous morality of the situation.'

'Don't bother.'

'How much?'

Arthur grinned at Terry and said, like a bad ventriloquist: 'The kid's a mug.' He then smiled blandly at Shades. 'Well?'

'A ton.'

Arthur looked as if he was going to have apoplexy. 'You gone round the twist?'

'I said, a ton.' Shades' voice hardened.

'Haven't you read your *Financial Times*? Don't you know recession is rampant in the Western world. We're all having to scrimp and scrape. But you, Shades, you want a hundred notes of sheer exploitation and wanton greed.'

'Fifty?'

Arthur turned to Terry again with his bad ventriloquist act, little aware that Shades could understand every word. 'I told you the kid's a mug.' He turned to Shades with a bright smile. 'Ten – and I'm being generous.'

'Leave it out.'

'What then?'

'Forty.'

'I said ten.'

'Thirty.'

'You're a fool to yourself.'

'Thirty, I said.'

'Twenty-five.'

'A score – and we touch hands.'

Shades thought hard. He did not consult the other kids and they seemed to be listening to him in awe, content that he should hold sway over the bargaining.

'All right.'

'You'll take a cheque?'

Shades looked affronted. 'No way!'

'Just testing,' said Arthur.

Arthur dug into his pocket and brought out twenty crumpled pound notes.

'O.K.?'

'We'll come back if we need more.'

'If you do – I'll see you get your arse kicked.'

'Who by?'

'My man here.'

'Oh, him.'

Shades put his fingers in his mouth and whistled his men out the telephone kiosks. Arthur then took Terry aside, while Petal and Sylvia looked on in amazement at the completion of the negotiations.

'I think he knows who's boss.'

'Yeah – he is.'

'Come on, Tel. Admit I had him.'

'I was deeply impressed,' said Terry ironically. 'Incidentally, we haven't discussed my fee yet, Arthur.'

'What fee?'

'Wages? Salary?'

'Oh,' said Arthur airily. 'You'll get your whack. You don't expect to be a partner, do you?' he asked in terms of amused amazement.

'Why not? I do most of the work.'

'Terry – my dear Terry –'

'Yeah?'

He put a hand on Terry's shoulder. 'See, you don't understand, Terence.'

'Understand what, Arthur?'

'The difference between senior management and the worker on the shop floor.'

'Oh?'

'It's all down to differentials.'

'Eh?'

'Have you heard that expression, Tel?'

'Yes, Arthur. I seem to recall I have.'

'It means – well, the difference between the soldier on the field, and the General on the staff.'

'No need to say which one I am.'

'Command decisions, you see. Do you understand it now? Arthur looked at his watch. 'Oh, I've got to fly.'

'You haven't said anything about money, Arthur.' The old feeling was coming over Terry – the feeling of resigned helplessness. But Arthur was half-way across the street, heading for his Jag. He stopped to point an accusing finger. 'You know what your problem is, Terry?'

'No?'

'It's just like young Shades.'

'What's that, Arthur?'

'Greed – wanton greed.'

'I see.'

'I'll be in touch.'

'Arthur –'

But the telephones in the kiosks began to ring and they set up such a racket that Terry was reminded forcibly of his dream. Arthur smiled and waved from the safety of his Jaguar.

'Nothing wrong with work, you know.' He roared off leaving Terry and Petal heading towards the blasting phones.

'He didn't say anything about me working,' said Sylvia.

'No,' said Terry. 'He didn't.'

Slowly Sylvia began to walk towards one of the kiosks.

'It's a miracle, isn't it?' said Terry to Petal as he opened the door.

'What is a miracle?'

'Arthur's rabbit,' he snapped, slamming the door.

Arthur walked briskly down the corridor towards the door with the name-plate on. He felt good, confident and sure that at last, as he had told Terry, he was senior management. When Arthur opened the door of the office, Ernie was standing there with a welcoming grin whilst the tiny man busied himself as usual behind the desk.

'Hallo, Arthur.'

'Good morning.'

'You've had quite a result, haven't you?'

'How do *you* know?' asked Arthur.

'Look at your pile of correspondence – very handsome. Be lucky, Arthur.'

'It's not a question of luck, Ernie. It's business acumen.'

'Oh yes.'

'Experience.'

'Mm.'

'Tenacity.'

'That's it.'

'And above all – courage.'

Ernie shook him by the hand as he left and a volley of imaginary trumpets sounded in Arthur's ears.

'What a clever feller, eh?' cried the tiny man, giving him a cynical smile. But Arthur did not notice and the trumpets resounded again.

'Don't worry about me, old friend.'

'I'm not.'

'I combine honest endeavour with enterprise.'

'Sure.'

'If the price is right there are always customers.'

'You bet.'

'Never mind about supplementary benefits. Get out and graft is my philosophy.'

The tiny man gave him a huge bundle of envelopes and Arthur whistled with appreciation.

'There you are, you see. It's all trust, you know.'

The tiny man leant over his desk and addressed Arthur in a furtive whisper, 'A guy was asking for you.'

Arthur immediately lost his confidence. In a worried tone he said: 'Who?'

'He wouldn't say his name.'

'But –'

'He looked official like.'

'Like what?'

'He wouldn't say his name.'

'So you said.'

'He looked official like.'

'You said that, too.'

'He had a raincoat.'

'And?

'Well – you can spot 'em, can't you? It's the Terylene, innit?'

'What did he want?' Arthur tried not to betray his anxiety, but failed. As he talked he opened a couple of envelopes and a cheque fell out. Arthur looked surprised.

'He didn't say.'

'You must have – did you pick up anything?'

'Right away I thought – it's gotta be Mr Plod.'

'Oh my Gawd!'

'Or even worse.'

'Like what?'

'The dreaded VAT man.'

Arthur blanched and the tiny man continued with relish, 'They knock on the door in the early hours.'

'Oh yeah?'

146

'You hear terrible things, don't you? About the VAT man.'

'Yeah.'

'Anyway, I thought I'd mark your card.'

Arthur tried to regain his composure. 'I'm most grateful, but everything I'm doing is above board.'

'Of course.'

'All paid up.'

'Why not?'

He stuffed the envelopes into his pockets. 'Must be getting on – probably send one of my staff in next time. Too busy to make these journeys.' Arthur hurried out of the office. 'Cheery-bye.'

'So long.'

Left alone, the tiny man gave vent to a tiny laugh.

'I got him going,' he muttered, well pleased with himself.

'Oi!'

'Yeah?'

Ernie turned to see he was being hailed by an official-looking man in a Terylene raincoat.

'You a friend of Mr Daley?'

'No.'

'You know him?'

'Very slightly.'

'Do you know which is his car?'

'Er –'

'I'm sure you do.' The man smiled threateningly – in an official way.

'Yeah. Course I do.'

'Then –'

'It's over there – the Jag.'

'Thank you. I'm most grateful.'

'It's a pleasure.'

Hurriedly, Ernie departed, knowing he had shopped Arthur.

Arthur stood in the reception area of the office block, scanning the cheques and postal orders that the envelopes had contained. Then he walked out to the street entrance and paused. The man in the Terylene raincoat was prowling round his Jag. Arthur remained frozen in the reception area until the man began to move away. Slowly Arthur stepped into the street, but as he did so, the man suddenly took renewed interest in the car. Frozen again on the pavement, Arthur spied a cruising cab and hailed it.

'Where to, Guv?' asked the cabbie, turning round to see Arthur crouching on the floor. 'You O.K?'

'Just a little warm,' said Arthur desperately.

'Warm?'

'The glass – it reflects the heat.' He doubled up on the floor again, well beneath the window level. 'I'm allergic to light,' he said.

'You planning on getting out?'

'Now?'

'When I drop you?'

Arthur considered the situation. 'If I keep low.'

'Want a blanket or something?'

'No thanks.'

'You're not a celebrity?'

'Well –'

'TV star?'

'Just a successful business man.'

The cabbie again regarded Arthur's crouched position. 'Where to?' he repeated impatiently.

'The Winchester Club.'

The cabbie set up his meter and drove on.

'Right nutter,' he said to himself warily, wondering if Arthur would cause trouble en route.

In the Winchester, Arthur regained confidence on his favourite stool. Dave was the captive audience.

'There I was, more or less surrounded.'

'It was a stake-out, was it?'

'Oh yeah – very carefully planned. Must have been dozens of 'em.'

'But you evaded them?'

'Course.' Arthur gave a modest shrug.

'How did you do it?'

'It was just one of them James Bond things.'

'You wore a frogman's outfit?'

'Eh?'

'He often does.'

Arthur shook his head impatiently.

'None of that – just ordinary raincoats.'

Dave stared at him, puzzled. 'What do you mean, Arthur?'

'What I say – ordinary raincoats.'

'In disguise?'

'I knew right away – one of 'em was a right wally.' Arthur smiled at the recollection. 'You know, Dave, they have to get up early in the day to find Arthur Daley.'

'Arthur –'

'Yeah.'

'Why were they wearing raincoats?'

'They always do.'

'I see.'

'I had 'em sussed.'

But Dave was no longer giving Arthur his undivided attention.

'Hallo, Mr. Sprott. Long time –'

'Hi Dave. How about a bottle of light ale?'

'Coming up.'

Arthur turned, annoyed at his flow being interrupted. Then he almost fell off his stool. Just by his side was standing the man with the Terylene raincoat.

'Now, Arthur,' said Dave, 'I still can't understand this business about the raincoat – Hey Arthur –'

But Arthur was already heading towards the exit. Then Sprott saw him.

'Oi!'

Arthur was still beating a retreat.

'Daley, innit?' But Arthur was gone.

With as much dignity as senior management would allow, Arthur cantered across the street outside the Winchester. But even after his recent jogging experiences, Arthur was unable to elude Sprott who was after him in a few seconds and soon had his hand on his coat collar.

'At your age,' said Sprott, 'you'll do yourself a mischief running like that.'

For a moment Arthur wished he had taken up his recent jogging invitation more readily.

'I beg your pardon?'

'Come on, Daley.'

'Who are you?' blustered Arthur. 'I think you've got the wrong man.'

'I don't think so.'

'You trying to mug me or something?'

Mr Sprott flashed a warrant card and Arthur's indignation quietened.

'Ever seen one of these before?'

'It's not a Fulham season ticket, is it?'

'In the motor.'

'Hang about!'

'I said – *in* the motor, Daley.'

'I don't go with strangers.'

'Why not?'

'Didn't your mum ever tell you that –'

Sprott gave Arthur an evil grin. 'My mum said knee 'em in the privates.'

'Did she? I don't consider that –'

'*Get* in.'

'Well if you're gonna be like that.'

'You going?'

'If I have to.'

'You have to.'

Sprott began to hustle the unwilling Arthur to a saloon car. He opened the front passenger door and unceremoniously dumped Arthur on the seat. He then turned round to the driver's door, shouting as he did so:

'Don't try anything, Daley.'

'I don't understand,' said Arthur.

But directly Sprott climbed behind the wheel it was very clear to Arthur that he was having difficulty in controlling his anger.

'Well?' said Arthur.

'Shut up.' Sprott made no attempt to drive and Arthur

produced his full magisterial tone of outraged injustice.

'I think you should know that I am one of the most respectable businessmen in the borough – indeed throughout the Greater London area and I am not used to –'

'Shut up.'

'I beg your pardon?' But Arthur was beginning to quail.

'You owe me money,' said Sprott in a hoarse whisper.

'Me?'

'You.'

Sprott had a manic expression on his face and suddenly Arthur felt instinctively that he was neither from the Income Tax nor the VAT.

'Could I ask –?'

'Where's T.P.?'

'Is this official business?'

'Answer the question.'

A kind of Dutch courage overtook Arthur. 'I must ask you – is this official business?'

'No.'

'Where we going?'

'You'll find out.'

'To the nick?'

'No.'

'Then –'

'Where is he?' asked Sprott quietly.

'He's ill.'

'You his partner?'

'We have certain common interests.'

'I said – you his partner?'

'In a way.'

'I see.'

'You don't work round here?' asked Arthur, unsuccessfully trying to put the conversation on a less threatening level.

'I don't work anywhere.'

'Retired, are you? Of course, I'm semi–'

'I got kicked out.'

'Redundant?'

Sprott snarled at Arthur. 'T.P. and me were going to work together.'

'Nice,' said Arthur in his most social voice.

151

'I gave him money.'

'Yeah?'

'*My* money. He was going to get an office. I fancied that – a little office with three phones.'

Arthur started.

'Now *you've* got the office.'

'I don't know what you're on about.'

Sprott suddenly grabbed Arthur's jacket.

'You owe me money.'

'How dare you!'

'Don't give me that.'

Arthur was now extremely frightened, despite the fact that they were sitting in Sprott's car in broad daylight. Arthur considered that Sprott had a crazy glint in his eye – and he didn't like it.

'I don't know anything about your arrangements with T.P.'

'It's your office, innit?'

'Well?'

'Come *on.*'

'In a sense.'

'What does that mean?' His grip hardened.

'What I say – in a sense.'

'The office. It's mine.'

'Look –'

'I tell you – I own it.'

'The telephones –' said Arthur feebly.

'All three of 'em.'

'It's an expensive suite.'

'I'll tear it into shreds.'

'Now don't do that –'

'Why the hell not?' Sprott was beginning to look even more manic.

'I'm sure we can come to a reasonable arrangement.' Despite his rising fear, Arthur managed to give Sprott an optimistic smile.

'What do you mean?'

'What I say. I've always been a reasonable –'

'Where is it?'

'The office?'

'Come on –'

'I'll show you,' said Arthur magnanimously. 'All I hope is that the staff are at their posts.' Specially Terry, thought Arthur desperately.

Sprott's anger seemed to increase on the way to the station and Arthur grew even more agitated as Sprott drove erratically and extremely fast. When they were almost there, he snapped out, 'What is it?'

'Eh?'

'Short-term lease?'

'Oh yes. Short lease.'

'What else?'

'What do you mean?'

'Other amenities?' Sprott snarled as he accelerated.

'Oh, it's very handy for transport,' said Arthur evasively.

'What kind of transport?'

'Trains, you know.'

'Yeah?'

'And helpful neighbours.'

The station was looming ahead and Arthur felt a sinking in the pit of his stomach. Sprott wasn't going to like this – and Arthur hoped that Terry would be immediately available. Suppose he was in the pub? Arthur's heartbeat quickened. Sprott wasn't going to like anything.

'Just park by the station,' Arthur said in a squeaky voice.

'Not much of a neighbourhood.'

'Short-lease,' whimpered Arthur, jumping out of his passenger door as Sprott parked. 'Very short-lease.'

Once out of the car, Arthur dashed over to the telephone kiosks. 'Thank Gawd,' he said as he saw Terry inside one of them. Thumping on the door, Arthur yelled, 'Terry!'

But he was talking decisively and concentrating on the phone.

'Terry!'

Still no response and already Sprott was walking purposefully towards the kiosk. His eyes were little hard nuggets of suspicion that was rapidly turning to hatred.

'Terry!'

Again there was no response.

'For Gawd's sake!'

Finally, Terry opened the kiosk door, looking annoyed. 'I'm on the phone.'

'So I see. Look Tel –'

'Listen, Arthur. I'm trying to run a business. Shop floor – you know –'

'I'm being threatened.'

'You're senior management – take some decisions.'

'Terry – I'm being threatened.'

'And I thought it was something new!'

Terry closed the door, leaving Arthur transfixed and Sprott gaining on him. Then Arthur saw Shades and the other kids.

'This is too much,' he said.

'We need some more dough,' said Shades. 'What you gave me weren't enough.'

'Get lost!'

'You want trouble?'

'No.'

Sprott was still gaining, looking around him, with his lips moving soundlessly.

'Where's my dough?' asked Shades.

'All right,' said Arthur. 'I'll talk.'

'We don't want talk – we want money.'

'Just a minute.'

'Now!'

'Can I introduce you to the new landlord?'

'Who?'

'Charming guy.'

Sprott came up unbelievingly to Arthur, his eyes blazing.

'You said this was your office.'

'*You* said it was.'

'On a short lease –'

'Well – you've got certain outgoings, like.'

'Like what?'

'Where's my dough?' asked Shades, and the other kids, knowing that Terry was otherwise engaged, began to crowd in.

Then Petal emerged from one of the kiosks.

'Like Petal,' said Arthur.

'It hasn't been so strenuous today,' she smiled.

'Then there's the stationmaster,' confided Arthur to Sprott. 'He's on the firm.'

'This is bloody ridiculous,' said Sprott.

'Then there's toilets on the platform,' continued Arthur.

But Sprott could take no more. He lunged at Arthur, knocking him backwards into a telephone kiosk.

'You're a con man,' he shouted.

'Not at all,' said Arthur panting for breath. 'You don't know the other outgoing.'

'What's that?'

'Terry.'

'Who's Terry?'

'Well he takes care of all the aggravation – physical or otherwise.'

'Oh yeah?'

'I assure you – he's most useful.' Sprott now had Arthur pinned up against the telephone kiosk.

'We'll see, shall we?'

'Terry!' Arthur howled.

'Where's our dough?' asked Shades again.

'Get lost, kid!' yelled Sprott.

'We're in on your game,' replied Shades, not in the least shaken by Sprott's glazed expression.

'You know, Daley,' said Sprott, getting his twitching face very close to Arthur's, 'you owe me.'

'Please desist,' spluttered Arthur. 'I'm a prominent local businessman.'

'You'll be a prominent local stiff,' snarled Sprott.

'Terry!'

'Yes, Arthur?' Terry kicked open the door of the telephone kiosk. 'Did you call me, sir?'

'I think so,' said Arthur, breathing heavily.

Sprott looked up at Terry and the manic glint in his eyes became subdued. 'Who the hell are you?'

'I'm minding the office,' said Terry.

'What office?'

'It's a nice little business.'

Sprott stared hypnotically at Terry. 'What the hell do you mean?'

The telephones began to ring simultaneously in all three kiosks.

'And it's all yours.'

'Answer those damned phones,' said Sprott.

'Why?' asked Terry. 'They're probably for you.'

Arthur and Terry walked down the hospital corridor, heavily laden with baskets of fruit and rolls of magazines and newspapers.

'You can say what you like,' Arthur muttered. 'It's a good earner.'

'Yes Arthur – I know it. I've worked the shop floor.'

'The voice of experience.'

'Certainly the voice.'

'There are none more gullible than your average punter,' said Arthur philosophically.

'Don't start,' warned Terry. 'The old boy needs a rest.'

'I'm very sensitive to that,' admonished Arthur. 'I've been ill myself. Remember?'

'I remember,' said Terry.

'Anyway, it was a nice little number.'

'Yeah.'

'You like the gee-gees?'

'That's why I'm skint.'

'You've always got on with dumb animals –'

They were now walking down the ward – towards an empty bed.

'My Gawd!'

'He's gone,' said Terry reverently as they stared down at where T.P. had been. 'I wonder if St Peter *does* take credit cards.'

'Eh?'

'Nothing, Arthur.'

'He was a great man, an inspirer of souls.'

'He certainly inspired you.'

'A backroom boy – of course.'

'Of course.'

'But I'm grateful to him.'

'Yeah.'

'What about a wreath, Terry?'

'What about one?'

'You'll have to sub me.'

'*What*?'

'Well – he didn't deliver before he went.'

'P'raps it was sudden, Arthur.'

'He could have set us up for another week.' Arthur sounded very aggrieved. 'He could at least have done that.'

'Arthur, you're a –'

'Hallo, you two scallywags.'

'No,' said Arthur. 'It's a voice from the grave – from beyond.'

They both turned to see T.P. in a wheelchair, pushed by his daughter, Fenella.

'Where's me money, Arthur?' asked T.P. with a wry smile.

Recovering from the immediate shock, Arthur said:

'You look so well.'

'Got to move on.'

'Where to?'

'Switzerland.'

'What happens there?' asked Terry, looking at Fenella, She shrugged and her Father replied, 'Expensive clinics and an awful lot of banks.'

'It's not my idea,' Fenella said.

'You'll get nicked,' Terry replied.

'I'll tell you what,' said Mooney to Arthur.

'Yes my old mate?' Arthur's voice was warm with bonhomie.

'I'll phone you.'

PART FOUR

'God rest his soul.'

Arthur adjusted his black tie, whilst Terry opened the door of the Jag for him.

'You all right, Arthur?'

'I'm in mourning, Terence.'

'What? For Jimmy South?'

'It was a tragic end.'

'To be found upside down in a cement works? Nasty!'

'Don't talk about it now, Terry,' Arthur said in a hushed and reverent voice. 'It's not decent.'

'You hated him.'

'I respected him.'

'He was the biggest villain on the manor.'

'He was misguided,' said Arthur sadly. 'He had strayed from the rocky path we all have to tread.'

'Some go piggy-back,' muttered Terry as they watched the last of the mourners leaving the Wembley Crematorium. A thin drizzle was descending on their subdued clothing, except in a few cases, where umbrellas protected white, smug faces. Arthur sat in the back of the Jaguar and lit a cigar. He shuddered.

'Death worries me, Tel.'

' Not ready to meet your Maker yet, Arthur?'

'I've too much to do to go yet.'

'We none of us know when we'll be called,' intoned Terry.

Arthur shuddered again.

'With my health –' he began.

' 'Allo.'

'What's up?'

'Here comes the second biggest villain on the manor.'

'Oh my Gawd!' Arthur looked uneasy as a large man appeared with a shining bald pate. He wore a black astrakhan coat and carried a parasol – an eccentricity that made him somehow deeply sinister. 'Tommy La Roche!'

'Wonder what he wants with you, Arthur?'

'He can't want anything,' snapped Arthur. 'I didn't have no business with him – so what can I do for his partner?'

'P'raps he's just coming over to thank you for your condolences, Arthur.'

'Yeah, that's it. We sent a nice wreath.'

'It would've been, if it hadn't been a florist's reject.'

'I'm not a rich man,' said Arthur, 'not like Jim. Besides, it's the thought that counts.'

La Roche knocked on the window of the Jag, as a light rain mist began to descend on the crematorium gardens. Arthur wound down the window, smiling artificially.

'Hallo, Arthur.' La Roche's voice was gravelly, expressionless.

'Mr La Roche. Good to see you – but I regret the occasion.'

La Roche said nothing and there was an uneasy silence, broken only by the muffled sound of traffic.

'You did a bit of business with Jimmy recently,' said La Roche eventually.

'Me?'

'Come on, Arthur, spit it out.'

'I didn't do no business with him. But I might have done him a favour.'

'What favour?'

'I rented some storage space to him.'

'Oh yeah?'

'Weeks back.'

La Roche cleared his throat and a smell of damp grass wafted into the car.

'I had it spare,' said Arthur.

'What did he put there?'

'Now, I couldn't answer that,' replied Arthur. 'I always respect confidentiality.'

'Eh?' La Roche came nearer, sticking his head through the window. We got trouble, thought Terry. Maybe not now, but definitely later, unless Arthur plays ball. But he didn't.

'I don't know what he put there.'

'It's your space, Arthur,' said La Roche.

'Look,' said Arthur, 'Jim came to me for a favour – like they all do.'

'I'm sure they do,' said La Roche, his voice a little harder.

'I don't enquire.'

'I see. But it's there now, is it?'

'No.'

162

'What?'

Arthur bowed his head reverently. 'It was the last time I saw Jim. When he came and removed the goods.'

'When was this?'

'Couple of days before his tragic end.' Arthur's voice trembled a little.

'You there when he took 'em?' asked La Roche.

'No, sir.'

'You just let people go in and out of your lock-up without a by-your-leave?'

'In some cases.'

'How do they get in?'

'I let them have a key.'

'Did he return it?'

'He did, God bless him.'

La Roche smiled quickly. Then he said, 'I'll be in touch, Arthur.'

'Always ready to see a pal of Jimmy's,' replied Arthur with a sickly smile.

Slowly, La Roche walked away and soon he was lost in the damp, cotton-wool atmosphere. Once he had gone, Arthur drew up his coat collar and said to Terry, 'Get me out of here.'

'What's up, Arthur? Someone walk over your grave?' asked Terry thoughtfully.

'Don't joke about death,' said Arthur. 'It's no laughing matter.'

'Who's joking?' returned Terry.

'What's up, Arthur?' Terry repeated as he pulled the Jag up in front of Arthur's flat. Arthur had been strangely quiet in the back of the car and his cigar had gone out. He looked damp and subdued.

'Nothing, Tel. Death affects me – I'm a sensitive man.'

'There's more to it than that, Arthur.'

'Eh?'

'Why don't you come clean?'

'I told you, Terry – I have respect for the grim reaper.'

'La Roche has rattled you, hasn't he?'

'Now why should he do that?'

'What have you really done with Jimmy's stuff? I

remember it coming in – but I don't remember it going out.'

'You can't be privy to all my affairs, Terence. I'm a busy man.'

'You're a frightened one.'

'Terence.' Arthur stared at him from the plush interior of the back of the car. He looked crushed and out of sorts. 'You must not try to interpret my feelings.'

'I know you, Arthur.'

'Who do you think you are? An agony aunt?'

Terry shrugged. 'You don't want me to hang around?'

'No thank you.'

'Sure?'

'Yes. I want to be alone.'

'Touch of the Garbo's eh?'

'You don't understand, Terry. A man has died in the prime of life. I wish to cogitate.'

'That sounds nasty.'

Arthur frowned. 'Death has no dominion, Terry.'

'Eh?'

'I'm afraid that's above your head, old son.'

'Arthur –'

'Yeah?'

'Wasn't Jimmy about your age?'

'I beg your pardon!'

'Wasn't Jimmy about your age when he croaked?'

'I didn't realise my age was such public knowledge.'

'I could make a pretty good guess at it – and I knew Jim's.'

Arthur hauled himself out of the back of the Jag and stood on the pavement, a crumpled figure in a hired black suit. 'Good night to you, Terry. I shall now spend some time in quiet thought and meditation.'

He walked slowly into the house while Terry stared after him quizzically. What was up? he wondered. He had never seen Arthur so subdued – or was he just plain scared?

'Where's Arthur?' Dave asked Terry two days later in the Winchester Club.

'That's the question I was gonna ask you.'

'I haven't seen him – which is very, very strange for a man of unabstemious habits.'

'I've spoken to him on the blower.'

'Is he ill?'

'No – he said he was staying at home for a bit.'

'With 'er indoors? What's he done – fallen in love all over again? Are they having a second honeymoon?'

'I don't think that's a safe bet, Dave.'

'Then, what?'

'I think he's had a bit of a run in with La Roche.'

Dave whistled. 'That could be nasty. I didn't think Arthur was mixed up with the likes of him.'

'We went to Jimmy South's funeral.'

'So did all the crooks in London.'

'Thanks.'

'And half the filth.'

'Yeah, well it's not the filth he's afraid of.'

'Afraid?'

'He's running scared, Dave. Seems Jimmy dumped some stuff on him a couple of days before he croaked.'

'You know what it was?'

'No – but I saw a stack of crates in the lock-up.'

'Then?'

'Then they were gone.'

'And La Roche wants 'em?'

'Something like that.'

'You reckon Jimmy took 'em out?'

'I don't know. I've got an awful feeling he didn't.'

'Because he croaked?'

'Yeah.'

'And so Arthur – disposed of 'em? Would he have been fool enough to do that?'

'You know Arthur.'

'And now?'

'He's lying low.'

'So what now?'

'I dunno. But I'm gonna keep an eye on the lock-up.'

'What about La Roche?'

'He might come around for a little look-see.'

Dave poured out two large scotches and gave one to Terry.

'What's this? A celebration?'

'Thought you might need a bit of Dutch courage,' said Dave.

'Blimey.'

The lock-up was a scene of complete devastation. Nearly every crate and package had been overturned and ripped open and the contents strewn around the floor. The filing cabinet had been up-ended and, once again, most of its contents had been either scattered around or torn up – as if someone had finally lost their temper at the end of a fruitless search. Terry stared at the wreckage, making up his mind that he would have to go and invade Arthur's meditation in the flat. But as he was walking out, some sixth sense made him step back inside. He was too late, however, to close the door and the two heavies came in fast.

'What the hell do you want?' asked Terry, looking at the knife one of them carried in his outstretched hand.

'Just a bit of information.'

'What about?'

'Your boss.'

'So –'

'He had a pile of crates in here a few days ago.'

'Did he?'

The man with the knife advanced slightly. He was in his late thirties, heavily built with a rather fussy little beard. His colleague was younger.

'Yeah – he did. Now they're gone.'

'I'll take your word for that.'

'We want to know where they are.'

'They belong to a friend.'

'They would. Well?' He advanced again, holding the knife out threateningly.

Terry looked round him. 'I thought you'd already had a look-see for yourselves.'

'We did.'

'Then you know there ain't no crates.'

'We thought we'd ask you.'

'I can tell you nothing.'

'No?' The man came a few steps nearer Terry.

'You sure?'

'Yeah.'

Terry poised, ready for trouble he knew was coming. Then he heard the sound of distant police sirens. Both of the heavies paused – and the sirens came nearer.

'We'll be in touch,' said the man with the beard and they disappeared abruptly through the door.

I bet you will, thought Terry as he heard the sound of a hastily revving engine. A few seconds later, the sound of the sirens intensified and there was a squeal of tyres outside the lock-up.

'Here we are again,' said Terry philosophically.

'Arthur had a bit of a clean-out?' asked Detective Inspector Chisholm.

'I dunno – I just got 'ere!'

'Oh yes?'

'It's all a bit surprise to me.'

'It would be,' Chisholm looked around him gloomily picking up a cluster of black knickers. 'Fell off the back of a camel?' he asked.

'I wouldn't know,' said Terry firmly.

'Anything missing?'

'Arthur knows the stock.'

'And where is Mr Daley?'

'At home – he's not too well.'

'I am sorry about that. Arthur's got quite a delicate constitution nowadays, hasn't he? What with one thing and another.'

Looking around him cautiously, Arthur left his flat and walked the few yards to his Jag. Once inside it he felt safe, but on the streets he knew he was only too exposed. With a sigh of relief, he inserted the key in the door, climbed in and sat behind the wheel, his eyes closed and his breathing deep.

'Hallo, Arthur.'

'Oh my Gawd!' For a moment Arthur felt as if he was

having the major coronary he had always feared. He couldn't breathe and his whole body was bathed in an instant cold sweat.

'Nice to see you out and about again.'

Arthur made an inarticulate noise that sounded like the bleating of a wounded animal.

'Now we want you to drive us.'

'Where?' Arthur managed in a falsetto.

'To see a man about some crates.'

'I don't know nothing about any crates.'

'No, well p'raps the drive will help your memory.'

Arthur switched on the ignition, ground the gears and the Jag leapt forward uncertainly.

'Don't try anything, Arthur,' said the man in the back patiently.

'I'm not.'

'Just nervous are we?'

'I'm not a well man. I mustn't be subjected to any strain – doctor's orders.'

'Oh dear. Well, I'm sure we'll all make this as little of a strain as possible.'

'Where am I going?'

'Down Wapping way, Arthur, just to have a good look at old Father Thames.'

Ten minutes later, Arthur brought the Jag to a shaky halt outside a boarded up pub. A crude sign stated 'DUKE'S DEMOLITION LTD' and he could hear the rattling of a compressor.

'This is where we get out,' said the man in the back. 'You'll not try a runner, will you, Arthur?'

'Who – me?'

''Cos if you do, I've got a little automatic here, with a silencer – and I'll kneecap you – and that won't be a nice experience, will it?

Slowly, Arthur clambered out of the Jag, shadowed by his stowaway. Once on the pavement, Arthur turned to see a slim young man with a punk hair-do and a broken nose.

'Where we going?' asked Arthur.

'The old Red Lion. Sorry the bar's closed, but I'd be obliged if you'd enter by the saloon door.'

Arthur cautiously entered the building to find daylight streaming in from where the roof had been and most of the partitions already demolished.

'Down there.'

The young man pointed down a flight of rickety stairs that were covered in debris.

'That's not safe,' said Arthur.

'Neither am I, Dad. Now move it.'

Arthur stumbled down the stairs into the darkness below.

'She says he went off in the Jag,' said Chisholm, emerging from Arthur's flat. 'Been hanging round her feet for a couple of days.'

'He's not been well,' said Terry defensively.

'No?'

'Been under a lot of strain recently.'

'Course he has. But I happen to know Arthur's been looking after something for somebody. At least he was for a bit.'

'I'm not with you.'

'A certain somebody who's unfortunately recently deceased.'

'You mean Jimmy South?'

'Clever boy.'

'What would Arthur have of Jimmy South's? He was too big for him.'

'Oh this is only small. But small enough to be interesting.'

'Well,' said Terry, 'Arthur will surface somewhere.'

'He might not do that, my old son.'

'Why not?'

'Arthur's done a naughty to the South mob. They won't like that.'

'Jimmy's dead.'

'Don't be naive, Terry.'

'You mean his mates?'

'So let's drop in at the Winchester. We might find Arthur's taken refuge there.'

'Refuge?'

'Terry – there's something you should know.' Detective Inspector Chisholm smiled sweetly.

'What's that?'

'Arthur's on the run – well and truly on the one foot in front of the other caper.'

'What are you gonna do about it?'

'I want to see where he runs.'

The cellar was almost in complete darkness when Arthur managed, with some assistance, to descend the steps. Once there, he groped his way to a wall and hung on to it, breathing heavily. The place smelt of stale beer and other substances, vaguely animal in origin. For a while, there was almost total silence until the young man said, 'Switch on the light, Arthur.'

'Eh?'

'It's just to your right.'

Obediently, Arthur groped against the wall, feeling the light brush of cobwebs and the patter of a spider as it ran over his hand. He almost screamed aloud.

'What's up?'

'Bloody spiders!'

There was a throaty chuckle from somewhere else in the cellar and Arthur realised that there was another person in there with them. It was not a pleasant thought.

'He's not been here for three days,' said Dave.

'Funny – 'er indoors said he left in the Jag,' replied Terry while Chisholm merely looked frustrated.

'Maybe he had some business to attend to,' said Chisholm. 'He'd have wanted to tank up.'

'How you misjudge the man,' sighed Dave.

Chisholm grunted. 'I've never misjudged Arthur,' he replied.

'There's always a first time,' mumbled Dave.

Arthur eventually found the light switch and the cellar was flooded with a dim, yellowish light. At first there was no sign of anyone else – just heaped-up beer crates, an old pump, a battered horsehair sofa with the horsehair leaking out, and a couple of old and rusting Aladdin stoves. Once again Arthur heard the throaty chuckle.

'Well, Arthur,' said the young man, 'feeling ready to meet an old friend?'

'What's going on?' shrilled Arthur. 'I'm a respectable business man. I can't be lured down to cellars.'

'Why not, Arthur?' asked a familiar voice. 'You're neither respectable nor are you a business man.'

'I'll have you know –' Arthur began indignantly. Then he exclaimed: 'Oh my Gawd!' The colour drained from his cheeks and a muscle in his right cheek began to twitch. 'Oh my Gawd!' he cried again and began to shake.

'There's no need to call on the Deity, Arthur. I'm sure I can answer most of the more immediate questions about your future.'

Jimmy South stepped out from behind a screen, smiling gently at Arthur.

Chisholm and Terry were standing outside the Winchester.

'He's in dead trouble, Terry.'

'With you?'

'No – with the South mob. They'll take him apart.'

'What's he done?'

'The whisper is that Arthur flogged the South crates when he heard Jimmy had snuffed it.'

'Arthur wouldn't do a thing like that.'

'Wouldn't he?'

Terry was silent.

'Look,' said Chisholm, 'find him. Quick.'

'You're dead,' whimpered Arthur.

'Officially.'

'What do you mean?'

'What I say, Arthur. I'm officially dead.'

'I saw you burn. I was at your funeral.'

'You saw a coffin slide out. I wasn't in it.'

'Who was?'

'No-one who need concern you, Arthur.'

'I can't believe it.'

'I'm alive, Arthur – and I want those video recorders.'

'Eh?'

'Come on – where are they?'

'I don't know nothing about 'em.' Arthur made a pathetic attempt at recovery. 'I must say, it's good to see you looking so well, Jim.'

'Shut up, Arthur.'

'You were too young to die.'

'Where are they?'

'I don't know –'

Jimmy South advanced a few paces towards Arthur.

'You remember me delivering them to you, don't you?'

'Yeah.'

'They're not there now.'

'They must have been nicked.'

'By you.'

'Look, Jim, I was looking after them recorders – if they're gone –'

'Which they have.'

'Someone must have broken into my lock-up and nicked 'em. Person, or persons unknown.'

'Not unknown, Arthur.'

'Eh?'

'We know the person – it's you.'

'But –'

'You sold 'em to Danny Foster, didn't you?'

'Look Jim –'

'Didn't you?'

'I certainty didn't,' said Arthur feebly.

'Because Danny Foster says you did.'

'He's lying.'

'No way.'

'I deny –'

'And he gave you five grand, didn't he?'

'I wish to state here and now –'

'So where's the five grand, Arthur?'

Suddenly Arthur collapsed and sat down heavily on a beer crate.

'I spent it,' he said.

'You what?'

'I had some debts –'

'Five grand's worth?'

'Thereabouts.'

'Who to?'

'Micky the Monk. I owed him – took a lot of stuff on sale or return. And he wouldn't take it back.'

'I'm not interested, Arthur. You heard I'd bought it – and flogged the stuff. Now I want the money.'

'I'll get it back for you,' said Arthur desperately.

'From Micky? You won't have a chance.'

'I'll get it some other way.'

'You will an' all – because I've had a few little problems.'

'Like being dead?' said Arthur recklessly.

'I don't like jokers,' said Jimmy, 'they're liable to get cut up.'

Arthur said nothing.

'I needed to be dead, right? Too many of 'em closing in. So – I was off to the Canary Islands with a new I.D.'

'Very pleasant climate.'

'I'm sure it is, Arthur, but I may not get there.'

'Why not, Jim?' said Arthur. 'You're a resourceful man.'

'I know I am, Arthur. But someone let me down over money. Now I need that five grand for travelling expenses. Get it?'

'Yeah.'

'I'll give you forty-eight hours, Arthur.'

'What?'

'Find the dough, Arthur. I can hold out here for forty-eight hours. No longer.'

'But I know where the stuff's gone – you've got to believe me, Jim.'

Jim South looked across at the young man with the beard.

'This conversation's getting repetitive.'

The young man with the beard walked slowly across to Arthur and then with great precision took him by the throat.

'The position is this, Arthur. Jim needs the money in forty-eight hours.'

Arthur made a rattling sound as the young man increased the pressure on his windpipe.

'And *you* have to *find* the money in forty-eight hours.' He increased the pressure. 'If you don't – I'll kill you.'

He suddenly released him and Arthur fell to the floor, gasping for breath.

Jimmy South grinned down at him. 'Happy hunting, Arthur.'

A few hours later, Arthur strode into the Winchester with all the bonhomie of a desperate man.

'Where the hell have you been?' yelled Terry. 'We thought you'd been kidnapped.'

Arthur smiled icily. 'Now what gave you that idea?'

'You went to earth, Arthur,' said Dave.

'Oh yeah?'

'Even Chisholm's been making fond enquiries.'

'I find that very touching.'

'So where have you been, Arthur?' asked Terry. 'I've searched everywhere for you.'

'I find that very touching too, Tel.'

'Shut up, Arthur.'

Arthur put an avuncular arm around Terry's shoulders.

'My dear boy – I've been in conference.'

'You've been hiding out with 'er indoors.'

'That was thinking time.'

'I see. What's up?'

'Something rather special.'

'Oh yeah?'

'A good work!'

'From you?'

Arthur laid a printed handbill on the bar in front of Terry and Dave. I read:

> SAVE THE KILIKO INDIANS
> DON'T LET THEM DIE
> £5,000 WILL SAVE THIS
> PRIMITIVE TRIBE OF THE SOUTH
> AMERICAN RAIN FORESTS.

GRAND SPONSORED BATH-TUB
JOURNEY. SPONSOR TERRY McCANN
AS HE ROWS A BATH-TUB UP AND
DOWN THE LENGTH OF OLD FATHER
THAMES.

SAVE THE KILIKO INDIANS
DON'T LET THEM DIE

Terry looked up from the handbill, his eyes almost popping out of his head.

'No,' he said. 'No!'

'Come on, Tel,' said Arthur admonishingly. 'A big, strong lad like you, and you won't take part in one of the most important conservation projects of our time.'

'That's right, I won't.'

'Shame on you.'

'What's in it for you, Arthur?'

'I beg your pardon?'

'I *said* – what's in it for you?'

'I don't understand. I would have thought it was obvious.'

'You collect five grand – and send it to South America?'

'I told you, it's a good work.'

'You've never done a good work in your life, Arthur,' said Dave blandly.

Arthur looked shocked. 'How can you say a terrible thing like that?' he asked.

'Because it's true,' said Terry.

'I'm very hurt, Terence. As a prominent local businessman I've done my fair bit for charity.'

'When?'

'And now I have my chance to contribute to world aid.'

'Who are these Kiliko Indians?' asked Dave.

'They were drawn to my attention by a prominent anthropologist.'

'Who?' said Terry.

'He advised me of their need.'

'What is their need, Arthur?' asked Dave.

'They're on the way out – dying from a common virus. They need medicine – fast.'

175

'Five grand won't do much,' said Terry.

'It's but a small contribution,' said Arthur. 'Prominent businessmen up and down the country have been asked to raise the money – amounting to millions. I feel a duty incumbent on myself as a man of charity – of benevolence.'

'Then why don't *you* get in the bath-tub?'

'Don't be foolish, Terence. I'm not a fit man – like yourself.'

'I'm not doing it, Arthur.'

'It is your duty. Children are dying, they need the antidote.'

Terry paused. 'Who approached you?'

'Professor Eisemeyer.'

'Who the hell is he?'

'I told you – a distinguished anthropologist.'

'And he's approached other people?'

'He has – prominent businessmen, like myself. Men renowned for their liberal outlook, their compassion and their inventiveness.'

'You've got that all right, Arthur,' said Terry.

'So the least you can do is to get in the bath-tub.'

Terry was silent. Then he said, 'How you gonna raise the dibs?'

'Multi-national companies. Conservation groups.' Arthur airily waved his handbill.

'So where do I go?'

'You'll do it?'

Terry grinned. 'I hope it's for a good cause, Arthur.'

'What better than preventing the suffering of little ones?'

'You're very noble, Arthur,' said Dave. He blew his nose noisily.

Terry said: 'How many weeks have we got?'

'Eh?'

'How many weeks we got to book the sponsors – and for me to train?'

Arthur laughed. 'You don't seem to realise the urgency of the children's needs.'

'So?'

Arthur looked at his watch. 'It's three fifteen.'

'Yeah?'

'You start at five.'

'What?'

'Terry – will you stop being selfish?'

'Arthur – this is bloody ridiculous!'

'Even now a small child is gasping for breath in a jungle.'

'Where?'

'Every minute counts.'

'But the money –'

'Will be pledged in the next few hours.'

'Who by?'

'My own business contacts.'

'They couldn't raise daisies.'

'Leave that to me, Terry. The ceremonial start will be from Wapping Step at five. Be there, Terence, and dress suitably.'

Arthur downed the last of his vodka and strode from the bar, leaving a bewildered Terry to say to Dave:

'Do you think he's finally gone off his block?'

'This is London Sounds on One Nine Six.'

Arthur sat behind the microphone, while the producer introduced him to the disc jockey.

'This is Sammy Styles, Mr Daley. He'll be interviewing you.'

'Pleased to meet you.'

'Hallo, Arthur. Good of you to come on the programme.'

'It's a pleasure.'

'Fascinating cause, isn't it?'

'It certainly is – and an urgent one.'

'Yes – I gather they're dropping like flies. Now pledges will be coming in during the course of the show and I gather we're going over live to Wapping Steps to see your noble paddler off on his journey. Tell me, Arthur, are you really expecting him to circumnavigate the Thames in a day and a night?'

'A night and a day actually, Sammy. Well – you know we hope he'll be sponsored for every mile he completes, so we'll just have to see how well he does. I don't expect miracles – but he will be paddling through the night.'

'O.K., Arthur. Now the light's coming up and I'm going to chat to you on the air. Righteho?'

177

'Righteho,' said Arthur, lighting his cigar.

'This is London Sounds One Nine Six – welcome to the Sammy Styles Show.' He played a burst of music. 'And my first guest is prominent London business man, Arthur Daley, who is organising a bit of Marathon Thames paddling in aid of relief for the Kiliko Indians of South America. Arthur – tell us all about it.'

Arthur cleared his throat. 'Thank you Sammy. It's good to be on the prog. Well – it's all a bit of a dash because the needs of the Kiliko are immediate. My colleague, Terry McCann is going to have a bit of fun paddling up the Thames in a bath-tub.' He laughed heartily, joined by Sammy. 'It's quite a sight,' Arthur commented.

'Is he gonna give himself a scrub as he goes?' asked Sammy jocularly.

'There won't be time for that kind of thing,' replied Arthur, as both Sammy and the producer winced.

'We want sponsorship by the hour – right up until the deadline of tomorrow midnight.'

'And that's a must,' said Sammy, 'or these Indians will not receive sufficient medical aid. And what will happen to them, Arthur?'

With a catch in his voice, Arthur said quietly: 'It's quite simple, Sammy – they'll die.'

'I see – well, we can't let that happen that's for sure. Can I ask you, Arthur, is this only the tip of the iceberg?'

'Yes – I just happen to have got it together quicker than anyone else, for over the next few months, professional business men like myself will be sponsoring other events in aid of these simple people, who stand in such deadly danger from a Western imported virus.'

'It's good to know that there are people around like you, Arthur, who are prepared to put their energy into such an important piece of conservation.'

'I'm for people,' said Arthur, 'I'm just into them.'

'Yes,' said Sammy Styles, 'it's pure humanity at work. And I hope you are all going to support the bath-tub rescue. Because I certainly am. O.K., Arthur, where do they get their sponsorship forms from?'

'From the foyer of your own radio station – and from the departure point at Wapping Steps.'

'And we hope you come in your thousands. Arthur Daley – human being par excellence – the very best of luck to you.'

'Thank you,' said Arthur. 'Thank you, one and all.'

The D.J. played a record and turned to Arthur.

'Bully for you, mate.'

Arthur drew a xeroxed sponsorship form out of his pocket and smiled at Sammy.

'Will you be so good?'

'Certainly.'

He scrawled a figure on the form with a flourish. It was not until Arthur was in the producer's office that he saw Sammy had put himself down for 10p a mile. How mean can you get? thought Arthur as the producer said:

'Right, let's see how the foyer situation goes – and then we'll run you down to Wapping in the radio car.'

'Most kind. But I must slip out for half an hour. Got to get something.'

'Anything we can do?'

'I have got to buy a bath,' said Arthur. ' You could bring it down on the roof of your car.'

The producer smiled a little frostily. 'What a good idea,' he said.

'In training, Tel?' asked Dave.

Terry had spent the afternoon in the Winchester and was now on his third lager. 'I'll keep going on booze,' he confided.

'It's good of you to do it.'

'I must be crazy,' he said.

'You know,' said Dave, 'I never thought Arthur would be capable of doing a thing like this.'

'I don't think he is.' replied Terry.

'The bath's in your foyer,' said Arthur to the producer who sighed miserably. 'That's all right, innit?'

'Fine.'

'Then we can strap it to the roof of your radio car and get it down to Wapping.'

'Absolutely fine. One small thing –'

'Yeah?'

'We've had quite a few people coming in for sponsorship forms while you were out.'

'That can't be bad.'

'No, but I notice on the bottom of the form it says that all money must be handed in by midnight tomorrow. That's tricky – he'll just have finished.'

'It's the urgency of the situation. You must appreciate that.'

'Of course.'

'Children may die.'

'Yes.'

'They *will* die unless medical aid can be rushed into the rain forest.'

'I was only querying the sheer practicality of it all.'

'That's all right. I put a notice in your foyer.'

'Did you?'

'Yeah – and I'd be pleased if you'd broadcast it. There's something important I forgot.'

'What's that, Mr Daley?' said the producer with growing tension in his voice.

'I'll be here in person in your foyer from midnight through till dawn – and beyond if necessary. Picking up the sponsorship money. It will be my own personal vigil.'

'I see. Well that's most noble.' He looked at his watch and said, 'I think we'd better get you and your bath-tub down to Wapping.'

'Most kind,' said Arthur.

'I'm sending a reporter with you, of course.'

'It'll be quite an event.'

'Yes,' said the producer, 'it's become that already.'

At five p.m. a small crowd had gathered on Wapping Steps and the bath-tub, with a plastic paddle in it, was bobbing gently by the wharf. Terry stood beside it, wearing a track suit and a life-jacket. He felt particularly foolish. Arthur scurried about the radio car. With him was an attractive young girl with a tape recorder.

'I haven't had time to introduce you to Terry yet,' said Arthur. 'He's just raring to go. Terry may I introduce you to Miss Tracey Jones. She's going to interview you.'

'I'd like to interview you, Arthur,' said Terry.

The bath-tub looked totally unstable and the paddle a child's toy – which it was.

'Now, now,' said Arthur. He turned to Tracey. 'He's full of fun.'

Tracey pushed the microphone into Terry's face and said brightly: 'Terry McCann – you've volunteered for a tough task. What made you do it?'

'I was thinking of all those little children in the South American rain forest – waiting for medical aid.'

'And now you're going to paddle as hard as you can up the Thames in a bath-tub? Are you looking forward to it?'

'It's all great fun.'

'Yes, I'm sure it is – and every mile that Terry paddles more money will be raised for the Kiliko Indians. Well, we've got quite a crowd down here on Wapping Steps and many of them have already received their sponsor forms. Beside me, local business man, Arthur Daley, is dishing out more forms in addition to his many other duties. Arthur Daley, can I just snatch a few words?'

'With the greatest of pleasure.'

'Now, your contribution to this scheme is five thousand pounds – do you hope that Terry will raise all of this?'

'He'd better –' Arthur hastily corrected himself. 'He's going to have a jolly good try. Terry knows that every mile he paddles brings in more money – for the Kiliko Indians and their desperate plight in the Amazon rain forest.'

'Thank you, Arthur Daley. And now Terry McCann is getting into his bath-tub. It's looking bit shaky and so is he – whoops – he nearly had it over, but Mr Daley and some of the spectators are holding it for him – and yes – yes – he's in control. Yes – he's slowly, very slowly – beginning to paddle downstream. He's called out something to Mr Daley – couldn't hear what it was – but there we have to leave the Kiliko Indians sponsored bath-tub marathon and return you to the studio.'

'Arthur,' shouted Terry across the water.

'Well done,' said Arthur, 'keep it up!'

'You didn't put any food on board.'

'No.'

'Or drink.'

'Keep paddling, Tel.'

'I'll starve – or die of thirst.'

'I'll follow you up in the Jag.'

'Where's our meeting place?'

'I'll track you down. I'll bring a couple of pork pies and a bottle of lager.'

'Thank you, Arthur. I'll always remember your generosity.'

He began to turn in circles again and Arthur shouted at him urgently, 'Get on course.'

'It's not easy, Arthur.'

'Straighten up.'

Terry said something quietly that Arthur did not hear. One of the spectators did, however, and there was a flurry of laughter as she repeated it to her friends. Suddenly a big motor-boat hove into view and began to bear down on Terry in his tub. Arthur watched it for a few moments with mounting excitement.

'BBC, I expect,' he said to Tracey. 'I phoned 'em you know.'

'Don't see any cameras,' she said.

'Or the press. I called 'em all.'

'Aren't they a bit near?'

'Near?'

'Yes, they're causing such a wash, they'll have him over.'

'Oi,' yelled Arthur, 'they're too near.'

'They're still running at him.'

'Change course, you idiots,' shouted Arthur.

The crowd also screamed out, but the big motor cruiser did not alter course at all.

'It's going to hit him,' said Tracey.

A few seconds before the impact, Terry looked up to see a slightly, but not instantly recognisable, face ducking down behind the cock-pit cover of the cruiser. As it rammed him amidships, Terry recognised that slightly familiar face. It was La Roche.

'He's a goner,' said Arthur fatalistically as the cruiser buried both the bath and Terry in a curl of foam.

'He didn't have time to jump,' yelled Tracey as the crowd became hysterical.

'My Terry,' moaned Arthur. 'My poor brave lad.'

The cruiser ploughed on with a considerable turn of speed and began to roar away, leaving a wake behind it that dashed itself against the wharf, soaking the onlookers.

'Get the police,' someone shouted. But Arthur's attention was only on the surface of the water. It bore no sign of either the bath, or Terry.

Desperately fighting for breath, Terry swam under the hull of the cruiser, diving deep again to avoid the deadly thrust of the propeller. For a moment he thought he was finished as he received a glancing blow to the head that almost knocked him unconscious. Then he felt himself rising and he struck out for the surface, feeling at any moment his lungs would burst. After what seemed like an eternity of pain he finally broke through the grey suffocating water and once again saw the London skyline.

He also saw Arthur, standing on the wharf, his head bowed.

Choking and spitting out water, Terry shouted:

'All right, Arthur, no need for another funeral!'

'Well – that was short-lived,' said Tracey as she helped haul the sodden and bleeding Terry onto the wharf-side.

Arthur shrugged. 'I've had it.'

'What do you mean?'

'You can always organise it for another time,' said Tracey.

'Eh?' said Terry, still bringing up water.

'The ambulance will be here soon,' she said in a jolly voice.

'What's that you –' he spluttered, looking up at Arthur.

'It'll be too late,' said Arthur. 'Too late for the rescue.' He looked as if his last hour had come. 'It's my funeral,' he said to Terry.

*

183

'How are you feeling?' asked Dave as Terry drank a large brandy.

'Fine.'

'They kept you in overnight?'

'Only to put a few stitches in the cranium.'

'No brain damage?'

'Nothing to damage. There can't be after the things I do for Arthur.'

'Chisholm's been here.'

'Oh yeah?'

'He's gone to fetch Arthur.'

'Where is he?'

'Hiding behind her vacuum cleaner, no doubt.'

'I wonder why –'

'What's that?'

'Never mind.' Terry turned to the door. 'Talk of the devil!'

Chisholm came in with a beaming Arthur.

'How are you Tel?' Arthur asked, putting his arm round his shoulders.

'Apart from nearly drowning and nearly getting a fractured skull – great! Why are you looking so cheerful?'

'It's always good news,' said Arthur, 'when villains are brought to justice.'

Chisholm smiled. 'Had a bit of a coup,' he said.

'What's that?' asked Dave.

'I'm about to tell you something in confidence,' said Chisholm. 'And I'll come down like a ton of bricks on anyone who takes all this further than this room.'

'I'm the soul of discretion,' said Dave.

'Likewise,' put in Terry.

'Mm – well Arthur knows.'

'And I'm a trustworthy client,' said Arthur smugly. Terry and Dave raised their eyebrows.

'When thieves fall out,' said Chisholm, 'fun begins for us coppers.'

'Give us more,' asked Terry.

'Well – the late lamented Jimmy South ain't dead after all.'

'What?' said Terry, staggered. 'I saw him cremated!'

'Appears he faked the death to get out of the country fast. Matters were pressing.'

'Who was in the coffin?' asked Dave.

'Some minor villain they wanted to top. Anyway, Jim was holed up by one of his associates in the East End while they got some money together to send him out.'

'What then?' asked Dave.

'We got a call last night saying where he was – someone grassed him so we went and picked him up. Simple as that.'

'Who grassed him?'

'Haven't the faintest. But the whisper says Jim fell out with one of his partners. So they didn't want him to leave the Mother Country any more. Thought I'd tell Arthur – as he was having a bit of trouble with 'im.' Chisholm looked round him as Dave said:

'Can I offer you a half, Mr Chisholm?'

'You can, David. I think this calls for a small celebration.'

Terry looked across to Arthur's cheerful countenance.

'You celebrating too, Arthur?'

Arthur smiled sadly. 'I'm a charitable man,' he said, 'no-one's gonna be celebrating in the rain forest, are they?'

'But a villain has been brought to justice, Arthur,' said Chisholm. 'I'm sure you'll drink to that.'

'I'll always drink to that, Mr Chisholm,' replied Arthur blandly.

Minder – Back Again

PART ONE

Terry had jogged four miles when he heard the shout. He paused, panting, trying to make out who the hell it was. Terry didn't feel like company – he just felt like collapsing on his bed with a nice cup of tea.

'I've been trying to get hold of you for days.'

'Well – if it isn't Justin James,' said Terry sourly. He was confronted by a good looking brash young man, exuding considerable nervous energy and standing outside a greengrocer's shop as if he owned it.

'Where is he?'

'Who?'

'The great man. Signor Corleone. *Numero Uno*. Daley.'

'Oh, 'im.'

'He's giving me a blank.'

'So what's new?'

A housewife was inspecting the fruit and vegetables just behind Justin.

'Sprouts are beautiful,' he said. 'Fresh today – straight off the boat.' Justin returned his gaze to Terry. 'Where is he then? He's never at home, the lock-up's engaged all the time. I belled him at the Winchester, but he weren't there neither.'

'He must have gone invisible,' said Terry, wondering how he was going to get away from Justin. But Justin was persistent.

'You look knackered.'

'Thanks.'

'Jogging?'

'No – I'm body popping.'

'Funny man.'

'What do you want to see Arthur for?'

'I want to see him because we're all gonna be rich.' He picked up a nectarine and gave it to Terry. 'These are lovely.' Then his voice became confidential. 'Tickets. *Capisce*? This is the big one, Tel.'

'Is it?' Terry bit thirstily into the nectarine.

'I've been working on it for weeks. Arthur would be very impressed.'

'He's only impressed by one thing.'

3

'Yeah – that's what I'm on about. Money in the bank. But it's too big for me, see. He's got muscle.'

'Arthur!'

'Well – he's got you.'

'He's not a gangster, you know,' said Terry, enjoying the nectarine. 'He's a name – he's a face.'

Suddenly the greengrocer appeared behind Justin. 'That'll be twenty-five pence.'

'What?'

'Twenty-five pence,' he repeated firmly.

'Look here,' said Terry indignantly. 'I thought you worked in this joint.' But Julian was otherwise occupied with the greengrocer. Grudgingly he handed him the twenty-five pence and then turned back to the woman who was just about to enter the shop.

'Don't go in there, love,' said Justin. 'They're robbers.'

The greengrocer took immediate exception to that comment. 'Shove off or I'll chin you.'

Justin took a step back. 'Don't start on me, mate. If you're looking for trouble, I've got the right man here.'

Terry grabbed Justin's arm. 'Behave yourself.' He smiled warily at the greengrocer. 'Sorry pal – he hasn't had his breakfast yet.'

None too gently, Terry steered Justin away from the shop. 'You've got more front than the Albert Hall,' he told him.

Justin treated Terry to a lovely, wide smile. 'I get by though, don't I?'

Strolling towards Terry's flat, Justin expanded on his scheme. 'We can take over – we can break the monopoly. Of course, I'm not just talking about football – it could be anything – Wimbledon, Covent Garden Ballet, Chelsea Flower Show, boxing – the sky's the limit.'

'And what do you think Little Phil, King of the Touts, will do? Abdicate?'

'He's had a good run. The king is dead – long live the king. I'm gonna get my act together when I'm away.'

'Where're you going?'

4

'Inside.'

'That's nice.'

'I'm on bail – didn't you know? Crown Court next week. Me brief reckons six months. No problem.'

'That's good to hear.'

'It's an open nick. Be a doddle. That's why I want to settle up the tickets thing.'

'So you can get another stretch when you come out?'

'That's what I'm trying to tell you – it's legal. They advertise in *The Times*, don't they? Wait till Arthur hears about this – he'll be over the moon.'

'He usually is,' said Terry dourly as he passed a man with a briefcase coming out of his block of flats. Then the man stopped and said:

'Mr McCann?'

'Maybe.'

'You're a difficult man to get hold of.'

'What name did you say?' Justin asked with mock innocence.

'McCann.'

'Nobody of that name lives round here.'

But Terry intervened quickly. 'Leave it out, Justin. I am over twenty-one. What's your problem, pal?'

The man gave Terry an envelope. 'We have written to you several times, sir – but what with the post these days. . . So the office decided a letter by hand would be better.'

'I'm honoured.'

'It's all self-explanatory. Good morning.'

He hurried away, leaving Terry curiously opening the letter. Justin read it over his shoulder. 'Don't stand for that,' he said.

'No?'

'I mean – the income tax people can't *do* that. Give 'em a blank – you're not –'

'Justin?'

'Yeah?'

'What's the Italian for "shut up"?'

'I'm only trying to help.' He sounded aggrieved.

5

'Yeah – I understand that,' said Terry. 'But you give me a headache. *Comprendo*? *Ciao*, Justin.'

Terry walked stiffly towards his front door but Justin dashed after him. 'What about Daley?'

'Send me a letter – by hand.'

'Come on, Tel. I've gotta see him. You promised.'

Terry put the key in the lock, but Justin persisted, 'You'll be seeing him later. What about lunch? All down to me.'

'Don't give me lunch, mate. You had a hard time paying twenty-five pence for a nectarine.'

'I got dough.'

'Yeah?'

'Yeah – course I have. Me and Daley – you gotta understand, Tel – we're made for each other.'

'You are?'

'The young tiger and the old fox. And we're *all* gonna earn out of it.' He drew Terry in, anxious that he shouldn't think he was being left out. 'I'll book a table at Mario's. I mean – Arthur eats, doesn't he? Tel, doesn't he? Tel –'

Terry propped himself up on the doorpost, more exhausted by Justin than his jog. 'OK.'

'You'll fix it?' Justin looked at him with wide-eyed enthusiasm and Terry felt even more drained.

'I'll phone you.'

'If I don't hear from you – it's on.'

'You'll be at your penthouse?'

'Actually, I'm back at me mum's.'

Terry opened his door. 'That's great.'

'And Tel –' Justin began to run off down the street.

'Yeah?'

'It's the best thing you've ever done. *Ciao*.'

Joc Eldon wasn't pleased.

'Move it, super-star,' he told Steve Benson who was doing as little training as possible and was determined to do less. As trainer, there was not much love lost between him and Benson, largely because Benson was in his early thirties, had five England caps – and no chance of getting another. A dozen other players of the Third Division squad were training on the pitch, but none of them matched Benson's idleness. Even now he was skiving.

'It's the ankle.'

'You can walk to the bar,' said Eldon unsympathetically.

'Only if you're buying 'em, darling,' replied Benson condescendingly. Then he saw Justin hurrying over from the grandstand and, ignoring Eldon, Benson slouched over to meet him.

'Oi – this is supposed to be a training session.'

'Who told you that? I'll be back in a sec.'

'Who's this?' asked Eldon as Justin came into range. 'An agent for Real Madrid?'

Benson turned, treating Eldon to a cynical grin. 'No – he's my counsellor from Alcoholics Anonymous.'

'I'll give you three minutes.'

'Thanks, boss.'

Justin seemed surprised by Eldon's attitude and said so:

'You don't have to take that, do you?'

'I do.'

'But why?'

'Because I can't get into the First Team, that's why.'

'They can't even lace your boots.'

'Sure. Anyway – what's the score on your man?'

'Daley? We've got a meet.'

'You sure he's OK?' asked Benson, doubtfully.

'He's very big,' said Justin, reassuringly.

'I've never heard of him.'

'Maybe not. But he's a very well known man.'

'OK,' said Benson, his enthusiasm regained. 'I've got two thousand tickets for the England–Scotland match. Cash on the nail – face value – and you sell them for whatever you can get on the open market. And by the way –'

'Yeah?'

'You fix your own price.'

'Double, treble, even more, eh? Them Jocks – they'll rob banks to get football tickets.'

'That's why it's big,' said Benson. 'I could be a marked man for this. See – I've had a nice business with Little Phil. What I do is collect tickets from players in London – I mean, they always have tickets for the big games. But what do I get? Peanuts.'

'Little Phil takes you for granted.'

'You're right there.' Benson grinned. 'Why should I make him any richer? If I had the dough I'd buy the tickets meself. But I haven't. And you, my son, are potless.'

'Slightly embarrassed.'

'Skint.'

'Happens to us all.'

'Yeah. Anyway – I'm relying on you. I don't know any villains – you do.'

'I know 'em all,' said Justin proudly.

'Get me the best,' snapped Benson.

'Oi,' yelled Eldon. 'You still chewing the rag?'

The Jag nosed through the traffic whilst Terry took the brunt of one of Arthur's black moods.

'Terence – I don't *like* young people. So I certainly don't want to meet one of them.' Arthur drew on his cigar, cursing the traffic.

'He ain't "young people". He's a person – and he ain't a representative of the whole flaming generation, Arthur.'

'You seen 'em?'

They glanced through the window. 'There's one – and another. Both sexes, ain't they?'

'Don't come the jokester with me, Terence. They know it all, don't they? Slovenly, rude, opinionated.'

'This one reckons he's got Steve Benson in his pocket,' interrupted Terry.

'Old Benno?'

'Yeah – fair player.'

'Fair?' said Arthur wonderingly. 'He's brilliant. Even when he's had a few the night before, he can still pop the goals in.'

'That's right,' said Terry soothingly.

'And this – Justin. He's a pal of Benno's, is he?'

8

'You bet.'

'He's buying lunch?'

'He says so.'

'You sure he'll pay? I mean – I don't want to be put in an embarrassing situation. I'm a respectable businessman.'

'Yes, Arthur.'

'So – on your head be it, Terence.'

'Thanks, Arthur.'

He parked the car outside the restaurant and leant back for a moment in the driver's seat. 'You know something?'

'What?'

'You're taking the initiative, Terry. I'm not sure I like that.'

'We're talking about money, Arthur. Lots of it.'

'You take the initiative more often, then.' Arthur lit his cigar again and opened the door. 'I need money,' he said.

The interior of the Italian restaurant was smart, cool and inviting. As Arthur and Terry came in they saw Justin immediately, for he cut a distinctive appearance. He was wearing a light-weight suit, a good shirt and tie and there was a floppy handkerchief in his breast pocket. Justin, radiating confidence rose to his feet as Arthur trailed over to him, looking enigmatic.

'The great man. Don Daley, Numero Uno.' Justin took Arthur's hand and kissed it.

'Blimey.'

He hurried on, before Arthur could say anything else. 'You know what this is?'

'My –'

'This is one of the greatest days of my life.'

Terry winced in the background.

'No kidding. Sit. Sit.' He sounded a little as if he was talking to a dog. 'A glass of Soave, eh? How did I know you'd like Soave?'

Arthur shook his head bemusedly.

'I just knew.' Justin poured the wine and Terry grinned. He had never seen Arthur at such a loss for words.

9

'This is Justin – Arthur.'

'Pleased to meet you,' said Arthur weakly.

'He's sizing me up,' said Justin to Terry.

'Eh?'

'The old fox.' He squeezed Arthur's arm. 'I still can't believe it – me sitting with you, Arthur. Now – you don't mind me calling you Arthur, do you?'

'That's fine – Justin,' said Arthur in a voice of deep strain.

'I'll tell you what.' He continued to squeeze his arm.

'Yes?'

'In my book, you're a hero. I mean – you're up there with the stars. Bogie, Edward G, George Raft. Did you know him?'

'Who?' asked Arthur vacantly, but Terry could see that he was warming to the praise.

'George Raft – when he came to London.'

Arthur smiled modestly. He was beginning to enjoy himself. 'We had a few words.'

'I bet. I said to Terry – Terry, you're privileged to work with Arthur Daley.'

'When was that?' asked Terry cynically.

'Told you dozens of times,' continued Justin, quite unabashed.

'Now, Arthur –'

'Yes, Justin.'

'You can help me.'

'I can?' For a moment Arthur looked a little suspicious. Then he succumbed to Justin's charm as the talk swept over him.

'You've got it all – knowledge, experience, wisdom.'

'Well –'

'I'm just climbing the ladder, a mere apprentice. It's like Leonardo da Vinci – he had the idea, grand design and then he had all those wallies, apprentices, I mean, putting in a nose or a tree or a bit of sky. They were learning, weren't they? Learning from the master. And that's why I'm grateful to break bread with you, Arthur.'

'Talking about bread,' said Terry, breaking into the sycophantic chat. 'Any chance of seeing the menu?' But he could see that Arthur was purring.

'Sorry, Tel,' said Justin. 'I was getting carried away.' He waved at the Head Waiter. 'Mario.'

Terry looked at Arthur. He seemed swathed in a reverie. Then he caught Terry's eye and sighed. 'You don't understand ambition, Terence. This young man is right.'

'Oh, yeah?'

'The kind of advice that I can give him is rather special. You don't get it in college.'

Mario appeared and much to Terry's relief, he was brandishing menus. '*Signorini.*'

'Mario,' said Justin, 'I want you to meet Mister Daley. Mister Arthur Daley. He is a man of respect – is that the expression?'

'It is the expression.' He bowed low to Arthur. 'I am delighted to meet you. Many people talk about you.'

Arthur straightened his tie and beamed. 'Do they?'

'Arthur Daley,' continued Mario, 'I would rather have you in my restaurant than Egon Ronay. Please – enjoy yourself.'

He's a pro if nothing else, thought Terry as Mario left the menus and hurried on to greet another customer in different, but somehow similar effusive tones.

'What a nice man,' said Arthur.

'Mario's great.' Justin's enthusiasm was making Terry tired again.

'Just as well.' Terry wanted to put the boot in – anything to break up the sickly enclave. 'His partner was after you a year ago. Remember?'

Arthur looked at him glazedly.

'You sold a Merc to him.'

'Who?'

'What's his name? Angelo? The one who sent a solicitor's letter to you.'

Arthur sighed and then smiled at Terry patronisingly. 'As usual, you've got it all wrong. Thaz man had a little caff in the Harrow Road. How did *I* know it was stolen?' Arthur looked injured. 'Even the judge said I was a pawn in the game.'

11

'Yeah,' replied Terry. 'Pity the jury decided you was a lobster.'

'I still got away with a three hundred pound fine, didn't I?'

Arthur looked guardedly at Justin, wishing he had not admitted to that.

Justin squeezed his wrist again, this time very excitedly and Arthur drew back in pain. 'That's what I was saying to you, Arthur.'

'What?'

'How you can help me. After all, you know all the dodges.'

'I'm not sure that –'

'In fact you're an utter, thorough, unmitigated *rogue*.'

'I beg your pardon?'

'That's why I admire you.'

Arthur smiled sweetly at the dubious compliment.

'You've got him in one,' said Terry.

A pained smile crossed Arthur's face as he looked down the menu. 'I think I'll have the spaghetti bolognaise,' he said reflectively. 'Now,' he began in a business-like tone, turning to Justin. 'I gather you have an offer that I may have to reject.'

Meanwhile, down at the football ground, Little Phil sat beside the driver of his Cadillac. They drove into the car-park and he got out, standing grandly by his car in an enormous astrakhan coat that seemed to swamp his tiny body.

'Hey!' Little Phil spotted Benson walking towards his Sierra. He looked up unwillingly and then slowly began to walk towards him. Little Phil treated him to a cold smile.

'Suddenly I don't hear from you?'

'I've been busy.'

'Busy? You don't even play.'

'Now look –'

'I don't even see your name in the papers anymore. We had a meet last week and you didn't show. What's up? I've been generous to you, Benno.'

'You kidding? I get buttons.'

12

Little Phil poked a stubby finger into Benson's chest. 'Most people don't want to know about you.'

'I see.'

'But I'm a sentimentalist. I remember you when you was a fine player.'

'How would you know?' said Benson with a sneer.

'Don't get clever with me, pal.' Little Phil was gradually losing his temper. 'We need to have a serious discussion.'

'What about?'

'The tartan army – what else?'

'I'm having negotiations with other people,' snapped Benson.

'You what?'

'You heard.'

'There *are* no other people. If people want briefs for Wimbledon they come to me. Don't give me all that stuff about other people.'

'They're well connected,' said Benson uneasily.

'With who?'

'Top men. Kings of the underworld.' He was defensive now.

'You mean they gotta sauna club in Upper Norwood?'

'They got muscle.'

'See Cedric over there?' said Phil menacingly, pointing out his burly driver. 'You want to know about muscle? And there's a hundred more where he came from. You tell your friends that.'

Justin poured more wine.

'You see – old Benno's got this friend who works in the office at Wembley Stadium. Now this friend –' He paused to see Arthur hanging on his every word and even Terry was beginning to look interested. 'He can get two thousand tickets for the England–Scotland game.'

'Nicked, you mean,' said Arthur knowingly.

'No.'

Arthur looked at him in surprise.

'He's got to settle the books. You know people have to apply by post to get the tickets, right? What's more, you have to live

13

in England to stop all the Scotties from flooding the sacred turf. I mean – the Jocks are going to appeal to the Race Relations Board. Well, what he does is this – he ignores some of the letters. That's the beauty of it, see, he ignores 'em. Then he keeps two thousand tickets to his self. It's legal – they don't care as long as they get the dough. And I said to Benno – there's only one man who can handle this – Arthur Daley. He's got the contacts, the muscle, the organisation. And sod Little Phil.'

'Er – how much?' asked Arthur tentatively.

Justin smiled at Terry. 'No messing about with the Guv'nor, eh?' He turned back to Arthur respectfully. 'Sixteen grand for two thousand, eight pound seats, plus a drink for him, say two grand. We're talking, Arthur, about eighteen grand.'

Arthur stared at him with spaghetti dribbling down his chin. 'How much?'

'Eighteen –'

'Yeah,' said Arthur sadly. 'I heard it.'

Terry gave a wry grin. 'I'd like to hear that again,' he said, happily conscious of Arthur scowling at him.

'You'd treble that in a week,' said Justin. 'Even more.'

Arthur spoke slowly and carefully. 'Let's get this straight – you want me to lend you eighteen grand.'

'Not lend – it's an investment.'

'Is it now?' Arthur looked devastated.

'We'll split the profit – obviously you'll get the lion's share.'

'Thank you.'

'I thought you'd grab the idea.' Justin's enthusiasm was undiminished by the parchment grey hue of Arthur's face. 'It's like printing money, innit?'

'Ah,' said Arthur leaning back in his chair, 'the impetuosity of youth.' He turned to Terry, gave a sad smile and then addressed himself to Justin again. 'You want to know about wisdom, Justin?'

'From your lips.'

'Then let me give you this advice – first sus it out. If someone offers you a bargain – there *has* to be a catch in it.'

'Not in this one. Honest,' reassured Justin.

'That's the catch.'

'Eh?' For the first time Justin was thrown.

'When I hear the word honest,' said Arthur, 'I reach for my solicitor.'

'You've got to trust me.'

'Why?'

Justin considered for a second. 'You're right – who needs trust? I'm being very naive.'

'You are, my man, you are.' Arthur was censorious and patronising all at the same time.

Justin treated him to an eager smile. 'I'm learning. Now I've got two thousand tickets for a football game.' He paused. 'Got any contacts in Scotland?'

'Naturally,' said Arthur grandly.

'I mean – big contacts.'

Arthur turned to Terry and said commandingly, 'Tell him.'

'What?' Terry gazed at Arthur uncomprehendingly.

'Tell him about Big Hamish.'

'Oh him.'

'Well –' encouraged Arthur.

'Yeah,' Terry hesitated. 'He's big – 'bout five foot ten. He's violent. He's –'

'Never mind,' said Arthur hurriedly returning his attention to Justin. 'He's a personal friend of mine, is Hamish – the top man, chairman of the board. Know what I mean?'

'Phone him.'

'Eh?' Arthur looked as if the pace was getting too much for him.

'Phone him. Mario.' Justin beckoned back to the head waiter. 'Show the gentleman where the phone is.'

'At once, *Signori*.'

'He's learning,' said Arthur to Terry as he rose majestically to his feet. 'Learning fast.'

Little Phil was sitting in the big back seat of the Cadillac, in a pensive mood, while Cedric drove him through the traffic.

15

'You try to help,' he said. 'You really try.'

'You always help people, Phil,' said Cedric supportively. 'You don't get credit for your charity work either.'

'True. People don't know about that, do they?'

'That's because you're an anonymous benefactor, Phil.'

'I don't get any recognition for it, do I?'

'You should get an OBE.'

'It's orphans and widows,' muttered Little Phil, 'and bloody dishonest footballers. Who's Benno's pal, then?'

'Oh, 'im.'

'Who's 'im?'

'Justin something. Right ice-cream.'

'He is, is he?'

'Flash git – no form.'

'Never mind,' said Little Phil and was silent for a while. Eventually Cedric asked him:

'Something you'd like to tell me, boss?'

'Something I'd like you to do.'

'Say the word –'

'Why don't you give this flash Justin a pull?'

Arthur returned from the telephone, gracefully thanking Mario as he passed him.

'My pleasure, Signor Daley.'

'Incidentally – I've always had a passion for Italian merchandise.'

'Yes, *Signor*?'

'There's an item in one of my warehouses.'

Mario immediately looked cagey.

'An espresso machine.'

'They are very good –'

'Almost brand new, this one,' confided Arthur. 'The same model they use in the snack-bar in the Vatican.'

Mario looked at him, suddenly dazed. 'The Vatican?'

Arthur gave him a virtuous smile. 'So they say. Mark you, I'm not suggesting that it's been sanctified.'

'I'm pleased to hear that.'

'But, if you're interested –' Arthur began to walk back to the table.

Mario put a restraining hand on his arm and whispered, 'Signor Daley –'

'Yes?'

'How much?'

'Well, now.' Arthur passed him a visiting card. 'Someone's always there. Do drop in.'

Justin anxiously gazed at Arthur as he arrived back at the table. 'What gives, Arthur?'

Nonchalantly, Arthur sat down and picked up his glass. 'Nice drop of wine, that.'

'Hamish?' asked Justin, anxiously pouring out more.

'Oh yeah – Hamish,' said Arthur ruminatively. 'He was having his mince and toddies, wasn't he?'

'Was he?' asked Terry innocently.

'And when he's done his rhubarb and custard you know what he'll do?'

'What's that?' Justin was hanging on Arthur's every word.

'He'll jump on an inter-city.'

Later that evening, Arthur, Terry and Justin were waiting at Euston Station for the Glasgow Express to arrive at platform twelve. Arthur was saying to Justin: 'You'll like Hamish – bit of a rough diamond, but his heart's in the right place. And he doesn't have too much rabbit – yes Justin?'

'You're the Guv'nor,' said Justin. 'Like a teacher to me.'

'You booked him a hotel?' Terry's voice had a sudden suspicious note to it.

'Not really,' said Arthur innocently.

'So?'

'I thought he could kip at your drum.'

Terry remained silent, watching the train draw in.

'OK?' asked Arthur hopefully.

'No.'

'Terence – he's a colleague.'

'He growls.'

'What?'

'I said, he growls.' Terry was scanning the arriving passengers now. 'Then he attacks. I had three fights when he came here last yea~'

'Just high spirits,' said Arthur dismissively.

'Yeah – Teachers, Bells, Chivas Regal and any other spirits he can get hold of.'

'I've never heard him growl,' said Arthur.

'You don't listen, do you?'

'This him?' asked Justin, nudging Arthur.

'No.'

'He looks like a growler – big bloke.'

'That's not him. Where the hell is he?' Arthur was beginning to look worried. Then a large gentleman, smartly dressed with an overnight bag, glasses and a nasty scar down his cheek, walked over to Arthur and said:

'Mister Daley?'

'Eh?' Arthur took a step back, temporarily thrown and instinctively exhibiting his timid nature.

'My name's Alisdair.'

'Oh yeah?'

'He's not coming.'

'What?'

Alisdair looked round furtively. 'I must ask you not to shout.'

'Who are you?' Arthur hissed.

'I've just told you.'

'Where is he?'

'I've just told you.' He looked helplessly at Terry and Justin. 'Is he a cretin or something?'

Terry was just about to reply, when Arthur said: 'What are you doing here?'

'I'm Hamish's proxy.'

'Who?'

'His stand-in. Hamish is in hospital.'

'What's he picked up?'

'Two broken legs, broken wrist, dislocated shoulder, multiple cuts and abrasions.'

'Street accident?'

'Aye,' said Alisdair quickly, 'It was in the street.' He nodded at Terry and Justin. 'This the gang?'

Grudgingly, still thinking about Hamish's mysterious street accident, Arthur introduced them. Alisdair turned back to Arthur. 'Hamish said that you were a good man to do business with.'

Arthur bridled, while Justin said, 'Numero Uno.'

'You what?' asked Alisdair suspiciously.

'You're talking to the top man. Arthur's met them all – George Raft, Murder Incorporated. He's nation-wide, coast to coast. You ain't talking to some little Gorbals tearaway, you know.'

Alisdair gave Justin a strong stare. 'Who is he?'

'He's with me,' said Terry.

Alisdair treated them to a frosty smile. 'Just before Hamish lapsed into unconsciousness –'

'Poor chap,' said Arthur respectfully.

'– he muttered something about tickets. He didn't say anything about a hotel room.'

Arthur gave Terry a pointed glare. 'Hamish usually made his own arrangements.'

'Fine,' said Alisdair, 'so have I.'

'Oh yes?'

'I've booked at the Hilton.' He began to walk towards the exit. 'I expect you know the way, Mr Daley.' Arthur followed him as if mesmerised.

'I'll tell you one thing, Arthur,' said Terry.

'What's that?' asked Arthur, feebly.

'He don't growl, does he?'

Terry sat in the front passenger seat of Arthur's Jag, while Justin stretched out in the rear. They were parked outside the Hilton.

'Ain't we on the firm?' asked Justin a little plaintively.

'No.'

'Why not, Terry?'

'It's high finance time now, innit?'

'Yeah – but is he going to stitch us up?' Justin sounded restless, insecure.

'Who's us?'

'Me and Benno. I mean – is the great man honest?'

'No.'

Justin suddenly sat up. 'Now you tell me.'

'Work it out for yourself.'

'I'm learning, Terry.'

'Well – let the Deputy Head take over. Are you paying attention, Justin?'

'I'm all ears.'

'Arthur's been around for a long time and he knows the worth of a pound. Know what I mean?'

'No.'

'Anyway – what's your problem? Yesterday you had nothing and tomorrow you *may* have a few bob. That's fair enough, innit?'

Justin spoke reluctantly. 'I s'pose so.'

'Don't worry about Arthur,' Terry said matily. 'It's the other guy you should be worrying about.'

Inside Alisdair's luxury hotel room, all was quiet, all was calm as the high level negotiations took place. Alisdair, with his suit jacket draped over a chair, was tucking into room service, whilst Arthur, too mean to add to the bill, watched him reflectively.

'That's a bit steep, Arthur, isn't it?'

'Is it, Alisdair?' Arthur's voice was warm, friendly.

'Thirty-five grand?' He did a quick calculation. 'That's about seventeen pounds fifty pence per ticket.'

'That's about right,' said Arthur cheerfully.

'It's steep. My people won't like that.'

'You still have a handy profit. Some of the Jocks would commit murder for a ticket. Present company excepted, of course,' added Arthur hastily.

'Aye,' said Alisdair after a meaningful pause. 'I reckon they would.'

Arthur, still anxious to appease a social gaff, said: 'A figure of speech.'

'No.'

'Eh?'

'You got it right first time.'

'They love their football,' said Arthur enthusiastically.

'Now wait a minute. Just for a second – let's forget the tickets. I just want you to think about the logistics, Arthur. Yes?' Alisdair flung his napkin down on the table and began to pace around. 'Shall we say – ten – no, twenty thousand punters are converging on Wembley from Scotland.'

'Why not?' said Arthur, trying to get comfortable.

'Now, let's assume each punter has got one hundred pounds in his pocket – and that would be a liberal assessment.'

'Quite.' Arthur cleared his throat.

'I see an army on the move.' Alisdair's eyes were very bright as he continued to pace up and down. 'One hundred pounds times ten thousand equals one million pounds.' He stood back in awe of his own calculations. 'A million, Arthur – I'm giving you a million. All of it.'

'Very generous, Alisdair.'

'All you have to do is to get the money out of their pockets. Look man – from the moment they cross the border they're fair game. They have to be fed, sheltered – and more importantly – refreshed.' He paused and turned to Arthur with near religious zeal. 'It's a remarkable prospect, is it not?'

'A remarkable prospect indeed.' Arthur echoed the words with awe and with greed.

Alisdair smiled and said, 'Want topping up, Arthur?'

Arthur stared at his glass, still thinking of the prospect. 'I could handle a drop,' he said.

Alisdair poured him another glass of champagne. Then he spoke slowly, confidently. 'Tickets are a mere bagatelle. A drop in the limitless ocean. What I am suggesting is a huge exercise, a major operation.' He leant forward confidently.

21

'You see, Arthur – you have to realise that the world is ruled by accountants now and,' he added hastily, 'a few entrepreneurs like yourself.'

'I assume I'm talking to an accountant?' said Arthur with a quick smirk.

'You've got it in one, Arthur,' Alisdair replied. 'We want to get together an attractive package. Say – two nights in London, decent bed, continental breakfast, a couple of hand-picked clubs and a ticket for the game.' He paused to consider the deal. 'People will pawn their videos to get to Wembley. It'll be a weekend of a lifetime.'

'I like it,' replied Arthur. 'I like it. Incidentally, a pal of mine has three thousand autographed photos of Charlie Nicholas. They'd make a nice souvenir, wouldn't they?'

Alisdair gave him a mirthless grin. 'Why not, Arthur. You're the kind of guy we need. You know this city. We can guarantee the bodies, but it's up to you to bury them.'

'You're suggesting a partnership?'

'That's it. Mind you, I still have to meet other people.'

'Like who?' asked Arthur with instant suspicion.

'Do you know a man called Phil?'

'Oh yeah. He's a very good man if you want to go to the Royal Ballet.' Arthur tried to look casual. 'But if you want briefs for England and Scotland – I'm your man.'

'We've worked with him before,' said Alisdair doubtfully. 'He reckons he can get any amount of tickets . . .'

'Does he?'

'Aye.'

'He's a dreamer,' commented Arthur patronisingly, 'old Phil. He doesn't realise that I've taken over –'

'I like your confidence, Arthur.' He paused and then leant forward again, this time with the kind of directness that made Arthur wary. 'Are you ready to go to Glasgow?'

'Well –'

'Put the tickets on the table, meet my associates and shake hands?'

'There's a few details I have to settle first.' Arthur shifted uneasily and took a long draft of champagne.

'In principle, I mean?'

'Oh yeah . . . in principle. And Glasgow very soon,' said Arthur, 'very, very soon.'

'Maybe tomorrow?' asked Alisdair.

'Glasgow, eh?' Arthur gave a glum smile.

'The natives are really quite friendly.'

'Who said?' asked Arthur uncertainly.

Terry watched Arthur leave the hotel. For a moment he stood by the kerb, preoccupied, chewing at his cigar. Then he ambled slowly round the corner, as if he were sleep-walking.

'Now what's he doing?' asked Terry rhetorically. He opened the door and bellowed: 'Oi, we're over here!'

But there was no reaction from Arthur as he turned the corner. Cursing, Terry got out of the car and walked briskly after him.

'Arthur – where you going?' he said when he finally caught up with him.

Arthur continued to walk slowly, reflectively, along the street. 'I'm thinking – you know, oiling the old grey matter, considering things.'

'You can do that in the motor.'

'With young Justin committing GBH of the Donalds?'

'I've never seen you thinking, Arthur,' said Terry wonderingly.

'You may scoff, but this is a command decision. Have you ever dipped into your pocket and come out with eighteen grand? Course not,' he said before Terry could answer. 'It's beyond your experience, innit?'

'Well – I've had a pull from the Inland Revenue.'

'What's that – two bob?' asked Arthur sneeringly. 'They probably owe you. I'm talking about *real* money.'

'Have you got real money?'

'Course I have. That's not the point. My dough's tied up.'

'Can't you get it from your bank?'

'Oh yeah,' said Arthur with withering sarcasm. 'How about this for starters. Please mister bank manager – I've got two thousand hooky football tickets.' He paused expectantly, looking at Terry questioningly. 'I mean, it ain't exactly an extension for the kitchen or a new roof. Anyway, I'm borrowing me own dough. I've got to sell the tickets. You've got to realise, we're into a high risk venture, Terry. What happens if Alisdair's pals don't want to buy?' Arthur's eyes dilated with horror at the thought. Then he continued looking glazed. 'Or maybe they do, but we get hi-jacked on the way back to London.' He plucked at Terry's sleeve. 'All kinds of things can happen. An earthquake? What happened to Hamish the Growler? Who knows? So that's why I'm schlepping around the environs of Park Lane and thinking, and thinking, and thinking. Can't you understand, Terence, I'm thinking. So just leave me alone.'

Arthur turned away abruptly and walked down the street, leaving Terry calling after him. 'Should we wait?'

'Obviously,' said Arthur impatiently. 'I'm not going to think all night, am I?'

Cedric lumbered up the stairs of the council block. Once he had reached the scruffy, graffiti-strewn landing he began to look for a number. Eventually he found it, but before he could knock, the door opened. A woman stood there, looking harassed. She was in her early forties and still bore some vestiges of tarnished glamour.

'Who are you?' she asked brusquely.

Cedric gave her what he hoped was a winning smile. 'Justin about?'

'You police?' she asked.

'Not me, love. I'm a friend of Justin's – me and Steve Benson.'

She turned and shouted into the flat. 'Justin – it's for you.' She returned her jaundiced gaze to Cedric. 'I'm late for work – I hope he's heard me.'

'Don't you worry, Mrs James,' said Cedric reassuringly, 'I'll give him a yell.'

'Could you? I'll miss my bus. Ta-ra.' She walked quickly to the staircase and Cedric walked into the flat.

Glancing into the living-room, he saw no one, but along

24

the hall was a closed door. Cedric opened the door to find Justin in bed, sleeping peacefully. With sudden dexterity Cedric grabbed the mattress and pitched Justin on to the floor.

'All you ponces lie in bed all day. Look at you with your mum going out to work and all.'

Justin grabbed at the bedclothes, blinking in the hard light of day.

'Who are you?' he asked blearily.

'Who am I? I get up early in the morning and then I hit people.'

Justin stared at him unbelievingly and Cedric continued with his disarming explanation.

'I work for Phil,' he said. 'I bet you don't work?'

'I'm self-employed,' replied Justin trying to gather up his ruffled composure – and pyjamas.

'What as? A thief?' Cedric asked unpleasantly. Then he came up very close to the still sprawling Justin and stood over him menacingly. 'You're thieving my livelihood.'

'What?'

'I mean, Benno tells me that you're a go-between and you know the missing link. Who is he?'

'Ask Benno,' said Justin feebly.

'He doesn't know him.'

Justin draped the bedclothes over his shoulders. '*Numero Uno*.' He stated.

'Who's he?'

'The man who's going to slaughter you and your gu'nor.'

Cedric thought about that statement for a while. Then said quietly, 'What I'm going to do is smother you with your duvet. Fancy that?'

Justin stared at him, wondering just how serious he was. 'If I tell you, you'll be out of here in two seconds?'

'Try me.'

'Arthur Daley.' Justin spoke with great confidence and a long pause ensued. Then Cedric repeated with a grin:

'Arthur Daley?'

'Yeah. I thought you'd be worried.'

25

But Cedric didn't seem worried at all. Instead he giggled, even guffawed. Justin looked disturbed for this was a far cry from the reaction he had hoped for.

'Dear oh dear,' said Cedric, tears running down his cheeks. 'I think I'm going to wet meself.'

'You wouldn't say that to him?'

'Why not?'

'Well, you wouldn't.'

'I would. Him and his punch-drunk pal and his relatives and his creditors who are many, and his debtors, who are few – the whole bunch of 'em.' Cedric began to laugh again and, to Justin, it was not a pleasant sound.

'Yeah?' asked Justin, his confidence draining.

'Oh yeah,' said Cedric, squatting down beside him on the floor. 'So why don't you tell me all about it?'

Theo Warren was bald, fifty, confident and friendly. He sat behind his executive desk as if it fitted him – as if it was part of him. Sitting uneasily opposite him was Arthur, staring at a chart on the wall which was covered by zigzag lines and numbers.

'What's all that about, Theo?'

'It's a graph – assets, capital, deposits – it's to encourage the customers.'

'Yeah, but what does it mean?'

'I don't know. It looks good, doesn't it?'

'It's brilliant.' He grew silent. 'I went to your other place, the bank.'

'Not anymore. I only run a bank for a year, Arthur – otherwise the Fraud Squad get busy. It's a time-share property company now. You don't want an apartment in a baronial castle in Wales, do you?'

'Whereabouts?' said Arthur chattily.

'We don't know yet. Now I hope you don't want a mortgage, Arthur.'

Arthur, not to be hurried, looked around him. 'This outfit a good earner?'

'Good? I tell you what – it's going so well I'm thinking of

turning it into an honest business.'

'Never!'

'No, never. You see – and you know this yourself – there are those who take and there are those who are taken. It's all greed.' He winked at Arthur and then gazed at him affectionately. 'We offer a nice rate of interest and we're competitive. And we're the leaders in the field. Now, if the other societies put up their rates it would be to the good of the public, wouldn't it?'

'Yeah, I suppose so. But you don't pay out.'

'That's a different thing, Arthur. I'm talking about the principle. We offer good value.'

'So I believe.' He glanced around him more warily now. 'Er, I understand you're financing some – projects?'

'Money's the game, Arthur.' Theo whispered.

'Of course.'

'My lips are sealed. But try this: four characters who didn't have two bob between them put up a scheme. Have you got any collateral, I asked them. A safe vault, they said. You couldn't get any better collateral than that, could you? They wanted twelve grand for the laser welding equipment and the protective clothing. A first class investment, I thought. And as it was I got it back in three weeks. So what's your problem, Arthur?'

Arthur looked taken aback. 'I'm not a robber, you know,' he began to protest.

'Some say yes, some say no.'

Arthur ignored him. 'I'm a simple general dealer and I need eighteen grand for two or three days.'

'What for?' Theo asked solicitously.

'Do you trust me?'

'No.'

Arthur frowned and tried again. 'I've got tickets. Wembley. For the England–Scotland do. What I don't need is any welding equipment.'

Theo considered for a moment and then said abruptly, 'OK. Three and a quarter per cent per day.'

Arthur began to do complicated calculations on his

27

fingers. 'That's five hundred and eighty-five quid.'

'Give us a chance, Arthur,' Theo protested. 'I haven't even got me calculator yet.'

'The figures are OK – don't you worry about that,' said Arthur reassuringly. 'If I need it for a week you're copping twenty-two and three-quarters per cent interest.'

'Why don't you go down to the Woolwich?' Theo checked on his pocket calculator.

'I think it's diabolical,' said Arthur.

'It depends on what side of the desk you're on. You're good at sums, Arthur.'

'Five per cent for three days, eh?'

'That's a bit strong, Arthur.'

'Well, I'm not going to knock you, am I?' Arthur's tone was all injured innocence.

'Never been known. One way or another we always get paid.'

Arthur looked at him in surprise. 'Theo! We're friends!'

Theo shook his head.

'Come on,' said Arthur, but Theo still shook his head.

'We're acquaintances. Three per cent for forty-eight hours. And then three and a quarter per day.'

'Yeah, OK.' Arthur sounded defeated.

Theo rose triumphantly and took his cheque book from a drawer. 'We'll have to go to my bank.'

'Haven't you got cash here?'

'You must be kidding. The villains who come into this place?'

Arthur smiled sadly. 'That's the world,' he said. 'It's a wicked place.'

Another business conference was taking place in a different part of town, but this one was a little more formal. There was no friendship here – merely the Income Tax Inspector and Terry, gripped by mutual interest.

'You missed the tea-lady, Mr McCann. You don't mind if I drink my coffee?'

'Sure – go ahead.'

28

'You do understand that this is not an investigation? I'm only trying to elicit information. The thing is–' He hesitated. 'We seem to have lost track of you, Mr McCann.'

'Really?'

'How would you describe your occupation?'

'Tricky, innit? Just odds and ends.'

'Self-employed?' he asked blandly.

'I just get by.' The reply was casual.

'Freelance?'

' I dunno.'

'What I'm trying to get at is your income – haphazard as it may be.'

'That's the word,' said Terry frankly. 'It's so haphazard that I don't know what it is.'

The income tax inspector gave a patient, resigned smile. 'Should I try another tack? Have you a PAYE code number?'

'What's that?'

'Precisely. We'll ignore that then.' He was beginning to look tired and pressed a button on his desk. 'Unemployment benefit?'

Terry shook his head.

'Social security supplementary benefit?'

Terry shook his head again.

'You don't contribute to national insurance? Or, as we used to call it – stamping your cards?'

Terry shook his head yet again, but the Inspector was determined to be thorough.

'Mortgage, HP? Credit cards? Pension fund?'

'None of them,' said Terry.

The Inspector stared at the desk-top and picked up his pipe, filling it thoughtfully with tobacco.

'You've cracked it, haven't you?' he muttered.

'Beg your pardon?'

'The system. You haven't got a number. You're not a statistic. You're a spirit – a spectre. They hardly know about you. Where were you when they did the census?'

'I was out.'

'I bet you were.' He gazed at Terry as if he was an entirely new species – unrecorded man.

The door opened and an attractive young woman entered, carrying a file and some letters. She put them down on the desk.

'Thank you, Miss Demosthenous,' said the inspector, smirking at her.

Terry was spellbound, for Miss Demosthenous had, without doubt, the best legs in London. As she made a graceful exit, the inspector lit his pipe and glanced at Terry.

'They're amazing, aren't they? The best legs in the Department of Inland Revenue and she's not a bad typist either.'

'Fantastic,' said Terry.

The Inspector paused, his mind reluctantly reverting to other matters. 'You know what you are, Mr McCann? You're the invisible man. Where's your identity? What happens if we have a war? You'll dodge it, won't you? We've been after you for seven years and during that period you must have had some job – just some job.' He sounded as if he was beginning to plead.

Terry thought, then he said, 'Well, last week, for example, I was minding a pub for two nights because they thought there might be some bovver. I got fifteen pounds in cash for each night, plus a drink and a couple of sandwiches. I don't need an account for that, do I?'

'What are you saying?' The inspector looked wild-eyed. 'Are you some kind of itinerant bodyguard?'

'I'm an odd job man.'

The Inspector exhaled a whiff of tobacco and picked up the file left by the exquisite Miss Demosthenous.

'Daley,' he said and Terry winced at the all too familiar name.

'Does that mean anything?'

'Who did you say?' he asked despondently.

'Mister Daley – are you his gardener?'

'His what?' he gaped at the Inspector, unable to take in this latest gambit.

'Gardener – as in Percy Thrower.'

30

'He hasn't got a bloody garden.'

The inspector's eyes gleamed. 'Hasn't he now?'

Terry made a quick recovery, realising that he had made a mistake. 'Mind you, he's got a big balcony and he does like a daffodil and a, er, Busy Lizzie. Actually, he's well into horticultural affairs.'

The Inspector gave Terry a manic grin. 'Minding the flowers, eh?'

'You've got it. How much do I get?'

He looked down at his file. 'Let's have a look. Oh, yes. The financial year April 1982. Fifteen hundred pounds. That's more-or-less thirty pounds a week. It's creeping up, isn't it? What with the occasional stint at a boozer, any other odds and ends and suddenly you're liable to pay tax.'

Terry sat there in gloomy silence.

'Unless you wish to state that Mr Daley is falsifying his claim and his books?'

'Mr Daley wouldn't dream of doing that – he's as honest as the day.'

'You don't do any other gardens?' asked the Inspector eagerly.

'No,' said Terry. 'I'm not into digging up the earth. I'm a speciality man – balconies only. Of course, at a stretch I'd do a window box, as well.'

'That's nice to know,' said the inspector, busily making notes.

An impatient Arthur drummed his fingers on the pub counter. He kept glancing at his watch and sighing, showing all the symptoms of a busy man who was deeply frustrated by time being wasted. So when at last he saw Terry entering, Arthur's mood was sour.

'Long enough, weren't you?'

'Was I?'

'This is a big day for me. I've just put my life on the line.'

'Not on the clothes-line in the garden by any chance? Is there a drink going?'

'No – we're on a tight schedule.'

31

'Oh yeah?' Then he began to chant, 'Arthur Daley, quite contrary, How does your garden grow?' Terry paused and said angrily, 'You owe me fifteen hundred sovs.'

Arthur drained his glass. 'What're you talking about?' he asked innocently.

'The trusty old retainer.'

'Who?'

'Me.'

'I don't understand, Terence.'

'The one with manure on his wellies – the gardener. You've been just a bit too clever this time, Arthur. You're sussed.'

'You didn't grass on me, did you?' asked Arthur worriedly.

'No, I didn't. And you haven't got any in your bleeding garden either.'

'Now, Terry –'

'Listen, Arthur,' said Terry bitterly. 'You dropped me right up to the neck in your compost and you'll get away with it. But I won't, 'cos I'm going to be assessed now.'

'You don't understand –'

'I understand fifteen hundred sovs.'

'You'll get a drink out of it.'

'What? A watering-canful?'

Together, in uneasy companionship, Terry and Arthur walked towards the door of the pub.

'It's more important,' said Arthur.

'What is?'

'That I'm solvent.'

'Who says?'

'Me. I'm the brains of this organisation, you know.'

'Hang on.'

'Eh?'

The beautiful Miss Demosthenous had just entered the pub by another door and Terry had swung round to feast his eyes on her legs. 'Fantastic.'

'What?'

'Those legs – she should get the Nobel Prize.'

Arthur sighed a world-weary sigh. 'Terence. We're talking about serious things and you're rabbiting on about legs. Is that the only topic that exercises your mind? No wonder you're at the bottom of the heap. Handyman and occasional gardener . . . dear oh dear . . . you've got to do better than that.'

'Arthur,' said Terry patiently.

'Yeah?'

'Shut it.'

The Jag was crowded. Arthur drove, Terry sat beside him and Justin and Benson were in the back.

Arthur glanced back at Benson and said, 'Old memories, eh, Benno?'

Through the windows they could see the twin towers of Wembley Stadium in the distance.'

'Yeah.'

'I was always a great fan of yours,' said Arthur nostalgically. 'Why Greenwood didn't use you more I could never understand.'

'Bit of an expert are you, eh?' Benson said in a surly voice.

But Arthur was oblivious. 'As a matter of fact, I know 'em all – Mooro, Greavesie, Banksie, Ballie, Bestie, Webbo, Robbo, Stroller, Chopper and Sniffer – I know 'em all.'

'And Groucho and Harpo,' put in Terry helpfully.

'Who did they play for – Orient?'

'Odeon, wasn't it?'

Suddenly Arthur caught hold of the joke. He didn't like it. 'A bit of a jester, eh?' he said sourly. 'Well now, where do we meet the man with the tickets?'

'In his office. You give me the money and I give it to him. I'm in and out in three minutes,' said Benson.

'I don't even meet him?'

'He's worried –'

'*He's* worried –' Arthur stared at Benson in the mirror but it was not direct enough so he turned round in his seat, unconcerned about the road. 'I've got to give you the eighteen grand in cold blood and –'

Terry started as a pedestrian brushed the car. 'Arthur – you almost killed someone,' he pointed out.

'So what?' snarled Arthur. 'What's more important – life or money?'

With that little homily, he drove into the vast, almost empty car-park of Wembley Stadium, steering the Jag towards the entrance steps. They all got out of the car, but Arthur beckoned Terry and walked away from the other two leaving Justin and Benson to watch them suspiciously. Arthur took an envelope from his inside pocket and gave it furtively to Terry.

'Eighteen grand – I'm trusting you.'

'Do you think I'm going to do a runner?'

'Who knows? With that kind of dough. No – I'm talking about Benson. I mean, he was a very elusive player, wasn't he? A bit quick in the box and very greedy, as well. So, listen – you give him the dough and you wait for three minutes. If he don't appear you break doors, windows and shout and scream.'

Terry looked bewildered. 'He's got to talk to the man, hasn't he? Three minutes isn't enough, Arthur,' he protested.

'All right, four.'

'Five minutes at least. Maybe he wants a cup of tea.'

Arthur looked at him in amazement. 'Why?'

'Well – people do *have* a cup of tea, you know.'

'You sound like somebody in a war film.'

'You make everybody nervous – that's the trouble with you, Arthur.'

He took the envelope from Arthur who watched him handle it apprehensively. 'Don't drop it!'

'That's what I mean –' said Terry. He walked up to Benson and together they climbed the steps to the entrance, watched by an all too anxious Arthur.

Terry and Benson's footsteps echoed as they tramped down the wide, desolate corridor, usually thronged with people on match days, that skirted the stadium. Benson pointed to a staircase.

'It's up there,' he said pointing out a door marked OFFICE at the top of the stairs.

Terry glanced around before giving the envelope to Benson. 'Arthur's a bit worried about you.'

'Where can I hide?' said Benson reassuringly. He stuffed the envelope in his pocket and grinned. 'Be fair. We're all on the same side,' he said and ran up the staircase.

Terry moved over to a point where he could see the pitch and gazed down on its empty desolation. Then he glanced up at the vaulted ceiling, suddenly finding everything very oppressive.

Meanwhile, Arthur was prowling around the Jag, chewing his cigar. Justin was ready with his pupil/master relationship well to the fore.

'You've probably done things like this before, haven't you, Arthur?'

Arthur made an effort at coolness. 'All the time.'

'What was it like in the war?'

'You mean the fighting and everything?'

'No. I mean all the dodges – petrol, clothing coupons and things. What about chocolate?'

'I was doing my bit. Six gallons of petrol and you could live like a king. A dozen bars of fruit and nut and you thought you'd done something against the Hun. Mind you – it was tough.'

'I bet.'

'You couldn't hang around . . . of course the others were tucked up in their air shelters. But not me. I was on the streets, braving the buzz-bombs, bobbing and weaving, trying to get a crust.' Arthur paused to reflect on his past glory. 'I suppose we were the unsung heroes of our finest hour.'

'I wish I'd been there, Arthur.'

'You'd have loved it. I was a harum-scarum nipper in the university of hard-knocks. But then I got captured.'

'The Germans?' asked Justin with awe.

'National Service,' said Arthur flatly.

'I bet you were a commando.'

'Yeah – very similar – pay corps. I always like to be where the money is.' He looked up at the building and started to chew his cigar again.

'You all right, Arthur?' asked Justin.

'Just playing a waiting game,' said Arthur as he accidentally bit off the end of his cigar.

Terry's nerves twanged as Benson rushed down the staircase. He gave a quick glance to the right and left – and then passed a package to Terry, who tucked it into his jacket. Then they both began to walk briskly to the exit.

A few minutes later an excitable Arthur was ripping the package apart in the back of the Jag, while Terry drove. Then, as if holding up some religious artefact, he picked up the first ticket, fondled it, examined it and held it up to the light.

'Gold dust,' he said, almost salivating. Then his paranoia returned. 'Anybody following us?'

'No. Why should they?' asked Terry.

'When them little Jocks see this lot – they'll drool,' he chuckled.

'You're drooling a bit yourself,' pointed out Terry.

'Why not, eh? Now we're off to bonny Scotland.' He turned to Justin. 'Get me the briefcase, son.'

Justin picked up the executive briefcase from the back seat and humbly handed it to Arthur.

'I don't want to go to Scotland,' said Benson unhappily.

'Then you don't get weighed-in,' replied Arthur mercilessly, putting the tickets in the briefcase and locking it.

'Why?'

'I need help. I mean –' He gazed at Benson in annoyance at his lack of understanding. 'D'you think I'm going to the mean streets of Glasgie on me tod? They don't take prisoners up there, you know. What chances have I got with two thousand tickets?' But Benson was still looking uncooperative. 'I'll tell you what, I'll end up wearing a Blue Circle overcoat and having a quick paddle in the Clyde.' He gave Benson an admonishing look. 'For a few days, Benson, it's down to man-to-man marking.'

Neurotically, Arthur then tried to open the case just to check the tickets were still there. He twiddled the locks – but in vain.

'Oh my gawd,' he said, 'I can't remember the combination.'

Terry was instructed by Arthur to hire a minibus for the great trip North, so that he could be flanked by all his troops. Arthur drove, with passengers Terry, Alisdair and Benson, as they had yet to pick up Justin from the tender clutches of his glamorous mother.

'They all use them in Scotland. Very handy vehicle, you know – when they're shooting,' Arthur explained to his passengers.

Alisdair, looking up from his *Financial Times*, said, 'What d'you mean? We don't shoot in Glasgow.'

'I mean in the *country*. Up in the lochs and the braes and the Alps. With the lairds on their estates when they shoot pheasant and grouse and smoked salmon.'

Alisdair looked at Arthur's back grimly and Terry wondered how long he would contain himself.

When they drew up outside Justin's flat, Arthur said to Terry, 'Give him a shout.'

Terry got out of the minibus and approached Justin's flat. He knocked on the door and it was answered by Mrs James.

'Is he in?'

'He'll be back in a minute,' she said. 'You'd better wait.'

Reluctantly, Terry went inside, followed by Mrs James, who was wearing a dressing gown. After a quick glance in the mirror, she patted her hair and said, 'He's off to Scotland now, is he?'

'Couple of days.'

She lit a cigarette. 'I usually work – but if he's out of the house I try to relax. It's so quiet.'

'Oh yeah?' said Terry cautiously.

'More trouble, I suppose?'

'I wouldn't think so,' he said trying to reassure her – and failing.

'It's trouble,' said Mrs James. 'I can smell it.'

'You worried about him?'

'He's so restless. I mean why can't he be unemployed like everybody else? He's on remand, you know.'

'Six months, he reckons.'

'I'd be delighted if he went away for two years.'

Terry looked at Justin's mum in surprise. 'You don't want that, do you?'

'Don't I?' she said cynically. 'If he's palled up with Arthur Daley he'll probably be away for ten years.'

'You know Arthur?'

'Years ago. Right Jack the lad – bit like my Justin. Mind you I was just a kid then. I worked at the Cabaret Club in Jermyn Street. I didn't have a lot of luck – I was the hat check girl and suddenly people stopped wearing hats –'

'Arthur still wears a hat,' said Terry innocently.

'He would. Then I was a cigarette girl – and all of a sudden people stopped smoking. That's when I decided to have Justin.'

'That was nice.'

'I couldn't think of anything else to do. Want a drink?'

'Bit early for me.'

Notwithstanding, Mrs James opened a sideboard and took out the sherry bottle. The front door opened and she hurriedly put back the bottle as Justin appeared, carrying an overnight bag.

'Sorry, Tel. I suddenly realised I didn't have a bag. Nice, innit? Came from Gucci.' He glanced at his mother and then returned his gaze to Terry. 'Didn't she give you a cup of tea?'

'We've got to shoot,' said Terry hurriedly.

'Be right with you,' said Justin, dashing into his room.

'Busy boy, isn't he?' commented Mrs James. 'He was good at scripture in school, though.'

'Oh, that's handy,' said Terry, stuck for a reply.

'There's only one Archbishop isn't there?'

Terry nodded.

'I could have been croupier but for him. I mean Justin, not the Archbishop. Everybody was swinging down the Kings Road and there I was dusting talcum on his bum. I took a wrong turn somewhere.'

To Terry's relief, Justin appeared in the doorway. '*Avanti* . . . OK?'

'Nice to meet you, Mrs James –' Hurriedly Terry went to the door, while Justin said to his mother:

'You haven't been talking to my friends, have you?'

'Just "hallo",' she said casually.

'I've told you – don't talk to my friends, right?' He was about to follow Terry through the door, but he hesitated: 'You haven't got a tenner, have you?'

Defeated, Mrs James pointed to her handbag.

Arthur's minibus, driven by Terry, sped past a sign pointing to the North. Traffic was busy and so far they had all failed to notice that they were being followed by Little Phil's Cadillac.

'Got your passport, Terry? And your phrase book?' asked Arthur, who seemed to be in rare good humour.

'What you on about?'

'All foreigners from now on. Nobody speaks English north of Tottenham. Didn't your mum ever tell you that?'

'Pack it in, Arthur, I'm trying to drive.'

'Oh, is that what you call it?'

A few hours later Arthur's directions came to grief when the minibus left the motorway at Birmingham's spaghetti junction.

'You're barmy, Arthur,' said Terry.

'I'm telling you we should've stayed on the M1. Everyone knows the M1 goes to Scotland.'

'Yeah, but not Glasgow.'

'That's in Scotland, innit?'

'I give up. You'll drive me potty.'

Alisdair interrupted with an edge to his clipped voice. 'M6

for Glasgow – Terry's right, Arthur.'

Arthur shrugged, 'If you'd only consulted me earlier.'

'We did,' said Alisdair menacingly.

Back on the right motorway, Arthur took over the driving amidst an oppressive silence. But he did not allow this to affect his sunny mood. 'Cows,' he said, looking out at the open countryside.

'Do what?' asked Terry sleepily. Alisdair did not deign to reply and Justin merely looked bemused, while Benson slept.

'Cows.'

'Oh . . . great.'

'Don't knock cows.'

'It's just that they're not the most riveting topic of conversation.'

'I don't know so much – there's milk, cream, cheese and . . . er . . .'

'Yoghurt,' added Terry.

'There you are, then.'

'Yeah and that's it. End of conversation.'

There was a long pause while Arthur stared ahead. In the end he said, 'You're right.'

'Any chance of driving slower?' asked Justin. He looked ill.

'I'm only doing seventy . . . that's all.' Arthur seemed indignant.

' 'Cause I feel a bit sick.'

'Gawd. Open the window.'

Alisdair shifted away from Justin. 'Don't you dare spew over my *Financial Times*.'

'It's just a bit close in here.'

'Don't think about it, Justin,' said Arthur. 'It's all in the mind. Just concentrate –'

Justin burped. 'What on?'

'Why don't you collect numbers? You and Terry could have a competition – who can get the most Maestros?' He sounded happy in his generosity.

'Have you got any Smarties – for the winner?' asked Terry.

'You can have a touch of haggis when we get there,' Arthur promised.

Meanwhile, a few miles behind them, Cedric drove Little Phil in his Cadillac with both speed and restraint. Soon, they were crossing the Scottish border, still keeping their distance from Arthur's minibus. It was a good thing they did, for the minibus was beginning to cough and wheeze and Arthur began to nurse the clattering vehicle along, much to the disgust of its passengers.

'Overheating,' said Arthur.

'Amongst other things,' replied Terry.

The others maintained a pessimistic silence.

'There's a service area coming,' said Arthur. 'I might drop in.'

'I should,' said Alisdair, 'before the whole thing conks out.'

'Up your kilt,' muttered Arthur.

'What was that?' The edge had returned to Alisdair's voice and this time rather more sharply.

'I said – jolly good idea,' said Arthur. 'I'll soon get us back on the road.'

'On foot?' asked Terry unhelpfully.

Ten minutes later, the bonnet of the minibus was up and Arthur was in deep conversation with a middle-aged mechanic, a roll-up stuck to his lower lip.

'Can you have a look at this, squire?'

'Gasket,' said the mechanic without even looking under the bonnet.

'You haven't had a look at it yet,' said Arthur plaintively.

'Gasket – and the thermostat,' he added.

'I'm in the trade, squire,' Arthur stated knowingly. 'How long?'

'Couple of hours.'

'I'm going to Scotland.'

'Are you in the AA?'

'I told you – I'm trade, squire.'

41

But the mechanic was not impressed. 'It's still got to be two hours. I've got to get the spares. There isn't another garage for twenty-two miles.'

'I'll tell you what, squire . . . there's a good drink in it.'

'Thanks . . . it'll be about one hour and fifty minutes.'

Arthur gave him a searching look.

Meanwhile, Benson, Justin and Alisdair were about to enter the restaurant. Terry, anxious for news, came over to Arthur, overhearing the last part of the conversation.

'What's all this *squire* business?'

'We're in the North. The rustics love the touch.'

They walked together to the entrance of the restaurant. Then Arthur froze. 'Where's the tickets?'

'I thought you had –'

In a flash Arthur was gone, running back to the minibus. Terry followed him casually. Frantically, Arthur wrenched open the driver's door. He scrabbled in the back and retrieved his precious briefcase. When he returned to Terry, Arthur looked almost ashen.

'Don't you ever do that again.'

'Me?'

'You've gotta take care of your old Arthur.'

'Oh my Gawd.' Terry looked as if he was literally squirming.

'We're in Scotland now, the bad lands, with Apaches lurking around every corner.' Arthur glanced about him. 'Look at it – it's a wilderness. No wonder that Adrian didn't fancy it and he didn't have any football tickets.'

'You're a bit edgy, Arthur.'

'No wonder. We should've had an armoured car.' He patted the briefcase and looked around him again. 'We're talking about fifty grand at street value. Never mind about illegal substances – them wee Jocks would kill for these. And that Alisdair . . . Always reading his *Financial Times* – what's he up to? You should keep your eye on him.'

'Yes, major.'

Arthur began to march back towards the restaurant. Then, once again, he froze.

'Now what's up?' asked Terry.

Arthur pointed a shuddering finger. 'Look!' he gasped as Little Phil's Cadillac drove into the service area and parked. Arthur looked wildly at Terry. 'Did you see his little eyes? Now you wonder why I'm worried? This has got to be the furthest north he's been beyond Hendon Way. *He's* after *me*.'

And Arthur began to run for cover.

The five gallant travellers had gathered together in a corner of the garish motorway cafe. Dominated by their plastic world, they were subdued. Under the yellow neon, they ate without pleasure and talked dispassionately.

'What I really fancied was a Pina Colada,' said Justin. No-one replied.

Alisdair wiped his mouth. 'I think I'll call Glasgow,' he said, going to the door.

'Follow him,' whispered Arthur to Terry.

'Why?'

'To see what he's doing?'

'He's going to phone somebody. What's the big deal?'

'I just want to know,' said Arthur between gritted teeth, his eyes alive with paranoia and suspicion.

But Terry clearly wasn't going to move. Arthur grabbed the briefcase and walked to the door. Outside the entrance to the toilets, there were two public pay phones. Alisdair was talking into one of them. Hurriedly, Arthur returned to the corner table and whispered urgently to Terry:

'He's talking to somebody on the dog and bone.'

Terry looked at him. 'So that's how he does it.'

'Eh?'

'I thought he was going to shout. But he uses the phone instead.'

Arthur sat down heavily. 'I wonder who he's talking to?'

'How do I know?' said Terry irritably.

Arthur scowled at him, picked up his plastic cup and grimaced as he drank. At that moment Cedric came in. He saw them and gave Arthur a patronising smile. He then went to the counter and bought two teas.

43

Justin glanced at Arthur. 'D'you know him?'

Arthur nodded.

'And what about you?' asked Terry.

'Well I . . . I had to tell him –' Justin said uncomfortably.

'What?' Arthur's voice was hollow.

'About us – and the tickets.'

'Thank you!'

'He was going to give me a hammering. So I told him –'

'What did you tell him?' asked Arthur in a distant voice.

'You have to settle with *him* – I said. The guv'nor, the don of all dons. He wasn't all that impressed.'

'You didn't say it in Italian, did you?'

'I haven't got to that bit in the phrase book. Anyway, you're not worried, are you? What about the old days when you was in gang warfare at Brighton racecourse?'

'That was before the war.'

'Was it? Well, what about the street corner bookmakers – the shoot-out at Mister Smith's – you know, the what-d'ye-call-it family, and the what's-'is-name twins –'

Arthur studied Justin for a moment with confirmed distaste. 'Justin, your yearning for nostalgia is almost morbid.'

'I'm just trying to learn, aren't I?'

'The first lesson is to say nothing to nobody.' He leant back in his chair and closed his eyes as if trying to blot out the harsh realities of the material world.

'He was gonna strangle me,' said Justin excitedly.

'Particularly to people who are going to strangle you,' said Arthur in a sonorous voice. Then instinct made him open his eyes and he was back to reality.

Cedric was approaching him, carrying plastic cups and two fruit buns. He stopped three or four yards away from their table. 'Phil would like to see you,' he said.

'I'm here,' said Arthur with a detachment he didn't feel. He gave a quick glance to Justin just to ensure that he knew he was in command of the situation.

'We tried to find you last night,' said Cedric. 'Went to the usual haunts, but you had an early night. Imagine you on the high road to Scotland –' He ended on a note of wonderment.

'It's the Winchester Annual Trip,' said Arthur.

'Well – Phil's in his Cadillac, looking at the afternoon film.'

'What's that? *Stranger in the Night*?' asked Terry innocently.

'Mister Daley is in a meeting,' said Justin.

Cedric leant forward threateningly. 'I'll shove this fruit bun down your throat if you don't watch it, sonny.'

Justin turned to appeal to everybody. 'See what I mean?' His voice rose hysterically.

'Justin – reduce the volume,' said Arthur censoriously. He looked up at Cedric. 'I'll be there directly.'

Cedric stared at Justin for a second and then went away. Before he was out of earshot, Justin said:

'Yeah – and *buona notte*.'

Cedric hesitated, scowled and then walked on.

'That's "goodnight",' said Terry.

'Is it . . .? Well, he didn't know that, did he?'

Arthur lit a cigar and then rose majestically to his feet, nodding at Terry as he did so. Reluctantly, Terry also rose. Arthur was ready to meet Little Phil.

As they walked towards the door their progress was interrupted by a dishevelled young Scots fan, wearing a tam-o'-shanter and tartan scarf.

'Hey Jimmy . . . gie's a light?'

Arthur offered the glowing tip of his cigar and the fan lit his cigarette.

'Nice game, was it?' asked Arthur casually, trying to ensure that the still observant Justin did not think he was in too much of a hurry to obey Little Phil's summons.

'What game?' asked the fan.

'I assume you've been at a football match?'

'That was two years ago . . . Hamburg. D'you think they've kept my job open?'

'No, but you'll get a nice Giro cheque.'

Arthur continued his stately progress to the door, followed by a yawning Terry.

As Terry and Arthur walked towards the car park, Arthur

said, 'He'd have bought a ticket.'

'Yeah – but what about Little Phil?'

Arthur gave the briefcase to Terry. 'Guard this with your life.' He straightened his jacket. 'And don't worry about me. I'm bigger than Little Phil.' Arthur touched Terry's arm and gave a brave smile. 'I'll be okay now – just cover me.'

'I will,' said Terry dramatically. 'Just get out of the burning sun, Arthur – and watch his right arm.'

Frowning at Terry's frivolity, Arthur walked alone towards Phil's Cadillac.

As Terry walked back to the restaurant, a group, of young people passed him. Amongst them, he saw a girl smile.

'Sorry – do I know you?'

'Inland Revenue.'

Terry started back. It was Miss Demosthenous from the Inland Revenue. Instantly, he looked at her legs, only to discover she was wearing jeans.

'How are you?' asked Terry, but too late, for she had hurried on.

Justin was washing his hands in the toilets when Alisdair burst into the room. His first action was to grab Justin and fling him against the wash basins.

'You're a lucky man.'

Justin sprawled on the floor, staring up at him in terror. 'You gone potty?'

'I've got egg on my face and you're going to have blood on your throat –'

'Leave it out. What have I done?' On his hands and knees Justin tried to crawl to the door. As he did so, he received a sharp, painful kick on the backside from Alisdair.

'You must think we're mental up here, don't you?'

At that moment the doors opened and a traveller entered. He was suitably surprised by what he saw.

Alisdair gave him a sweet smile and said, 'We're just friends, you know.'

'Well, in that case, I'll come back later.' The traveller

closed the door firmly behind him and from his position on the floor, Justin said:

'You've got the hump, haven't you?'

'I'm a civilised man, an accountant. I don't do things like this. I don't kick people around toilets.'

'Then why don't you stop?' Justin asked.

'I went to an Academy – I've got letters after my name.'

'Which ones?'

Alisdair aimed a wild kick at him, which Justin just avoided.

'Forgeries! How could you do it?' Alisdair's voice was calmer.

'Them tickets?' Justin stared at him in surprise.

'I've been on the phone since we came here – they know, they know.' He ended on a declamatory note.

'Who knows?'

'My people – they've got contacts, friends at Wembley. They know.'

'Blimey,' said Justin.

'They've checked the postal applications and there are no missing tickets. You're flogging forgeries.'

Justin sagged against the wall. 'I don't believe it.'

Alisdair looked at him with the bitterness of a disappointed father. 'You're just a *boy*. Oh aye . . . you've mixed with the wrong people all right – Arthur Daley, Terry McCann –'

'They don't know about it, either. Benno – he got them into this.'

Alisdair gave a resigned scowl. 'I remember him when he was playing – always diving in the penalty box.'

'Well – he can't claim "foul" this time.' Justin tried to get on his feet, backing off as Alisdair came towards him. But this time he was trying to help him.

As Alisdair pulled Justin to his feet, he said, 'Sorry about the violence.'

'Well,' said Justin, 'it wasn't very nice.'

Alisdair gave Justin a wild look. 'We don't *do* this in Glasgow,' he said.

47

'Of course you don't,' said Justin respectfully.

The autograph hunter was a young man with an obsessive air and Terry knew they were in for a real dose of ear-bending when he arrived in the swirling gloom clouds of their table.

'I thought you were Steve Benson,' he said giving Benson a grubby piece of paper.

'I am,' he said, signing his name.

'I saw you against City about ten years ago. Two late goals and then you got booked. Not many like you now, eh Steve?'

'Thank you,' said Benson. The young man smiled gratefully and went away, whilst Benson grinned up at Terry, his mood lightening a little.

'He's got a good memory . . . eh?'

'Ever thought of getting into management?'

'What, with my record? They want stable characters – they don't want guys like me – been in the gossip columns, in court, into scrapes – I'd be a bad influence. And if you're going to say "Why don't you get a pub?" – I've had a couple, plus a restaurant and a sports shop.'

'America?'

'They don't want to know. Got any other ideas?'

'Mini-cabbing?'

'Lost me licence two years ago –'

Benson saw Justin and Alisdair approaching. 'We're talking about my career, Justin. They shoot horses, don't they?' he said cheerily.

But Justin was in no mood for jocularity. 'Shooting's too good for you,' he said.

'What?' Benson was astonished.

'You're just a professional toe-rag, ain't you?' remarked Justin sweetly.

Meanwhile, inside the large Cadillac in the Service Area's car-park, Little Phil and Arthur were watching a portable TV set.

'I like George Formby as well,' said Arthur.

48

'And Will Hay. I mean, it's better than racing,' said Little Phil nostalgically. Then his mood changed. 'Have I done anything against you?' he asked.

'Never, Phil,' replied Arthur resolutely.

'I got an electronic carving knife from you couple of years back. No complaints.'

'That was a snip. I'd like to get some more if I could.'

'Course you would,' said Little Phil generously. 'To each his own. For your own reasons you've diversified into electronic carving knives, motors, antiques, hi-fi, whatever. And now tickets as well. Myself, I concentrate on one market – a business I know – tickets.'

'You're an expert, Phil. The best scalper in the game,' said Arthur with all the respect of one pro for another.

Little Phil replied patiently, 'I don't like that word scalper, or even tout. I think of myself as a ticket *broker*. You want to go to *The Mousetrap*, not my taste, but I can fix you up. Russian ballet, which I *do* like, or two together for old blue eyes' umpteenth farewell concert – no problem. Give me a bell and I'm happy to comply.'

'You're well known for it,' remarked Arthur with the same professional respect.

'Precisely. I've got four hundred tickets for the England-Scotland game, but that's not enough. Then I meet you on the motorway by chance and you say you've got two *thousand*. You see, Arthur, it's all a question of *respect*. I'm known as the man who runs the ticket market – that's why I'm going to Glasgow. Suddenly, Arthur, you're a threat.'

'Me?'

'And a threat has to be curtailed – or destroyed.'

Arthur considered his statement for a few seconds. Then he said, 'As you explain it, I can understand your problem.'

'Not my problem – your problem. It's peace or war, you know that, Arthur.'

Arthur spoke in a measured, reflective tone. 'To be honest, Phil, I'm not all that crazy about the ticket business. I don't trust them little Jocks anyway.'

'You have to understand minorities, Arthur.'

49

'And you've got the gift. You can have 'em.'

'I can?'

'Yeah, you can have the two thousand eight pound seats for thirty-five grand.'

Little Phil smiled as if he had just heard a very good joke. A little old perhaps, but very good. 'You're talking silly money, Arthur. I'll give you half.'

'I need a small margin of profit,' Arthur protested.

'Twenty.'

'Twenty-five?'

'Arthur – we're business men –'

At that moment, Cedric rapped on the car window. 'It's Benno,' he mouthed.

Looking out of their cosy eyrie, Little Phil and Arthur watched Benson pass them, running like an Olympic sprinter. A few paces behind him was Terry.

'Taking exercise, are they?' asked Little Phil.

'He ain't jogging,' replied Arthur.

Benson was running down a slip road now with Terry hard on his heels. Avoiding a stream of traffic, he jumped over a fence and ran on into a woodland, with Terry closing on him.

'You can't run all the way to London,' Terry shouted.

But Benson showed no sign of hearing and the race became something of a steeplechase as they both tore through the wood, leaping over felled branches and tangled briars. Gradually, Terry narrowed the gap until Benson, aware that his stamina was at an end, turned to kick Terry and grab at his jacket.

'You'll get booked for that,' panted Terry as he brought him down. They both sprawled on the ground – in the middle of a large puddle.

As he lay in the water, feeling it seep into his clothes, Terry said, 'I hope you haven't spent all that money.'

Meanwhile, in the Cadillac, the atmosphere had changed perceptively. Little Phil seemed to have been very shaken by the enthusiastic athletics he had just witnessed.

'What about our deal then, Phil?' asked Arthur hopefully, knowing full well that all could be lost.

'Oh, I don't know.' His eyes returned to the flickering screen. 'There might be a stewards' inquiry now.'

Arthur closed his eyes. It was true – reality was too disappointing. He needed a holiday.

Arthur drove the minibus in the slow lane back down the motorway with Terry beside him. Justin and Benson were in the back. Alisdair, with tight lips, had hitched a lift north.

Finally, Arthur broke the silence by saying, 'How could you do a thing like that, eh?'

'I don't know,' said Benson.

'A professional foul?' asked Terry.

'Something like that. You get desperate, don't you?'

'What about that bloke at Wembley?' asked Arthur. 'Your contact?'

'There wasn't a contact. I stashed the tickets in the loo the night before,' replied Benson disconsolately.

'It gets worse.'

'We nearly got away with it.'

'*We?*' asked Arthur. 'What do you mean, *we?*'

'You would've taken the dough.'

'I almost had a deal with Little Phil.' Arthur sounded reflective.

'But that would have been dishonest, wouldn't it?' put in Terry.

'I didn't know that they were forgeries – not at that point.'

'Anyway, you'll get your money back,' said Benson consolingly.

But Arthur was not to be appeased. 'And what about the three per cent interest on the eighteen grand? The petrol and the new gasket, thermostat and cups of tea and pies and biscuits and all the aggravation?'

'That's right,' said Justin. 'In the old days it would've been a kneecap job, wouldn't it, Arthur?'

Arthur scowled at him in the driving mirror.

Justin continued unabashed. 'I'll tell you what, Arthur. I'll make it up to you when I come out. I mean, we're going to be partners anyway, so –'

'Justin.'

'Yes, Arthur?'

'I don't want to see, or hear from you ever again.'

'You must be kidding? Just as we were getting on so well.'

'As they say, Justin. This is *finito*.'

Justin sat there, unable to believe what Arthur was saying.

Terry tried to translate. 'I think he means *ciao* – and all that.'

PART TWO

Dreams of big money had always haunted Arthur, but after the Wembley tickets fiasco he went to ground for a while, nursing his disappointment and cursing Justin.

Terry, meanwhile, with little to do for Arthur, was forced to resort to the part-time work he had so vividly described to the income tax inspector.

'Can't you find nothing to do?' asked Big John officiously as he bustled past Terry.

'All seems very quiet – apart from the music.' Terry looked around the night-spot with its young band, centre stage, and its gyrating dancers on the floor. It was an all too familiar scene, for he knew there was no money in bouncing. It was something he was forced back on every time Arthur licked his wounds.

Big John paused, sensing a challenge in Terry's casual attitude. Asserting himself, he said, 'Well keep an eye on that little team at the bar. They look like trouble-makers to me.'

Terry glanced in the direction of the bar, seeing a group of youths laughing and drinking. They looked harmless enough, but to keep the peace, he said, 'Anything you say, chief.'

Big John went on his way, whilst Terry glanced at the bar again. But there was no problem.

The final thundering chords came from the band, the sweating musicians took their bow and the crowd cheered. Then they trooped off stage with their instruments.

Backstage, Chris Lambert picked his way carefully among the instruments and amplifiers. He was one of a new breed of impressarios – young, brash and confident. As he arrived the young members of the group were mopping themselves down, swigging coke and packing up their gear. Chris walked up to their leader.

'Good gig, Barry. You'll definitely get an invite back.'

'Great.'

He handed Barry four fivers.

'Twenty?' he asked in surprise.

'Something the matter?'

'We were told we were getting seventy.'

'Who told you that?'

Barry turned to his drummer. 'You said seventy, didn't you, Sammy?'

'That's what you said, Chris, when I fixed the gig.'

Chris's reaction was one of both astonishment and amusement. 'Seventy? I said seventy? Hey, John, they think they're superstars.' He turned round as Big John loomed out of the shadows. Then he continued, looking reassured. 'Be sensible. How can I pay a bunch of kids like you seventy?'

'Twenty's hardly worth our while,' said Barry unhappily. 'Knock off the transport and we're left with about two quid each.'

Chris shook his head sadly. 'I don't understand you kids,' he said paternally. 'You spend most of your time on the social security and I give you a chance by putting you on in a big establishment. I give you exposure to a large public, an opportunity to build up a personal following. What else can I do? You do want an invite back, don't you?'

'Naturally,' said Barry defensively.

'Then take your twenty.'

Barry took the money and stuffed it into his shirt pocket.

'And show a bit of gratitude as well,' said Big John softly.

'We don't want any aggravation, John. It's been a genuine misunderstanding – right, Barry?' said Chris.

Barry gave him a resigned look. 'Sure,' he said.

Chris smiled engagingly. 'I think you went down quite well. Really nice.'

'Thanks.'

'So listen. Drop in in a couple of days and we'll talk about another gig. OK?'

'Yeah, OK.' He paused. 'Thanks a lot, Chris.'

'It's OK. See you fellers.' Chris gave a cheery wave, then he departed with Big John at his side.

Once they had gone, Barry turned to his band. 'What a stitch-up,' he said.

It was the end of a sweaty evening. The record faded out, the lights went up and the disco suddenly became its barren and tawdry self. Almost instantly the bars were shuttered, glasses were gathered in and ashtrays emptied. On the PA a voice, originally welcoming and full of bonhomie, snarled. 'OK, we're closing the club now. That's all for tonight.'

Most customers took the hint and began to depart, but one remained disgruntled: for young Alan had suddenly realised that not only was the disco finished, but his glass had gone and with it, a double Bacardi and Coke.

'It doesn't matter, Alan,' said his girl-friend when Alan began to protest.

'Doesn't matter? You're kidding, I've just lost a full Bacardi and Coke.' He turned to the massive bulk of Big John who was chivvying the punters out as quickly as he could. 'Excuse me. I had a full drink there. They seem to have taken it away.' He was polite, but forceful.

'Well, we're closed, ain't we? We're not an all-night bloody drinking club.'

'But I hadn't even touched that drink.'

Big John jabbed a finger into the boy's ribs. 'Shut up and get out.'

'Listen,' he said reasonably, 'I had –'

But this seemed enough provocation for Big John to grab him by the shirt front. 'You trying to make trouble?'

'I'm going to complain about you,' said Alan indignantly. 'Take your hands off me.' He tried to push Big John away – a fatal move for Big John immediately slammed him against the wall.

'Cheeky sod,' said Big John. Then, as Alan rebounded from the wall, he punched him in the face and blood burst from the boy's nose. The girl-friend screamed as Big John piled into Alan again. Two of their friends watched in horror, but made no move to interfere as Alan's girl-friend continued to scream her head off.

'Come on the lot of you . . . out of it,' said Big John as he half dragged, half carried Alan to a side exit, while his girl-friend yelled:

'I'm going to report you to the police.'

'Shut up, you little slag, and get out.' He favoured her with a particularly brutal grin as he shoved her through the exit and slammed the door. Glaring round at any other customers who might be loitering, he saw Terry, who, drawn by the commotion, had arrived on the scene and was cynically watching Big John.

'You was a big help.'

'Well, they didn't exactly seem like the Wild Bunch, did they?' he said drily. 'Now who do I see about getting paid out?'

'Me.'

'Well?'

Big John pulled a wad of notes from his pocket, peeled off two fivers and handed them to Terry.

'It's three of them innit?'

'Tenner.'

Terry came a little closer to Big John who, despite his size, looked wary. 'Plus five for the VAT,' he said.

'Now look, pal –'

Terry came a little closer. 'Never mind "look". Mate of mine asked me to stand in for him. Three fivers – that's what he said and that's what I walk out of here with. OK?'

There was something about Terry's quiet confidence that worried Big John. Grumbling, he extracted a grimy looking fiver. 'And tell your pal, if he can't make it any more, *I'll* find a deputy.'

'With the money you're paying you'll probably get Muhammad Ali. Tara, chief,' said Terry as he headed for the door.

Big John watched him go, mentally marking him down.

Terry sat beside Arthur as he drove his Jag slowly through the crowded streets. He seemed to have recovered something of his optimism – always a sign to Terry of impending trouble.

'You will get yourself involved in these dopey jobs.'

Terry had just been giving Arthur a dour account of last night's action at the disco.

'Dennis wanted a night off.'

'He's going to have two years off,' said Arthur complacently.

'Eh?'

'Didn't you see the papers? There were four of 'em. They thought they'd had it away with a Belgian juggernaut and there were six Old Bill sitting in the back.' Arthur paused. 'Your name was up for that an' all.'

'That's nice.'

'I told 'em. Not my Terry. He don't want to know about pickaxe handles and shooters – not him.'

Arthur turned the Jag into a mews that had arches running below a railway line. Most of them were filled with workshops and small warehouses – all of which were grubby and run-down.

Arthur slowed the Jag down and said, ' "Not that we've joined the other side," I said. "All we've done is like Sweden in the war – we've declared our neutrality." ' Then he braked sharply. 'Blimey.'

Parked across the mews was a police Rover 3500 with a uniformed constable standing by the car. Examining the doors to a lock-up storeroom was a plain-clothed detective who looked all too familiar.

Terry turned to Arthur. 'What have you been up to, Arthur?'

'Shtum, Terry. Very, very shtum.'

Arthur got slowly out of the car and approached his old friend, Detective Sergeant Chisholm, who smiled up at Arthur in the friendliest manner. 'I never knew this was your gaff, Arthur?'

'I never said it was. Something the matter, Mister Chisholm?'

'We've got no record of you as landlord, tenant or registered key holder,' he said, ignoring Arthur's badly concealed irritation.

'What's the problem?'

'You've had the burglars round – that's the problem.' He chuckled slightly.

Arthur stared at the door. It was double padlocked, but the hasp for one of the padlocks had been severed.

'Catch 'em?'

Chisholm grinned and shook his head. 'Patrol car spotted 'em. But we're not sure ... were they coming out, or still trying to get in? It *is* your place, is it?'

'Sort of,' said Arthur cagily.

'Well, let's have a look inside and we'll see if they got away with anything –'

'I don't think that's necessary,' said Arthur very quickly as Chisholm gave him a knowing look.

'What've you got in there, Arthur?'

He shrugged as if to diminish Chisholm's interest. But he only served to increase it. 'Odds and ends. Very nice of you fellers taking an interest. I'll let you know if there's anything missing.'

Arthur made no move to open the padlock and Chisholm waited patiently, but determinedly. 'We'll just have a peek, Arthur.'

'I'll take an inventory,' said Arthur. 'Don't bother yourself, Mr Chisholm.'

Finally, and regretfully, Chisholm realised he was getting nowhere with Arthur – for the moment, at least.

'I wonder what they'd be after, Arthur?' he asked ruminatively.

'Gawd knows, Mister Chisholm. Probably just kids. You know what the younger generation is like nowadays.'

'I still think we should have a look though.' He was trying again for the last time.

Arthur gave him a reassuring grin. 'Normally, I wouldn't mind, Mister Chisholm. But the place is such a mess.'

There was a long pause, at the end of which, Chisholm said dryly, 'All right, Arthur.' He turned away regretfully, walked to the car and then glanced back at Arthur. 'You'll be well insured, I suppose?'

'No worries.'

'The Royal?'

'No.' He pointed to Terry. 'Himself.'

Terry was leaning against Arthur's car and he gave Chisholm a pleasant nod.

'Just remember, Arthur, if you're going away for the weekend, don't forget to inform your local police station,' said Chisholm.

Terry smiled and muttered to him, 'Then you're a certainty to get your gaff turned over. See you, Mister Chisholm.' Terry joined Arthur as they watched Detective Sergeant Chisholm get into the car. As he did so, a man in overalls in the workshop next door, quickly slipped a pile of car number plates under some rubbish. The visit had been unwelcome all round.

Arthur watched the police car leave the mews. He took a key ring from his pocket and inserted it into the undamaged padlock. 'No wonder Sir Keith Joseph's always on about law 'n' order, Terry. Everywhere you go there's tea-leafs.' He opened the door and stepped into the darkness.

Arthur switched on the light, illuminating an Aladdin's cave of treasures, all of which he regarded as highly saleable commodities. One wall was stacked high with unopened cases of Smirnoff vodka, another with TV sets, transistor radios, washing machines. There were three clothes rails with Oscar Jacobson suits and neatly packaged shirts were in piles on the floor. A stack of books in one corner and a display rack of ties completed the range.

Arthur beamed at Terry, anticipating compliments. But he did not receive any. 'You're at the long firm again,' said Terry.

'What're you talking about? I paid for all this lot.' He looked very offended.

'Bent gear. You're going to get us nicked again.'

'Terry, this is all strictly kosher.'

'Then why didn't you want the law to have a look?'

For a moment, just a brief moment, Arthur looked a trifle

61

uncomfortable. 'Cos it's nothing to do with them, that's why. Do you think they have the law nosing around every five minutes at Harrods?'

Terry sighed deeply, not believing Arthur for one moment. Morosely, he glanced round at the merchandise.

'Nice suits,' said Arthur encouragingly. 'Swedish. You like a nice Oscar Jacobson, don't you?' He selected a suit from the rail, slipped the jacket from the hanger and offered it to Terry. 'That's about your size.'

Despite himself, Terry tried on the jacket.

'Nice. Hundred and thirty in the shops. You look the business in that, son. No problem.'

'Good cut,' Terry said grudgingly.

'Yeah – you can have that one for seventy.'

'How much?' asked Terry looking shocked.

'All right. Give us fifty then,' compromised Arthur.

'Bent gear –'

'Terry, on my landlord's life. The whole lot is straight,' said Arthur vehemently. 'I got bills of sale, receipts – everything.'

'Where?'

'The feller's bringing them round. All I done was buy a job lot and the container burst –' Arthur's explanation was a trifle rapid.

Terry was silent and Arthur said, 'Obviously, it's all export stuff.'

'Export!' He examined the jacket. 'These are *from* Sweden.'

'Exports and imports. That's what I mean. What about these then?' With a sense of triumph he flourished a book from the stack in the corner. 'Five hundred digest versions of *Great Expectations* by Charles bleeding Dickens. You can't say *they're* Swedish, can you?'

Terry gazed at him thoughtfully and then gave up, giving Arthur the opportunity to briskly start the next move.

'Now, what we got to do is to think about shifting it all and getting some better locks for that door.' He sat down on a pile of shirts. 'And then,' he said, 'we've got to work out who sussed the gear was here and tried to get in.'

Terry was trying on another jacket. 'Course it wouldn't be

a few pals of the bloke you bought it from?' asked Terry innocently.

'It might be,' said Arthur with sudden, surprising honesty. 'That's why we've got to start clearing it, fast.'

An hour later, Arthur's Jag pulled up outside a large pub. Arthur then lifted out two cases of Smirnoff and stacked them in Terry's arms. 'I'm knocking these out for two pounds a bottle. That's about right, isn't it?'

'You go in tonight and have three doubles and you'll 've bought one back. How about that?' He went over to the pub, pushed the door with his foot and went inside.

Meanwhile, the true impact of Terry's remark dawned on Arthur. 'Bloody publicans. Three weeks and I'll be out of pocket.'

Inside the large music lounge just off the main bar of the pub, Freddie, the landlord, was sitting at a table listening to a girl singer accompanied by a pianist. He was looking pained, for although the girl was young and attractive, her singing was atrocious. The pianist was labouring not only to keep in time with her but also to keep in the same key. Sitting beside Freddie was the girl's boy-friend and agent, a little hustler in his mid-twenties. He was whispering:

'She's into nostalgia . . . see.'

'Yeah,' said Freddie.

Meanwhile, Terry was stacking the Smirnoff boxes by the bar, almost unable to believe how badly she was murdering the 'sixties ballad. Then Arthur appeared behind him, carrying the last of the boxes.

'Good way to close a pub, innit?' said Terry.

But there was no immediate response from Arthur and when Terry glanced at him, he saw Arthur was transfixed.

'Now that's what I call a song, Terry.'

'Eh?'

'And a knock-out bird an' all.'

'Not exactly a Capital chart-climber, is it?'

'Don't tell me you know about music for gawd's sake,' said Arthur. 'That was . . . erm . . . 1965 if I remember correctly.

Liz Taylor and what's-'is-name – the Welsh feller in the film.'

'Sixty-five?'

'Yes – the year Cassius Clay changed his name after dumping Liston in one minute of the first. I can't be faulted on my history,' he said sanctimoniously.

'Same year I dumped big Keith Perkins,' said Terry brightly.

'Who?'

'Top man at Burston Road Secondary Mod. He was good at history an' all.'

As they spoke the singer laboured to the end of the song, dragging the last word out for several beats too many. There was silence while she smiled hopefully in the direction of Freddie. Until she heard solitary clapping.

It was Arthur, beaming and unperturbed by the general lack of enthusiasm around him. 'Beautiful, knock out!' he exclaimed.

The girl have him a quick, nervous smile. 'Ta.'

Freddie shot a glance at Arthur. Then his jaundiced gaze returned to the girl. 'Well, darling, we're basically a rock and roll pub. So . . . er . . .'

'So you don't want to know . . . You're all the bloody same you lot . . .' She sounded tearful as she fled from the stage.

'Oi,' said Arthur, starting up after the girl, and laying a restraining hand on her agent's arm. 'Leave it to me, son . . .' He brushed past him and hurried after the girl into the street. 'Just a minute, luv,' he yelled.

The girl hesitated as Arthur puffed his way alongside her.

'What's your name, love?'

'Sharon – but I'm not free.'

'I thought you were.'

'Now look, sunshine –' She tried to make off again but Arthur added:

'Musically speaking, I mean.'

'Eh?' She paused again.

'Don't let that lot upset you.'

'They don't appreciate nothing good them sort.'

'Course they don't,' said Arthur reassuringly. 'But it's only a boozer, isn't it? I mean, Friday night it's full of yobboes. Your style's more some West End nighterie. Know what I mean?'

'Yeah, well that's what I think too,' she said and began to cry.

Arthur pulled out his silk handkerchief. 'Now, come on, why don't you dry them little tears. Got a motor?'

She shook her head.

'Then I'd better give you a lift home, eh, Sharon?'

Sharon spotted Arthur's Jag and was suitably impressed. With a quick smile, she nodded, dabbing at her cheeks with Arthur's hankie.

'Nice hankie.'

'Pure silk, innit? Got a couple of dozen of them indoors. Just to match all the different suits.'

Arthur gallantly walked round and opened the passenger door for Sharon. Twirling his keys, he walked round to the driver's side. Showbiz suddenly had its appeal.

Driving Sharon down the Fulham Road in his Jag, Arthur gave her a brief grin and received a coy smile in return.

'Are you in the business then?' she asked.

'I'm Arthur Daley.'

But although Arthur was hoping for instant recognition, he didn't get it.

'I'm Sharon Nightingale – not my real name of course.'

'What, Sharon?'

'No,' she giggled, 'Nightingale, but it sounds better than Dobbs anyway. But I thought you must be in the business, being so appreciative and all.'

Arthur spoke in a slow measured tone. 'I've got a lot of contacts in the – er – business, Sharon. Clubs and hotels mainly. I was having a drink with Jimmy Saville the other night at a little charity dinner we was at. Contacts is the name of the game, Sharon.'

'I know,' she said rather dolefully.

'So I could probably be a great help to you in your career.'

She nodded uncomprehendingly and Arthur, noting her

puzzled expression, tried for clarification. 'You need the right promotion,' he said. 'Proper handling –'

'That's what I think.'

'Married?'

'No.'

'Feller in the pub with you? Boy-friend?'

'Nothing like that. He wants to be an agent. He went to Pitman's Business College and everything.'

'That's nice.'

Then Sharon gasped. 'D'you see that?'

'What?' He instinctively braked.

'In that shop window. A really nice dress. Beautiful I mean.'

'Blimey. I thought you was witness to a robbery or something.'

'You couldn't stop – just so I could have a look, could you?' she asked.

'Course I could,' said Arthur gallantly, putting the car into reverse. There was some impatient horn-blowing from a car behind as the driver swerved wildly to avoid the Jag, but Arthur was quite impervious to it all. 'And you, china,' he said as the driver sped past him, giving him a generous measure of words and gestures.

Looking from the car into the window, Arthur sought the price tag and found it – a mere £120.

'It's like you said, Arthur,' said Sharon. 'Presentation is everything in this game, isn't it?'

'Course it is. Look at the gear that Shirley Bassey wears,' he said unconcernedly. 'It'd look beautiful. Why don't you try it on?'

'Oh, Arthur, should I?'

'When you're with Arthur Daley, sweetheart, it's cabaret time. Live a little . . . eh?'

But Arthur wore an expression of resignation as he helped Sharon out of the car.

Terry was underneath the arches at work on the doors of the lock-up, fixing a massive padlock on the inside. He glanced up as Arthur's Jag drove down the mews.

'Long lie-in?' asked Terry cheerily as Arthur got out.

'Some chance of that with 'er indoors 'oovering round the bed. I didn't get in till gone four.'

'Dear oh dear – not the singing scrubber?'

'What d'you call her?' He looked outraged.

'Sorry,' said Terry quickly.

'That is a very special young lady, Terence.'

'And what's her speciality?'

Arthur frowned. 'That's all you would understand – something like that. She's just a nice girl and good company at that.' He walked into the storeroom followed by Terry. There he began to examine a large pile of jeans.

'What else has she got?' persisted Terry.

'Enormous talent.'

Terry gave Arthur an old-fashioned look. 'I thought you was going to say something else for a minute.'

'You would do. I thought Jackie Strong was coming for these jeans.'

'He was and he did. But then he said those jeans with the famous label were made in Albania and'd last about two weeks. He has his reputation to think of. His reputation as an honest trader down the market – or so he says.'

'He was selling Christian Dior perfume the other week made by a little Paki in his council flat kitchen by QPR stadium, no less,' said Arthur sourly.

'You was talking about "talent",' said Terry hurriedly changing the subject.

Arthur turned on him, his eyes gleaming. 'That girl is going to be a superstar. As her manager, I'll give it two years before we'll be tax havening it in the Cayman Islands.' He sounded very confident.

'You got more chance of caravanning.it down on Canvey Island,' said Terry realistically.

'You know what you know? Nothing,' said Arthur sweetly. 'What you forget is I've still got a few friends in clubland. A few favours still outstanding. So I'm going to start making a few calls.'

'Like where?'

'Top places – like the Blue Gardenia.'

'The *what?*'

' "The what?" he says.' Arthur gave Terry a deeply patronising glance. 'Only one of the most exclusive nighteries in the West End. Jermyn Street. You know where that is, don't you?'

'Arthur –'

'They have top Americans in the cabaret.'

'Arthur –'

'It's the haunt of royalty.'

'Arthur –' said Terry yet again, determined to interrupt.

'Yes,' said Arthur wearily.

'They closed that in the swinging 'sixties.'

Arthur looked dumbfounded.

'And all the other places like it.'

'The Golden Bangle –' said Arthur desperately. 'There was a lavish floorshow there.'

'Yeah, well the lavish floorshow now consists of a geezer putting on records and debs and rock stars eating hamburgers and chips.'

'All those beautiful places,' he reflected nostalgically.

'Yeah, and we lost India an' all.' Terry was not sympathetic.

'Don't wind me up on history,' said Arthur irritably.

'Sorry.'

'See, I don't do the West End much these days.'

'No,' commented Terry bleakly.

'Well, how do they make it then? All these kids . . . Top of the Pops and all that?' Arthur's voice took on a strident note.

'How would I know?'

'The place you was working in the other night. That was music, wasn't it?'

'So they said. I suppose all the groups start in pubs like that,' said Terry vaguely.

Arthur rose up in a brisk and business-like manner. 'All right. What's the guy's name? The head man?'

'How do I know? I was on the subs' bench for a bouncer.'

68

'You should make it a point to *know*,' said Arthur reprovingly. 'That's how you get on in the world.' He started for the door, but Terry was anxious to detain him.

'What am I supposed to be doing now?'

'Sorting out all them metric sizes into the approximate English equivalent.'

'Eh?'

Arthur paused, tapping his forehead. 'Think about it. Give them muscles up there a chance of a workout.' With a brief smile, Arthur disappeared, leaving Terry cursing behind him.

At the disco, the sound system was being tested and balanced. As a result, strange noises darted from various areas of the building and there was an occasional burst of recorded music.

Meanwhile, a couple of cleaners were at work – one pushing a jumbo size vacuum cleaner and the other wiping tables and chairs. All this activity tended to emphasise the tattiness of the sordid, evil-smelling cavern.

Big John led Arthur across the deserted auditorium. As he walked, Arthur gazed about him sceptically. There was no doubt about it – this was a far cry from Jermyn Street and nightingales singing in Berkeley Square.

As if sensing his mood, Big John said, 'When you get five hundred screaming kids in here and all the psychedelic lights are going it all looks a bit different.'

'Glad to hear it,' said Arthur addressing the bulk of Big John's rear quarters. He flinched as a particularly dreadful noise screeched from one of the mammoth loudspeakers. Then they headed towards a staircase and Arthur was ushered into Chris's office.

Autographed photographs of pop stars past and present were on the walls whilst executive toys littered the desk. Behind the vast polished surface sat Chris. His shirt was open almost to the waist and a St Christopher medallion dangled on his chest.

Arthur sat himself down in front of the desk, whilst Big

John lurked in the background.

'You probably know my name well enough. Arthur Daley.'

Chris didn't even bother to look up and began to play with one of his executive toys. 'Can't say I do really,' he said carelessly.

'Little bit out of my manor really. But I've got this fantastic girl singer.'

'Mebbe you should let me decide that –'

'What?'

'Whether she's very good. Got a demo?'

'Eh?'

'Cassette.'

'Just take my word for it.'

Chris continued to fiddle with his toy. Then he glanced up, showing Arthur the stainless steel magnetic gadget. 'They copulate, see. Like a praying mantis, only she don't turn round and eat him. Now, what exactly is the deal, Mister Daley?'

'I'd like her to go on here, so a few people can hear her. She ought to have a good band and all that.'

'Got it. Got it. You're talking about you paying us – not us paying you?'

'Mebbe I am. Depends, dunnit?'

'What on?'

'Your offer.' He was annoyed at Chris's offhand attitude and was beginning to show it. 'You get that toy for Christmas?' Arthur asked with an edge to his voice.

'Friend of mine – got to number five in the charts.'

'We get a lot of presents,' said Big John complacently.

'Only way to do business, isn't it?' replied Arthur confidently. 'Favours done – presents given. Then everybody's happy.'

Chris spun one of the stainless steel gadgets. 'OK,' he said in a brisk voice. 'You want the record companies here, you want booking agents, television, the musical press people. That takes a lot of arranging, you know. There are phone calls, drinks – that kind of thing.'

'All of that,' said Arthur vaguely.

70

'You'll need backing from top musicians, so that'll be three hundred for a start. Then there's my time, my staff's time, all the arrangements, the hassles, my reputation and joint management if I like her –' He paused for breath.

'Well, what does it add up to?' Arthur asked in a voice of doom.

'Six readies.'

'Well –' said Arthur beginning to try and beat him down. But Chris was quick to prevent him.

'No arguments, no haggling. Six hundred up front or that's it.' He paused. 'If she *is* a good chick singer you could end up making a fortune. It's the year of the chicks, everybody's saying that.'

Arthur forced a grandiose smile. 'Why else would I be interested? A man of my experience?'

That night found Arthur locked in a passionate clinch with Sharon in the front of his Jag. After a while, she gently disengaged herself.

'I'd better go now, Arthur.'

'Don't I get a cup of coffee?'

They were parked outside a house in a part of the Fulham Road that was still not classy.

'Oh, I'd really like to – but it's the other girls –'

'All right, darling, I understand. We'll soon have you out of this place, anyway.' He spoke confidently.

Sharon opened her eyes wide. 'Arthur, you've been so wonderful to me.'

'It's nothing,' he replied modestly.

'I mean – that Chinese meal. I never had nothing like that before.'

'Well, they know I like a good King Prawn in there.'

'And then going on to the Music Box. I mean that is really, really unbelievable.'

'Well – I told you – I'm well known, respected. You'll most likely end up with a record contract.' He adjusted his tie casually.

'No,' she gasped.

'Well, I've got a lot of record people coming down . . . most of them are personal acquaintances . . .'

Sharon threw her arms round him. 'Oh, Arthur –'

'When we get things sorted out, maybe we'll slip away for a few days. Been to Marbella?'

'It's all racing drivers down there, isn't it?'

'Sure – course, I know a few of them and all. James Hunt and Nicky what's-is-name.'

There was a short silence, then Sharon said, 'You know what we were saying earlier – 'bout the difference in ages and everything?'

'Yeah?' asked Arthur cautiously.

'I don't think it matters. I mean, all the stars do it, don't they? It's like they need a more mature man.'

'And you are a star, my darling,' said Arthur romantically sliding towards her. Quickly, Sharon gave him a peck on the cheek. Her hand was on the door handle.

'You won't get into trouble or nothing?'

'Sorry?'

'At home, I mean.'

A mental picture of 'er indoors swam into Arthur's mind. 'Sharon, my darling, I told you . . .' he said. 'I know how to handle everything.'

'That's good, Arthur,' she said as she slipped hurriedly out of the car.

Terry was in bed asleep when Arthur knocked on the door. He stirred, Arthur knocked again and Terry tumbled out of bed. He hitched on his Y-fronts and went to the door.

'Yeah?'

'Me.'

Wearily, Terry opened the door, switched on the light and admitted Arthur.

'What time is it?' asked Terry yawning.

Arthur glanced round the flat, taking in the fact that the place had not been cleaned for some time. He wrinkled his nose in disgust. 'Gawd almighty, you live in this filth? It's a quarter to five.'

72

'Late night or an early start?'

Terry went back to his bed and curled up, wishing that Arthur was just a nasty dream. But he wasn't – he was for real.

' 'Er indoors only locked me out, hasn't she?'

'Thought you had her well trained?'

'I gave Sharon a bell from home – must have been ear-molling on the extension.'

'Yeah, I seen the movie.'

Arthur scowled at Terry and brushed a few newspapers off the couch. 'Well, don't I get a cup of tea or nothing?'

'Only if you brought your own tea-bag.'

Arthur took off his jacket. 'You got a duvet or something?'

'There's a tartan travelling rug in the airing cupboard.'

'Where's that?'

'In the kitchen under the shelf with the marmalade.'

'Gawd. This is a carsie.'

Terry said sleepily, burying his head under the blankets, 'Next to the kitchen . . .'

Arthur scowled, went through to the kitchen and looked around for the rug, opening cupboards and making a great deal of noise.

'Simon come about those jeans?' asked Arthur poking his head into the bedroom area.

Terry was silent.

'Hey,' Arthur repeated loudly, 'Simon come about –'

Terry sat up, annoyed. 'Course he bloody well did. Said they was Albanian and also pointed out you spell Levi with an I not a Y.'

Arthur came back into the room, shaking the tartan rug.

'What they all got against Albania? They was on our side during the war.' He looked at the rug in horror. 'Hey, this has got stuff all over it.'

'I burst a bag of wheat germ over it.'

'Got every other kind of bleeding germ as well,' he muttered, taking off his trousers, folding them neatly and putting them over the back of the sofa. Then he sat down heavily. 'I might get a flat with that Sharon,' he pronounced.

'Hallo, young lovers wherever you are,' yawned Terry. 'Anyway, you been married twenty-eight years,' he said.

'Well – she got her cards tonight. I told her.'

'Thought she locked you out.'

'She did. I shouted through the letter box.' Arthur tried to settle on the sofa. 'This cushion could do with a visit to Sketchley's and all.'

But there was no response from Terry.

'Hey!'

'What?'

'Get me up at quarter to eight.'

'What for?'

'Well, I've got to get the kids to school, haven't I,' said Arthur petulantly.

'Oh yeah – I forgot that.'

'Forgot what?'

'If they don't turn up in a Jag, they get expelled, don't they?' Terry pulled the hanging light switch. 'Now, Arthur, why don't you get some kip?'

Well before the disco opened for business, Sharon was on stage with Barry's group. Whilst she waited, they were having a blow and producing some excellent rock and jazz.

But Sharon thought they were never going to end and when they eventually did, she wasn't in the best of moods.

'I don't suppose there would be the slightest chance of us rehearsing one of *my* numbers now, would there?'

Barry, the leader and keyboard-player, glanced up. 'Oh, sorry love. What d'you want to do?'

' "Who Can I Turn To?" ' she said flatly.

Barry paused. Clearly, he was not very familiar with the tune. 'Yeah – well, what key?' he asked vaguely.

'Well, I don't know, do I? You're the one who's supposed to know about things like that.'

'It's this one, isn't it?' He picked out the melody with one finger.

'Yeah, but it's too high – and I do it very slow.'

Barry stared at the keys for some time. Then he said,

'Okay – as the man said – you try it and we'll follow you.'

But already the lead guitar player was muttering, 'I won't. I've never even heard of it.'

Meanwhile, Arthur, looking much smarter than usual, was propping up the bar of the Winchester. Terry stood disconsolately beside him.

'What do you mean, "you don't fancy it"?' snapped Arthur.

'Well, it's not my scene is it? I don't like that kind of music.'

'Terence – have you forgotten I am launching a star?'

'Yeah, but you're not going to get riots down there, are you? You'll be doing all the glad-handling and that. There's no need for me.'

'I thought you might want to share in a moment of triumph,' said Arthur huffily.

Terry protested. 'I'm saying good luck and everything. But I've been doing that metrication all day – and I've got a meet with a bird at nine.'

'So bring her down.'

'I promised her a Greek meal.'

'So have a quick doner kebab and chips and bring her down.'

'She's into soul music. Look – I'll see how it goes.'

'Very considerate of you.'

Terry lowered his voice. 'By the way – the sofa tonight – probably not on. Know what I mean?'

'Did I ask?'

'No. But –'

'Hotels all over the place, y'know.'

'T'riffic. No problem.'

Arthur sipped his drink meditatively. 'And might I enquire – who is this little creature who makes you forsake your friends?'

Terry gave a modest shrug. 'Air hostess.'

'Oh, not the little blonde number?'

'Yeah.'

'Oh well, she's not exactly jet set, is she? Not – "I'm Penny . . . fly me to Dallas, Texas".' Arthur was enjoying being condescending, whilst secretly worrying where he was going to lay his head for the night if 'er indoors shut him out again.

'No. Her name's Rita and she's on the London-Manchester shuttle service.'

'She don't exactly need to be fluent in three languages for that, does she?' Arthur said sarcastically.

'No. But at least she don't sing,' said Terry quickly.

'Thank you, Terence,' replied Arthur. 'It's good to know who your friends are. Particularly when you need a little support.'

As Sharon wavered her way through "Who Can I Turn To", Arthur prowled the balcony area of the disco impatiently. She was wearing his dress and it was this additional expense, on top of everything else, that made him worried for there were only a dozen or so patrons in the whole place. Finally, Arthur went to the bar.

'Vodka and Slimline and where's all the people?'

'Monday night, innit. Anyway, most nights they don't come in till the boozers close,' said the barman.

Suddenly, Arthur spotted Big John. 'Oi.'

'Yeah?'

'Where are they?'

'Dunno.'

'The faces, the record producers – the guests?'

'Didn't show.'

He walked away, while Arthur glanced dismally over the balcony as Sharon finished her song – to no applause whatsoever. Arthur, outraged, turned to hear a young bloke say:

'They'll be doing Come Dancing next week . . .'

Arthur returned to the bar where his drink was waiting. 'Stick another vodka in there,' he told the barman desperately as Sharon said into the mike:

'Now I'd like to do a beautiful love song called "Shadow Of Your Smile".'

Barry turned to the band, glad that he could recognise the

76

tune. 'One and two and three and four . . .'

Raggedly and slightly apart – the band and Sharon began but then the worst happened and Sharon dried, whilst the band played on. She stared round the vast auditorium with its scattering of punters, tears running down her cheeks. For a moment Sharon stood there frozen, and then ran off the stage.

'Oh Gawd,' said Arthur, taking a long swig of vodka. He ran down the stairs whilst the DJ quickly spun a record and the disco filled with music that was clearly much more acceptable.

Once backstage, Arthur found Sharon sitting on a bench sobbing her heart out. Quickly, she put his arms round her.

'All right, darling – now don't you fret about anything.'

'They're pigs, Arthur . . . they're all pigs. They don't appreciate nothing,' she wept.

As Arthur tried to console her, Barry arrived.

'Sorry, Sharon, we just wasn't very much together.' He sounded genuinely apologetic, but Arthur was furious.

'You ought to get nicked with a band like that.'

'Wasn't our fault.' Barry was defensive now.

'Well, whose fault was it then?'

'She just hit a few bum notes.'

'Bum notes? Well, you're not exactly Mantovani, are you?'

'Who?'

' "Who?" he asks. Mantovani – a man who could play anything with a bloody big orchestra and all.'

'They're difficult sort of numbers for a group like ours.' He was once again apologetic and Arthur wagged an angry finger at him.

'Look – for three hundred a throw you should be able to get through the Warsaw Concerto –'

'For what?'

'Your bleeding fee,' said Arthur ungraciously.

Barry, however, looked totally bewildered. 'We got twenty-five quid between us and that's a fiver more than we got last time.'

Arthur stared at him, unbelieving. 'What'd you say?'

'Twenty-five.'

Arthur took out his silk handkerchief and threw it at Barry imperiously. As he hurried towards the stairs, he shouted, 'Dry her tears.'

Arthur was very much out of breath as he flung open Chris's office door and stood panting on the threshold. Chris was behind his big executive desk, with Big John sitting on the sofa. Both had large drinks in their hands as they stared at the enraged Arthur, who said in a measured voice, 'You've turned me over, you –' He advanced a few tottering paces.

'Just calm down, Mister Daley,' said Chris casually.

'Calm down? Six hundred you've had off me –'

'She went on. She went off. Not my fault.' He shrugged as if to finalise the whole business.

'And the people? All the celebs? The record producers?' Arthur's voice spluttered and died away as he leant on the desk for support, badly out of breath.

'They didn't show. Invites, telephone calls. Did I try my best, John?'

'Fingers to the bone, we worked,' said Big John grinning.

'You're lying.'

'That's nice,' said Big John.

'I want my dough back,' yelled Arthur.

Chris spoke slowly and carefully. 'All I can suggest is that you put the matter in the hands of your legal advisers.'

'I don't have legal advisers. I have people who come round and punch your head in,' said Arthur threateningly.

Slowly, Big John levered himself up from the sofa and placed a meaty hand on Arthur's shoulder. 'Mister Daley. That is a very nasty threat –'

'Made in front of witnesses,' said Chris officiously. 'Perhaps you'd show Mister Daley to the door, John?'

Big John squeezed Arthur's elbow with less than loving concern.

'That is a two hundred pounds suit,' protested Arthur.

'Then we don't want to get it all messed up, do we?' replied Big John, still holding Arthur's elbow, now in a grip of iron.

'You don't know me, do you?' said Arthur with attempted dignity.

'We have heard the name,' replied Chris reflectively. 'What was that old election slogan? "Yesterday's people." That's the trouble, Mister Daley – times change. See you, eh?'

Big John led Arthur to the door and it was only when he was in the corridor that Arthur found the strength to say, 'Up yours.' But by that time the office door was closed and, anyway, Arthur's voice was very soft.

Terry was sorting out some shirts in the lock-up next morning, trying to arrange them in neat piles. From time to time he jotted down a calculation in a notebook.

'So that's . . . one inch equals two and a half centimetres and a bit. And that's two and a half into forty is . . . erm . . .' he was saying somewhat desperately to himself as an enraged Arthur blew in. 'I think I cracked this metrication –'

'Yeah? Well, forget it.'

'What? After all –'

'They had me over, Terry.'

Terry's indignation turned to smiles. 'No Stars on Sunday?'

'That Chris is going to be seeing a few stars.' He glanced at one of the shirts. 'Forty – that's a seventeen collar, near enough.'

'Oh, nice –' said Terry, 'I thought it was the chest size.'

But Arthur's anger continued to mount as he recalled the humiliating events of the previous evening. 'They tucked me up very nice with a bleeding awful band. As to producers and record execs – they had about ten squatters in the place sharing a half pint of shandy between them.'

'That's show business, Arthur.'

'That's a diabolical business. Six hundred sovs. That little flash Chris stole my money. And that, my son, is a crime – a liberty. So you forget about metrication and go down there and give him a pull.'

'Get the money back?'

'Right.'

'And suppose he don't want to pay?'

'Then he gets a spank. And he keeps getting spanked till he does want to pay.'

'Hmm,' said Terry derisively.

'What d'you mean "hmm"?'

'I mean them days are over.'

'What?'

'Putting the frighteners on people. Doing favours for guys. Collecting bad gambling debts – it's all gone, like the Blue Gardenia.'

'What do you mean – gambling debts! This man *stole* from me.'

'He ripped you off – and that's *your* game. How many mug punters have you had over? You thought you was on a good thing with Fulham's answer to Tina Turner and you backed a loser. All right – tough.'

'He threatened me.'

'What was he going to do? Hit you with his silver bracelet?'

Arthur shook his head and walked restlessly round the storeroom, occasionally shooting an angry glance at Terry. 'This is marvellous, innit? I mean, you are supposed to mind out for me. And here I am with a genuine grievance and you don't want to know. How's that going to sound around the manor? What does that do for my image?'

'What image?'

'Listen, sunshine. I am a highly respected person –'

'And where would that be – "sunshine". A few afternoon drinking clubs? Car auctions? A few old villains with long memories?'

Arthur gave Terry a long, hurt look. 'I don't know what's got into you. I mean, have I done you a favour or three?'

'Four even.'

'Looked after your Mum when you were away?'

'Sure.'

'Dropped round with a few prezzies?'

'Nice set of dralon curtains as advertised on Police Five – she wouldn't be without them.'

Arthur gave Terry a tolerant smile. 'Set you up when you came out?'

'You're getting there, Arthur. Now you're setting me up to go back inside.'

'I'm asking you to return a few favours,' said Arthur patiently.

'I'm doing that right now – in metric an' all.' He waved a shirt under Arthur's nose. 'What's a thirty-six?'

'Fifteen, fifteen and a half – I dunno. Won't do your reputation any good either.'

'Well it might do with the prison after-care service.'

'I am not asking you to go and shoot the geezer. Just a bit of friendly retribution.'

'That's not my game and you know it, Arthur.'

'Well, what is, I wonder?' He put in unpleasantly. 'Certainly not conversion tables. The man has nicked six hundred out of my pocket and what you're saying is I should stand for that, eh?'

Terry scowled as he tossed a bundle of shirts across the table. 'No, I'm not.'

'Well, what then?'

'I dunno. Solicitor's letter. I mean, six hundred – that's high finance, innit?'

Arthur was so disgusted that he lit a Panatella. 'Just sussed it – bottle job. That it? Happens. You've said it yourself in the past – "always going to be somebody better". Now it has come to pass,' Arthur paused for effect. 'That Chris is well protected so you've made your decision. Swallowed it.'

'Look.' Terry held up his hand. 'Trembling, eh? The guy he's got down there – I'd have him over in ten seconds, including the count.'

'Course you would,' replied Arthur, pausing for effect. 'Then you give that little Chris a whack and walk out with the money – and you get a nice drink out of it.'

'And Chris calls the Old Bill and I'm up on assault, demanding money with menaces. Haven't you got it yet, Arthur? I'm not doing it. End of message . . . right?' His tone was final, decisive and his message received a stony look from Arthur.

'Right – end of job and all.'

Terry looked at him for a moment, suddenly realising that, for once, Arthur meant what he was saying. 'Obviously, redundancy money is out of the question –' He pocketed the notebook and pen, but Arthur was too quick for him.

'My biro and notebook,' he said coldly.

Terry, headed for the door, flinging the biro and notebook in the direction of the workbench. 'Yeah – I'd hate to get caught ripping you off for a biro and a notebook. I mean – you might put a contract out on me.' He slammed the door behind him, leaving Arthur staring after him.

When a disgruntled, very upset Arthur phoned, Sharon was in bed with Barry. This, however, was something she did not confide in her impressario, as she put her finger to her lips whilst Arthur spoke reassuringly into the phone.

'Hallo, my love . . . how are you . . ?'

'As well as anyone could expect after last night,' she complained.

'Don't you worry about it. We'll get something together. Mebbe we'll have a bit of a meal tonight . . . eh?'

'Don't really know that I can tonight, Arthur –'

'Why not?'

'I was going to rehearse, see.'

'Where?'

'Not sure. You know Barry? The keyboard player.'

'Barry?'

'He's going to teach me all about chromatic scales and that.'

'But he was diabolical.'

Barry waved a clenched fist towards the phone, but Sharon again put her finger to her lips.

'No – he's good. He really is. And he's a good contact. See, last night wasn't his fault. Tell you what – can you phone me later? And I'll tell you where I'm going to be. You know – I'm thinking of doing a whole new act.'

'Whole new act? All right, my love, don't you worry. I'll call you later. Bye.'

'Byyyee.'

She hung up and turned back to Barry.

'He's a right creep,' said Barry.

'He's been like a dad to me,' reproved Sharon.

'More like a sugar-dad.' Barry took her in his arms.

Terry returned to his flat depressed, angry and equally as upset as Arthur at their parting. But once inside, he was amazed to find that the familiar tip had become a clean, sparkling little palace. Then with a rush of pleasure, Terry saw his air hostess girl-friend walking out of the kitchen.

'Thought you were working?' she said in the Northern accent that he loved.

'Penny, love – you do all this?' he said delightedly.

'Well, you can't say it didn't need it.'

'I think I'd better have you living in.' He took her in his arms.

After a while, she said, 'You're spoiling my uniform. I've got to look fresh and alluring for all those fellers who want to fly me to sun-drenched Manchester. Where have you been?'

'Having a row with Arthur,' said Terry, flopping into a chair.

Penny looked surprised. 'Your best friend? Great pal . . . man who's like a dad to you?'

'Yeah – well he wanted a favour that could land me back somewhere I haven't been for a good few years.'

'Then don't do it.' She gave him a quick kiss on the cheek. 'I'd miss you.'

Terry sighed. 'But a pal is a pal is a pal –' He broke off, staring into space.

'Somebody hurt him?'

'Only where he feels it most – in his pocket.'

'Look, pardon the expression, but I've got to fly. I've got three days off in eight days' time and I thought I'd spend it in London. We could have a lot of fun if you're not in Wormwood Scrubs. And I'll tell you another thing –'

83

'You love me, right?' asked Terry grinning.

'Yeah – but get some new bags for your vacuum cleaner.'

When she had gone, Terry leant back in the chair. After a moment he got up, glanced in the mirror and patted his hair.

'Know what you are, son? You're a right old charmer,' he said to himself.

Then Arthur's face swam into his mind and he winced.

In the Winchester Club that afternoon, Arthur was off-loading his troubles on to a sympathetic Dave.

'To tell you the truth, Arthur, I'm sorry to hear it,' Dave said.

'It happens,' Arthur replied gloomily. ' "Foresake not an old friend", as the good book has it. And that's what he's done.' Then he said quickly. 'Dave – I'm not asking you to take sides. All I'm saying is that if Terry'd been where he should've been it would never've happened. I was heavily outnumbered. Outgunned, you might say.'

Dave lowered his voice. 'They had shooters out?'

'Figuratively. I'll put it no stronger than that.'

The doorbell of the club rang and Dave turned to a slim, elderly man who sometimes acted as a helper. 'Get that, Jimmy.' Dave turned to Arthur. 'Squeeze another one in there, Arthur?'

Arthur's glass was full, but he quickly took a couple of sips. 'Why not?' he said recklessly.

Jimmy reappeared alone, looking worried. 'It's Vic Piner.'

'Well, just leave the door closed.'

'Says he's got a meet with Arthur –'

'Yeah, that's right.'

'Leave it out, Arthur,' said Dave sharply. 'The man's barred.'

'He'll be in my company. I'll vouch for him – all right?'

'You're joking.'

'We're going to discuss a little business.'

'Sorry. Not here. No offence to you, but the man has upset too many people. He don't come in and that's it.' Dave's voice, for once, was absolutely definite.

'Well, I'm certainly learning something about friends today,' he said bitterly. 'Cheers.' Arthur drained his glass and headed for the door. Behind him Dave raised his eyebrows at Jimmy. Arthur was in deep water.

Vic Piner leant against Arthur's Jag which was parked just outside the Winchester Club. Vic looked like what he was – a thug, a bully and a nutter. There was also an aura of evil about him which Arthur detected all too well.

'You're not all that popular, Vic.'

He became immediately aggressive. 'He slag me off, that Dave?'

'Take it easy,' said Arthur quickly. 'Just said you were barred. He cast no aspersions upon you in person. I think we'll have to have a cup of tea somewhere.'

Arthur got into his Jag, opened the passenger door for Vic and waited for the reaction.

'Tea?' asked Vic in a voice of awe.

'Well, are there any licensed premises in the manor where you're not barred?'

Vic shrugged and clambered into his seat. 'No,' he said.

'Wonder why?' asked Arthur innocently as he drove off.

'I get picked on a lot,' said Vic by way of explanation. 'People look at me and say "Who's he think he is?" So I tell 'em. My brother is the same. So you got to stand by 'em ain't you? I mean – family and all.'

'Oh yes,' remarked Arthur. 'The family's a very precious thing.'

'You want some geezer done over, do you?' Vic came straight to the point.

'Just persuaded to pay a little debt.'

'Drop by my brother's yard then,' said Vic invitingly.

Arthur hesitated. 'I don't think it needs the whole family Piner.'

But Vic seemed impatient to be family minded. 'It's only round the corner,' he said. 'Let's drop by.'

Apprehensively, knowing he was getting further and further into something he couldn't control, Arthur drove to the Piners' scrapyard. Then they both got out of the car, Arthur reluctantly, and began to walk towards a shed at the end of the yard.

Vic's brother, Henry, was bigger and more vicious looking than Vic – if that were possible.

'Henry,' said Vic enthusiastically. 'Show Arthur your collection.' Henry looked pleased and pushed a couple of cabinets aside to reveal a trapdoor. Opening it he displayed a collection of weapons which included bayonets, swords, two sawn-off shotguns and a couple of dockers' hoods. Vic reached down lovingly. 'That's an antique, innit – Austin Seven starting handle. And this –' he pulled at a gleaming bayonet – 'World War One that is,' said Vic in hallowed tones.

'I keep 'em nice,' remarked Henry, as if he was talking about a stamp collection.

'They – they all been used?' asked Arthur looking worried.

'Oh yeah. Like depending how much you want to hurt 'em,' Vic said in a matter of fact voice.

'Yeah, but any one of these things could kill somebody,' pursued Arthur, sweat breaking out on his brow.

'Easy,' replied Henry.

'I don't want anybody killed – just frightened a bit,' pleaded Arthur.

'Well – you tell him you're going to kill him, that'll frighten him, won't it?' said Vic logically.

'He only owes me six hundred.'

Vic paused. 'Let's say he only owes you three hundred now. See what I mean?'

Arthur gave Vic the bleakest of smiles for he could see only too well what he meant.

Whilst Arthur was getting into a situation he couldn't handle, Terry and Dave were having an urgent whispered conference in the Winchester.

'You don't tell him I told you though. You don't say I phoned. But that Vic – they wouldn't even fancy him in Broadmoor,' Dave told him.

86

'OK, but Arthur's over twenty-one. He's made his decision.'

'Terry – your old pal could be up on a murder conspiracy charge.'

There was a long silence during which Terry thought deeply. Then Terry said, 'You ought to've heard the birds sing an' all . . .'

Once Terry had made up his mind, he acted fast. Arriving at the disco entrance, he quickly looked up and down the street, hoping to see Arthur's Jag. But there was no sign. As Terry hesitated, Big John opened the disco doors and spotted him. He spoke ungraciously. 'What the hell do you want?'

'Anybody called to see you, guv'nor?'

'What's it to you?'

'What's it to *you* more like it –'

He brushed past Big John, who made a grab for him. But he neatly side-stepped and slammed Big John up against a wall.

'Now listen – I'm doing you a favour. You keep these doors shut, right, 'cause you've got a lot of trouble heading this way and you want to be well clear when it arrives. In other words – lock 'em.'

Such was the note of real urgency in Terry's voice that Big John hurriedly closed the doors.

'Where's what's-'is-name – Chris?'

'Up there.' He pointed to the stairs. 'Oi,' he said as Terry disappeared up them. Lumberingly, he followed only to discover Terry confronting Chris in the middle of his electric shave.

'Right, now listen –'

Startled, Chris backed away and began to shout for Big John.

'Never mind John. You're gonna need half the Airborne Division if you don't listen to me.'

Chris then saw that Big John was at the door, but was making no attempt to tackle Terry.

Seizing his opportunity, Terry began to bash his point

home. 'You had Arthur Daley over –'

'It was his own fault.'

'All right. Good luck. Now Arthur's a bit tight with his money as you may have noticed.'

'If you've come in here threatening me –'

'Shurrup. Heard of Vic Piner?'

There was a blank look from Chris, but Big John nodded sagely.

'Well, muscles has heard of him. He's a nutter. Mad Vic – not vapour rub. This guy gets on your chest and he stays there, and you'll need more'n that St Christopher medallion to get you home safe.'

'He's right, Chris,' said Big John looking uneasy.

'What's he going to do then?' asked Chris reluctantly.

'He's gonna take the money and then give you a hiding just for the fun of it.'

'And what's your angle?'

'Oh, you're one of them, eh? Everybody's got to have an angle? Well, mine's simple – Arthur's an old pal and I can't afford the petrol to go and see him wherever they lock him up. And second – I don't see why you should get your legs broken for being a bit too greedy.'

Then they all froze as a determined banging suddenly began on the front door.

'Oh, Christ,' said Big John, 'this is it.'

'Not if you keep your cool,' said Terry. He ran lightly out of the office, hurried down the stairs, listened and then heard a movement in the auditorium. Tiptoeing inside he saw, under a few working lights, dim shadows of Arthur and Vic crossing the auditorium towards the main staircase. Deliberately, Terry cleared his throat and they turned abruptly to face him.

'Bit early for the dancing, aren't you?' he said smiling, beginning to walk towards them.

'What you doing here?' asked Arthur with hostility.

'Chatting with my old pal, Chris, who tenders his apologies and says you left this behind in his office.' He tossed a neatly taped bundle of notes over to the astonished

88

Arthur. 'Four hundred. He reckons he was due a twoer just to teach you a lesson and putting up with hearing the bird sing. Fair?'

'Reasonable,' said Arthur.

'Of course it's been a wasted journey for poor old Vic here.'

Vic glared at Terry, maniacally enraged. Arthur began to back off.

'You just nicked my job –' spluttered Vic.

'Job? You're not even on the firm.'

'I was on three hundred.'

'What's that? Hundred a year?'

At that point Vic went crazy. 'Bastard!' he yelled and dived at Terry. But Terry simply wasn't there. Vic moved again. They grappled, fell against the console and the lights began to flash, a tape of rock music automatically played, drowning Vic's heavy breathing. So far, he hadn't landed a punch and Terry was handling him with ease. Arthur watched with cautious admiration.

Terry suddenly broke the clinch, pushed Vic back and hit him on the chin. He thudded to the floor and stayed there.

'Arthur, I'm surprised at you. I always thought you was a good judge of a fighter,' Terry said as they both stared down at the prone figure of Vic.

Arthur nodded and smiled wryly. 'Yeah,' he said.

Terry then crossed to the fallen Vic and knelt over him, bringing him back to consciousness with a few face slaps. Vic stared at him muzzily.

'Hear all right?' asked Terry.

'Yeah,' he said, wincing with the pain.

'I'll do a deal with you. You and your brother don't start a war and I won't tell a soul that it only took one good right hand to knock you spark out. OK?'

Vic nodded unhappily.

'Together,' said Arthur, 'we're very clever.' They were driving towards the lock-up in Arthur's Jag, with Arthur triumphantly at the wheel.

'Putting mad Vic onto him, that wasn't too clever, was it?'

'Wasn't it?' said Arthur vaguely.

'Well, was it?' demanded Terry.

'Soon got you working, didn't it?' he replied truculently. Then Arthur saw something that he didn't like. 'Oh, my Gawd.'

Once again a police car was outside the lock-up, but this time the big wooden doors were wide open. Detective Sergeant Chisholm was waiting as Arthur hurried agitatedly from the car and Terry followed more casually.

'Did you this time, Arthur. Cleared you out,' said Chisholm cheerfully.

Arthur glanced into the empty storeroom with an expression of acute loss on his face. Then, instantly, he recovered his ability to bluff. 'Nothing in it anyway,' he said airily.

'Nothing?' asked Chisholm.

'Just a few odds and ends – that's all.'

'All we found was a few records – musical that is, not criminal.' He laughed quietly at his own joke.

'Well, Arthur's very partial to a bit of music,' said Terry.

'Matter of fact, Mister Chisholm, I used to be in the business. Managing a girl singer.'

'What happened to her?' asked Chisholm.

'Well, you know – kids these days. She ran off with a tone-deaf piano player.'

Arthur walked into the storeroom with Terry following, pausing only to make a weary gesture of resignation to Chisholm. 'That's show business, Mister Chisholm,' he said.

PART THREE

Following their rift, Arthur had decided to behave so generously towards Terry that they both found it completely exhausting. Eventually, Dave couldn't stand it any longer as they slapped each other's backs in the Winchester.

'When are you two love-birds gonna stop cooing?' he asked hopefully.

'What do you want?' asked Terry. 'Blood?'

'You don't understand, Dave,' said Arthur. 'You've never experienced true bonding.'

'True what, Arthur?'

'Bonding, Dave. Together we're a team. Apart we're rubbish. Isn't that so, Terry?'

'Yes, Arthur.' It was strange to have Arthur so compliant, so generous. He was waiting for the bubble to burst so that they could return to their old relationship. But Arthur was still so pleased to get his money back that it was as if he had sworn eternal friendship. It was all a bit wearing.

'You see, Dave,' said Arthur, waxing philosophical. 'A true partnership gives and never minds the cost.'

'Eh?'

'And when in doubt, turns inwards, seeking strength. Then it's out to conquer the evening. See what I mean?'

'It's truly wonderful,' said Dave.

'Ah – you can mock. But you cannot break our glass walls with your stones. We are invincible. And what about another Dave? Fill 'em up and let's drink to the team.'

'You're very silent, Terry,' said Dave as he poured vodka for Arthur and lager for Terry.

'I was just basking in the warmth of it all,' he said. 'Getting a tan in the sun that shines out of Arthur's – whole being.'

Arthur smiled benignly. 'And we can share a joke, too.'

Dave asked, 'So all this minder business is out of the window, is it?'

Arthur looked perturbed. 'You're speaking in riddles,' he said. 'I'm a simple cove.'

'Yeah – what I mean is – you're equal partners now, are you?'

Arthur paused, reflecting on the beauty of it all. 'Terry

still looks out for me – he's the younger man.'

'You share and share alike?'

'I give him part of my crust.' Arthur looked at his watch. 'I must be toddling off.'

'Got some business to do, Arthur?' asked Dave.

'I'm a busy man.'

'Not got another chick who's gonna be a pop star?' Dave's face creased into the suggestion of a smile. Terry grinned, but Arthur frowned.

'That's in poor taste – don't take the piss out of my benevolence,' he remonstrated.

'Sorry, Arthur.'

'Where you going?' asked Terry.

'Bit of business in Southall.' Arthur downed the last of his vodka.

'You didn't tell me about that.'

'Just needs a bit of preliminary reconnaissance,' He hurried out of the bar.

When Arthur had gone Dave said to Terry, 'That'll be a tenner for the drinks.'

Terry froze and then his hand went reluctantly to his pocket.

'All in the spirit of true friendship,' said Dave happily.

Southall seemed the lively centre of a new Bombay. Greengrocery shops spilled on to the pavement, butchers' shops had meat on one side and video tapes on the other and the gift shops had windows bursting with gaudy Indian jewellery. There were Indian banks, cafés, restaurants and a smell of spice overlaid the petrol and diesel fumes of the passing traffic and the blander aroma of fish and chips and hamburgers.

Arthur parked his Jag and began to look for an address. A stranger in a strange land, he was uncomfortable – and would have been much happier walking down Fulham Broadway. But he plodded on, passing a Sikh reading an Indian newspaper on the street corner.

Then Arthur recognised the address he had been

searching for – a radio, TV and video shop. Walking cautiously inside, Arthur faced the owner – an elderly Hindu. Suffering from the cold, he wore mittens, a long scarf and a Husky waistcoat. His English was shaky and he gave Arthur a deeply suspicious look, partly because he had met him once before and also because he was deeply suspicious anyway. Life in England seemed far more devious than life in India and, to Ajit, Arthur seemed to be the very epitome of deviousness.

'All right, guv'nor? Shamy about?'

'No.'

'Is he coming back?'

'Don't know.'

Arthur looked at a TV monitor set showing an Indian film. 'Nice, eh? You remember me – Mister Daley?'

'Yes.'

'We met once before.'

'Yes.'

Arthur paused. Did he detect a lack of communication? Then he said, 'I've got a meet with Shamy.'

'Yes.'

'Well, where is he?' he asked with an edge of impatience.

'Not here.'

'I've got that. He's not here. Let's start again.'

'Shamy running.'

'Yeah, I know he's a bit slippery. But where? Home? The bank? Betting shop? Boozer? –'

Ajit pointed to the street.

'Running – out there?' asked Arthur.

Ajit hesitated, locked the till and then shepherded Arthur to the door. 'There.'

Arthur looked down the street. 'Gone for a cup of tea?'

'Tea?'

'Thank you kindly.' He nodded at the till. 'Don't get cold, you get back to the old Jack and Jill.' Arthur then began to hurry down the street towards an Indian cafeteria.

Walking in, he made the predictable discovery that all the customers were Asians. At a corner table sat Shamy. He was in his late twenties, casually dressed, handsome and full of confidence. Directly his eyes fell on Arthur, he gave a start of annoyance. Then his features rearranged themselves into a warm smile. Shamy stood up and shook Arthur by the hand.

'Arthur – nice to see you.' He turned to the owner of the cafe. 'Rajiv – a cup of tea for Mister Daley, please.'

'The old feller said you was running.'

'You know me, Arthur. Busy, busy. I've got things to do.'

'It's your shop, is it?'

'Yeah, more or less,' he said uneasily. 'The old bloke, he's just a peasant. He can hardly speak English. What does he know about hi-fi and videos? He had two goats and a field of of rice in the old country and he's still got the peasant mentality. Shrewd, mind you. A lot of them are like that. He'll probably be a millionaire in a couple of years.'

'Talking about millionaires,' said Arthur slowly.

'I know what you're going to say and I've got it. OK?' Shamy gave a quick, wary glance around him. Then he fished out a wad of twenty-pound notes. 'Monkey, right? You did me a right favour. Those reconditioned sewing machines were a real winner.'

'The old values,' said Arthur nostalgically. 'They don't want to know about home-made dresses in this country. Young wives – they want coffee mornings with their Tupperware, but they can't even darn a sock. Your womenfolk have got their priorities right. I couldn't sell those sewing machines in Fulham.'

The waiter brought them a cup of tea as Arthur pontificated. 'They hardly know how to thread a needle and some of them can't even thaw a couple of fish cakes. How's your good lady these days?'

'Still working at Charlie Chester's Casino. She's doing roulette and blackjack now.'

'Nice.' He paused. 'She'll probably leave now that you're doing well.'

'I don't know about that, Arthur –'

'Don't be modest. I've known you for a few years. What can I say about you – a ne'er-do-well? Could I go farther? A tea-leaf? A drunkard? A gambler, a cheat, a sponger and you were prone to make up pork pies, as well. Oh yes, you were an all-round ponce, sure enough.'

Shamy looked a little disappointed. 'Well, nobody's perfect, are they?'

'I know what's happened? You're back with your own folk – you're at home.' Arthur looked delighted with this little piece of wisdom and he gave Shamy a sickly smile.

'I'm just a Londoner,' shrugged Shamy.

'You may think so, but all that dashing around the West End doing the Find the Lady, living in Whitechapel – that wasn't *you.*'

'The only reason I left was because the Bill gave me a lot of aggro and I got mugged three times – 'cause they thought I was a Paki.' He spread his hands. 'What could I do?'

'Well, you won't have that here, will you?' Arthur sipped his tea. 'And they make a nice cup of tea as well. I'm proud of you, Shamy.'

'Thank you – that's real praise. Incidentally, have you got any video machines?'

'Well –'

'Do you know anything about that game?'

Arthur laughed patiently. 'Do I? I was a pioneer, wasn't I? I've still got two tapes of "Dixon of Dock Green" – that's how long I've been in that area. Are you expanding?'

'Indians do love a film.'

'I've heard that,' said Arthur, shaking his head wisely.

'They make more films in India than in Hollywood.'

'You surprise me –'

'They'd rather have a video than an Oxfam parcel.'

Arthur stared at him. 'You *have* changed, haven't you? What you've got now is imagination – a world view.'

'Ambition – that's what it is.'

'It's nice to hear that.'

'Nobody makes money by working –'

'Ah,' said Arthur, 'that's where you're wrong, see. Look at your compatriots with their little newsagent shops.'

'Yeah, I have,' said Shamy. What do they get after twenty

years? A lot of old newspapers – that's what.' He smiled sadly across the table.

One phrase blazed across Arthur's mind – he's got it sussed.

As Arthur came out of the café, he noticed that an Indian traffic warden was sticking a parking ticket on the windscreen of his Jag.

'And a poppadum to you, darling,' muttered Arthur, but the traffic warden ignored him as she crossed to the other side of the street.

Inside a betting shop in Fulham, Terry was waiting for the girl settler to count out a winning bet.

'Five hundred and twenty-four. Who's a lucky boy then?'

'No luck in it, it's skill,' said Terry. 'Cheers.' Delightedly, Terry turned away from the counter. As he did so, he stuffed the money into his pocket and almost bumped into another punter who was wearing the worst wig in the world.

'Blimey,' said Terry. 'If it isn't Syrup.'* The middle-aged Syrup's wig was a grim travesty of the hair-style of Englebert Humperdink.

'Was that Arthur's winnings?' he asked.

'No . . . mine.'

'Handy.'

'Yeah. My first yankee –'

'I done hundreds of them.'

'Me too – but this is the first I've won.'

Syrup paused. 'I've done me lot.'

'There you go. And I know what you're going to say next.'

'No, I wasn't. You wouldn't like to sub me till tomorrow?'

'Well, what's happening tomorrow?' asked Terry dubiously.

'I don't know,' admitted Syrup.

'I'll give you a fiver.'

'Make it a score, eh?'

Terry hesitated.

---

*Syrup – syrup of figs – wig.

'I wanted to get some things. Bread and milk and some sweets for my little girl –'

'She's about twenty-nine,' Terry reminded him.

Syrup looked offended. 'Well, she still likes sweets, don't she?'

Terry palmed him a twenty pound note. 'Don't spend it all in one shop,' he said.

'You're a very generous man.'

'I know that,' said Terry briskly, but Syrup still wanted to talk.

'Gonna share you winnings with your mate Arthur, then?'

Terry looked at him in amazement. 'I wouldn't share a tent with Arthur.'

Ajit was studying a document given to him by a Mr Mitra, who was soberly dressed and looked like a bland accountant, when Shamy entered. Ajit looked up belligerently.

'Sorry I'm a bit late –'

'You go,' said Ajit.

'What's the matter?'

'Go . . . go.'

'Why?'

Mitra intervened, looking officious. 'Mister Desai has dispensed of your services.'

'Who are you then?'

'I'm his financial adviser and I've just advised him that you're too expensive. You want to be a partner, not an employee, don't you?'

Ajit suddenly lunged at Shamy, shouting, 'Thief, bloody thief.'

Shamy fended off the blow, muttering, 'He's a nutter.'

Mitra tried to calm Ajit and then said, 'You've been trying to dip in the till.'

'No chance. He's always got the key in his pocket.' But now Shamy's temper and sense of injustice was rising. 'I've helped him. Brought him lots of customers –'

'He wanted to call the police. There are many things missing,' said Mitra in schoolmasterly tones.

99

'Shoplifters.'

'Yes, and they're all your friends. It was you suggested that he should accept cheques and many have bounced – your friends again.' Mitra paused to let his censorious comments sink in. 'You took deposits on two TV sets and a music centre and the addresses are false.'

'It could happen to any shop.'

'Fifteen video tapes are missing.' He was almost intoning the list of offences now.

'He doesn't organise things. Anyway, he's a crook. He pirates tapes.'

'That is a very serious accusation. You must go.'

'Any chance of having my wages?' asked Shamy innocently.

Ajit moved purposefully towards him again and Shamy backed off.

'No wages – you had my money,' said Ajit, fighting for control.

'Yeah, well you might have given me money – but you gave no peace of mind.' He backed away to the door. 'You know what your problem is, don't you?' Shamy said to Ajit. 'You're a peasant – that's your problem.' He opened the door. 'You may have a BMW – but your brain is back with a bullock cart and a handful of patna rice. Cheers.' Shamy slammed the door, leaving Mitra to pour soothing words of comfort into Ajit's ears.

Back in the Winchester, Arthur was in his usual corner, holding forth with a magisterial account of his journey to darkest Southall. Terry sat beside him, while Dave served drinks. Across the bar sat Detective Sergeant Chisholm, listening quietly, but pretending to read his newspaper. Next to Terry sat Syrup, looking weirder than ever in his badly fitting wig.

'You see,' lectured Arthur, 'your Indian likes to graft. Up in the early morning to open his paper shop. Gets the kids off to school. Still open at 10 p.m. more than likely. You ought to have a look at Southall; it's a thriving place. Mind you, there's thousands of 'em. Brown faces – it's unnerving, you know. I only saw one white face and I think he was Richard Attenborough.' He turned to Dave. 'And one for yourself, Dave.'

Terry sat there worrying – was Arthur going to do the disappearing trick again, leaving him to pay? He knew he had to be on his guard or all his winnings would quickly disappear.

Dave nodded and glanced at Chisholm, wondering if he should be included in the round. Arthur shook his head quickly.

'I seen an Indian playing the bagpipes – years ago,' said Syrup.

'And?' asked Terry.

'You wouldn't think they'd bother.'

'Give one to the Syrup,' said Arthur unwillingly, anxious to return to the subject. 'You see, your friend and my friend – old Shamy – he's even got the flavour of hard work. Dashing around like a good 'un –'

'I don't believe it,' said Terry.

'I met him once. He was going down the hospital. They were going to X-ray him, just to see if he had a day's work about his person. Two pounds seventy, Arthur.'

With relief, Terry saw Arthur reaching for his wallet. 'He was dead worried when they brought in the three-day week. He thought it was compulsory –'

'You may scoff – but he's a different man now,' said Arthur with confidence, pulling out a twenty pound note and giving it to Dave. 'He's got incentives now. Just shows you, you *can* change a leopard's stripes –'

'You don't spot too many of them, do you,' said Terry drily, but Arthur ignored him.

Meanwhile, Dave was inspecting the twenty pound note, putting it up to the light and pursing his lips.

'I put it down to marriage,' continued Arthur oblivious to Dave's activities.

'He only married her because she had a steady job.'

'What a cynical man you are,' said Arthur, attacking him

for the first time in days. 'Just because your personal relationships are based on the physical rather than the spiritual, do not mock the state of matrimony. He's become a better man.'

Just as Terry was about to tell him why he hadn't, Dave interrupted. 'Could I have a word?' he said to Arthur, holding up the twenty pound note.

As he did so, Chisholm looked up, suddenly interested.

'It's not a wind-up, is it?' asked Dave humbly of Arthur.

'Eh?'

'If I didn't know you better –' Dave paused. 'I may have to rephrase that, Arthur. You wouldn't do this to an old friend? You wouldn't, would you?' He ended on a pleading note.

'Do what?'

'Just tell me that you didn't do it? Have a butchers.' Dave was becoming emotional.

Arthur grabbed the note and examined it against the light. 'I don't believe it.'

'You'd better. It's phoney as a glass eye.'

Arthur winced and his eyes darkened with disappointment and anger. He muttered to himself, 'He's done me up like a kipper.'

'Who?' asked Terry solicitously.

Then Arthur froze, realising that Chisholm was hovering like a hawk ready to pounce on a field mouse.

'Never mind,' said Arthur quickly.

'It's time I was moving on. I'll settle with you later, Dave.'

'Eh – will you, Arthur? Right.'

But Arthur's ruse was too late and Chisholm was amongst them. 'Do we have a little problem, Guv'nor?' he asked Dave.

'Not really, Mister Chisholm,' replied Dave uncomfortably, whilst Chisholm moved nearer to Arthur.

'I trust the bold Arthur Daley is not passing off counterfeit currency?'

'Me? Would I do a thing like that?'

'You don't want me to answer that, do you? May I?' He offered his hand to accept the note. Arthur gave the note to Dave, who passed it to Chisholm. The whole process was

102

becoming a bit like a game in a children's play. At the same time, Arthur surreptitiously pulled out a wad of twenty pound notes and palmed them to Terry who palmed them to the Syrup.

'A fine piece of work, this,' said Chisholm having finished his examination. 'Any more where that came from, Arthur?'

'I didn't even know I had that one, Mister Chisholm. Some of these villains – I don't know.'

'I'm in a bit of a quandary. Obviously, you've broken the law.'

'I haven't lodged a complaint, Sergeant.'

'But I'm a witness – and I've got the evidence.'

'Yeah – but I didn't know it was bent.'

'All I know is that there are thousands of them in London. Ignorance of the law is no excuse – you know that – of all *people*. I think I'll have to nick you.' He moved nearer to Arthur, a sardonic smile on his face.

Arthur looked desperate and gabbled, 'Mister Chisholm – be fair. I'm a victim of circumstances. I've been turned over by some nasty little villain who has exploited my gullibility.'

'Where did you get it?'

'Ooh, I don't know. I'm a businessman. Money goes through my hands hour by hour.'

'Me too – sometimes. Incidentally, you still owe me two pounds seventy, Arthur,' put in Dave, anxious not to lose out.

'Dave – please. This is a crisis,' reprimanded Arthur.

'Yeah, I know – I'm out of pocket,' he said.

'In the book –'

Dave began to moan, whilst Chisholm looked on with the pleasure he took from other people's conflict. 'That bloody book is getting bigger than one of Harold Robbins'.'

'Well . . . I'm off then. You'll be all right, Arthur,' said Syrup.

'Thank you, Syrup.'

Chisholm brandished the note. 'You have an obligation as a citizen. It is your duty to help your local police –'

'He's asking you to grass,' said Terry helpfully.

'And why not?' snapped Chisholm, rounding on Terry. 'I

suppose that's a contemptuous word in your little vocabulary? What's wrong with giving a bit of information to us occasionally? I don't understand you people.'

'No, you don't,' said Terry. 'But just think it's a bit like the old school tie.'

'Yeah, that's why half of them would grass their granny,' Chisholm replied sarcastically.

'I have to agree with that, Mister Chisholm,' said Arthur sanctimoniously. 'It's the trend, innit? I blame the newspapers, see. If you can't rob a bank at least you can write an article about it in the *Sunday Times*. Not that I would know those sort of people.'

Then Terry said quietly, 'Syrup.'

'Eh?' asked Arthur, still very agitated.

Terry dashed to the door, hoping that he could grab Syrup but he was too late.

'What's all that about?' asked Chisholm menacingly.

'Search me, Mister Chisholm.'

'Yeah, I might. All kinds of things would leap to the eye.' He folded the twenty pound note and put it in his pocket.

'Are you gonna keep that?'

'Of course I am. You weren't going to use it?'

'Well, I thought I'd keep it as a souvenir.'

'And put it under the floorboards with the other souvenirs?' asked Chisholm sweetly.

'You should remember you're speaking to a respectable businessman,' said Arthur. There was sweat standing out on his forehead and he absentmindedly mopped at it with a silk handkerchief.

'Feeling warm, Arthur?' asked Chisholm.

'It's a little close in here, Mister Chisholm. I've told Dave he always keeps the place too hot.'

'I've got a place where we can cool you down, Arthur. It's called the nick.'

'Be reasonable, Mister Chisholm.'

'Yeah – I may be lenient this time, Arthur. But I'm watching you, right?'

'Yes, Mister Chisholm.'

'I'm watching your every move.'

The beautiful friendship between Arthur and Terry was over
as the argument raged in the Jag, driven badly by a tense
and impatient Arthur.

'And then you lose the Syrup!' Arthur was raging on.
'Gawd knows where he is now – the Mayfair Wig Centre? Or
even Los Angeles. He's always fancied a syrup like Gene
Kelly's.'

'He can't use the dough anyway,' said Terry defensively.
'Any idiot would recognise those hooky notes.'

Arthur treated him to a grim scowl. 'But I took 'em.'

'That's what I mean,' said Terry. 'You'd have to be a special
kind of idiot.'

Arthur pumped the horn as he tried to overtake a car. 'I
trusted that horrible Indian,' he moaned, ignoring Terry's
insult.

'Yeah, you reckoned Shamy was a changed man.'

'That's because I've got compassion in my heart. Do-
gooder? That's not my style. I'm going to "do" him – and do
him good.' He glanced contemplatively at Terry, every bit
the hard man. 'And I don't want any soft-hearted stuff from
you. I want the old one-two. I want to see him splattered on
the pavement, teeth in the gutter and plenty of claret an' all.'

Terry smiled sardonically, amused by Arthur's sudden
blood-curdling threats. 'It could be that he's got a reasonable
excuse.'

'How could he?' Arthur sounded completely outraged. 'He
took a liberty.' He reflected for a while. 'No – not a liberty.
We're talking about wickedness, a crime beyond human
weakness – it's – it's *inhuman*.'

'It was only five hundred . . . wasn't it?'

'There you go,' said Arthur, 'a simple lad, you are. Trust –
that's what we're talking about. I don't give 'em invoices,
bills, receipts . . . I give 'em my hand and my heart.'

'I think they'd rather have a guarantee.'

'A mere slip of paper?' Arthur placed his hand on his heart.
'I give 'em my honour.'

'And you're about to ram this motor into a van,' warned Terry as Arthur steered wildly, his rage increasing all the while.

'You know what to do.'

Terry and Arthur were walking down the street towards the radio and video shop where they hoped to find the defaulting Shamy. Arthur had lost none of his fury.

'I'll have a chat with him,' said Terry mildly.

'I've told you what to do. The man needs a spanking.'

'Arthur –'

'Never mind, Arthur! He cheated me. He got me into bother with Chisholm – of all people. So he has to be taught a lesson. I don't want you to hang him, draw him, and quarter him. Just a reasonable retribution. Gawd help us – haven't you even seen Clint Eastwood?'

'Yeah – I'll throttle him with spaghetti.'

They arrived at the shop doorway and, strangely, Arthur's desire for confrontation appeared to subside as he hung back.

'Well, aren't you coming in?'

'Er . . . well, you'll be better on your own – I'm too generous hearted a man to witness such violence.'

Terry gave a dismissive snort and he went into the shop whilst Arthur, left to contemplate, lit up and watched Terry talking to Ajit. Then he glanced away and vaguely watched somebody crossing the road. Somebody familiar. It was Shamy, arguing with another Asian. In sudden panic Arthur fumbled with the door of the shop. 'Terry . . . Terry,' he yelped as Terry waved him away, still deep in conversation with Ajit. Failing to disturb him, Arthur bawled across the road.

'Oi – Shamy . . . Hey! You!'

Shamy turned, looked startled and said something quickly to his companion. Then he quickened his pace whilst Arthur turned back to the shop and began to pound desperately on the window. After what seemed like an eternity, Terry sensed Arthur's impatience.

'He's over there,' Arthur mouthed through the glass, with

an elaborate display of mime. When Terry came outside, Arthur said, 'Shamy –'

'Yeah – he's had the elbow,' said Terry.

'He's over there – you berk,' bellowed Arthur.

Terry glanced in the direction of Arthur's shaking finger and saw Shamy cutting down a side-street. Immediately, Terry ran across the road, with Arthur following him, yelling, 'Move it Terry – get your skates on.'

Shamy was running up the street and was about fifty yards in front of them.

'Don't let him get away,' shrieked Arthur, clutching at his hat and panting desperately.

'Shamy,' shouted Terry.

But Shamy wasn't going to stop. He glanced back as Terry sprinted behind him and then dashed into the front garden of a semi-detached cottage, scampering up the path to the small back garden. But Terry was closing in on him, encouraged by Arthur, now in the middle distance.

Shamy jumped over the low fence into the adjoining garden and over the next fence and the next and the next. After a few hundred yards of this massive bout of hurdling, Shamy was almost exhausted, panting, his heart pounding, his head aching. All the time he could hear Terry coming – and all the time his pace was slowing. Then Shamy stumbled and sprawled on his back, facing Terry with a beguiling smile.

'Hallo, Terry – I didn't realise it was you.' He finally managed to gasp out, effecting a look of pained surprise.

'Who did you think it was?'

'I know so many people –'

'And all of them running after you?'

Shamy gave a resigned smile. 'That's the story of my life, innit? How's Arthur?'

Arthur, meanwhile, was trying to track down the athletes by invading a number of different back gardens. In one of these he was discovered furtively lurking by an Indian housewife.

'Are you the man from the council?' she asked.

'Certainly not, madam.' He tipped his hat and beat a dignified retreat, leaving her staring after him in bewilderment.

Back in the street, Arthur saw Terry and Shamy. Slowly, menacingly, Arthur approached them.

'D'you want to hit him? Should I hold him?'

'What a deplorable suggestion.'

Terry looked surprised. 'I thought you wanted blood, Arthur.' •

'We're civilised people. I'm sure there's a simple explanation . . . isn't there, Shamy?'

'Oh, yeah – course there is,' said Shamy relieved.

Arthur preserved an icy calm. 'I can't imagine what it is but nevertheless, I will listen to it.' He pointed to a pub down the road. 'Shall we imbibe?'

As Terry, Arthur and Shamy approached the pub, Shamy paused.

'There's just one thing.'

'Yeah?' asked Arthur suspiciously.

'There might be some people in there who I don't want to see.'

'Then have a little shufti – is that the word?'

Shamy agreed and opened the door, wondering why Arthur was being so helpful.

All the customers in the pub were Asian and the television was showing an Indian film. Once Shamy had had a good look round he said, 'OK.'

But Terry noticed he seemed surprised.

Arthur, Terry and Shamy sat down at a table.

'Terence,' said Arthur commandingly.

'Yeah?'

'Lay in some drinks.'

'Suppose he makes a dash for it?'

'I'll mind him.'

'You?'

'Besides,' Arthur smiled benignly at them both, 'I don't s'pose Shamy is in any mood for any more running.'

Reluctantly, Terry went to get the drinks. When he returned he found Arthur and Shamy sitting in deep silence.

'Chummy,' he said.

'I'm just waiting for a witness,' said Arthur grandly.

Shamy burst into agitated speech. 'See, I didn't know they was dodgy notes –'

Arthur gave him a patient smile. 'You're lying, Shamy.'

Shamy considered this for a moment and then he said, 'Yeah – you're right.'

'Did you make them yourself?'

'No, I bought them. A fiver for each note.'

'Oh, nice. You told me that the shop was yours too.'

'I never said that.'

Arthur's smile became definitely frosty. 'Oh yes you did.'

'Did I? Well, to be honest – I must've lied.'

Arthur stared at his glass and then glanced at Terry, who shrugged. 'See, you bought sewing machines from me and you sold them for – I assume – a handsome profit?'

'That's the point, Arthur – I owed money. Just ordinary debts, you know, a tenner here, a tenner there, plus cards, the gee-gees, gas bills, rates, the simple things. I worry about my wife, too. She works so hard and we needed a break so we had a couple of days in Eastbourne.' He paused. 'So I had to borrow some dough – then I needed some shoes.' Shamy appealed to Terry, 'You know what it's like –'

' 'Specially shoes.'

'Have you got *any* assets?' asked Arthur impatiently, returning the meeting to the agenda.

'Nothing.' He looked desperate. 'I'm one of nature's debtors, Arthur. I was in the red from birth.'

'Then you must've run up a few bills, eh?'

'To be honest, Arthur. You're at the end of a long line.'

'Aren't you ashamed?' asked Arthur sanctimoniously.

'I am – I am.' Shamy bowed his head.

'Well,' said Terry, 'as the man said . . . Annual income ten grand, annual expenditure nine and a half grand, well, I wouldn't call it happiness, but you can get by, can't you? Annual income ten grand, annual expenditure about twenty-five grand – and we're not only talking about misery, but a handful of aggravation.

'Nicely put, Terence,' said Arthur patronisingly.

'I'd drink to that,' said Shamy.

'If only you could call a round.' Arthur's voice was hollow.

'Might, in a few days.' He looked at them furtively. 'I've got a possibility –'

'Don't tell me,' said Arthur.

'I'm thinking of going into show business.'

'Yeah? Pantomime?'

Arthur frowned at Terry who was grinning and saying, 'Show business – Arthur's the expert in chick singers, if you're interested.'

'Ignore him,' said Arthur. 'He has a sense of humour.'

'Honest, Arthur,' said Shamy, 'I'm talking about the movie business.' His voice became a whisper. 'Video. Should I cut you in?'

'I'd love that . . . wouldn't I?' said Arthur sarcastically.

'They love a video.' He nudged Arthur and pointed towards the television screen. 'They make more films than Hollywood, you know.'

'All I want is my five hundred,' said Arthur resolvedly.

'Don't you trust me?'

Arthur stared at him – he just couldn't believe what he was saying. 'The simple answer,' began Arthur, but he was interrupted by a voice bellowing in his ear.

'You Shamy?'

'Oh, Christ –' Shamy half rose to his feet as a huge Sikh lunged across the table and almost knocked Arthur out of his chair.

'You owe me money,' said the Sikh.

'Don't you threaten me – I'm in the middle of a business meeting.' But Shamy looked far from confident.

'I don't give a damn about your white friends –'

'Tel?'

'They can't protect you –' He gestured to the other customers. 'These are all my countrymen.'

'And these are *my* countrymen,' said Shamy.

110

'Gawd help us,' sighed Arthur. 'Now he's gonna start a race riot.'

Shamy managed to talk his way out of his conflict with the Sikh – but only by promising to pay him in thirty-six hours. Grudgingly the Sikh had agreed – but Arthur and Terry knew he had about as much chance of getting his money back as Shamy buying him the Khyber Pass.

Now, Shamy, Arthur and Terry were standing in front of a shop window in Southall that displayed a vast mound of video tapes – all of Indian films.

'Look at that one,' said Shamy. 'It's like *Gone With The Wind* with a dash of *Dallas* and *Death Wish*. Biggest thing since – I don't know. If you've got a film like that, it's a licence to print money.'

'You know all about it.'

'I was just trying to get some easy money. But as you said, nobody gets money without working.'

'*He* said that?'

'Yeah, I think.'

'It is the cornerstone of my philosophy –' said Arthur pompously.

'Look,' Terry's voice was incredulous, 'you took some sewing machines from one place to another place, that's not exactly philosophy.'

'You have to think about it,' said Arthur.

'I agree with you, Arthur.' Shamy was quick to curry favour.

'What?' asked Terry outraged.

'What *he* said. You've gotta work, you have to seize the opportunities. Like I've got –' He began to whisper urgently. 'I've got this tape – the biggest Indian film ever.'

'*E.T.*, *Gandhi*, you name it –'

'Then you're gonna be rich.' Arthur walked on, he simply didn't want to know about any more of Shamy's schemes.

'But I need help. I need –'

'I know what you're going to say . . . You're gonna say you need money?'

111

'Well, sort of –'

'Goodbye.' Arthur walked briskly away with Shamy tugging on his sleeve. 'Terence,' said Arthur, 'this man is molesting me.'

'This is the best offer you've had today.'

'He is importuning me –'

'A few measly pounds –'

'There's a by-law against this.'

'Arthur!'

Arthur walked to his car and Shamy looked at Terry. 'You understand, don't you?' he said desperately.

'Well, just for once,' Terry said in a considered voice, 'he may be right.'

'Why can't people trust me?' asked Shamy naively, looking at Terry, hoping he would confirm his honesty.

'You've got a reputation and it ain't for honesty.'

'All right – all right. Occasionally, I tell fibs –'

'No . . . you're a liar.'

Shamy considered that for a moment. 'Yeah. All right. But I'm in an 'ole. I know that – but how can I get out?'

Across the road, Arthur got into his Jag and shouted to Terry. 'Let's go.'

'Listen – just give me half-an-hour of your time tomorrow – thirty minutes, that's all. A jam-jar from A to B – is that a terrible request? We're friends . . . not friends – *mates*! Would you do that for me? I've got to collect this tape – I'm skint, I haven't even got the fare for a cab. Tomorrow, eh?'

To avoid any more pleading, Terry agreed.

'You're one of the good guys, Terry.'

'Don't I know it – an' all.'

An impatient Arthur was revving up, when Terry opened the passenger door. Shamy then came up to Arthur and stood optimistically by the bonnet of the Jag.

'Any chance of a lift home, Arthur?'

There was a long moment before Arthur delivered his considered and crushing reply.

'Piss off.' Then he gunned the engine and Shamy stepped away.

'Cheers, Arthur. I was gonna walk anyway.'

The Jaguar disappeared down the road and Shamy began slowly to walk home. But he had not gone far when an elderly Indian shouted at him from across the road, 'Shamy, I want to see you –'

Shamy gave him a tentative wave. 'I've got to dash,' he said and began, somewhat wearily, to run. His legs felt very stiff, but Shamy knew that he had to keep running.

'It's important,' yelled the Indian.

'Yeah, I know. See you.'

'Bloody man. Where is my money?' He began to limp after the rapidly disappearing Shamy. But gradually the gap widened.

Arthur was muttering fiercely to himself as he drove the Jag through the dense traffic.

'What did you say?' asked Terry.

'I said, I'm getting soft.'

'Well, when were you hard?'

'In my prime. Before I met you. Nobody took liberties in those days. That little Indian would've been odds on for a kneecap job.'

'Leave it out, Arthur.' Terry was adamant. 'You'd faint if you saw a bare kneecap, never mind the blood.'

A few miles away, Chisholm was parking his Sierra outside the Wigwam Hair Centre, a down-market wig shop. Chisholm glanced at the models in the window and his companion, D.C. Jones, said, 'I don't think they're my style.'

Without deigning to comment, Chisholm marched into the Hair Centre where he stood for a while examining the wad of twenty pound notes whilst the owner watched him. He was a large burly man with hairy arms, an open-neck shirt, displaying a hairy chest, and a handsome head of hair.

'Can I help you?' he asked.

'I don't see why not,' said Chisholm, showing his identity and explaining his business.

The owner, whose name was Mr Henry, went to check the

till. When he returned, he said, 'Fifteen of them. Three hundred.'

'Didn't you check them?'

'You don't, do you. You wouldn't think a man with a scalp problem would do that.'

'Could you describe him?'

'Well, he's wearing, at this moment, one of our Roger Moore's. Very popular, completely waterproof.'

'Waterproof?'

'Keep the rain off.'

'Off what? Their brains?'

'You can swim with a Roger Moore. We have our exclusive, special adhesive –'

'Well, apart from glue on his scalp, are there any other distinctive features?'

'I'd call him nondescript – more-or-less.'

'No scars, moles, a big hooter and dodgy eye?' asked Chisholm disappointedly.

'As I say – nondescript, average . . . a face in a crowd. Mind you, I'd recognise his scalp anywhere.'

Chisholm gave a manic smile of angry frustration. 'We don't have a file of cranium prints.'

'There is one thing – what you might call a clue. He left his other wig.' He rummaged in a drawer, coming out with the soiled, battered Engelbert Humperdink creation. 'A cheap nylon hairpiece,' said Mr Henry fastidiously. 'Circa 1972, an early, I would say – Engelbert Humperdink. I'm afraid it needs renovation.'

Chisholm carefully picked up the greasy looking wig. 'Renovation? It's got real dandruff.' His lips were parted in disgust.

'Not in the best of condition.'

'I've seen nicer rats down the old East Indian Dock, Jonesie – try this on.'

'Me? What have I done?' said Jones indignantly.

'D'you want a list? We are trying to picture the face beneath this – this apparition. Try it.'

Mr Henry helped Jones to fit the wig on his cranium.

114

Eventually, Jones looked in a mirror and started back. 'I feel like a real fool.'

'True . . . true.' Then he reacted. 'The Syrup!'

'What? Who?'

'A person known to the police.' He turned to Mr Henry. 'I will have to take this Irish into custody. Have you got a plastic bag or something?'

'Course. You mean, you know the culprit?'

'Oh, yes. I suppose you could say that he's got a price on his head –' Chisholm smirked whilst Jones hooted with polite laughter.

Mr Henry took the wig off Jones and put it into a plastic bag. 'It's an incredible piece of deduction, Sergeant. Incidentally, have you ever thought of having a hairpiece yourself?'

'Why?' Chisholm gave him a sour glance as Mr Henry looked at his head.

'Well, I hope you don't mind my saying so, but you are receding a bit, sir, almost to the point of vanishing.'

'I get by,' said Chisholm, a strained look on his face.

'I'm sure, but it is a disability. Socially, even professionally. I'm sure that your macho image would be enhanced with, say, the Burt Reynolds model that we offer. Or even the Starsky, which is very popular with the upper ranks at the Yard.'

'I was going to suggest that to you, guv,' said Jones happily.

'Were you?'

'Yes, I was. But –' Jones's voice trailed away as he recognised that certain strange gleam in Chisholm's eyes. Jones spoke quickly. 'Only joking, guv. Should I carry the plastic bag?'

Shamy arrived home at his flat a shaken man.

'Gayle?'

'In the kitchen. You want tea?' yelled a girl's voice.

'Please.' He took off his jacket and saw a handbag on a chair. 'Anything happened?'

'Just a sec.'

Taking advantage of his girl-friend's absence, Shamy quickly opened the handbag and took out a purse. He grabbed a few pounds, closed the handbag, went over to a dresser and opened a drawer. Inside there was a wad of twenty pound notes. He counted them and then stuffed them into his pocket. 'Have you taken some twenty pound notes from that drawer?'

'Yeah.' The mystery voice entered the room, carrying two cups of tea, revealing herself as an attractive blonde in her late twenties. 'I took forty pounds to pay the gas bill; they were going to cut us off.' Gayle gave Shamy the cup of tea and kissed him on the cheek.

'And they took 'em?'

'Why not?'

'Well, you know –'

'What, exactly?'

'You shouldn't have used them.'

'Oh my God!' Gayle suddenly realised what she had done. 'Are they duds?'

Shamy sat down and nodded. 'There are hundreds of them around.'

'They even gave me change.'

Shamy grinned. 'Then we've got a result, haven't we?'

'Haven't you got any shame?'

'Don't start all that again – I'm having a run of bad luck.'

Gayle slumped miserably onto the sofa. 'There's even more. Some other bloke was trying to get hold of you . . . Kamal, or somebody.'

'I only borrowed £50 from him.'

'Well he wants it, and he's bringing his brother tomorrow.'

'I tell you what – I'll never borrow from him again.'

'I don't somehow think he'll let you.' Gayle looked at Shamy with an expression of pity mixed with amusement. She knew him so well. 'I dunno, why can't you work like all other Indians?'

'You'd like that – wouldn't you?'

'Yeah. You don't even like curry! *Everybody* likes curry.'

'Some English people don't like it; and I'm one of them. You've got all these romantic views of the East, the Taj Mahal—'

'You thought it was a caff in the Commercial Road.'

'And you see too much television. Come on, be nice to me, eh?' He leant across to her, hoping that she would be less abrasive. She hesitated and then hugged him.

'What am I going to do with you?' she asked, this time torn between love and desperation.

'I've had a hard day, y'know.'

Chisholm was sitting in a steamy café at a dirty table, to which Jones had just brought two slopped cups of tea. He stirred his tea and stared at the street as he soliloquised.

'Did I let him off the hook? He actually had a dud twenty pound note in his hand. Bang to rights. And I let him get away. There should be no pity for the likes of Daley and his ilk.'

Jones said nothing, knowing that Chisholm wished to speak aloud and uninterrupted.

'The Syrup was talking to him. Then, a few hours later the same person turned over a wig-maker and scarpered with a Roger Moore look-alike toupee. Is that mere fortuitousness? I think not.'

'I agree, guv,' said Jones, thinking it was time to at least prove his existence.

But Chisholm didn't even hear him. 'Of course, there are more important things in life than nicking Daley. But at this moment I can't think of anything else. Daley—he's a thorn in my flesh, a tickle in my throat. I had hair when I started in this manor. I've had many encounters with Daley and most of them are nasty. I don't approve of his pathetic, trivial wheezes – gold-fish, Albanian sparkling wine or even flood-damaged bathing suits—'

'You have to laugh, though.'

For the first time Chisholm heard him. 'No,' he said.

'He got that micro-oven for our canteen.'

'Burnt offerings. I've always thought of Daley as a more

117

dangerous man. The idea of him circulating dodgy twenty pound notes is attractive – for the likes of us. Even better if he's actually *printing* currency of the realm.'

'That's a staggering thought.'

'Awesome,' said Chisholm with a kind of secret delight.

Terry honked the horn of his battered car and Shamy ran out of his flat and got in.

'Where are we going?' asked Terry, already cursing himself for weakening.

'Down the shops. I'll only be there for a couple of minutes. I've got to meet a guy –'

'What about?' asked Terry bleakly.

'A dog,' said Shamy.

A supervisor was checking an Indian film in a video factory. Around them were banks of cassettes and a familiar figure – Mr Mitra. Holding a cassette, Mr Mitra walked to the main entrance, on to the street and into his family saloon car.

Fifty yards down the road was another car – an old Cortina – and as Mr Mitra's saloon passed the intersection, the Cortina began to follow him. Unknown to him, the two occupants were plain-clothed police officers.

'I'll only be a couple of minutes,' said Shamy as he got out of Terry's car outside the video shop.

'Make it snappy,' warned the suspicious Terry. 'I'm not hanging around, you know.'

As Shamy stood outside the shop, he saw Mr Mitra's saloon pulling in. As he parked and opened the door, Shamy saw that Mr Mitra had the video cassette in his hand. Quickly he walked towards him and, in a sudden movement, grabbed the video cassette and shoved Mr Mitra into the shopway. Then he ran off towards the side street where Terry's car was parked.

At the same time, the Cortina skidded to a halt and the two plain-clothed police officers dashed to Mr Mitra.

'You're nicked, mister,' said one of them as he grabbed him.

'I've been attacked,' Mitra protested.

Shamy sat panting in the front seat of Terry's car. 'Let's go,' he said, gasping but Terry had no idea of what was going on.

'What's up?' he asked, his suspicion deepening.

'Nothing. I've just got to see somebody.' He gave Terry a quick, nervous smile.

Terry started the car and began to drive at normal speed. Shamy glanced through the rear window agitatedly.

'I've got away with it. Hey, how about that?'

'You nicked that video, didn't you?'

'Course not.'

'Then how come you're so excited?'

'No, I'm not.'

'Yeah?'

'Straight.'

Terry shrugged. 'You know what, my old son?'

'Yeah?'

'I don't believe a bleedin' word you're saying.'

Meanwhile, outside the video shop, the two plain-clothed police officers were frisking Mr Mitra.

'Don't you understand, I was mugged,' Mitra protested.

'He hasn't got it,' said one of the police officers to the other, in a disgruntled voice.

'Daylight robbery –' continued Mitra.

'Shurrup – you're a lucky man.'

'Can't we nick him anyway?'

The other police officer frowned. 'Not today,' he said.

'Who're you expecting to follow us?' asked Terry as Shamy kept looking through the rear window.

'Nobody.'

'Then why're you looking through the back window?'

'No, I wasn't.'

Terry gave him a very dubious glance. 'Where are we actually going?'

'What about your place?'

'No.' He was quite decisive. Then he said, 'You did nick it, didn't you?'

'Honestly,' began Shamy. Then he said, 'Yeah, I did. He nicked it anyway –'

'That's all right, is it?'

'Sort of. The only thing is, they know about it.'

'Didn't you think about that beforehand?' said Terry fatalistically.

'You don't, do you?'

'I dunno – you tell me.'

'Balaclavas and false beards – I can't be doing with them.'

'Now they're after you?'

'Yeah.' He gave a smile of resignation and even Terry had to laugh.

'What about Arthur? Could I stay at his place?'

'You must be kidding. You couldn't kip on his floor even if you paid his £500 plus 100 per cent interest.'

'He's so suspicious, isn't he? But I know a place,' said Shamy. 'It's not far from where you live.'

'Oh my Gawd,' said Terry. 'Can't we make it Birmingham?'

Terry and Shamy stood before the scruffy Paddington hotel reception desk.

'Both of you?' asked the middle-aged manager quizzically.

Shamy gave him a charming smile. 'We're not *all* that friendly. It's just me.'

'Got any luggage?'

'It's at the station,' said Terry.

'Thirty pounds a night. In advance.'

'Okay.' Shamy pulled out his wad of twenties and gave him two notes and the Manager lugubriously gave him a ten pound note as change.

'Room service?' asked Shamy hopefully.

'Continental breakfast – two pounds extra. You can have a curry across the road.'

Shamy gave him a bleak smile. 'Thanks.'

In the middle of the forecourt of Arthur's used car lot stood a Fiesta on which a scruffy looking character called Smudger was fixing a roof sign. It read:

DaLey

Driving School

Qualified Instructors Approved

Arthur beamed at him in an avuncular manner.

'It looks like a real driving school,' said Smudger happily.

'Well it is.'

'No disrespect, Arthur – but what's all that about, "approved"?'

'They all have that.'

'Yeah, but approved by who?'

'Me.'

Smudger grinned. 'Yeah, I've got it. This is gonna be a winner. Incidentally, have you got a licence for me? Just in case –'

'In case of what?'

'If I get a pull.'

'You're supposed to be a driving instructor,' said Arthur severely.

'That was years ago. I *had* a licence, but I lost it.'

'Well – apply for another.'

'It was in a different name, wannit?'

'You come in here as a bona fide instructor –'

'I never said that. I taught my brother.'

'He's in Ford Open Prison.'

'But *not* for a driving offence.'

'What for then?' asked Arthur gloomily.

'Stolen motor – but nothing wrong with his driving. Sweet as a nut.'

Arthur was about to make some condemning remark when the telephone began to ring. Arthur walked sullenly over to his caravan. 'You've misled me,' he said sadly.

But Smudger was unrepentant. 'You must've been Brahms that night.'

Once in the office, Arthur picked up the phone. 'The Daley School of Motoring,' he said in a posh voice.

'You what?' said Terry.

'It's a new venture, Terence,' said Arthur grandly. 'Can I help you?'

'You know what we were talking about – films?'

'If it's Shamy – the answer is –'

'All right, all right. But he wants to see you and we're not talking about phony notes.'

'Look, every time I see him it costs me money.'

'This time it won't,' said Terry.

'I'll see him,' returned Arthur. 'One little thing, has he got a driving licence?'

Downstairs at reception, the manager put down the phone and thought for a while. Then he went to the till and took out several twenty pound notes. He picked up the first two notes and examined them. Then he picked up the telephone and dialled.

Arthur, watched attentively by the manager, arrived at the hotel room half-an-hour later and immediately plunged into an argument with Shamy. At the same time, Terry was trying to convince Arthur to at least bend an unprejudiced ear.

'How much?'

'About three hundred and fifty.'

'Did you hear that? This man who owes me –'

'It seems a good deal to me,' said Terry calmly.

Arthur turned on him sarcastically. 'Have you gotta healthy bank balance? How's your investments? And the old portfolio – is that thriving? What are you into these days? Commodities, unit trusts, bricks and mortar?'

'Then don't ask me,' shrugged Terry.

'I won't,' said Arthur firmly.

'But I've got an idea that you don't understand what he's saying.'

'I understand it perfectly. He wants to go to Bombay and buy a video tape there.'

'That's not it! I'm selling – not buying.'

'That's what I said.'

'No, you didn't.'

Before Arthur started again, Shamy said, 'They can't get video tapes in India. See. This film is the biggest thing since sliced bread or instant rice. They copy them over here for the western market and Africa, for example. We're not worried about the shops in Southall, or Leeds or Bradford – we're selling to millions. Every village in India has got its own video. If I take six copies to Bombay, to a certain person, then we'll be rich. One hundred grand and for *me*, that's rich.'

Arthur stared at him, a certain comprehension dawning.

'I knew you didn't understand it,' said Terry looking blank.

'All I need is a return ticket to Bombay and a couple of pounds for food and hotel and Bob's your uncle.'

'It can't be that easy?'

'But it is,' said Shamy. 'It really is.'

If only Arthur had realised that Chisholm was downstairs examining twenty pound notes, he would not have been so interested.

'Indian – you reckon?' asked Chisholm of the Manager.

'Of that persuasion I would say.'

Chisholm turned to his constant companion, Jones. 'I think we're in luck. Would you like to lead the way?' he asked the manager delightedly.

'There's one little problem,' said Arthur. 'If you go to Bombay we may never see you again –'

'I don't even like the food. Are you going to help me or not?'

Then there came the gentlest of knocks on the door.

'Room service?' asked Arthur.

The manager stood back as Chisholm and Jones stepped over

the threshold and an expression of euphoria crossed Chisholm's face as he saw Arthur. 'It must be my birthday.'

'What a pleasant surprise, Mr Chisholm.'

'I bet it is. You can introduce me to your friend with the fistful of twenty pound notes.'

'Gawd help us,' said Arthur.

Shamy didn't wait for the introductions. He pushed Terry aside, bowled over Chisholm and dashed down the corridor like a whippet. Jones and Chisholm charged after him. The manager followed.

Arthur and Terry were alone in the hotel room. Terry picked up the video tape and put it in his pocket. 'What d'you reckon?'

Arthur gave an expressive shrug. 'I think Mr Chisholm's gone to take some exercise. I wonder if he's any good at hurdling?'

But Terry was not to be free of Shamy for long. That night he was woken by a tapping on the window. Terry dragged himself out of bed, went to the window and opened the curtain. It was, of course, Shamy. Terry went to the door and switched on the light. Shamy stumbled in, looking terrible.

'You been running all night?'

'Bloody freezing.'

'What time is it?' He asked as he closed the door.

'Five o'clock.'

'Great. You're taking a chance coming here, aren't you?'

'And you –'

'I haven't done anything.'

'You haven't got a fire?'

Terry switched on a double-bar electric fire as Shamy rubbed miserably at his arms.

'That copper was after the twenty pound notes, not the video.'

'That's enough, innit?' Terry went into the kitchen to make a cup of tea. 'Why didn't you go home?'

'Because the Indians are after me. I didn't know where to

go, so I walked the streets. This city's dead at three o'clock in the morning. Just four taxis and the odd patrol car. And you feel *guilty* . . . I thought, I'd mingle with the crowds at Paddington Station. Ever tried that?'

'Not really.'

'There's no trains. Half a dozen penny stamps and two old Bill walking around the place, you feel very conspicuous, y'know.' He warmed his hands. 'Is Arthur still on about me going to Bombay?'

'I think so.'

Shamy took out his wad of twenty pound notes and looked at them. 'I want to get rid of these.' He held them to the electric fire and Terry kicked a waste-paper bin towards him.

'Just before you burn up the house –'

Shamy stared down at the flames. 'Pity, I thought they were good.'

'Ever thought of getting a job?'

'Eh?'

'They usually say that to me. But you, you're in a different class.'

'I don't believe in it. If God wanted us to clock in every day he would've given us a time-card in our hands.'

'Yeah, but you have to work *hard* to avoid work.'

'Well, what d'you want me to be? Somebody like Arthur? I agree, he's a grafter – but is he happy?'

'When he has a roll-call every night, he's delighted.'

'But happy? I don't know. Happiness is the thing you do after work.'

The next day an attractive young woman called Denise was waiting beside the Daley School of Motoring car. Looking both aggressive and impatient, she kept glancing towards the caravan where Arthur was talking on the phone.

'She's here, Smudger,' he was saying. 'Your first pupil. Well, how long is that going to take? As quick as you can then.' He hung up and went outside, rubbing his hands together ingratiatingly. 'Alas, one of my instructors has been detained, but he'll be along in about half-an-hour.'

'Well, can't you take me?'

'*I* am the principal,' he said with dignity.

'You can drive, can't you?'

'Young lady. . . I, personally, have taught the highest and the lowest, advanced motorists and those who don't know the difference between a slip-differential and a windscreen wiper –'

'Well, you'll do then, or I'll have to push off.'

'Have you actually put down a deposit yet?'

'No.'

'Well, in that case – could I suggest a preliminary course of, say six lessons – at our introductory offer of sixty sovs.'

'Fair enough.' She brought out a wad of twenty pound notes and gave three to Arthur.

'Thank you, darling,' said Arthur and immediately checked the notes against the light.

'What's all that about?'

'You can't be too careful.'

'Well, give 'em back then. What am I – the phantom forger?' She tried to retrieve the money, which was difficult with Arthur clutching three of the notes.

'Did I suggest that?' asked Arthur calmingly. 'Never in a million years did I say that, luv. But there's hundreds of Sexton Blakes all over the place. Haven't you read about it in the local rag?'

'Well, I don't mix with those sorts of people.'

'Of course you don't. But there's some terrible scallywags in the world.' He took the notes and put them in his pocket. 'I'll start you off on the right foot by giving you a preliminary lesson. At least pro temp, as it were, till Smudger appears.'

Denise went to the car whilst Arthur followed, having another quick peak at the notes.

'I know the rudiments. I mean, I've failed the test four times. Of course, they're against me.'

'Who?'

'All of *them*. They don't like my attitude.' She got into the car and slammed the door, whilst Arthur slid warily into the passenger seat. Just as Denise was about to switch on the engine, he said:

'Now, now, young lady. Let's do it right. Check your door, seat belt and so on.'

'Yeah, yeah, yeah.'

Arthur was both pedantic and avuncular. 'I trust you have mastered the four principles of the internal combustion engine?'

'Eh?'

'Induction, compression, ignition –'

'And then bloody exhaustion.'

Arthur looked surprised. 'Very good. You obviously know quite a lot. I think we should go into the street and see what –'

Denise quickly switched on the engine, but Arthur was still not ready. 'Just a minute. I haven't finished yet. Right away, I see that you've missed a crucial point. Young lady, your mirror is your friend.'

'We're in a yard.'

'Doesn't matter. It should be automatic. Where're you going?' The car was creeping towards the road.

'I don't know –'

'Brake, brake –'

'Well, haven't you got one?'

Arthur pointed vaguely to the floor. 'The middle one . . . your foot –' He grabbed the hand-brake. '– Take off the other pedal –'

'Which one?'

'The one your foot's on.'

The car stopped dead.

'I don't know why you're so excited.'

'I'm not excited,' said Arthur practically gibbering. 'But you must understand it's quite difficult to stop the motor if you've got your foot on the accelerator.'

'Well, the other cars had pedals for the teachers as well.'

'Yeah, but that way you won't learn so much. My system – the Daley-way, every day's another day – you learn from your own mistakes. Like Fittabaldie and all the others.'

Denise ignored him. 'Can we go somewhere? I ain't gonna sit in a yard all day.'

'All in good time, my dear.'

'We could shoot down to Sussex to see my old dad. He knows you, anyway.'

'Who?'

'Big Alfie –'

'Alfie the Hammer?'

'Yeah and when I told him that I was having lessons from you he said – you should be with him in Ford Open Prison. Where're we going then?'

Arthur was a little taken aback. 'I think first I'll sus out your ability . . . gears, clutch, your road sense –'

'I know all that.'

'I'm sure . . . It's Denise, innit . . . But I'd like to see it for meself. Let's go down the street and then –' He looked alarmed as she gunned the engine. 'Not yet –' He grew a fraction calmer.

'All right.'

Arthur quickly fastened his seat belt, testing it, checking it and checking it again. 'Right . . . a nice bit of clutchwork, an easy gear-change and we're gonna go left . . . LEFT.' His voice ended on a high note and there was a sickening crunch as Denise engaged first gear. The car lurched ahead and steered to the right. Without heed to the passing traffic, Denise drove confidently out of the yard and there was a terrible sound of skidding as another car narrowly avoided them.

'I said, "left",' said Arthur weakly.

'What does it matter?' asked Denise happily.

Arthur looked dazed, as if he was on the verge of a nervous breakdown. 'I think it does. If I say "left" and then you turn – Oh my gawd . . . brake, brake –'

For a horrendous moment, it looked as if Denise was about to smash into a car in front. But, astonishingly, Denise not only avoided the car, but also overtook it.

128

'Very good,' said Arthur weakly, glancing into the rear window. 'Look at his boat – ashen, that's the word – ashen. You see, Denise, you might think it doesn't matter if I say "left" and you go right. Of course in the cosmic way it's not all that important, but for mere mortals, like meself, it becomes confusing. Do you understand?'

'Yeah.'

'There *is* a difference between left and right –'

Denise spoke abruptly. 'All right – sod it then – we'll go the other way.' She suddenly span the steering-wheel and executed a hair-raising U-turn.

A number of expressions passed across Arthur's face but the most recognisable were fear, agony, shock and mad, mad hope that soon this nightmare might come to an end.

Smudger was sitting on the caravan steps when the car, driven by Denise, shuddered to a halt on the forecourt. He got up and opened the passenger door. Inside Arthur was staring ahead.

'You all right, Arthur?'

'Yeah – good as gold,' he said, his voice distant and his eyes still fixed. Beside him, Denise yawned. She looked totally relaxed.

'You look a bit queer.'

'No, no.'

'I got the licence, see.'

'Nice.' Arthur unfastened the seat belt and got out of the car. He walked slowly towards the caravan with Smudger beside him.

'I mean, it's a good 'un,' Smudger whispered. 'Not in my name, obviously, but similar.'

'That's nice,' said Arthur again. He fumbled for his keys.

'Did you have a good lesson?' asked Smudger innocently.

Arthur stared at him for a moment. Then he closed his eyes. 'Smudger, it was awful. Never mind her dad, she ought to be locked up.' He decided not to unlock the door and instead went to his Jaguar. 'I'm going to my warehouse. I don't want to be here when you come back.'

'Right, Arthur,' said Smudger as he turned back to Denise and her demon driving.

When Arthur was about to open up his lock-up, he paused, detecting a presence. Mr Mitra was about two inches from his face.

Arthur smiled. 'Dear oh dear, you did give me a nasty turn.'

But Mr Mitra didn't answer. When Arthur looked closely he saw there was another Indian behind him – and another, and another. When he spun round he saw two more. For a moment, Arthur thought he was having a nightmare. Then reality intruded – there was something menacing about the Indians.

He smiled hopefully. 'Buying or selling, gentlemen?'

'Please open the door and enter,' said Mr Mitra.

'I was gonna do that anyway. Can I help you?'

'Absolutely. Lead on,' he said. Somewhat reluctantly, Arthur opened the door and the Indians filed in.

'Brothers?' asked Arthur.

'Brothers in arms,' replied Mr Mitra, closing the door.

Arthur sighed, feeling the world crowding in on him again.

'I understand that you have an article of mine.'

' I do business with lots of Indians –'

'My video tape?'

'That's what it's all about. I'm afraid you've got the wrong man. I deal in many things –'

'Shamy stole my video. I want it back. Please sit down.' He pointed to a chair and Arthur realised that he must comply. He sat down heavily. 'There is no nonsense about this,' Mr Mitra explained carefully. 'We are going to search this place piece by piece, brick by brick and – eventually – bone by bone.' He turned to his colleagues. 'Begin,' he said commandingly.

'I haven't got it,' said Arthur.

'They're very careful. Would you like a cigar?' He sat down

and offered Arthur an expensive cigar. Arthur began to cheer up.

'A man of discernment, I see.'

'Among other things. I'm also a wholesale tobacconist.'

'This could be your lucky day. Interested in some good cigarillos? Argentinian, as it happens. But with the political backlash, it's quite difficult to move 'em.'

'No, thank you.'

'Well, there's all kinds of things here –'

'I have three corner shops, four newsagents and a couple of Do-It-Yourself shops.'

'Paint? Five litre pots.' Arthur was ever pressing. 'Perfect for the handyman. These are very similar to the paint used by the council – what we call Institutional Green –'

'Stolen goods,' said Mr Mitra censoriously.

'Surplus stock,' replied Arthur indignantly.

Then one of the Indians called to Mr Mitra and said something in Urdu. He was carrying some boxes. 'Stack them up outside,' commanded Mr Mitra.

As the Indian went outside, Arthur said, 'Careful with them. Have they done this before?' he asked Mr Mitra.

Chisholm emerged from the Magistrates Court and walked to his car, carrying a piece of paper in his hand. Once inside, and with Jones driving, he gave an icy smile of satisfaction. 'They don't like it, y'know. A search warrant is like winning the pools in our game.'

'I never trust magistrates anyway, guv.'

'They're always worried about rights.'

'Whose rights, eh?'

'I can't wait to see Daley's boat. He'll be on the old trombone in two seconds.'

'To whom?'

'The whole team – the busy-bodies. Release, Split, The Samaritans, Mensa, Exist, The London Rape Centre, The Alternative Parents' Group, Gay Rights – the whole shmeer, including the Royal bleeding Automobile Club.' Chisholm looked lovingly at the warrant.

After a pause, Jones said, 'Going to the Federation meeting on Monday?'

Chisholm scowled at him. 'What have they ever done for me?'

A pile of boxes began to grow outside the door of the lock-up, whilst inside seven of the Indians were making a systematic search. Then, one of them uncovered a video machine and some cassettes beneath a pile of leg-warmers. 'Mr Mitra –' He showed him one of the video cassettes.

'Is this mine?'

'No, no, it's an old one.'

'What does it say?'

'*Gone With The Wind,*' said one of the Indians.

'Like so many other things in this gaff,' said Arthur sadly.

Mr Mitra crossed the room and took the tape. He picked up another cassette. '*To Catch A Thief,*' he read.

'One of the greats. Can I mark your card?'

Mr Mitra picked up another tape. 'You mean, this one?'

'No, no – that's not the title,' said Arthur hastily. 'What I'm saying is that these videos are from another era. I'm not interested in your sort of films.'

'Really? Well, Mr Daley, I am going to mark *your* card. Do you know about Ghandi?'

'One of your own.'

'He believed in passive resistance.'

'A noble sentiment. We need a bit of that these days, eh?'

'Not me. Kill the bastards,' he said.

'Fair's fair – that's a bit strong, innit?'

Mr Mitra put his arm round Arthur's shoulders. 'There are some Indians who believe in turning the other cheek and the meek will inherit the world. Silly sods. There is another tradition, Arthur – you don't mind me calling you Arthur?'

'An honour.'

'Warriors, for example. Juggernauts, the thuggee, and those chaps could certainly have a good row. In my youth I saw howling mobs, baying for the blood of young Tommy

Atkins. Not a pleasant sight, Arthur.' As Mr Mitra spoke, the other Indians gathered silently around Arthur. 'Have you got my drift, Arthur,' continued Mr Mitra. 'In other words – if I may use an apt expression – you're up the Khyber. You've got ten seconds.'

Arthur looked uneasily around the circle. Four seconds had gone before Arthur plucked up the courage to say, 'You've got it all wrong –'

'Six,' said Mr Mitra.

A loud knock interrupted their deliberation and at the same time the door burst open. Chisholm stood there, looking at Arthur.

'What's this then? A Dutch auction – or even a Doolali auction?'

'How nice to see you, Mister Chisholm.' He turned courteously to Mr Mitra. 'D'you know Detective Sergeant Chisholm, a leading local representative of the thin blue line?'

Mr Mitra gave Chisholm a pleasant smile. 'Well, I suppose you have lots of business to do. Good morning, Mister Daley, and to you, Sergeant.' Mr Mitra beckoned to his troops and in single-file they marched out. Each of them acknowledging Chisholm as they took their leave, muttering "Good morning". Chisholm looked at them suspiciously.

'See you again, lads,' said Arthur cheerily.

Chisholm stared at Arthur as the last Indian closed the door behind him. 'What are you selling now? Second-hand poppadums?'

'I also like to do my bit for race relations, Mr Chisholm.'

Chisholm ignored him and began to prowl around the lock-up.

'Can I help you?' asked Arthur, after a while.

But Chisholm only scowled at him, still silently pacing. Jones picked up a couple of transistor radios on a shelf and Chisholm looked at Arthur's desk. He opened a drawer, rummaging through the contents and was eventually interrupted in his task by Arthur.

'D'you mind? These are personal effects.'

Chisholm pulled the drawer out and tipped the contents on to the desk-top.

'It's a bit presumptious. I do have certain rights, you know.'

'Like what?'

'You're trespassing on private property. Unless you've got a magistrates' search warrant, sworn and signed and sealed –'

With tremendous satisfaction, Chisholm produced the warrant. 'All right? D'you wanna call the Law Centre, Citizens Advice Bureau, or Channel Four? I think not. The best thing you should do is sit down or, even better – get down on your knees and pray that we don't find anything.'

Arthur looked shocked. 'Mister Chisholm – what have I done?'

'All kinds of things. I was hoping to see a printing press –'

'Why?'

'Somebody's printing these twenty pound notes.'

Greatly relieved, Arthur sat down. He smiled. 'Would I do that?'

'Yes,' replied Chisholm curtly. He was rummaging through another drawer.

'After all these years. You *know me* –'

'Yes.' Chisholm's voice was still hard. He unfurled a roll of labels that he had taken from the drawer. 'Miss Selfridges? See – you'd do anything for a penny or a pound. And for a twenty pound note, you'd mortgage your soul.'

'That's a very offensive remark, Mister Chisholm.'

'I've been saving that up.' He started to pace around again. 'Why have I come to see you? Forged notes have been wafting around the manor – I first saw one in your own hand. At this moment a man is impersonating Roger Moore; he doesn't *really* look like him, but the hair is similar. This person is known as The Syrup, an acquaintance of yours, and he bought the Roger Moore toupee with fifteen dud twenty pound notes. Last night I attempted to apprehend an Indian who was trying to pass – guess what – twenty pound notes. What is the common denominator? All roads lead to Daley –'

Arthur looked relaxed and confident. 'Search, then, Mr Chisholm.'

Chisholm looked at him and there was doubt in his eyes. Could Arthur have escaped him again? Chisholm turned abruptly to Jones. 'Have you found anything?'

'All kinds of remarkable things, guv – everlasting pencils –'

'Just a gimmick,' said Arthur airily.

'Scotch . . . *Loch* Eim?'

'Jews say that.'

'Yeah, well, it's for the discerning Jewish Scotch drinker. I cater for many palates.'

'And most of them reprobates.'

The telephone rang and Arthur and Chisholm reached for it at the same time. Arthur won by a narrow margin. 'Daley Enterprises.' At the same time, Chisholm put the receiver to his ear. It was Terry.

'It's me. I'm with Shamy. He wants some dough to get his ticket, there's a flight this afternoon. We'll shoot over, eh?'

Arthur had little to say.

'Who's with you?' asked Terry, getting wind of trouble.

Chisholm spoke to him sweetly. 'You know me, McCann. Did you say "Shamy" – is that our Indian friend?'

Terry abruptly hung up.

Chisholm turned to Arthur. 'What is it with you people? Don't you trust me?'

Back in the flat, Terry sat by the telephone, glaring at Shamy. 'We've gotta go . . . Twenty minutes and Chisholm's gonna be here.'

'But where're we going?'

'I don't know. Bombay?'

'Where'd I get the dough?'

'You're being dead straight, yeah? No moody . . . you're going to sell that video and come back with the money?'

'Course I will. I mean, them twenty pound notes – I was desperate.'

'Well, you're desperate now.'

'It's different –'

'It bloody is.' Terry went into the kitchen and fished out a plastic bag in the saucepan. As Terry rinsed the bag under the tap, he said. 'This is the best thing that's happened to me for six months. A Yankee – my first ever. Four winners on the trot. Punters like me dream about that.'

'How'd you pull that out?' asked Shamy.

'I just fancied them. Usually, I suss out the form, read the papers, horses for courses, who's the form jockey. But this time, I just *knew*.'

'Just luck then?' said Shamy disappointedly.

Terry arranged the notes on the draining-board. 'Well, don't knock it – it's going to get you out of an 'ole. You got your passport?'

'I'll phone her.' He picked up the telephone with a flourish. Hope had flowered again.

But not for long, for a saloon car was parked a few yards away from Shamy's flat. Two Indians sat in the front, with Mr Mitra in the back.

In Arthur's lock-up, chaos reigned as Chisholm searched, little caring for niceties. A disconsolate Arthur watched Chisholm tip over a tea-chest and spill the contents all over the floor. But there was nothing – no notes, no printing press. Meanwhile, Jones was prodding at a hardboard panel in the wall.

'This is a likely place, guv,' he said.

Eagerly Chisholm came over, picked up a large screwdriver and levered the panel.

'Just a bit of damp,' said Arthur casually.

'Could be a secret panel,' said Chisholm with manic delight.

'Nothing secret about it.'

'We might find all kinds of things here.' Chisholm was literally licking his lips in anticipation. He ripped off the panel and a small cloud of plaster and dust settled on his suit. As he shook off the dust, he said, 'As you said, Arthur – damp.

You'll have to have the builders in.' He flung the hardboard panel across the room.

'Charming,' Arthur muttered to himself.

'Eh, what d'you say?'

'Nothing.'

'I hope you're not questioning my behaviour?'

'The iron hand in a velvet glove. It's like having Attilla the Hun for tea.'

Then Arthur heard a strange sound from the yard – a kind of crunching and clanking that was reminiscent of a demented tractor. Hurrying, Arthur went to the door only to witness the return of the Daley School of Motoring car – dented, battered and with only one wing. Smudger stood beside it. A dazed Arthur slowly approached him.

'She's a nutter, y'know,' said Smudger. 'No question about it. She's a nutter.'

Chisholm was framed in the doorway. 'Not your day, Arthur,' he said smiling.

Terry's car approached the international terminal at Heathrow and he entered one of the multi-storey car-parks. Some way back at the roundabout, Gayle's car was being followed by Mr Mitra's saloon. A few minutes later, Gayle met Terry and Shamy as they waited beside the entrance to the tunnel that connected the car-park with the terminal building. She ran towards them, taking Shamy's passport from her handbag, and throwing her arms around him. Terry pushed them towards the tunnel and then began to run.

'You got everything?'

'Apart from the ticket –' Then to Shamy's horror, he saw Mr Mitra and his heavies approaching.

'You go ahead,' said Terry. 'I'll handle these guys.'

Shamy hesitated.

'Go on. This is my game – your game's running.' Terry looked around him. Then ahead he saw a long line of parked traffic trolleys. He darted for one of these, rolling it down the tunnel, while Shamy and Gayle ran into the terminal building. Terry wheeled another trolley down the tunnel and then another, until a barrage of wheels tore into Mitra and his gang. Mr Mitra fell over but a bolder Indian kicked away one of the trolleys and ran after Terry. He grabbed at him, Terry sidestepped, flinging his arms round the Indian's waist and depositing him into a trolley, rolling it down the tunnel so that it collided with Mr Mitra, just as he was painfully rising to his feet.

Back at the lock-up, Arthur was alone, sitting in the middle of the chaos like a broken-hearted clown. The telephone rang and he walked wearily to answer it.

'It's Terry – Shamy's on the plane to Bombay and Gayle's with me.'

'Good for you.'

'What's the matter, Arthur?'

'That Chisholm – he's a wicked man.'

'You owe me money,' said Terry.

'I owe you money? What d'you mean – Bombay? I never said he could go. I wouldn't give him the fare to Bethnal Green.' Arthur hung up abruptly.

The next day, Syrup was to be seen on Arthur's lot, polishing the repaired 'learner' car. He was proudly wearing his new wig. Inside the caravan, Arthur said to Terry. 'He don't look like Roger Moore. Not in a million years.'

'He's thrilled to bits. He don't even mind if Chisholm nicks him.'

Then a taxi drew up by the car-lot. Gayle got out, saying something to the driver and walking quickly to the caravan.

'Hold on,' said Arthur, 'if she wants money, she's *your* friend.' He gave a gleaming smile to Gayle. 'Hallo, my darling – good news, like malaria or something?'

She slammed down a bulky envelope on the table.

'Yours. He cabled it and he's having a great time. He didn't get as much as he thought, but even so –'

'Why hasn't he come back?' asked Terry.

'He loves it so much that I'm going over as well. He's bought a ticket –'

'He said he'd be there for a day.'

'Yeah, but he reckons he likes it. Everything – the dust, the dirt, the heat and the squalor. It's magic. He's got a job –'

'That's the heat. It's affected his brain.'

'Anyway, there's two grand there and he said "thank you for everything". I've got to dash.' She quickly kissed Terry and went. Arthur stared at the contents of the envelope.

'Five hundred of that is mine,' said Terry slowly.

'And five hundred of it is also mine.'

'Then divi-up the rest –'

'I had all the aggravation –'

Outside, Chisholm had just parked his car. Syrup saw him and hid quickly behind a pile of oil drums. As Chisholm marched towards the caravan, Terry spotted and nudged Arthur who was counting out the money – in twenty pound notes. Arthur looked up, caught Chisholm's look of deep hatred and gave him a sickly smile.

PART FOUR

Terry walked across a vast graveyard of old cars, some of which were damaged or wrecked and others had just come to the end of their lives. Mounds of tyres, heaps of gearboxes and rotting hulks were piled on the ground, whilst looming above them were cranes, magnetic grabs, metal compressor machines – all the tools of the car breaking business.

Gypsy Joe was the boss here and he watched Terry come across his domain with all the pride of the king of a devastated country. At fifty, Joe was tough and wore a single ring in his right ear. While he was waiting for Terry he was prowling round the yard, seeing what he could rescue – be it a hub cap or a clutch pedal or a penny. Even now, Joe was poking into a heap of rubbish and picking up a Rover badge, dusting it and putting it into his dungaree pocket.

'Hi, Terry,' said Joe. 'I thought Arthur would come and see me personally.'

Terry smiled and handed over an envelope. 'He's expecting company.'

'Oh yeah,' said Joe, who had already opened the envelope and was counting the wad of twenty pound notes he found there.

'It's all there,' said Terry.

But Gypsy Joe wasn't going to stop counting. 'I can't read or write, but I can add and that's why I'm called the King of the Gypsies.'

'You don't still use that name, Joe? Gypsy?' said Terry cynically. 'I mean – you don't roam around a lot, do you?'

'Still got the caravan.'

'Yeah, I know,' said Terry. 'But its moored in the South of France, innit?'

'That's right,' replied Joe with a self-satisfied smirk. 'I've got it beside my villa.'

'That's what I mean. Don't reckon you're a raggle-taggle gypsy round the old camp fire any more.'

'Course not. I've got a nice house in Stanmore now and it's detached an' all,' he said proudly. 'But my heart is with my people, Terry – wherever they are.'

143

'Yeah,' said Terry drily, 'they've probably been evicted by the council, but obviously they can't have been evicted from Stanmore or you would have given them a nice site in your garden –'

'They can always ask me.' Gypsy Joe clapped Terry on the back. 'Let's go into the office.'

The office was a corrugated iron shed, highly ramshackle, caving in on the corner of the yard. As they passed a Mercedes Gypsy Joe pointed the car out. 'That's it,' he said.

'Not a lot of motor left,' said Terry.

'Nasty one – jumped over the barrier on the M4, right into a juggernaut.' Joe began to rummage through a pile of papers on his desk and finally he discovered the document he was searching for, which he put into an envelope. 'This is for Arthur. Vehicle document.'

'For what?' asked Terry.

'That one.' He pointed through the window to the wrecked Mercedes.

'He ain't buying that!' exclaimed Terry.

Joe smiled. 'I thought you were partners. He's putting in a "ringer" – a car from Germany; same make, different model. He's bound to make a handsome profit.'

'Haven't the insurance people told the Department of Transport?' asked Terry.

Joe said, 'You're a simple boy, Terry. Now the sad thing about that Mercedes is that the man forgot to post his premium. Some people are very unlucky – he broke five ribs and gawd knows what else and he got nicked for driving an uninsured vehicle. As it happens, I gave him a favour. Incidentally, Tel, if you ever see a write-off in your manor – you into a long 'un . . . just for commission.'

'Thanks,' replied Terry. 'I'll look round for any crippled drivers an' all.'

'They're like gold-dust.'

'Crippled drivers?' asked Terry.

'The vehicle documents,' explained Gypsy Joe patiently.

Terry went to the door. 'Yeah, sure. I'll see yer.'

'Wait a minute,' said Joe. 'You'll need the MOT certificate.'

Terry passed by the door, glancing down at the wrecked Mercedes. 'For that?'

'No – for the new one.'

'But, you haven't seen it.'

Joe looked at him righteously. 'Well I'm sure Arthur wouldn't sell a duff motor. It's trust – that's the name of the game in our business, Terry.'

Terry went out into the yard. 'Thanks,' he said, 'I'll remember that. It's a good word – trust.'

After his doubtful escapades in the Asian world, Arthur returned to more familiar territory on his second-hand car lot. He was expecting a ringer but he had time to spare for the odd punter. Directly he saw his unwary victim inspecting a Mini with a sticker on the windscreen saying, 'The Bargain of the Week', Arthur hurriedly walked over from his caravan office.

He began to peel off the sticker.

'Is it sold?' asked the punter immediately.

Arthur looked round as if he was surprised. 'Sorry, didn't see you, sir. Actually, my wife wants to buy it.' He gave a quick deprecating grin. 'No profit in it for me, eh? But there you go, if 'er indoors wants it – what can I do?' He paused. 'Were you interested in it, sir?'

'Well, I don't know. You reckon it's a good motor?'

'Good? Would I sell a vehicle to my own wife – or even to my own mother? No, this is one of the best. I had to go to the Duke of Norfolk's estate to buy that.'

'What – his own personal car?'

'Well, one hardly presumes that he's talking a lot of pork pies, is he?'

The punter was obviously impressed. 'Titled owner, eh?'

'Well,' said Arthur casually, 'he was wearing a deerstalker and a Harris tweed suit. I *assumed* that he was His Grace. We had a bit of conversation about horses. He's well into racing, as you probably know. Y'see, nice thing about the aristocracy is they like to keep their motors in good nick. Know what I mean?'

145

'He's probably got a garage,' said the punter naively.

'Well, he ain't going to park it outside his house, is he?'

The punter walked round the car. 'How much were you selling it for?'

'My wife would break her heart. Obviously, I was selling it to her for trade. Bad week for me.'

'How much did you say?'

'I didn't.'

'Oh.'

'I tell you what – I mean if you're interested, you are, aren't you?'

'Well, I –' his voice trailed off.

'Never mind "well". Her indoors set her heart on this little motor, given its pedigree. I'm a fool to myself – what with the financial climate and all that – I'll tell you what I'll do.' He clasped the punter's elbow and began to whisper confidentially.

MacFadyen, a hard forty-year old Scot, was driving a car transporter towards Arthur's car-lot. On board, the German Mercedes rocked gently – it was the ringer. But unfortunately, what MacFadyen didn't realise was that the nondescript van a few yards behind him contained two plain-clothed police officers, who were already reporting back to base the exact location of MacFadyen and his transporter.

'Rio Mary,' said one of the officers into a microphone, 'we've just picked him up – travelling eastward to Fulham.' But then the driver had to brake as a car ahead stopped for the red light.

'Sod it,' he said as MacFadyen's transporter jumped the lights.

A smiling Arthur was waving goodbye to the punter – and the Mini – when he saw MacFadyen parking his transporter. Arthur walked towards him. 'How're you doing, Frank?'

'Not so bad – and yourself?'

As MacFadyen climbed out of the cabin Arthur was

already looking at the cars on the back. 'Very handsome motors.'

'Great runners. In fact, my own wife wanted to buy the Merc, very clean car – too expensive for me.'

Arthur interrupted him. 'I've used that particular line this morning. Never lie to a liar, old son.'

MacFadyen grinned. 'I should've never said that to you. You're a bit too long in the tooth for that.'

'And they're all mine as well. Come on then – load off. I want to see this motor.'

MacFadyen started to lift down the ramp.

'Going up to Glasgow tomorrow?' asked Terry, emerging from the caravan with some new registration plates.

'Just going to relax here for a couple of days. I'm delivering the Porsche to a feller in Warren Street – have a few jars – maybe see my sister –'

'Nice motor. No problems?' asked Terry.

MacFadyen looked at him warily. 'Like what? Paid the customs and the tax. It's all down to Arthur now. If he's got the right logbook, it's a doddle for him. No come-backs if he's clever.'

'Oh, he's clever.'

'Would you like to come into the office?' said Arthur. 'Terry put them plates on.'

'How?' he asked simply.

'How? with a screwdriver – you have used a screwdriver before, haven't you? Documents – and put the right plate on the right motor.' He gave the documents to Terry and looked at MacFadyen. 'He's worse than two Irishmen.'

Terry said sarcastically, 'Have you got any tools in your workshop? I mean, things like screwdrivers, spanners, screws, bolts and nuts –'

'Now he's getting stroppy an' all. Go and borrow them.'

'No chance of actually buying them. Petty cash? A float?'

'Obviously, you'll be recompensed.'

'Yeah? I think I'll have a drink down the boozer instead. See you, Frank.' Abruptly, Terry left, exasperated, as usual, by Arthur's lies.

A few minutes later, Arthur was opening a briefcase stuffed with banknotes. He started counting with a bank clerk's expertise. 'That's the kind of problem we have in this country. Work? Where is he now – the honest English workman? He doesn't want to know about work. Graft? Not a chance. The sweat of the brow? No – it's all easy money now, the quick buck – as our American friends say. Years ago a man went to his workplace with a couple of slices of Hovis in his pocket and a nice piece of farmhouse cheese and he put in ten hours of honest toil. Now what do we get – luncheon vouchers! Sod it,' he said as he lost count. 'I'll have to start again now.' He licked his forefinger and rapidly began re-counting. 'What did we say? Seven grand?'

'I think we said seven grand five hundred and three hundred for the delivery charges.'

'You're more wicked than British Leyland,' said Arthur, as one professional to another.

Arthur would have been most agitated if he had realised that two Police Rovers were currently bearing down on him. In the second, Detective Sergeant Rycott sat with a large man named Inspector Klingmann, who had an impressive bearing and a hard intimidating scowl. He was an officer of the Federal Republic of Germany Police, on an exchange visit, an anglophile in tweeds, smoking a pipe. Beside him was Inspector Armstrong, middle-aged and sceptical.

As they neared Arthur's site, MacFadyen's car transporter drove past the police cars in the opposite direction. Then, as they pulled up beside the somewhat tatty-looking second-hand car display, the street became alive with policemen, plain-clothed men and uniformed officers. Police motor cycles stopped the traffic and a small crowd of curious onlookers began to gather.

Completely unaware of what was happening, Arthur was reading his newspaper when he looked up and saw Rycott approaching the hut. He smiled benignly, little realising that another officer was circling behind the caravan. Innocently, Arthur rose to welcome Rycott obsequiously, but an armed officer darted in front of him. 'Freeze!'

'Eh?'

'Keep your hands on the desk.'

Arthur saw Rycott standing behind him. Then he saw the full bastion of his armed colleagues. 'What's this then – a wind up?' But he was so surprised that he felt no other emotion but curiosity.

'You heard him. Hands on the desk.'

'It's me, Mr Rycott,' said Arthur, desperation replacing his curiosity.

'I know who you are.'

'Well, what's all this business. "Freeze?" It's Starsky and Crutch –'

'Do as you're told.'

Arthur then finally realised that Rycott was in earnest and he put up his hands. 'Can I ask why?'

'Shurrup,' said the armed officer.

'Am I being arrested?'

'Course not. We just want to talk to you –'

'Like this?'

'Down the road.'

'In the nick, you mean? Certainly not –'

Rycott gave him a wolfish grin. 'Okay, then do a runner. You wouldn't get to the pavement. There's ten armed coppers surrounding this place. At least one of them's gun-happy – got to be. Fancy your chances?'

Arthur stared at him in bewilderment. 'But what've I done? I mean, just give me a hint?'

'All in good time, Arthur,' said Rycott patiently. 'Now are you coming quietly?'

Outside Klingmann and Inspector Armstrong were looking at the gleaming Merc. They had opened the bonnet and seemed interested in the engine.

Klingmann glanced up as Arthur was escorted by two armed officers to a police car. Arthur mustered as much dignity as he could – given the fact that one of the officers was shoving him into the car.

149

When Terry returned from the pub, carrying a couple of screwdrivers and spanners, he discovered the Merc being lifted up on to a police break-down trailer. There were policemen still nosing around the site, whilst two uniformed constables were telling curious onlookers to keep moving.

Terry paused and crossed to the other side of the road. There was no sign of Arthur.

At the police station a shirtsleeved officer was about to take Arthur's fingerprints.

'Eh, eh – just a minute. I'm not having my dabs –'

'Why?'

'Why? Because I have certain rights.'

'They always say that.'

'I don't care about that.' Arthur was insistent. 'I still don't know why I'm in here.'

The officer wrestled gently with Arthur's hand. 'Well, I don't know, do I? Take his dabs – that's all they said to me. I mean, we've got to distinguish you from the other suspects.'

'What suspects?'

'I don't know, do I? Anyway – everybody should have his fingerprints. I mean, say you fell into the river and you lost your wallet. Drowned. Stone dead. How could we identify you? We're not talking about crime; we're talking about personal identity.'

'I never go near the river.'

'Car crash? Collapse in the street? I mean, it's common sense. I'm a great believer in identity.' He still continued taking Arthur's prints. 'We've got to sort out the goats from the sheep, eh?' he said, as if he was talking to a patient. 'Painless, innit?'

'Yeah, I know,' said Arthur caustically. 'You've got them, anyway.'

'Really? I'd have thought that you'd never been in a police station before. Tissue?' He offered a Kleenex box. 'Years ago we never had things like this – a dirty old rag. Hygiene – see? That's the thing these days. Sit down over there, sir.'

Arthur sat down on a bench. A few minutes later, another officer passed him and said, 'Don't sit there. Go over there –'

Arthur crossed to a chair by the corner. Then he called out to his retreating back. 'Excuse me! Could you please tell me what this is all about?'

'No idea, mister,' said the officer, without pausing.

Arthur fidgeted and clicked his teeth. Various police officers walked about the area, each looking purposeful and businesslike. Then another officer passed. 'I say, could I just ask –'

'I'm busy.'

'Oh, thanks,' Arthur said as the officer disappeared down the corridor. 'That's great, innit? The one time you need one they're all busy,' he muttered to himself. After a while, he peeped round the corner to see Rycott approaching. Arthur rose quickly.

'Mr Rycott, can I have a quick word?'

'No.' He was carrying a file.

'I can't have that. I am a law-abiding ratepayer –'

'Who says?'

'I'll ignore that. But as nobody knows why I'm here, do you think I can go now?'

'You must be joking? You're helping the police. You know, "a man is being interviewed by the local police." That man is you.'

Arthur stared at him. 'In that case I think I should phone my soliciter.'

'Why'

'Why? Are you cognizant of the common law of this country? Magna Carta – and all that? Habeas corpus, the inalienable right of decent Englishmen? May I suggest that you are well out of order, Mr Rycott?'

Rycott started to say something, but Arthur hurriedly continued.

'I haven't finished yet. When my brief comes down here *he* is going to give you and your superiors a right verbal thrashing –'

'Yeah, yeah, yeah – OK. What's his name?'

'Ivan Silkman, of –'

'You're kidding. He's doing eighteen months in Ford Open nick.'

'That's his brother, a headstrong lad,' said Arthur quickly. 'But Ivan is one of the rising lights in the legal profession.'

'I'll give him a bell,' said Rycott grudgingly.

'And quick.'

Rycott scowled and started down the corridor.

Arthur's complaining voice pursued him. 'I think I've been very decent to you people. I mean, fair's fair – but you haven't even suggested what the charge is.'

Rycott turned. 'We're working on it.'

'Like what?'

'I don't know – conspiracy maybe.'

'You what?' Arthur sounded shocked.

'Harbouring, illegal substances –? Smuggling drugs? Causing a riot? Oh and – that German motor hasn't got a MOT certificate – not a real one at least.' Rycott walked away, whilst Arthur looked dumbfounded. For a moment he didn't realise that another officer, this time the gaoler, was shepherding him towards a door.

'This way, please . . . sir.'

'Yeah,' he said absentmindedly. But it was not until he was walking down the white tiled corridor that Arthur realised where they were heading. 'Hey, what's going on?'

The gaoler lead him towards a cell. 'You'll be all right here, sir.'

Arthur began to pant. 'That's a cell.'

'Quite harmless. Excuse me.' He began to pull off Arthur's tie. 'And these, sir.' He undid Arthur's braces.

'Gawd help us,' said Arthur grabbing at his trousers.

'You'll be better in there. It's all hurry and scurry upstairs, you can't even hear yourself think . . . what with coppers running around and people being arrested, shouting and swearing. This is much nicer.' He smiled generously. 'You only have to knock if you want anything, sir.' With that he slammed the door closed, leaving Arthur a shocked, shuddering heap.

Arthur's Mercedes was being systematically dismantled. The doors had been removed and the bonnet. The car was on a hydraulic ramp with two mechanics busy removing the exhaust system. A plain-clothed officer was discussing progress with the shop foreman.

'Are you going to be able to put it all back together?' he asked jocularly.

'The Jerries can do it; why not us?' said the foreman. 'Incidentally, the shock absorbers are a bit iffy.'

'I don't want to buy it, Charlie. Let's just find the stuff, right?'

In Warren Street, the second-hand car market of London, MacFadyen was unloading a Porsche from his transporter. When it was finally set on the roadway a car dealer called Ronnie slid into the driving seat with MacFadyen beside him. Ronnie was very flash, with a chunky gold bracelet, half a ton of gold watch on the other wrist and a Dior gold tooth-pick dangling on his solarium-tanned chest.

Ronnie tried to back the Porsche into his garage-cum-showroom, but it was a tricky manoeuvre which annoyed him, for he liked to show off his driving. As he started the car backwards, he brushed an old parked car and swore. But when he saw MacFadyen grinning he laughed and said, 'That was nothing, believe me. Just a little scratch. He shouldn't have parked here anyway – this is for people in the trade.' He glanced around him. 'I know every car in the street and that wreck is a stranger. Probably a punter,' said Ronnie as he switched off the ignition.

'I'll have a wee look, just the same,' said MacFadyen suspiciously.

Ronnie squeezed MacFadyen's shoulder 'I'll tell you what. This isn't a bad motor. You know I drove a lot.'

'I can see that,' said MacFadyen with a straight face.

'Do a bit of rallying, know what I mean?'

'Is that right?'

'Yeah. I'm a member of The DrivingWheel Club – Jackie Stewart, Fittipaldi, the new French feller – I met 'em all.' He glanced round the interior of the car. 'Nice and clean, isn't it?' He pushed the stereo button on the radio. 'Nice music.' Ronnie got out and prowled around the car looking at the bumper. 'Told you – not a scratch. Hard to sell a motor in Glasgow.'

'Aye, but we're in London, aren't we?' said MacFadyen. 'Anyway, I've got a punter in Glasgow. A decent guy – managing director of a building business.'

Ronnie nodded making it clear that he'd heard it all before. 'Yeah – managing director – they all say that.' He gave a quick grin. 'No disrespect to you. Now, you were hoping to get ten and a half for this, weren't you?'

'That's what we said on the phone.'

'Yeah, I know, but now I see the actual motor –'

MacFadyen interrupted him, looking particularly evil. 'Don't piss me around – I did all the work and I've got contacts over there. They've even changed the number on the chassis and the engine. You've got to realise, German villains are very efficient. All you've got to do is stand by the corner and cop five grand for just wearing out your shoe leather.'

Ronnie gave him a cynical grin. 'As it happens, I'm hoping to get about eight grand. I like very, very expensive shoes, Frank.'

Terry walked into the solicitor's office and was immediately rebuffed by Karen, the receptionist. 'Sorry, we're closed now, love.'

'It's an emergency,' said Terry dourly.

'Oh, it's you, Terry. You in trouble or something?'

'No. Is he in?'

'He's gone shooting for the weekend. It's his new thing – he's gone right off golf. I think it's because he mixes with a lot of people who like shooting – robbers, you know what I mean?'

'Yeah,' said Terry. 'Have you got his number?'

'He doesn't want to be disturbed.'

'This is important – Arthur's in the nick.'

'Well, he's certainly not interested in Arthur. We haven't

154

had his last cheque yet or the one before.'

'Must have slipped his mind,' said Terry.

'I bet.'

'This is an emergency,' said Terry.

'You've already told me –' The telephone rang and Karen picked up the receiver. 'Sorry, he's gone for the weekend. Oh, hallo Sergeant Rycott –'

'Just a minute,' said Terry, 'let me talk to him.'

Hesitantly, Karen gave the phone to Terry.

'Mr Rycott?'

'Yes, Terry?'

'What's the SP on Arthur?'

'He's just helping us with our enquiries.'

'But what's the charge?:'

'Nothing yet – but there will be.'

'Will he be appearing in court?'

'If I've got anything to do with it,' said Rycott, 'he'll be in the Magistrates' Court on Monday.'

'Can I have him out on bail?' asked Terry.

'No chance – he's here for the weekend, while we pursue our enquiries. He wanted his solicitor.'

'Yeah,' said Terry, 'but he's not around, he's gone shooting.'

'That's nice,' said Rycott.

'Could I see him?'

'If you find out where he's shooting.'

'No,' said Terry patiently. 'I mean Arthur.'

'Maybe.'

'What do you mean, maybe, Sergeant Rycott?'

'What I say.'

'But look – if he hasn't got his solicitor there –'

'Listen Terry, said Sergeant Rycott, 'are you suggesting I'm not doing things by the book?'

'No, Mr Rycott. Not in the least. But I would like to see him.'

'Come down here and chance your luck,' said Rycott. 'If we've got time you might be able to drop into his cell for five minutes.'

Terry put down the phone and turned back to Karen. 'We're in stuk. Can't you possibly give me that phone number?'

'Sorry,' said Karen. 'And if you see Arthur, give him this envelope.'

'What's in it?' said Terry.

'His prior account.'

'Please help me.'

'I told you – Ivan needs his rest just as much as anyone else. Why don't you go down to the Law Centre?'

'That's for squatters and old ladies who are being evicted,' said Terry.

Karen closed her handbag primly. 'You do understand that there's one law for everybody, don't you?'

In the police station that was currently housing Arthur, Klingmann and Inspector Armstrong were studying a file, while Rycott looked on.

'Not guilty. Not guilty. Not guilty.' Klingmann's very correct English accent was beginning to show frustration. 'Excuse me, but do you ever convict people like this?'

'Well, he's a slippery character, Daley.'

'Slippery?'

'I think the Sergeant means that Daley is a very clever criminal,' said Armstrong.

'Obviously – I see here that he had a sentence for eighteen months, twenty-four years ago.'

Rycott looked over his shoulder. 'He had a couple of parking offences three years ago,' he said with a hopeful smile. 'You see, when I heard about it, I thought, well, it's not Arthur's usual game.'

'Sergeant, I want you to assist Inspector Klingmann in every way,' said Inspector Armstrong.

'Yessir.'

'This is an Anglo-German operation. So I want you to explain Daley's "usual game".'

Rycott began to speak slowly and carefully. 'Well, I mean – he's a rascal, no question about it. He's a scallywag – but, I

156

can't buy Arthur, I mean, Daley, as a drug dealer. For a start, it's dangerous.'

'That is because the stakes are high.'

'But he's a devout coward, sir. A dodgy motor, yes. But –'

Klingmann was annoyed. 'I have had very reliable sources and efficient methods.'

'In that case, why didn't you intercept the car in Germany?' asked Armstrong with a smile.

'Nobody is perfect, you know,' he snapped. 'Including here . . . Not guilty, not guilty, not guilty. What is the expression here? This man is overdue, yes?'

'Well overdue, sir.'

'And talking about overdue. I should be at a Police Federation meeting in a few minutes,' put in Armstrong.

'Another rise, sir?'

'In the pipeline, I think.'

Klingmann looked at them incredulously.

'Rycott will help you in every way, Inspector,' said Armstrong as he hurriedly departed.

'Well, how about a nice cup of tea, sir?' asked Rycott cheerfully.

'I do not wish tea. I would rather meet Mister Daley.' He paused. 'Unless he is already having some tea.'

Rycott smiled weakly. 'I'll wheel him in, sir.'

Arthur sat down in front of the desk gloomily. Rycott had just told him that they were unable to contact his solicitor because he was away – which left him feeling properly high and dry. There was a long pause whilst Klingmann studied some documents. The only light in the room was from a desk lamp. Arthur smiled hopefully and Klingmann looked up.

'Not guilty, eh?' he said with a sour smile.

'I beg your pardon?'

'Nothing. Do you smoke?' Klingmann offered him a pack of cigarettes although he was puffing a pipe himself.

'Cigar man. But they didn't leave my matches.' He gave a sideways glance at Rycott. 'Or me braces.'

'Go ahead,' said Klingmann.

Arthur took out a cigar, offering one to Klingmann who declined. Then the officer struck him a match.

'Apparently you have many friends in Germany?' asked Klingmann.

Arthur was still lighting his cigar. 'Never been to the place.' He straightened up. 'Is this about the motor? I am a bona fide motor trader. And anybody knows that I'm –'

'You are giving me answers and I haven't even given the questions yet.'

'Sorry – I'm usually quick, see.'

'Oh, yes, I realise that. Any man with your history of "not guilty's," I have to respect.'

Arthur gave him a strained smile and said, 'Am I assuming that I am talking to a German police officer?'

'This is true.'

'Charming.' He looked at Rycott. 'This is all down to the Common Market, innit? I mean – me – *me*, interrogated by a German. And they know a lot about interrogating, don't they?'

'Don't be cheeky, Arthur,' said Rycott firmly. 'He's just asking some questions.

'It's like Colditz.'

'Listen, any more of that and I'm going to nick you under the Race Relations Act –'

'That's for Lucozades – not for Jerries.'

'We're all brothers under the skin these days, Arthur.' Rycott turned to Klingmann. 'Sorry, Inspector.'

'Thank you. I repeat, who are your contacts in Germany?'

'I've told you. Just a simple car dealer, C of E, free enterprise – a true patriot. I was in the British Army, you know, King and Empire. I mean, Queen and Commonwealth.'

'All right, Arthur – we've got all your previous.'

'Who are the people you bought the car from?' asked Klingmann.

Arthur relaxed. 'That's easy – Old Frank.'

'Who?'

Arthur looked worried again. 'His name's Frank – I mean,

in my game it's all down to cash and first names. Everybody knows that. Got it – a receipt, no problem.' Searching in his pockets, Arthur found the receipt which looked indecipherable. 'Well, it's Frank – Frank somebody or other. There's a "M" there. "Mac" something. I don't know.'

Klingmann looked at the receipt and then gave it to Rycott.

'The tax people will like that. Are all your transactions like these?'

'That's down to my accountant, innit. He keeps meticulous books –'

'I hope you can remember *his* name.'

'Obviously. You see this name, this Frank. I can't understand his writing. I mean, they're not all that clever with writing and things, I mean, your Scotsmen. A bit handy with the roll-call and putting in the head and that's it.'

Klingmann stared stonily at him. Rycott smiled.

'My old mum is from Scotland.'

'I mean some of them. Old Frank – just an ordinary bloke, not your actual scholar. Can I see it again?' He paused.

Rycott gave him the scrap of paper.

'See that first name, Frank – that's quite clear. It's the other name, right? Mac – innit?'

'Mac – what?'

'I don't know – they've all got Mac's up there, haven't they?' He smiled. 'Got it – he came on the boat. Well, the passport people – they check all the names. That's your answer – documents. You people like that,' he said to Klingmann. Then he returned to Rycott and said, 'They love documents – Germans.'

'I don't care about the documents! I want to find out what's *in* the car. Drugs!' said Klingmann angrily.

'Drugs!'

'Narcotics.'

'I'm not into that. What do you think I am? The Fulham connection?'

'Why not?'

'Mr Rycott – tell him? Arthur Daley – a drug fiend? I don't

159

even trust one of them Paracetamols.'

'You could be a middle man though.'

Rycott grinned for he was enjoying this interrogation.

Arthur stared at both of them dazedly. 'That's it then. I don't say another word without my solicitor here.'

'I told you – he's gone shooting.'

'Then, I'm going.'

'Give us a chance, Arthur. This is a serious case. I thought you'd help us.'

'Of course I would. The man you're after is Frank What's-'is-name.'

'And we'll get him,' said Rycott. 'But in the meantime, I'd be grateful if you could dwell here for a while –'

'That's right – always help your local sheriff – correct, yes?' He beamed at his own heavy humour whilst Arthur glanced warily at Rycott.

MacFadyen was pouring champagne in a drinking club and clinking glasses with Ronnie, the second-hand car salesman, and Rita, who was young and sexy.

'To you, Rita,' said MacFadyen.

'Isn't he nice. I love your accent, Frank.'

'And I love your pretty face and your beautiful figure,' said MacFadyen leering. 'I bet you're a dancer.'

'You're right.'

'You was in the Royal Ballet, wasn't you?'

'Only for a bit,' she said. 'They're very stuck up, some of them. So I went to Tunisia with a group and that was more like modern dancing.'

'Ready for another one, Frank?'

'It's my shout,' said MacFadyen. 'Rita, do you fancy any more of the old bubbly?'

'Why not?' said Rita.

MacFadyen drunkenly lurched towards the small bar and Ronnie said to Rita, 'It's about time we got a bit busy on him, darling. He's got ten grand in his bin and that was only from me. Gawd knows how much more he's got on him, and he sold a nice Merc an' all.'

'Yeah, but I don't want him in my place,' said Rita.

'Course not – you gotta box clever. Take him to a hotel – George's gaff – he'll let anybody in; all the brasses use it.'

'Don't you call me a bloody brass,' said Rita indignantly.

'Course you're not,' replied Ronnie ingratiatingly. 'You're just in between engagements. Like between Swan Lake and the go-go at Marrakesh.'

Arthur lay miserably on his cot in the cell, with his shirt sleeves rolled up, whilst a doctor tested his blood pressure. He looked carefully down at the instrument as he unrolled the band around Arthur's arm.

'Well?' asked Arthur anxiously.

'You're fine.'

'Are you sure, doc?'

'Nothing wrong with you. You're as sound as a bell.'

'It can't be,' said Arthur disappointedly. 'I had a kind of turn.'

'What kind of turn?' asked the doctor.

'Well, I felt sort of dizzy like, with palpitations and apart from that, I suffer from claustrophobia –'

'Well,' said the doctor, with an ironic smile, 'this really isn't the place to be if you suffer from claustrophobia.'

'I told them,' said Arthur. 'I'm a nervous wreck. Usually I can have a nap anywhere. Not here.'

'Don't worry about it,' said the doctor. 'I'll give a tablet to the gaoler.'

'Don't give one to him,' said Arthur. 'I'm the one who needs it.'

But the doctor gave him a patient look. 'I'll give it to him and he'll give it to you. Do you understand that?'

'Yeah,' said Arthur.

'Goodnight.' Then the doctor went out and the gaoler appeared, telling Arthur that he had a visitor.

'About time an' all,' said Arthur picking up his jacket and walking behind the gaoler to an interview room in the station where Terry was sitting at a table.

'Where have you been?' asked Arthur.

161

'Well, give us a chance.'

'Why? I'm cooped up in here. Where's Ivan?'

'He's gone –'

'Yes,' said Arthur interrupting wrily, 'I know, he's gone shooting. But why?'

'I don't know,' replied Terry. 'Maybe he's joining the Israeli army. Why don't you sit down?'

'I will,' said Arthur and scowled at the officer who lounged beside the door.

After a pause, Terry said, 'It's a turn-up, innit?'

Arthur stared at him. 'Is that all you can say, when I'm in a situation like this, without a tie and no braces. I mean – I can understand prison riots now. I'm not kidding you – I'm stir crazy.'

'You've only been here for five hours,' said Terry.

'But it's the principle, isn't it. I'm a free spirit. I miss the buses.'

'What?'

'I miss the buses. I don't know why, but I have an obsession with red buses.'

'I think you're pregnant,' said Terry.

'Listen, Terry. This is a very big case. You do realise the Germans are after me, don't you?'

'What do you mean?'

'You know what they're like. Fulham today and brave little Belgium tomorrow.'

'Look – it's a simple case of mistaken identity,' said Terry.

'So was the case of the Count of Monte Cristo,' replied Arthur, 'and what about 'er indoors. What's she gonna say when she comes back from her sister's? The local paper will have a bonanza when they start putting up the headlines about a well known public figure in pokey. You've got to remember that my kids go to a private school and they mingle with scions of local personalities.'

'What about the stockbroker who's doing plenty of bird?' asked Terry.

'That's not the same,' said Arthur. 'That was business, not crime. Their talking about me as the mastermind of the

Fulham connection. And that's what happens when you do business with Scotchmen.'

'You were happy enough when you were stitching him up,' said Terry.

'Stitching him up!' exclaimed Arthur. 'Be fair, Tel – I was doing an honest deal. You do a favour – and then what? I had a feeling in my water with that man.'

'MacFadyen? Seemed a decent guy.'

'What? Give me the guy's name.'

'MacFadyen,' said Terry.

'MacFadyen, that's manna from heaven.' Arthur looked as if he was going to burst into tears. 'Why didn't you tell me before?'

'I've only been here a few minutes,' said Terry.

Arthur addressed the officer leaning against the door. 'Did you get that?'

'Eh?'

'Listen, officer. You're supposed to listen to our conversation. Did you get that name?'

'I wasn't listening.'

'Terrific, eh?' said Arthur to Terry. 'Anyway, I'll tell Rycott now that I've got the name.'

'Maybe I'll have a quick creep down Warren Street,' said Terry.

'Why?'

'"Cause he had a Porsche on the back of his trailer and I know he was going down there.'

'Blimey,' said Arthur, impressed. 'Full marks for observation. You really amaze me – not a lot, but just sometimes. Now get down there,' said Arthur theatrically. 'Find that man.'

'What about Rycott, the pride of the force?'

'Him,' said Arthur scornfully, 'he couldn't find a tart in a brothel.'

Terry walked down Warren Street, scrutinising the cars and rather crumby showrooms and garages. Dealers were chatting on every corner and the cars were parked bumper to bumper. Terry spotted the Porsche almost at once, jutting out from a garage entrance with a mechanic fitting a new registration number plate. Terry crossed the street and asked him, 'Guv'nor around?'

But Ronnie, hopefully spotting a punter, was already by his side. 'Handsome motor, eh?'

'Yeah.'

'You trade?'

'Sort of.'

'What's that mean?' asked Ronnie with a phoney smile.

'Always interested in an imported car from Germany.'

'What's that mean?' said Ronnie.

'You said that before,' said Terry with a grin.

'Who are you then?' asked Ronnie impatiently. 'VAT man?'

'No.' Then Terry spoke pleasantly. 'You met a feller from Glasgow yesterday –'

'What's it to you? I don't know nothing about the guy. I buy 'em and sell 'em. OK. See yer.' He turned away, walking back to his office, but Terry grabbed his arm.

'Just a minute – you're not being very nice, are you?'

'If you don't let go of my arm, you'll be asking for a slap.'

'Leave it out,' said Terry still smiling, but Ronnie swung at him and Terry grabbed the other wrist, pulling him towards the car.

'I don't know nothing about the guy,' Ronnie shouted. 'I just had a drink with him.'

'You know more than that.'

Ronnie turned to his mechanic. 'Gary, sort him out.'

But the mechanic wasn't having any. 'I clean 'em, you sell 'em – you sort him out.'

Ronnie tried to relinquish Terry's grip, but he wasn't strong enough and Terry pushed his face under the open bonnet. 'Come on, you're not helping me, are you?'

'Push off.'

'Nice clean engine –'

'Okay, it wasn't down to me. He went away with a brass.'

'Where?'

'Hotel in King's Cross.'

'What's it called?'

'Nero's Palace.'

Terry released him and Ronnie staggered back.

'Thanks,' said Terry.

Ronnie aimed a wild swing at him but Terry easily swayed out of distance. 'You should be nicer to people,' said Terry.

Back in the police repair shop various parts of the Mercedes were littered around the floor and the seats were propped up against a wall. A plain clothed man wandered into the shop and walked up to the foreman.

'Find anything?'

'Nothing.'

'What about the sump?'

'There wasn't even any oil in it – never mind drugs,' said the foreman sourly. 'But now we've come across a real problem.'

'What's that?'

'We're on double time.'

'Tell your guv'nor.' The plain clothed policeman walked slowly away.

When Terry stepped into the tatty reception area of Nero's Palace, Georgie, the obese owner, was having a cup of tea and checking his accounts.

'Yessir?'

'Looking for one of your guests. Mr MacFadyen?'

'That's a new one.'

'It probably is in here. Scotch? Tall. About forty.'

'Who are you? Old Bill?'

'I'm just a mate of his.'

'I've got a lot of residents.'

'He came in with a – you know – his wife.'

'I don't want a big party. The other two guys have already –' But he never finished the sentence for pandemonium suddenly broke out upstairs. 'Bloody hell,' said Georgie.

There was shouting, screams and the crashing of breaking

165

furniture. It was the latter sound that made Georgie, despite his weight, begin to ascend the stairs at a considerable speed. He was closely followed by Terry. But directly Georgie and Terry reached the landing, a door was wrenched open on the next floor and MacFadyen began to take the stairs, two at a time.

'Frank –' said Terry conversationally, as MacFadyen shoved Georgie aside. Then he hit Terry flush on the chin and Terry collapsed to the floor, whilst MacFadyen ran to the exit.

A few seconds later, Terry sat up against the wall, ruefully massaging his jaw.

'I thought you were a mate of his?' said Georgie.

'More like nodding acquaintances really.' Terry rose shakily to his feet, while, at the same time, two heavies, dishevelled and with multiple abrasions, stumbled from the room. One of them glanced at Terry and Georgie as they passed. 'Bloody nutters. All them Jocks are nutters,' he said.

When Terry and Georgie entered the room a girl lay naked in a disarrayed bed. The room was a shambles and she was fingering a nasty bruise on her cheek.

'Get your clothes on,' said Georgie. 'I run a respectable hotel.'

'I knew you'd say that,' she remarked sarcastically.

'That's right. I mean, this is a family hotel.'

'Don't give me all that crap. You run a glorified knocking shop.' She glanced at Terry. 'Who the hell is this?'

'I'm the man from the Michelin Guide,' said Terry.

'What're you going to give – a rosette or crossed fists?'

Terry picked up MacFadyen's hold-all.

'Nothing in there,' she said, but he had already found a tattered address book. 'I'm looking for his sister's address.'

'What's she? Female wrestler?' She took a cigarette and lit it, whilst Georgie rearranged the furniture. 'He had his money in his socks. No wonder he kept them on.'

'You're lucky. My pal's in the nick because of him.'

'Tough titty. He never even paid me. All I got was a right-hander.' With a touch of dignity she tidied the

166

bedclothes. 'I don't usually do this, you know.'

'And what about the two creepers –?'

'Not my friends.' She gave a meaningful glance. 'Were they, Georgie? They were after something he had.'

'You'd better go. Come on,' said Georgie.

'Don't talk to me like that,' shouted Rita. Despite her toughness, she was nearly in tears. 'He paid the room in advance. Blimey, with all this I'm due early morning tea and biccies.'

Terry pocketed the address book.

She eyed Terry. 'I don't suppose you're interested in a bit of business?'

'Not really,' said Terry unbelievingly. 'But I'll give you that – you're a trier! See you.' He went to the door quickly.

Arthur lay on his bunk, staring at the ceiling. He didn't even react to the sound of the lock rattling. The door opened and the gaoler ushered in Billy North, known as The Ferret. He was short, skinny and shifty.

'Sorry, sir,' said the gaoler absentmindedly to Arthur, 'busy night.' He slammed the door.

'Oh, my Gawd –' said Arthur.

'Arthur Daley! This is a real privilege – I mean – Arthur Daley!'

'Don't give me all that. You are privileged, as it happens. But I know *why!* Of all people – The Ferret!'

'I hate that name,' Billy said disappointedly. 'Why do they call me that?'

'Ever had a look in the mirror?'

'You can depend on me, Arthur.'

'You? You've got more grass than Kew Gardens.'

'Me, Arthur? Never. On my mother's eyesight.'

'She's dead. I was at the funeral nine years ago. And you – you wasn't even there.'

'They wouldn't let me out. I did a runner when me dad was buried. Can I sit down, Arthur?'

'No. Go and sit somewhere else.'

Unconcerned by the insult Billy sat on the floor. 'I had a

nice one tonight – jeweller's shop. Do you know, I got arrested by a dog.'

Arthur stared at him. 'On his own?'

'Clever, ain't they? Three law – but it was due to the dog.'

Arthur shook his head wonderingly. 'You're just a simple recidivist.'

'I'm inadequate – that's what they said.'

'Well, don't be so proud about it.'

'I'm just telling you what they said. I'm surprised to see you here.'

Immediately Arthur was alert. 'Well, here I am,' he said sourly.

'I've always respected you, Arthur,' Billy said ingratiatingly.

'Yeah?'

'You're a well respected man in the manor. Hard though.'

'Yeah.'

'Oh, no doubt about it – a hard man in business. Everybody knows that. That's why you've gone a long way –'

Despite himself, Arthur smiled. 'Very true, Ferret. I mean – Billy.'

'Don't get me wrong when I say "hard", not physical. I mean, you've got Terry and he's as hard as you can get.'

'Where was he when I needed him?' he muttered.

'What was that?'

'Nothing.'

'That's what I thought.'

'Eh?'

'You don't think that Terry's done something – well, you know – he hasn't put you in this spot of bother?'

Arthur sat up slowly and stared at the Ferret. 'Who told you to say that?' he asked softly with creeping suspicion.

'Oh, no –' He was beginning to look shifty.

Arthur stared at him with an expression of complete revulsion. 'You never concocted that theory all on your own,' he said menacingly.

Billy gave a guilty smile. 'I don't know what you mean.'

'As you say, I'm not a physical person, Ferret. Brain rather than brawn. But in your case, I could make an exception.'

Billy, who was only half Arthur's size, gave him a sickly smile. 'Sorry – no offence, Arthur.'

Arthur put on an assumed drawl. 'Don't mess with me, Ferret.' A little power was a good thing, he thought, particularly after he had just avoided a real stitch-up.

Terry stood outside the nurses' home, watching them bustling in and out. Then, taking courage in both hands, he approached a blonde nurse.

'Hallo. D'you know Bridget MacFadyen?'

'I might do.'

'Is she around?'

'Where did she find you?' asked the nurse grinning.

'I'm the phantom lurker.'

'I've been looking for you for years,' she said amidst the giggles of others.

'Can I get you on the National Health?' said Terry.

'All free,' said the nurse. 'Come with me.'

'Why?' said Terry cautiously.

'Because, you'll never get past security. Just follow me.' She took him round to a fire escape and pointed upwards. 'Be lucky,' she said with a smile. 'MacFadyen's in number 27.'

'Bless you,' said Terry as he went up the stairs.

Knocking quietly on the door of number twenty-seven, Terry waited hesitantly, not knowing how he was going to play it. Then the door was opened by a large and attractive girl with a mild Glasgow accent.

'You must be Bridget,' he said.

'What's it to you?'

'I'm a friend of Frank's.'

'Is there something wrong?' she asked alarmed.

'Not really, but could I come in for a minute?'

'That might be dodgy – you might be the rapist.'

'I promise I'm not.'

'Anyway, I can look after myself. You had better come in.'

She opened the door and he entered the tiny room. 'What's wrong?' she asked. 'I only talked to him twenty minutes ago.'

'I just left him,' said Terry.

'Then why did he give you my address?'

'It's a long story,' said Terry. 'Can I sit down?'

But suddenly, Bridget was both alarmed and suspicious. 'I don't believe he gave you my address.'

'All right then – I found it.'

'Get out.'

'Now, don't start screaming,' he said, but before he could finish the sentence, she had rushed for the door. 'I'm not going to hurt you,' said Terry. But to his surprise she did not scream, but punched him in the face. She shaped up like a real fighter as Terry side-stepped. 'Give us a chance,' said Terry as he ducked another blow. 'Where do you work out?' he asked her as she tried to knee him in the groin. 'Don't do that,' he said and grabbed her, putting her into a clinch.

'I'll scream,' she said.

'Not you,' replied Terry and pushed her away so that she stumbled into the other wall. 'You're never going to be raped, are you?'

But Bridget was ready to fight again. 'Only if you want to,' she said.

'Take a standing count,' shouted Terry. 'A friend of mine is in trouble and Frank can help him. That's why I've come.'

Bridget poised, ready to dart at him again, but this time she was listening.

'This pal – he bought a car from Frank, but now the police want to nick him.'

'Are you a copper?' asked Bridget with returned suspicion.

'No, I'm not. But for all I know, they're after your brother.'

'He's done nothing,' said Bridget quickly.

'How d'you know?' protested Terry. 'You don't know what it's all about yet.'

'My brother's a decent man.'

'I'm sure he is, but I've got to see him and all I'm asking is how to. Will you help me?'

'I might,' she said.

'It's important – honest it is. I mean, I'm not going to hurt him. Anyway, he can take care of himself – I'm sure it runs in the family.'

Bridget deliberated for a while and then she said, 'All right – I'll show you where to find him.'

Terry and Bridget walked down the street together.

'Have you lived here long?' asked Terry.

'About a year. I'd had enough of Glasgow.' She paused. 'Lived in Brixton for a week and the riots started. It was worse than Parkhead, so I got a job around here.'

'It's all right around here.'

'I've always been a great fan of Chelsea. Mind you, I don't like the colours. I support Celtic. I've met a lot of players at the hospital. It's handy for them – you know, the hospital what with their injuries and whatever –'

'In Fulham the players haven't even got a first aid box. A couple of corn plasters and that's it.'

'Where did you learn boxing?'

'Here and there. And you?'

Bridget scowled and Terry grinned to cover up. 'Don't hit me.'

They crossed the road, heading towards a pub.

'I'm the only girl out of a family of six.' She smiled. 'The survival of the fittest. By the time I was fifteen, I was punchy. The left jab isn't bad.'

'I've seen worse.'

'Now I'm a lover – not a fighter.'

Terry appraised her fine figure. 'A bit like myself.'

'Is that right?' She paused. 'I bet you like little, slim girls who drink German wine.'

'I don't know about that. And what about the fellers you like? Eighteen stone, bullworker muscles and a convertible Roller.'

'No.' She paused. 'You'll do,' she said smiling. 'I've got an awful thirst – I could murder a pint of Export.'

'Are you going to strangle it? Only kidding, Bridget,' he said quickly, opening the door of the pub.

171

In the police repair shop, the Mercedes was now totally dismantled – with wheels, tyres, wings and bumpers scattered everywhere. The foreman and his three mechanics were exhausted as a result of the intensive search.

'The thing is – I don't think we've got a manual for this particular model,' said the foreman, sitting on a stool and drinking tea.

'So, how are we going to put it back together?' asked one of the mechanics.

'That could be very tricky, but I'm sure we'll manage.'

'It's like putting together a jigsaw puzzle, isn't it?'

'That'll be all part of the fun of it.'

'Incidentally,' said the mechanic, 'the chassis number doesn't even tally with the vehicle document.'

'So what else is new,' said the foreman in a resigned manner.

Terry carried a pint and a half of lager to a table, where he sat down. Bridget picked up the pint and Terry, with an embarrassed smile took the half. A fiddler was on a small platform in the corner, playing a lilting romantic air.

'I really like you, Terry,' said Bridget laying her hand over Terry's. 'Have you got a steady girl-friend?'

'Not really. Is this a proposition?'

'You never know. Maybe you're too old for me. I'm only nineteen. Anyway – what do you do?'

'Not a lot,' he replied. 'You could say I'm self employed.'

'You mean, you're on the dole?'

'Certainly not,' said Terry , looking affronted. 'Look – I've had ordinary jobs. And plenty of guys would be happy to get any kind of job. But it's not for me. Some people think I'm pretty hard – being an ex-fighter and all that. But really, I'm for the soft options. I've no qualifications – except my fists – I don't want to punch a card, so what else can I do? I get by – that's all.'

'I think you need a good woman. Get yourself together. Hey, I know what, there's a job at the hospital – boilerman.'

Terry looked at her. 'Boilerman?'

'Lots of opportunities –'

'Like what?' Terry asked bleakly.

'Central heating fitter.'

'That's very nice of you, Bridget – I really need that –'

Back at the police station, Rycott was talking on the phone when a gloomy Klingmann took out a bottle of whisky and poured out two liberal measures into plastic cups. Rycott put down the phone and stared at Klingmann as he gave him the cup. Rycott swallowed and gasped. 'I usually have it with water.'

'I like soda – the English style,' said Klingmann.

'Yeah – well it's not the Ritz.' Then he began to berate Klingmann, who became more and more bewildered as he listened. 'I should've known – he's going to shout blue murder, just when I had him banged to rights.

'Forgive me – I do not understand,' protested Klingmann.

'D'you know, I can't even nick him on the car? Fraudulent logbook – what's that, eh? He hasn't even sold the car yet. It's times like this when I think about leaving the force. The humiliation. I don't think I can face Arthur. Do you think you could talk to him –?' Rycott looked up at Klingmann with all the fervour of a desperate man.

Bridget was still trying to convince Terry to take an ordinary job. 'I know what . . . why don't you open a little dry cleaner's shop?'

'You've got some great ideas, haven't you?'

'Just helping –'

Suddenly MacFadyen loomed over them. 'What's he doing here?' he asked menacingly, looking at Terry.

'We're discussing dry cleaning –' Bridget smiled up at him.

'Frank,' said Terry, 'I didn't have a chance to talk to you –'

'After my money, aren't you?'

'Look – Arthur's in the nick.'

'I'm not surprised.'

'They reckon that car you sold him was carrying some – you know – well, drugs.'

'Are you accusing me –'

'No, but obviously they want to talk to you.'

'Yeah. And then they're going to fit me up.'

'Look, it's probably –' said Terry cautiously.

'What?'

'Well, I don't know –' His voice trailed away.

'And what have you been saying?' he said to Bridget.

Bridget was annoyed. 'Don't you start at me, Frank. I can handle him any day,' she said to Terry.

Then he tried again. 'Look – please come down with me to the nick. It's just a misunderstanding. It'll only take ten minutes; I've got a motor round the corner.'

'And then what? I go with you and somebody else is going to mug me. All you cockneys are a bit fly.'

'Come on, Frank.' Terry stood up.

'Save it,' said MacFadyen and with sudden dexterity, he hit Terry on the jaw. For the second time that day, he went down.

'I'll tell your father about you,' MacFadyen said to Bridget. 'You're hanging around with the wrong people.' He didn't wait for an answer and turned, barging through the crowd.

'I thought you were good,' said Bridget to Terry, who was getting up groggily.

'He's done it again,' he muttered and then rushed to the door, pushing other people out of the way, and staggered out into the street.

When MacFadyen saw that Terry was after him he started running across the street and on to a passing bus. He stood on the platform, giving Terry a cheery wave, confident that he would never catch him now.

The bus accelerated and then stopped at a set of traffic signals as the lights changed from amber to red. By this time, Terry was a hundred yards behind the bus, his arms pumping, his teeth gritted. The lights changed from red to amber. MacFadyen looked worried, for Terry was now only a few yards behind the bus. The driver engaged gear, the bus lurched and Terry grabbed the rail. He was breathless and the conductor looked at him in amazement as he started up the stairs. MacFadyen was ready for him and kicked out as he reached the top, but Terry grabbed the rail and heaved himself on to the upper deck. MacFadyen momentarily lost his balance as the bus took a corner and Terry flung himself at him and they went into an erratic clinch.

The conductor told the few passengers to get off the bus. Then he ran round to the driver. 'There's a fight,' he said.

'Any good?'

'Not bad.'

'OK – keep an eye on it and I'll drive round to the nick.'

Arthur, with tremendous martyrdom, was sitting beside a desk in the police station and signing a receipt for his personal effects. Klingmann and Rycott looked both embarrassed and disappointed.

'As you know,' said Arthur, clearing his throat, 'I'm not a vindictive man –'

'I know, Arthur,' said Rycott quickly.

'But what can I say? Are apologies in order?'

'Well, I suppose so –'

'You've been a model interviewee. I have had a long career and you are one of the best subjects I've met,' said Klingmann with heavy approval.

'That's terrific. Obviously, you will be hearing from my solicitor.'

'I thought he was shooting –'

'Not for the rest of his life. Monday, maybe –'

'You've got to understand *our* point, Mr Daley. This international fight against crime is important. Don't you agree?' asked Klingmann.

'It's a moral dilemma, innit? The safeguard of the individual or the common good of the state?'

Klingmann puffed at his pipe. 'That is a fine philosophical point –'

'I should cocoa!' said Arthur indignantly. 'I mean – you pluck a man from his fireside –'

'It was a car site,' said Rycott quickly.

'Never mind,' continued Arthur, ' a law abiding citizen, a

local personality, a man known to give to admirable charities such as old folks, children, veteran footballers on their uppers, distressed show business people, stars of yesteryear who can't have a decent lunch at the Savoy Grill anymore. Me – respected, even *loved* by some –' He suddenly looked at Rycott. 'Are you listening to me?'

'Not really,' said Rycott.

'And why not?' Arthur said furiously.

'I've heard it all before.'

The fight continued as the bus pulled up with a screech of brakes outside the police station. The driver jumped out of his cab and dashed inside. A few seconds later, six policemen ran from the station to the bus.

At the top of the stairs at least two of the officers hesitated.

'Go on then – get 'em,' yelled the Sergeant.

'You must be joking,' said one of the policemen.

Swaying, but from punch-drunkenness now, Terry and MacFadyen still fought furiously. Then Terry got MacFadyen jammed between two seats and rained blows on him. Eventually the two of them collapsed on the deck – but Terry was on top.

'You're a hard man,' MacFadyen gasped.

Terry shook his head dazedly. 'You're a bit tasty yourself,' he said and fell back.

The police then moved in.

Arthur stood on the top steps of the police station. He lit a cigar and smiled. Klingmann and Rycott stood behind him. They all watched with fascination the battered, bloodied faces of Terry and MacFadyen as they were hurried towards them by an eager cluster of policemen.

'What's happening, eh?' asked Arthur lazily.

Terry freed himself for a moment. 'I've got him,' he said proudly. 'I've got MacFadyen!'

But Arthur was far from grateful. 'Where have you been? Never mind *him*. You left me on my own.' He drew on his cigar proudly, mentally hearing a burst of martial music. 'It was *me* against them. And you were no help. I've had a result. I'm out.'

'Well, you were innocent anyway.'

'Yeah, but they didn't know that!'

Terry turned to Rycott. 'What about me, Mr Rycott?'

'It's not down to me,' he said. 'He's *out* – you're *in*. Different case – a public disturbance, malicious damager to property, GBH? We'll think of something.'

'Arthur – tell 'em,' said Terry desperately.

But Arthur was preoccupied. 'Look I've got to go home to have a bath and a decent drink. I've had a very traumatic time.'

The police began to push Terry towards the entrance.

'Yeah, but I did this for you –'

'All right, all right. But you've got to fight 'em, Terry. Like me, fight 'em.'

Terry gave a bitter glance. 'I've gone right off you, Arthur,' he said as the door of the police station banged behind him.

'You'll be all right,' Arthur called after Terry. Then he smiled at Klingmann and Rycott. 'He's a good lad,' said Arthur, 'in his heart of hearts.' He walked slowly down the steps to the street.

Arthur was away and Rycott looked regretfully after him. Still, he promised himself, there would be another time. There *must* be.

Having shaved, bathed and washed his hair, Arthur went down to the Winchester for a quick one. He still felt exhausted and, however much he had washed and sprayed himself with deodorant, Arthur still felt he had the sour smell of the prison cell on him.

'What's up Arthur?' Dave was solicitous, vaguely kind and Arthur felt moved, almost to tears. It was so good to see a friendly face, to receive a pleasant word.

'An unfortunate misunderstanding,' said Arthur closing his eyes and sipping his large vodka. It was like nectar.

'Yeah – I heard about that. All over a motor wasn't it?'

Arthur opened his eyes, hissing sharply at Dave. 'It's a closed book now.'

'Is it?'

'It's not the kind of experience that I want to talk about, Dave – I think you have to understand that. I mean – a man in my position isn't used to that kind of experience and it takes a little time to recover.'

Dave shook his head sympathetically. 'I can understand that Arthur.'

'It's played on my nerves. Shaken me up.'

'Have one on the house, Arthur.'

'Well –'

'Go on – it'll do you good.'

'I'll accept a gift,' said Arthur, 'and it's good of you.'

'You've had a rough time, Arthur.'

Arthur sighed. 'You can say that again.'

'You've had –'

'All right, Dave. Don't get waggish. My recovery is going to be slow – I mean – I could be having a nervous breakdown.' Arthur took another long draft of vodka. 'I can feel the colour coming back to my cheeks, Dave. I'm losing the stir pallor.'

'I thought you were white, Arthur.'

'White? I was ashen.'

'Arthur –' Dave spoke after a full minute of restful silence.

'Yes?' His voice was soporific, unencouraging.

'I hear Terry's in there now.'

Arthur stared at him blankly. 'Yes?'

'Terry, Arthur. He's in there.'

'So I gather.'

'Anything you can do for him?'

'Me?' Arthur sounded outraged.

'Well – is there?'

'What can I do? He got himself into a fight on the bus. The situation's out of my hands.'

'Wasn't it connected with this car business?' Dave gently enquired and Arthur began to sweat with guilt.

'Very likely.'

178

'Ah – so there's nothing you can do?'

'What do you expect me to do?'

'You could go down there.'

Arthur's eyes opened wide with alarm. 'You mean – back to the nick?'

'You could just drop in,' suggested Dave hesitantly.

'Dave, you don't understand my position.'

'No.'

'My mental position.'

'Eh?'

'I've just suffered a nervous trauma by being incarcerated. I'm in no fit state to go back.'

'It's like getting back on a horse again.'

'What?'

Dave counselled him patiently. 'If you fall off a horse, you've got to get back on again.'

'Why?'

'To get your confidence back.'

'What do you want your confidence back for? I don't like horses.'

'Arthur –'

'I wouldn't be on one.'

'It's a figure of speech.'

'What have horses got to do with the nick, Dave. Are you out of your tiny?' Arthur looked at him with mounting concern. 'You're rambling.'

'What I'm trying to say, Arthur,' said Dave speaking slowly and carefully, 'is that if you walk back inside that nick you'll feel better.'

'Will I?'

'Bound to.'

'Why?'

'Because – if you walk inside that nick, you can bail Terry out.'

'Why should I do that?'

'Because you owe him one,' said Dave. He took out a ledger. 'Like you owe me twenty sovs.'

Arthur gave him a sickly smile. 'You mean I should take

my courage in both hands?'

'Take in what you like, Arthur,' said Dave leaning intently over the bar, 'but I still tell you – you owe him one.'

'Arthur – fancy seeing you again so quickly.' Rycott stood welcomingly in the foyer of the police station.

'I'm on business.' Arthur looked around him nervously.

'Trying to sell us something? Another Merc?'

'Very amusing, Mr Rycott.'

'You look nervous, Arthur. You don't find the atmosphere oppressive in here, do you?'

'Where's the Gestapo?'

'Herr Klingmann's time with us is over. He's gone back to his mother country.'

'Back to Colditz, eh?'

'Düsseldorf, actually.'

'Same thing.'

'Well – what can we do for you?' Rycott smiled helpfully. 'Come to confess have you?'

'I beg your pardon?'

'To any misdeeds.'

'I take that in poor part, Mr Rycott. As you may know – I've just been cleared of a grievous charge. This has affected my nerves and my business.'

'What do you want, Arthur?'

'I've come to bail out Terry.'

'Ah.'

'Well?' Arthur looked at Rycott quizzically.

'I'm not sure that's possible.'

'What do you mean?' asked Arthur suspiciously.

'We're charging him with a serious affray.'

'I'm sure in the circumstances you owe me,' stated Arthur firmly.

'I beg your pardon?'

But Arthur was firm. 'You owe me one, Mr Rycott.'

Back in the Winchester, Terry and Arthur drank to freedom. Dave was also in a jovial mood, although he didn't seem ready to offer as many drinks on the house as Arthur considered would justify a celebration. However, despite this slight shadow, Arthur was magnanimous when Terry asked:

'What kept you, Arthur?'

'I could have asked you the same question, old son.'

'When?'

'When I was in stir, Terry. When I was in chokey and waiting, wondering about outside assistance.'

'You took your time.'

'Dave will tell you I had to overcome my nerves, Terry.'

'Your *what*?'

'Dave – give Terence an idea of the state I was in.'

'Arthur was in a bad state, Terry.'

'What kind of state?' asked Terry unbelievingly.

'My nerves,' said Arthur. 'But I had to mount the horse again.'

'What horse?'

'If you fall off a horse, Terry, you have to get back on again.'

'Since when did you take up riding horses, Arthur?'

'It's a play on words. A speakeasy.'

Terry and Dave looked at him, both completely mystified.

'I had to regain my confidence to cross the threshold. Once done – I came galloping to you on my steed.'

'How many vodkas have you had, Arthur?' asked Terry.

But Arthur ignored him. 'You should be grateful, Terry.'

'I'm grateful, Arthur.'

Dave sighed. 'So it's a real reunion, is it?' he asked wonderingly.

'Is it?' asked Terry.

'We've got a great future, you and I, Terence,' pronounced Arthur. 'We're going a long way.'

Terry put a hand to his battered face. 'I feel I've been a long way already,' he said.

Minder – Yet Again!

PART ONE

Arthur's Jaguar nosed into the shabby mews and almost immediately he was wary. His antennae for trouble, and for personal threat, sent sharp warnings to his innermost being.

'Terry,' he said, 'I don't like the look of this. Not one bit.'

At the end of the mews, five young women, of both Asian and European origin, were carrying posters proclaiming 'We Demand Work', 'Official Strike' and 'We've been stitched up'.

'You must regard them as your sisters, Arthur. I know you're a man of the people.'

But Arthur was not listening. 'The enemy within and in our own metropolis,' he said.

'And not a slag-heap in sight,' replied Terry.

Arthur was not amused. 'Those people, Terence. They should be locked up. I'd give 'em hard labour.'

'That's what they want,' said Terry, waving at one of the posters.

With heavy indignation, Arthur braked, parked and then gave vent to his feelings. 'Look at 'em. The loony left, the militant tendency – there ain't a decent ratepayer among 'em.' He warmed to his theme. 'I can sus 'em out – squatters, one-parent families, rape victims, against our nuclear deterrent . . . And don't you scowl either,' he warned, turning admonishingly to Terry and then noisily opening the door. 'If there's one thing that winds me up it's strikers.'

'So I can see,' replied Terry. 'But I can't understand it, Arthur. I mean – we're all workers, aren't we?'

But once again Arthur took no notice, for all his self-protective instincts were predictably showing themselves. As Terry got out of the Jag, he grabbed frenziedly at his arm. 'You'd better walk beside me – on the right, on the right . . .' he gasped.

'Well, what're they gonna do?' Terry's voice was patient.

'Who knows – lumps of concrete, potatoes with razor blades . . .'

3

'They're girls –'

'That's all right, is it? After all, "the female of the species is more deadly than the male". Watch out!'

Angie, a spirited Cypriot woman and the leader of the pickets, approached them matily, but she did nothing to allay Arthur's apprehension.

'Good morning, brother. Is this a delivery, brother?'

'I'm not your brother,' replied Arthur defensively, 'not even your cousin, uncle or any other relation of yours.'

Angie, however, was not deterred. 'This is an official dispute. We're redundant.'

'No wonder you're striking,' said Arthur unhelpfully.

'All we're asking is support from other workers, like yourself.' She was a little sharper now.

'Me? A worker? I'm an employee, member of the Chamber of Commerce –'

Suddenly Terry could stand it no longer. 'I can guarantee that he ain't a worker. A grafter maybe but no worker.'

'Our governor's a crook,' replied Angie positively.

Arthur raised his eyebrows, adopting a school-masterly air. 'D'you know what you've said? Young lady, I trust you've got a good solicitor. That's defamation.'

'Then he can sue me, can't he?' she responded pertly.

Arthur glanced at Terry. 'He's a witness. Did she utter those defamatory words "he is a crook"?'

'Yeah, but everybody knows that.'

'A crook?' Arthur sounded incredulous.

'Well, he's a bit slippery, inne?'

'A well-known local businessman.'

'You said yourself "he's got more strokes than Oxford and Cambridge together" . . .'

'Just a turn of speech – and whose side are you on?' Arthur's suspicion surfaced quickly.

'One out – all out.' Terry smiled at Angie. 'One hundred per cent, is it?'

4

'Solid – the eight of us.'

Arthur waxed philosophical. 'Oh well, that's going to rock the economy, innit. Ignore her, cop a deaf 'un. They're just looking for publicity . . .' He began to walk on. 'And don't you call me scab.' He paused outside a seedy building with a notice proclaiming '*S & S Clothing Co.*'

Terry grinned at Angie. He clearly fancied her and she was quick to reciprocate. 'Don't you call *him* scab . . . cheers.'

Terry followed Arthur into the factory. Inside, the ancient building gave every appearance of a time-warp, a scene from the turn of the century. The walls were dirty and stained and the floor was littered with scraps of fine English worsted, lining and thread. The scanty furnishings consisted of a large cutting table, chairs, half a dozen antique sewing machines and several tailor's dummies with uncompleted gents' jackets. At the end of the warp was a dowdy office. By its door an elderly man waited to welcome Arthur and Terry.

Solly Salmon had been in the 'shmutter' business for forty-five years, and Terry often saw him as the authentic voice of two thousand years of ghetto wisdom. In other words, despite his suspicion, his cunning and his cynicism he still had a curious sense of wonder in him.

As Arthur approached, Solly burst into declamatory speech. 'Do I need this, Arthur? Flying pickets – at my time of life.' He began to mumble to himself and then became more articulate. 'Come in, come in. Now they want redundancy money. What's happening to this country? You can't sack a man now. I'm a boss – they're workers. I tell *them*, now they want to tell me.' For a moment he was distracted from his rhetoric as he ran his eye over Arthur's corpulent figure. 'I like your suit, Arthur.'

Arthur beamed at the compliment whilst Solly felt

his lapel. Then Solly stood back sighing, giving a shudder as he glanced at Terry's apparel. 'And *him* . . . is that for jogging? A marathon?'

Terry was wearing his usual casual gear and was for a moment discomforted as Solly and Arthur eyed him disparagingly.

'I've told him, Solly.'

'Don't you ever wear a suit?' asked Solly blandly.

But Terry decided to remain as unconcerned as possible. 'Weddings, funerals – and in court,' he said.

'That's the problem – nobody wants to wear a suit.' Solly threw out his hands in a gesture of despair. 'Arthur and Prince Charles are the only men in the country with four suits.'

'Yeah, but the other feller has paid for them,' pointed out Terry with feeling, earning a scowl from Arthur.

'Why don't you make a pot of tea for us?' he snapped.

Terry smiled. 'Why don't you?' But Solly was desperate.

'Terry please – even my secretary's on the picket.'

Reluctantly Terry went to the sink, asking casually: 'What's the strike about anyway?'

'Greed, Terry. Naked greed.'

'Whose greed?'

'You draw to the well and suddenly the well is dry.' Solly shook his head philosophically, neatly evading Terry's question.

Arthur was quick to give him support. 'Very true. You need a rainy day, Solly.'

Suddenly Solly became more animated. 'Come here – I'll show you something.' He beckoned Terry. 'And you. Come on.' Solly led them further down the factory and stopped beside a tailor's dummy. He then made what could have been the speech of his life. 'You know what this is?' he said, feeling the cloth. 'It's a bespoke suit.' He paused and reflected. 'A Savile Row suit is a gentleman's suit. You don't see gentlemen any more.' He began to become more excited. 'Arabs maybe with

6

terylene bedspreads, shwartzers with tribal robes – but no English gentlemen. They're hibernating in their country seats, worrying about death duties. In the old days they'd owe their tailors, run up a bill – now they don't even go to see them.' Solly was becoming even more excited now. 'You saw the flying pickets – Cypriots, Indians, Chinese – but no Lithuanians, Poles, Ukrainians. In the old days they couldn't speak English that well but boy – they could make a needle talk. And no strikes. That's what's happened to the English suit – it's on the way out and it's strikebound as well.'

'Makes me proud to wear an English suit,' said Arthur, unaware of any unintended irony.

'You got that one from Harry the Greek,' pointed out Terry.

Arthur, however, was not to be dissuaded. 'But it's a traditional garment, innit?'

Solly carried on, oblivious to all about him. 'I'm talking about eight hundred pounds, twelve hundred pounds. But I get peanuts. My man in Savile Row is bankrupt. It's the domino theory. One falls, we all fall down. Arthur – would you like to buy twenty bespoke suits?'

'But they're made for particular people.'

Solly ignored his protestations. 'You can sell anything. You're famous for it.'

Arthur beamed again, but this time a trifle mechanically. Meanwhile Terry was examining a particularly large jacket.

'Who's gonna find a punter for this? The guy's gotta be a giant.'

'There's always somebody,' reassured Solly.

'Even with my special talent you ain't going to solve your problem.' Arthur sounded humble. 'How much do you need?'

Solly gave an expressive shrug. 'I've been bankrupted six times. Up and down, up and down, Arthur.

The good champs get up and fight again –'

'Yeah, and some of them get knocked out as well,' put in Terry.

For a moment Solly looked dejected and sagged on to a chair, all his old spirit temporarily knocked out of him. 'You know what I need – an act of God.'

'Not another fire, Solly?' Arthur was jumpy.

'Flood? Pestilence? You got a good idea?'

'Earthquake?' Terry tried to make his contribution.

'This is serious, Terry,' said Solly, frowning.

'Mental breakdown,' said Arthur suddenly.

'Already did that. 1974 I think it was.'

'They recur, y'know.'

'Another one and they'll commit me. I've got a better idea. How about a burglary?'

'Thought you'd get into that eventually,' said Terry cynically.

'The perfect crime,' Solly was suddenly enthusiastic.

'Yeah perfect.' Arthur was not convinced. 'What're they gonna nick – twenty suits and a packet of needles?'

'Money.' Solly got up and beckoned them to the office. 'I'll show you.'

'I don't wanna know – not even for a joke.' Terry knew it was all happening again. He looked at Arthur hopelessly. Was he going to bite? You bet he was.

'You think I'm joking?' said Solly. 'At least take a look.'

Arthur was already hurrying towards the office, a gleam in his eye, pursued by Solly. Terry followed them reluctantly.

Once inside the squalid little office, Solly showed them a wall-safe and Terry's heart sank. Yes, it was all happening.

'You know about these things,' said Solly confidentially. 'Villainy – robbers, gangsters, burglars. And him,' he turned to Terry, 'he's been in prison.'

'And he don't want to go back in there again,' said

Terry firmly. 'But about your crimes?' he asked with a pleasant grin.

'Me? They weren't crimes – financial mistakes, misjudgements . . .'

'You've got the wrong blokes, Solly.' Arthur was anxious now and Terry felt a surge of relief. But would it last?

'I'm offering a lot of money,' said Solly and Terry knew it wouldn't last for Arthur's interest was caught immediately.

'Like what?' he asked all too casually.

'I'm going.' Terry was determined not to stay – not to get involved.

But Arthur was insistent. 'Just a minute, Tel. At least hear him out.'

'I don't want to.'

'Common courtesy at least,' said Arthur firmly.

'More like conspiracy.'

'Conspiracy means plotting. We're just chatting.'

'Chatting about doing his peter.'

Solly appeared not to understand Terry's dissent. 'All I want is somebody to break into the factory, blow up the safe and I'll claim that the redundancy money's gone.'

'That's all, is it?' scoffed Terry.

'He doesn't mean that – he doesn't *mean* an explosion.' Arthur didn't sound convincing.

'Blow – force – a *small* explosion,' insisted Solly. 'Nothing to frighten people – a whimper not a bang.'

'See you,' said Terry curtly, turning on his heel.

'Just a minute – you're being very impolite.' But Terry was walking away, down the debris of the factory floor. 'And you didn't even make that cup of tea,' shouted Arthur.

'What's wrong with him?' asked Solly innocently. 'Have I upset him?'

'He doesn't understand your humour. I knew you were joking but . . .' Arthur paused '. . . no, you weren't joking, were you?'

'Three grand, maybe?' said Solly meditatively.

'Three? I mean cash – no kites?'

'Of course. But I know I couldn't ask you to do it personally . . .'

'I should hope not.' Arthur looked prim.

'My suggestion is that you should be a sort of consultant. You could recruit the experts. It has to look good, obviously.'

'As you know, Solly,' began Arthur, 'I have contacts.'

'You're like the godson.'

'Godfather,' corrected Arthur.

'No, my godson – the one who's doing seven years at Parkhurst. He knew everybody. You see, I know about fires but burglaries are virgin territory. Still, it seems easy. Am I right?'

'No, you're not,' said Arthur. 'What happens in the morning when the Bill comes in? They want to know how much money was in the safe –'

'I'll say there was twenty thousand pounds in there. I'll even have a counterfoil from the bank.'

'And then you'll claim the insurance?'

Solly smiled sadly. 'With my record? I could try, but I'm not counting on it. I've worked all my life – am I going to change? They got good wages. Should I give them my life savings?'

But Arthur had been thinking fast. 'Incidentally, the three grand is for the safe breakers. My fee is a grand.'

'Why does everybody steal from me?' asked Solly plaintively.

Arthur Daley's pinstriped posterior slowly emerged from his Jag as he bundled up the suits on the back seat. Puffing a little he stood up, took out a silk handkerchief from his breast pocket and mopped at his brow. Arthur was not a worker. Seeking refreshment after his labours, Arthur strode purposefully towards the welcoming door of the Winchester Club. As he did so he noticed a ladder propped outside the club entrance. On the first floor level a painter was working and as Arthur glanced up he noticed how tall the man was. At once one of his ideas dawned.

'Excuse me. How big are you?' he asked enthusiastically.

The painter stared down at him as if sighting a madman – or perhaps some kind of sexual philanderer. 'I beg yours,' he choked.

Arthur continued unabashed. 'I might have something for you. What are you – about six four? Forty-six chest? Could have been made for you. A nice Savile Row suit.'

'I'm just an ordinary painter.' He was getting very worried.

'Don't painters have suits? Don't they go out of an evening? And it's your colouring as well . . .'

The painter craned down at the suit doubtfully. 'I don't think –'

'Try it on – it's only two hundred sovs,' said Arthur encouragingly.

The mention of the price seemed to put the man into a state of shock. He missed his footing, the ladder wavered, he grabbed at the upright and then slipped in an acrobatic stunt. Despite the twelve-foot fall, he managed to land miraculously on his feet.

'What's you say?'

'I said – for you it's a hundred and seventy sovs.'

'Who d'you think I am – David Hockney?' asked the painter indignantly.

'The footballer? He's much smaller than you,' Arthur said coolly, returning to the car, foraging about and flourishing the suit at his prospective client. 'Don't drip paint over it – but have a butchers at this.'

The painter was otherwise engaged, rubbing at his leg. 'I think I've done meself in – thanks to you.'

'That's okay,' replied Arthur distractedly, still running his hands over the suit.

11

'Bloody painful.'

'You've done your cartridge,' said Arthur in a professional voice.

'Have I?' He began to limp about, testing his leg. 'It's a funny old life innit?' he said reflectively. 'When I got up this morning I thought – I'll get a good eight hours on the old ladder. Have a couple of sherberts at dinner-time, a cheese and pickle sandwich. I wasn't thinking about me spring wardrobe. And then some raving wally tries to sell me a Savile Row suit when I'm twelve foot up a ladder –'

'Opportunity is a fleeting thing. Think about Fleming when he discovered penicillin.'

'Up the ladder at the time, was he?'

'Nobody checked that.' But Arthur had become bored with the conversation. Wishing to return to his sales tactics again he said: 'Tell you what I'll do – a hundred and fifty sovs. This could be your lucky day.'

'No, it's *your* lucky day.' Suddenly the painter lost his temper. Rubbing his leg again he shouted: 'If my leg was okay I'd kick you from here to next week.'

Arthur took a few steps back. 'Take it easy. You'd probably like a pinstripe, or something else.'

'You're right.'

'Well, in that case, see you down at Austin Reed,' said Arthur, beating a hasty retreat into the Winchester. Behind him the painter noisily began to sum up Arthur's character.

Arthur dumped the suits on the counter of the Winchester and Dave winced. As he began to protest, Arthur said: 'Dump them behind the ramp. Now, who's that bloke on the ladder?'

Dave looked at the suits meditatively. 'This place is becoming an oriental bazaar.'

'There's one for you there,' said Arthur reassuringly. 'What're you – forty-two?'

Dave declined with a quiet if resentful dignity. 'No thank you. I've still got the terylene mohair you sold me last year.'

Grudgingly Dave poured a vodka and slimline for Arthur who simply said: 'That was a steal.'

'Yeah,' replied Dave. 'I know the bloke who stole 'em.' He leant across the bar confidentially. 'Incidentally, your pal's in the corner. 'As he got the hump?'

Arthur glanced across at Terry who was reading a newspaper and drinking a lager. The newspaper was in front of his face. He didn't look friendly.

'What did he say?' asked Arthur trepidatiously.

'Not a lot. Apart from – half a lager. Those were his very words. He never even had a go at you – and that's unusual.' Dave began to examine one of the suits. 'You've got no labels on these, Arthur. In this establishment they like to see a label. Chester Barrie, Yves St Laurent, Tommy Nutter, anything. They love a name.'

And so they will. What about some of those fine old English names – Ashdown, Hudson and Huggins? What about Pillock Kilroy and Brainstorm –' He paused. 'I can buy labels at fifty a gross.'

Leaving Dave contemplating this idea with wonderment, Arthur took his drink over to Terry. He spoke to him furtively.

'I need you. Yes,' he said quickly. 'I understand your views. I'm not asking you to break in with a sawn-off shotgun. But you do *know* some unemployed thieves. Even them are having a hard time, scrimping and scraping, probably with nippers, a crippled grandma. This recession is hitting everybody.'

Terry put down his newspaper, sighed and whispered to Arthur: 'Any decent thief wouldn't want to know about it.'

'You're wrong there, young man. I don't need a decent one. They come in all sizes, y'know. Down market ones, sleazy ones, pathetic ones . . .'

'Beesley,' said Terry suddenly.

Immediately Arthur looked optimistic. 'And his brother? He's a nice bloke.'

'They did the Oxfam shop a couple of months ago –

13

that sleazy enough for you?' He sighed. 'D'you know what you're getting into, Arthur? Are you sure of your territory?'

'I'm just helping an old friend. A drink maybe – nothing else. I've gotta shoot.' He rose hurriedly to his feet, leaving Terry to contemplate impending disaster.

Arthur didn't hesitate – he went straight to the source of the action. Half an hour later he was sitting in the hub of the Beesleys' business empire – a caff called 'Snacks-U-Like'. It was tatty, had a thirties' decor and was, without doubt, sleazy. Billy was the spokesman; Benny the chorus.

'We don't do a lot now – since we got into catering,' said Billy.

'It's our new image,' put in Benny.

Arthur was gently patronising. 'Delighted to see young men striking out on their own,' he said.

'No staff, see. Staff steal. Nobody gets behind the jump. Know what I mean?' asked Billy.

'A family firm,' reassured Arthur with a benign smile. But Billy was not so sure.

'Not them – they're even worse. You see, Arthur, your mum is your greatest friend in life, I love her. And Benny's the same.'

'I'd do anything for her.' Benny cast an adoring glance towards the kitchen.

'Course he would. But my mum's been cleaning for people all her life. She picks up things – know what I mean. It's in her nature.' Billy grinned happily.

'Houses, shops . . .' said Benny apologetically. 'Only *little* things, Arthur.

'Well, that's all right then,' said Arthur, just a shade too quickly.

'She comes here once a week. Cleans the tables,' explained Billy.

Arthur looked at the greasy tables. 'Yeah?'

'Mops up a bit,' continued Billy. Ashtrays – that kind of thing. Nothing wrong with her sweeping.' He paused. 'But even though she's my mum she don't even sweep around the jack and jill. It's too tempting innit – what with her background an' everything?'

'That's very thoughtful, Billy.'

'Well, I'm a thoughtful man. That's why I'm a bit concerned about Solly's factory.'

'How d'you know it's his?'

'Fires and floods. A safe – it was only a question of time wannit? But we're talking about a specialist now. Gelignite's tricky stuff, innit?'

'What about your mum?' muttered Arthur hopefully.

Billy gave him a blank stare. 'She's a bit lightfingered, Arthur, but she ain't a thief.'

Arthur, who could sense hostility dawning in Billy's eyes, hurried in: 'My little joke.' He squeezed Billy's shoulder and went on: 'She's a jewel. I know that.'

'A jewel – you're right,' said Benny. 'I'll drink to that.'

But Billy was looking out of the window, a slow smile forming on his lips. 'Talking about drinking . . .' he said.

The man outside the dirty window was wearing badly creased clothes and carrying a paper bag – the kind that released prisoners often carry. Gently he tapped on the window and Arthur pronounced in a voice of doom: 'Scotch Harry.'

'Here's your specialist,' said Billy.

Arthur looked horrified. 'Not him! A pathetic petty thief, a bag snatcher, a failed – everything . . .'

'You ask him,' said Billy. 'He's your man.'

Scotch Harry walked into the caff jauntily. He wore a beaming smile and there was a bottle tucked into his pocket.

'This is all we need,' said Arthur.

But Scotch Harry was undeterred as he shook hands all round. 'This is great, eh? Old chinas. Isn't it magic this place? I heard youse were running it, boys. I didn't realise you'd have patrons like Arthur Daley.'

'Drops in for his tea,' said Billy enigmatically.

15

Scotch Harry hugged Arthur's shoulders. 'Great to see you, Arthur.'

Arthur smiled uncertainly.

'I was just telling Arthur about when you were an ace peterman,' said Billy.

'You must've known that, Arthur. I was the guvnor ... plastic, gelly, thermal lances – I was the bizzo. I did my time in that game.' He turned to Billy. 'Any chance of a ham roll?'

'Get him some tea,' said Billy magnanimously and Benny hastened to do as he was bid.

Scotch Harry sat down. 'I did all the banks in Glasgow. I was famous before I was twenty-five.' He cleared his throat and looked expectantly at Arthur. 'Anyway, what's the strength of this?'

'But you haven't done it for a while? Have you?' bleated Arthur plaintively.

Scotch Harry shrugged. 'It's in my bones. I was up for the big silver bullion job. But I didn't have a suit.' He looked dejected.

'I might have helped you there,' said Arthur instinctively.

'I could do with a suit,' continued Scotch Harry wistfully. He looked at his ragged, unkempt clothes. 'They don't take care of your clothes.'

'Who don't?' asked Arthur innocently.

Scotch Harry scowled at his naivety. 'I've been away. That's why you haven't seen me. Sixteen months – nae bother for me. I've just come out.'

Benny came up with a cup of tea and a ham roll. Harry grinned, took out his bottle and poured a generous measure into his cup.

'When did you get out?' asked Arthur.

'This morning,' said Scotch Harry through a mouthful of ham roll.

Arthur was already on his feet. 'See you chaps.'

'What's the matter, Arthur?' Billy seemed surprised.

'I'm off. If the man's come out of the boob half an hour ago it doesn't suggest confidence, does it?'

16

'Well, he's hungry, inne? And he's keen and he's cheap, What else do you want?'

Scotch Harry, still eating, appeared very confused. 'What's going on?'

'D'you want to work, Harry?' asked Billy with urgency in his voice.

'I'm brand new and I've got a lot of living to do. Are you the master-mind, Arthur?'

'No, I'm not,' replied Arthur irritably. 'Never, never say that. I'm just putting some work your way – that's all.'

'Never even seen you,' said Billy helpfully.

'I trust you'll remember that.'

'You saying that I'm a grass?' asked Scotch Harry with sudden aggression, but Arthur was not to be terrorised.

'You're not even on the firm yet – and you're talking about being arrested and grassing.'

'Scotch Harry's one of our own,' said Billy.

'Guaranteed,' asserted Scotch Harry. 'The thing about me is I'm always game – ready to do the bizzo – any time.'

'Yes,' said Arthur wearily, 'I'm sure you are.'

A confrontation was taking place outside Solly's factory. Terry had just appeared, carrying a couple of sewing machines when a furious Angie hurried up to him. The pickets were still on duty and clearly her mood was ugly – which didn't account for the rest of her, thought Terry.

'And where the hell do you think they're going?'

'Sold.'

Terry walked past her and put the machines in the back of a van. Angie followed him, suddenly losing interest.

'They're not worth anything anyway. We're the only ones who can make them work.'

'Arthur's bought them. He'll *make* them work.'

Angie looked very despondent. 'So the guvnor's

17

really done it, eh? We're slaved for him for five years.'

'Well, there you go.' He turned back to her and said in a softer tone: 'I'm just a hired hand, Angie.'

'Most of us are,' she returned, and walked slowly away from him, back to her doleful line of pickets.

Inside the factory, Terry was just about to pick up another machine when Solly appeared from the office.

'The girls reckon they're not worth anything,' Terry told him.

'So if Arthur doesn't sell 'em I'll buy 'em back,' said Solly undismayed. 'I'll be back in business in a couple of months.'

'I thought you were going to retire.'

'Me? Where would I go? Hove, Brighton? Sit in a hotel lounge, the TV room? I'm a doer, Terry, not a sitter. Who would I talk to? I like the cut and thrust of business, the arguments with the customers and the staff. I like cheating the tax man. I don't want to be rich, that's for young men when they've still got ambition. You know what I mean?'

'No,' said Terry. 'I haven't got ambition.'

'Then you're lucky or maybe you're wise. But I can tell you one thing: my only ambition is to exist. I'm even going to miss those flying pickets.'

Terry began to move towards the door. He was getting tired of Solly's rhetoric.

'Did Arthur tell you about tonight, Terry?'

'No, he didn't. And I don't want you to tell me either.'

'In that case . . . shtum.'

'I can't if I don't know anything, can I?' said Terry, going for the door, fast.

'What's the time?'

'1.40.'

'Let's move it – and for Christ's sake keep quiet.'

The night was dark, with only a pale sickle moon illuminating the shambling figures of Scotch Harry.

18

Billy and Benny as they prised open the window of Solly's factory and scrambled inside. Cautiously they tiptoed into the office and were just about to look for the safe when Billy whispered:

'What's that?'

'It's me. I'm just pocketing a couple of pairs of scissors. Mum'd like them,' said Benny.

'For God's sake,' replied Billy. 'Harry – get on with it.'

'All right. But it takes time, you know, to do a good job. Ah, here's the little beauty.'

He'd found the safe. Digging in the pocket of his old mack, Scotch Harry dragged out sellotape and a piece of plastic. Then he began to apply them to the safe.

Blimey, thought Billy, as he trailed two terminal leads from a plug socket on the wall. He actually seems to know what he's doing. 'You've done this before then, Harry,' he said, impressed.

'These old safes – they're a doddle,' Scotch Harry replied modestly. 'I hope he's put the dough in.'

'Three grand. If we could do one every night we'd be laughing, eh?' Billy's voice held a kind of religious awe.

'That switch off, right?' asked Harry as he draped a blanket over the safe door. 'Now, stand back, lads.' He checked his preparation and then went over to the plug. 'Just a wee muffled bang – that's all ye'll hear. Nothing to worry about.' He flicked the plug and nothing happened.

'That it?' asked Benny innocently.

But Scotch Harry was not perturbed. 'Nae sweat – must be one of the wee wires.' He walked towards the safe, and as he did so there was a blinding explosion. Suddenly the blanket was alight and dense smoke filled the room. Billy and Benny began to cough and gasp. For a moment there was no sign of Scotch Harry, then Billy saw him lying like a shapeless, smoking bundle on the ground.

Still coughing, Billy ran over to him – only to find Scotch Harry was scorched from head to foot.

19

'He ain't brown bread, is he?' asked Benny from a safe distance.

It was well after the witching hour in the Winchester Club. Dave was making desperate attempts to clear up the bar, but his efforts were considerably hampered by the presence of his three remaining members: Terry, Arthur – and a very drunk Detective Inspector Chisholm who was slumped by the bar. He was waxing philosophic – repetitively philosophic.

'I'm a peoples policeman. My role is preventive rather than detentive,' he was saying, his voice considerably slurred.

'And you're going to bore for England any minute,' pointed out Terry quietly.

'What did you say?' There was a sudden note of aggression in Chisholm's voice.

'It was the echo.'

'I'm trying to close a club, Mister Chisholm,' said Dave plaintively.

'I know. You don't understand coppers . . .'

'How's that?' asked Terry.

'Look at the environment I live in – tarts, pimps, grasses, muggers, rapists, transvestites, shop lifters. Is that a cross-section of human life? I ask myself. No wonder I have to drink occasionally.'

'And you've had a few tonight –'

'And why not? I live with the litter, the flotsam of life. I'll tell you what – a nice, straightforward, honest-to-God villain is like a breath of air.'

At that moment the door bell rang and Dave looked up in relief. 'That's gotta be your taxi, Mister Chisholm.'

'Yeah. Give me a fiver then.'

'Allow me.' Arthur grandly pulled out his wallet as Dave hurried to the door.

Chisholm stared at Arthur warily. 'This is not a bribe, you know.'

'Not for a second,' protested Arthur. 'Terry, give the gentleman a hand.'

With studied pleasure Terry took Chisholm's elbow and steered him towards the door.

'You took a wrong turning in life, Terry – that's all.'

'But you didn't help me, did you?'

'G'night . . .'

'Goodnight to you, Mr Chisholm,' said Arthur formally. 'And a safe journey home.'

When Chisholm had lurched through the door, Arthur turned to Dave and said: 'Not in the best of shape.'

'I should bar him,' replied Dave. 'He upsets people.'

'Yes,' said Arthur. 'Particularly when people are discussing business and him earholing – it could lead to all kinds of nasty misunderstandings.'

Just as Chisholm's taxi drove away, a car stopped outside the Winchester and Billy got out. He was pale and shaking as he yelled to Benny: 'Get him out!'

Benny began to drag Scotch Harry out, propping his blackened figure in a shop doorway, just as Terry was walking back into the club.

'What's this?' he asked, staring at the shadow in the doorway.

Billy did not waste words. 'Get Arthur,' he said.

Seconds later a flurried Arthur Daley appeared.

'You're not going to like this,' Terry told him.

A few minutes later, an ashen-faced Arthur sat behind the wheel of his Jag while Terry bundled Scotch Harry onto the back seat. Of Billy and Benny there was no sign.

'Look at the state of him,' said Arthur woodenly, but Terry only snapped: 'Let's go.'

'But where?'

'Start the car, Arthur. Drive.'

Automatically Arthur did as he was told, the sweat

21

running down his forehead and into his eyes.

'I've never seen such a mess. Can't you take off your jacket? These are real leather seats. I don't want him to die in my motor – it's bad luck.'

'Bloody bad luck for him an' all.'

'Is he breathing?'

'Aye,' said Scotch Harry, suddenly coming to, 'but I canna see.'

'Ah Gawd – he's blind. What did you do, for Gawd's sake?' Arthur was beginning to drive erratically.

'Just a minute,' said Terry as he wiped at Harry's face with a handkerchief.

'It must've been a different plastic – new stuff – helluva bang,' muttered Harry.

'Great,' said Arthur, cheering up a little. 'At least you got the dough.'

But there was no reply from Harry and a note of anxiety crept into Arthur's voice.

'You *did* get it?'

'Couldn't open it. Did the bizzo and the door wouldn't budge.'

'He needs a doctor,' put in Terry but Arthur was not sympathetic.

'I need a doctor. Did you hear what he said? You can open a fifty-year-old peter with a tin-opener. The dough's still in there. What are we gonna do? I've never –'

He was interrupted by a revelatory shout from Scotch Harry: 'I can see again!'

'Is it a miracle?' asked Arthur vaguely.

'Just a hankie,' said Terry.

'Just as well. I wasn't going to have a whip-round for a dog.'

There was a gasp from Scotch Harry, followed by a moan.

'You okay?' Terry was very concerned, particularly when the reply was only: 'Arrrgghh.'

'He's probably got concussion,' said Terry.

22

'That must've been twenty years ago,' muttered Arthur.

'Harry?' persisted Terry.

'Arrg,' was the only reply.

'Let's take him to the hospital, Arthur.' It seemed a reasonable enough suggestion but it caused Arthur to have near apoplexy.

'I can't do that. I'm well known, inni? I'm a public person, a local character. I give presents to kids in that hospital at Christmas . . .'

'They'll think you've brought Santa Claus.'

'He's got a burned boat, not a white beard. I know – we'll dump him on a skip.' Terry tried to interrupt but Arthur swept on, seemingly anxious to show a fraction more humanity. 'Just a minute, we'll leave him not necessarily on a skip, some comfortable place, and then we get on the trumpet for an ambulance . . .'

'We're taking him to the hospital,' said Terry firmly, and Scotch Harry, anxious to capitalise on the drama, yelled:

'Get me a priest!'

'I didn't know you're a Catholic,' said Terry baffled.

'Course I'm not,' said Harry firmly. 'But they get a better deal. I mean, if you're going to die they know how to do it – I mean the full five course bizzo. Who knows who's running the gaff upstairs, eh? I'm just hedging my bets.'

'This is great,' complained Arthur. 'The biggest crisis in my life and we're into a theological discussion.'

Scotch Harry suddenly lunged forward, grabbing at Arthur's shoulder. 'I'm dying, you know,' he stated.

Arthur turned to Terry in alarm. 'Get his filthy stained hands off me. He's in a coma or something.'

Terry restrained Scotch Harry with some difficulty. 'I think he knows what he's doing. He just wants to strangle you. Take it easy, Harry.'

Scotch Harry reluctantly subsided on the back seat. 'What I really need is a drink.'

'Well, in that case you ain't gonna die,' said Terry cynically.

'Can't people die and drink at the same time? I've hardly had a drink for sixteen months. I mean, I'm a born again drinker.'

Arthur, however, was not reassured by Scotch Harry's sudden need. 'See? All that rabbit, he's not all that ill. A wash-up, a couple of soluble asprins and he'll be as good as new.'

'He's still going to casualty,' said Terry. 'Just drive. Now listen, Harry, don't tell 'em anything. No name, no address, where you been, what happened. Nothing – right?'

'I know the score.'

'I'm going to check your pockets.'

And he did so, wading about in what was left of Harry's clothes.

'Letter, cards . . .'

'Listen, when I go to work I'm the man from nowhere. I'm the pro, the bizzo.'

'Yeah. You and your pals are just gas meter thieves,' said Arthur in a deeply depressed voice. 'Pros? That's what's wrong with this country – you can't get a decent pro any more. They all live in bloody Spain.'

Scotch Harry looked much worse in the bright lights of the hospital casualty reception area. His clothes were scorched and tattered and his face was blackened.

'In the name of God,' cried out an Irish nurse, running out from behind the reception desk, 'what's happened to him?'

'Dunno – just saw him in the street,' said Terry.

'Just sit him down there for a minute.'

Terry helped Harry to a chair.

'It's Terry, isn't it?' said the nurse enquiringly.

'Er – yes,' replied Terry, his heart sinking.

'You're always in here,' she continued. 'Of course you get into an awful lot of scrapes, don't you?'

'Not me.'

'Anyway, I'll see him in a second.' She went back to the reception desk and Terry hissed:

'You don't know me.'

Scotch Harry seemed offended. 'I know the drill. Tell you one thing though – my wife'll be worried. Shouldn't she be told – in case anything happens?'

Terry nodded in the most compassionate way he could.

'Eighty-two Frankel House – that's my address,' said Scotch Harry in a voice of hollow doom.

'You'll be okay,' said Terry, some of the compassion leaving his voice. But Harry was determined to provoke a touching farewell.

'Just in case the old ticker fades out – tell Arthur I'm sorry and see you – you're a pal.' He lay back with his eyes closed.

'Cheers,' said Terry, squeezing his shoulder.

'Jesus – that hurts!'

'Just testing,' said Terry and promptly walked away.

A moment later the nurse returned. 'Where's your friend?' she asked.

Scotch Harry stared at her in shock. 'Arrghhh,' he said.

'Now, what's your name?'

But Harry was not prepared to say anything but 'Arrrgggh'.

Arthur was parked outside the hospital. He was slumped in the front seat of the Jag with his hat tipped over his eyes. When Terry breathlessly arrived, Arthur started the engine and abruptly took off.

'It took you long enough,' he said grudgingly.

'Well, I couldn't leave him on the floor, could I?' protested Terry.

'Why not?' asked Arthur bleakly.

'Because one of the nurses recognised me.'

Arthur immediately flew into a tantrum. 'Oh my Gawd! That's it, innit? That's what happens when you're nice to people. We'll be up the steps in no time.

25

I'm not having it . . . What about my reputation?' he spluttered. ' 'Er indoors'll go mad. Can you imagine that? No. It's going to be a Spanish number. I'll be with all the others –'

'You haven't got that kind of dough,' said Terry with amusement.

'Haven't I? I'll get by.' He glanced around the streets flooding by the window. 'Incidentally, where are we going?'

'Scotch Harry's missus –'

Arthur exploded: 'No way!'

'We've got to tell her.'

'Why? She'll read it in the papers.'

'You're all heart, Arthur,' replied Terry. 'Left, left – and then right.'

'Wives are very strange. They get excited, they can't handle the Old Bill, they *say* things,' said Arthur paranoically.

'Doesn't matter. You've got the responsibility. I mean – you're the leader of the gang.'

But Arthur was not to be mollified and his hands shook on the wheel as he hissed at Terry: 'Don't you *ever* call it a gang. It's just a loose collection of inadequate individuals. And it's certainly not my gang, – I hardly know any of them.' He began to mutter to himself and Terry could just make out the extraordinary sentence: 'Is this the end of little Ricco?'

'Eh?'

'Edward G. Robinson said that in a movie.'

'And?'

'He died.'

'I'm a friend of Harry's,' said Terry, ringing the doorbell in the corridor of the council flats. He had left Arthur crouched furtively in the Jag.

'Who?' came the suspicious voice from the other side.

'Is that Mrs Stuart?'

'Aye.'

'Mrs. Margaret Stuart?'

26

'Aye.' There was apathy in her voice now.

The door opened suddenly and she stood there – a middle-aged woman wearing a dressing gown and curlers.

'Harry thought you'd be worried because he didn't come home when he got out of prison.'

'How d'you mean?'

'He came out this morning.'

'I didn't even know he was in the jail.'

'Oh. You must have realised he wasn't here?'

'Hey, Mister – I haven't seen him for eight years.'

'Were you worried?'

'Well, I was for about a year,' she said reflectively. 'I mean, he only went out for a can of lager. Mind you, he's never been a reliable man. What's he been up to then?' she asked curiously.

'Oh – this and that.'

'Aye, that's him. Is that why you've pressed the bell at four o'clock?'

'No – he's had an accident.'

'Anything serious? I mean, terminal?' she asked frostily.

'Probably not.'

'You win a few, you lose a few, eh son?'

'S'pose. At least I gave the message.'

'Yes, you did. And here's one for him – tell him he owes me ten grand maintenance and he can drop dead as well. G'night, son.' She closed the door.

Detective Inspector Chisholm parked his car outside the factory and he and Detective Inspector Jones got out. Chisholm paused for a second, massaged his forehead, watching the pickets parading up and down.

'Headache, guv?'

'A bit frail. I had a few drinks in that well-known den of thieves, the Winchester Club, last night.

'Socialising, guv?'

'Would I do that? I'm a twenty-four hours copper, even when I'm sleeping I'm thinking . . .'

27

'And vice versa guv.'

'I beg your pardon?'

'Only kidding,' said Jones hastily.

'Your Celtic humour doesn't travel. Witty with the sheep, but not all that clever in the metropolis. Perhaps you can use your silver tongue with these bolshie strikers?'

'They're not suspects, are they?' said Jones, anxious to please.

'Who knows? In this life of ours everybody's suspect.'

He pointed at the pickets. 'Look at 'em – they have fathers, don't they? Brothers? Cousins? Malfeasance runs in families, y'know. Check the names, run'm through the computer. But don't disturb me.' He quickly walked away in the direction of the factory door, leaving Jones to rather dolefully interview the pickets.

In the factory, Chisholm, his head aching violently, prowled around the safe, looking at the buckled door. As he prowled, Solly watched him with mounting anxiety.

'Mm.'

'Bad?'

'What you've got here, Mister Salmon, is a shambles.'

Solly shot him an uneasy, questioning glance.

'This is the work of incompetent gas meter thieves, rank amateurs – kids maybe.'

'Not even experts?'

'Why should they be experts?'

'Well, why not?' asked Solly a shade too quickly, and Chisholm gave him a rather suspicious glance.

'Well, it's not exactly the most inviting premises in the manor. Why have a go at this place? How much did they get?'

'I don't know. They didn't open it.'

Chisholm turned the handle and the door fell off its

hinges and clattered to the floor. A stunned silence followed as Chisholm stared into the charred interior. 'As I said – gas meter thieves. They've even incinerated the booty. How much did you say?'

'Twenty thousand pounds,' said Solly quickly.

'Really?'

'Probably more.'

'Ashes to ashes. It don't look like twenty thou of ashes to me. How many people knew you were carrying that kind of dough?'

'Nobody.'

'No clients, reps – friends?'

'I swear to God.'

'Your wife?'

'Becky's going to rob me? An old woman –'

'I'm not exactly pointing the finger. I just want to know. The strikers?'

'Who knows? I don't know,' said Solly defensively.

Jones knocked on the open door and put his head round it.

'Mess, innit, guv? Got the names.'

'What did those pickets have to say?'

'Not a lot. No visitors for several days. One bloke from the union and a couple of old friends of ours . . . sewing machines and suits –'

'Who?'

'Daley and McCann.'

'Well, well, well! You didn't tell me that, Mister Salmon, did you?'

Solly hesitated. 'Arthur and Terry. Didn't I tell you that?'

'Friends, are they?'

'Not friends – not *real* friends.'

Chisholm's headache miraculously disappeared and he was beaming. 'Suddenly I see blue skies, sunlight on the horizon.'

'Not their style, guv? I mean safebreaking?'

'Why not? Safes contain money – ipso facto – Arthur

29

Daley isn't far away from that commodity.'

'I can't imagine Arthur doing anything like this,' said Solly.

Chisholm paused. Then he said quietly: 'Mister Salmon, your business is tailoring, mine is investigating.'

'Very eloquent, guv. And of course you're absolutely right.'

Chisholm looked sharply at Jones. He was never quite sure whether Jones was an idiot or a sycophant.

Arthur drove his Jaguar out of a car-wash, got out and inspected the gleaming bodywork with meticulous care. Suddenly he became aware that the Beesley brothers, Billy and Benny, were standing beside him and their car was inconveniently parked across the exit.

'Got all the mess off, Arthur?' said Billy.

'Oh, very droll. You scarpered off a bit sharpish, didn't you?'

'Well past my bedtime –'

'And me an' all,' put in brother Benny.

'Is Scotch Harry dead?' asked Billy pleasantly.

'How do I know. He's a health hazard. That man can damage your brain. An expert you said – he couldn't open a kid's money-box.'

'He had a bad night.'

'Billy – society gets the kind of thieves we deserve. It's a metaphor for this benighted country of ours.'

'Eh?'

'Let it pass, Billy,' said Arthur wearily. 'Let it pass.'

'What about our dough then?'

'You don't expect money as well? It's still in the safe, innit?'

'Have you had yours?'

'Of course not. Haven't you heard of the old theatrical expression – no show, no dough?'

'That's not fair,' said Billy threateningly.

'Fair, he says.' Arthur's sarcasm was lost on both of them.

'What happens if Scotch Harry grasses? We're odds on for a three-year stretch.'

'At least,' replied Arthur comfortingly.

'And what about you?'

'Me? I didn't do it. We agreed from the start. You're not suggesting that I'm . . .'

'I am,' said Billy and Benny grunted in agreement.

'Well, in that case,' said Arthur, hurriedly opening his car door. He was about to get in when Billy squeezed his right arm and Benny the left.

'Are you threatening me?'

'Not in a million years, Arthur. I mean, we're equals, ain't we?'

'All for one — one for all . . .' He paused and then remarked, 'Like the Three Stooges.'

'You owe us, Arthur.'

'Take it easy on the threads,' exclaimed Arthur boldly.

'Sorry,' said Billy.

Arthur shrugged with renewed confidence.

'Thank you. I'll have a little chat to Solly but I don't have high hopes.'

'That's not enough,' said Billy dejectedly.

Arthur got into the car, this time unmolested. 'D'you fancy a couple of suits?' he asked blandly.

Chisholm and Jones were shown to Scotch Harry's screened-off bed by the Irish nurse and a young doctor.

'You may be surprised. He looks like the invincible man,' said the nurse.

'You mean the invisible man?' asked Chisholm.

'Whatever you fancy, sergeant.'

'He's quite ill,' put in the doctor.

'We won't disturb him. It's just a question of identity,' said Chisholm reassuringly as the nurse opened the screen.

'Blimey,' said Jones, 'it's a mummy.'

Scotch Harry was completely swathed in bandages and only his eyes and mouth were visible.

'We don't know his name?' whispered Chisholm.

'He wouldn't say. The burns suggest an explosion,' replied the doctor.

'Irish?'

'He certainly isn't. Look at him,' said the nurse.

Chisholm gave her a curious glance. 'Can it hear?' he asked.

'Oh yes.' The doctor's voice was officially expressionless.

Chisholm put on his bedside manner – which closely resembled a Gestapo doctor interviewing a malingering slave labourer. 'Now, what have we got here – a safebreaker or an urban terrorist?'

There was no reaction from Scotch Harry.

'Can it talk?'

'Possibly.' The doctor's voice was chilly. He found Chisholm's manner offensive.

'Have we got an address?' asked Chisholm, looking deeply into Scotch Harry's worried eyes.

'Arrrghh,' was his only reply.

Chisholm turned to the doctor. 'Foreigner, is he?'

'Who knows, Mr Chisholm.'

Chisholm stared into Harry's eyes again. 'I know him,' he said with quiet authority.

Scotch Harry gave him a startled stare. 'It's them minces. Can't hear him, can't see him – but there's an aura of wickedness.'

Chisholm looked up at the others. 'It's a copper's instinct. He's a wrong 'un.'

'You're amazing, guv,' said Jones.

Chisholm turned on him angrily. 'You taking the piss?'

'No guv – would I do that?'

Ignoring him, Chisholms said: 'We can confirm my view by taking his dabs.' Chisholm picked up Harry's bandaged hand. 'All right, doctor?'

'I'm afraid not. His hands have been dressed.'

'Not even his pinkie?'

The doctor shook his head. 'It is my professional view —'

Chisholm interrupted him brutally. 'They always say that. Unless their houses have been turned over recently. Have we got his clothes?'

'Just tatters. I put them in the incinerator,' replied the nurse.

'No I.D.?'

'Nothing.'

Chisholm bent hungrily over Scotch Harry again. 'I know you, pal – seen those eyes.'

'I've seen them too. It was one of those Walt Disney nature films, like when a coyote was trapped.'

'Good judge.' He straightened up. 'We'll be back, my old friend. And we won't be bringing any grapes. Thank you,' he added, nodding curtly to the doctor. As he and Jones walked towards the exit, Chisholm paused and looked back at the nurse as she drew the screens together again. 'By the way, how did he get here – under his own steam?'

'He looked awful.'

'On his hands and knees?' persisted Chisholm.

'Somebody helped him,' she said reluctantly.

'Oh yeah?' Chisholm was very interested.

'A man said he met him in the street.'

'And who was this Good Samaritan?'

'I wouldn't know his full name, but I've seen him around . . .'

'And?'

'He's called Terry.'

Chisholm gave Jones a broad smile. 'Well, well, well – there's about two thousand Terrys in this manor, but for some reason a particular Terry leaps to the mind. Obviously you'd recognise him if you saw him?'

'I suppose so. Has he done something wrong?'

'All the time, my dear,' said Chisholm cheerfully.

* * *

33

Detective Inspector Jones parked his modest Ford Escort in the street behind Terry's flat. As he strolled towards the entrance he saw Terry saying farewell to a woman in her early thirties. She was strikingly attractive.

'Where d'you get 'em?' he asked as she walked away.

'Copper's wife,' Terry told him. 'She couldn't abide the violence and left him.'

'You're pulling my leg, aren't you? Got a couple of moments?' Terry did not vouchsafe a reply so Jones blundered on. 'Mister Chisholm would like to see you.'

'He knows the address.'

'He wants a little chat. Just down the road.'

'What for?'

'I don't know,' said Jones unconvincingly. 'He just needs some information.'

'I don't have to come down there . . .'

'Come on, Terry. Don't give me a hard time. I'm just a working copper.'

'Every time somebody loses his dog I get pulled in.'

'Helping the local police. That's what it's called.'

'And what happens if I don't come?'

'I'll arrest you.'

'What charge?'

'You know the drill, Terry,' Jones told him wearily. 'Obstructing an officer? Avoiding arrest? Got a TV licence? I don't know – molesting a policeman's wife? Anything else *you* can think of?'

'No,' said Terry unwillingly. 'Not offhand.'

Chisholm gave Terry one of his characteristic supercilious sneers. 'Hear your name all over the place, Terry.'

'Popular name.'

'Oh yes – yes indeed,' he said ruminatively. 'Haven't been here for a while, have you?'

Terry ignored him. Behind him Jones leant against the closed door like a watchful weasel.

'It always happens,' continued Chisholm.

'What always happens?'

'The same faces. In this manor there's what – say, three hundred of 'em?' Jones nodded in agreement. 'The real rascals, the dyed-in-the-wool scallywags. If this was a police state – and thank God we don't live in one – I could have that lot behind bars and then ordinary people could roam the streets without hindrance.' He paused. 'But alas, we have rules and laws, arrest procedures, habeas corpus and all that cobblers. Three hundred of 'em in custody, in every manor, we could then contain petty crime.' He paused again and then added reflectively: 'This is my pipedream, Terry. I don't like running around after robbers and thieves, conspirators and receivers . . . Surely there's more to life than that, eh?' Chisholm gave Terry an icy smile. 'I understand you're into safe-breaking now?'

'Me?' Terry sounded completely astonished.

'Could I phrase that better? Apparently, you were hanging around a clothing factory yesterday.'

'I was collecting some sewing machines,' replied Terry angrily.

'That was earlier. You see – this is what happens with your unfortunate history. You're in the frame . . .'

'For what?'

'You know.'

'No, I don't.'

Chisholm spoke with heavy irony: 'You didn't know that there was twenty grand in the safe?'

So indignant was he at this comment that Terry knocked an ashtray off the desk. 'How the hell should I know?'

Chisholm looked at the ashtray on the floor and nodded as Jones who retrieved it. 'I trust we're not getting violent.' He turned to Jones. 'Was that a violent act, Taff?'

'A bit impolite, I'd say.'

'Can I go now?' asked Terry coolly, standing up.

Chisholm smiled. 'You must be joking! I haven't

35

asked you about the hospital yet. I have a remarkable description of you from an accident victim.'

'Who's he?'

'Just a victim,' said Chisholm airily.

Terry smiled. 'You mean you don't know his name?' Suddenly he realised he had the advantage. 'I don't know why you're asking me all these questions about last night.' Terry spoke with rising confidence. 'Safes, robberies – or whatever – I've got the perfect alibi.'

'Such as?'

Terry savoured the moment. 'I was with *you*, Mister Chisholm.'

Chisholm stared at him blankly.

'Remember the Winchester? A bit of "afters"? Incidentally, you owe Arthur a fiver.'

'That is a private matter.' Chisholm's face was drained of colour and Jones looked very interested.

'I just thought I'd remind you,' said Terry smugly.

Chisholm furiously dug into his trouser pocket, but couldn't find what he was searching for. Angrily he turned to Jones. 'Got a fiver on you?' 'he muttered.

'Yeah.' Jones pulled out a fiver and nodded at Terry. 'You mean I should give it to him?'

'Yes,' snapped Chisholm.

Terry took the fiver with a grin. 'Turn-up, innit? It's usually the suspect corrupting the officer. Now, what else were you saying?'

Inside Arthur's car, Terry was checking the contents of a plastic bag which contained a suit, shirt, shoes, tie and underwear. They were parked outside the hospital entrance and Arthur was looking worried.

'I'm not going in.'

'I didn't think you would. It's your pal though. But I'm the one who's being hassled by Chisholm.'

'You're in the clear.'

'He wants a body, doesn't he? And we can't guarantee on Scotch Harry.'

'He's as good as gold. One of our own.'

Terry shrugged and opened the car door. 'That's what I mean,' he said drily. 'Don't run away now.'

'Are you questioning my bottle?' asked Arthur angrily.

'Yeah.'

'Have I ever let you down?'

'Yeah.'

'I'll give you five minutes,' said Arthur nervously.

Terry got out and spoke to Arthur as if he was training a puppy. 'You *stay* till I come back.'

'What happens if you're captured?'

'You *stay*.'

Terry walked to the hospital entrance. Then he looked back at Arthur and hissed: '*Stay* – Rover.'

Terry, carrying the plastic bag, walked down the long hospital corridor until he found what he was looking for: a store room. Furtively opening the door, he left the plastic bag inside, looked around him – and hurried away.

Scotch Harry was sitting up in bed, swathed in bandages, when Terry came in with a cheery greeting to the ward sister.

'Afternoon, sister. How's my cousin – over there?'

'Much better.' She hesitated. 'But perhaps you can tell us his name – he seems to have a speech problem.'

'He's had that since he was a kid. Roland, that's his name. Surname's – er – Brown.'

'Brown?'

'Brown – yeah. Can he walk and everything?'

'Of course he can. He'll be fine in a few days.'

'Thank you very much.' He walked over to Scotch Harry and leant on the bed. 'Harry?'

'I'm magic,' he whispered. 'Great to see you. Chisholm was around, but I didn't say a dickie bird.'

'But he'll be back. Fancy doing a runner?'

37

'You know me – I'm game for anything.'

'I've dumped some clothes in a bag in the store-room down the corridor . . .'

'Okay.' Harry winked. 'Suddenly I feel like a leak.'

Arthur was taking a constitutional around his Jag when Chisholm and Jones arrived at the hospital entrance.

'Arthur!' said Chisholm in a voice of sudden relish, and Arthur smiled weakly. 'Not ill, are we?'

'One of my usual good deeds, Mister Chisholm. ' 'Er indoors is visiting a neighbour.'

Chisholm gave him a long and searching stare.

'Nice drink last night? No hangover?'

'No, thank you,' said Chisholm primly.

'Incidentally, you haven't got my fiver?'

Chisholm scowled. 'I gave it to McCann. He hasn't turned you over, has he?'

'Course not.'

With another suspicious glance Chisholm turned towards the hospital gates, 'You're like a saint, Arthur,' he said as he followed Jones inside. 'What's he up to eh?' asked Chisholm as they walked down the corridor.

'You never know with Arthur, do you?' said Jones enigmatically and Chisholm gave him a dismissive sneer.

As they clumped away the store-room door opened and Terry peeped out, watching their retreating backs. When they were out of sight, he and Scotch Harry walked quickly down the corridor. Harry was wearing a Savile Row suit two sizes too big for him and looked a ludicrous swamped and bandaged figure. They hurried through reception, surprisingly attracting little attention, and joined a flurried Arthur in the Jag.

'What's happened to his hands? They been amputated?' asked an immediately alarmed Arthur.

Harry shot his cuffs and showed his bandaged hands. 'Nice bit of suit, eh?'

'Beautiful,' replied Arthur. 'Suits you down to the ground.' He turned to Terry. 'Where's my fiver from Chisholm?'

'I was going to give it to you . . .'

'Oh yes,' said Arthur cynically.

'Course I was.' Terry's voice was too innocent.

Chisholm and Jones sat gloomily beside the empty bed.

'He'll probably come back,' said the ward sister.

'Why?' asked Chisholm bleakly.

'They all come back at teatime.'

Chisholm was not to be appeased. 'I've heard about the National Health. They take off wrong legs, misplace gall bladders and now you can lose a patient without much difficulty. Thank God he wasn't ill.'

Arthur, Scotch Harry and Terry walked apprehensively towards Harry's flat. Arthur was carrying a large bunch of flowers. At the corner they stopped and Arthur thrust the flowers into Scotch Harry's hand.

'You stay here for a minute. I'll just charm her.'

'Wanna bet?' said Terry.

But Arthur was in a confident mood. 'Leave it to me.' Arthur approached the flat door and pressed the bell while the other two lurked out of sight.

The door was opened by Scotch Harry's wife. Arthur was all smiles as he announced: 'Mrs. Stuart? I have good news for you. A shock maybe – but good news.'

'Are you the man from the papers – is it the bingo?'

'Almost, my love,' he said romantically and was just about to gush on when Scotch Harry, unable to contain himself any longer, broke cover and thrust the flowers in her face.

'It's me, hen.'

'God help us? What is it?' She stared at Scotch Harry in his outsize suit and bandages in horror.

'I thought you'd say that –'

' "Home is the sailor, home from the sea.

And the hunter home from the hill!" ' said Scotch Harry as he tried to kiss his wife.

'Is it some awful disease? Get him away from me,' she screamed, trying to struggle out of his clutches.

Arthur laid a restraining hand on Harry's arm. 'Now don't go over the top,' he said.

Margaret was staring at Harry's bandaged face. 'Is it catching? It's no' scabies or anything like that?'

'He's all right, Mrs Stuart,' said Terry calmly. 'Can we come in?'

Seemingly numbed, she led them into the living room.

'He's not staying here, is he?' asked Margaret Stuart warily.

'Of course I bloody am!' said Scotch Harry indignantly. 'Is it not my home?'

'You've been eight years away.'

'It's still ma *home*. She's never satisfied, see,' he said, turning to Arthur and then looking round the room proudly. 'I furnished this whole place,' he said, eyeing the spartan furnishings with affection. 'The best years of my life were spent in here.'

'He's off his rocker,' said Margaret. 'The best years of his life were in Barlinnie, the Scrubs and his bookmaker's wee shop.'

Scotch Harry turned to Terry. 'She's no memory of the magic moments. Don't you remember me as a young, dashing, tall guy . . .'

'It's thae bandages. He's always been that size.'

'Hang about, eh? Let's settle down.' Terry was still trying to be the peacemaker while Arthur watched the events rather vaguely.

Suddenly exerting himself, Arthur turned to Harry. 'That's right. You sit down in your favourite easy chair,' he said reassuringly.

'I've never had one.'

Arthur steered him to a chair. 'Well, in that case – this one's good enough.'

Terry took Margaret's arm. 'And you sit here.'

Scotch Harry and Margaret sat in opposite corners, with their seconds beside them.

'When the bell rings, come out fighting,' said Arthur loudly.

Scotch Harry rose to his feet. 'See, she doesn't understand.'

'Not yet,' said Arthur. 'You're not in the ring. Mrs Stuart, for a few days, at least, he wants to stay here. You see – if he walks down the street he's gonna be captured, and it's not just him . . . There are *others*. Terry, for example, and *me*. When he takes off the bandages – Bob's your uncle, he's as innocent as the next man. Apart from that, when he was in hospital, he was calling for you. It was very touching, wasn't it, Terry?'

'Oh yeah,' said Terry quickly, 'it was. That's why I came to see you last night.'

'Och – I'm that moved.' Margaret smiled. 'Did you call out for me, Harry?'

'I often do, hen. She's the bizzo, eh?' he said to Arthur.

Margaret was not impressed. 'Well, what's in it for me?' she asked coldly.

Scotch Harry looked embarrassed. 'These are my friends.'

'You're pathetic,' pronounced Margaret.

Attempting intercession, Arthur said: 'You're protecting your own husband.'

'What's in it for me?' Margaret insisted. 'If he's that valuable there must be a price.'

'Look, hen – you're bargaining for my body!' protested Harry.

'What do they call it – blackmail?'

'Arthur, you tell her. We don't do this. In the underworld we've got a code.'

'Is that right?'

'Aye.'

'Let's talk money then.'

Scotch Harry spread out his hands in a hopeless

gesture. 'Now I realise why I left her. She's worse than Ma Barker.'

'Harry is not a wealthy man,' said Arthur.

'It's all right for you. I mean there's the food, and I've got to arrange the flat. And what about Suzie?'

'Suzie who?'

'Your married daughter,' said Margaret with an impatient shrug. 'Remember her?'

'Oh aye – *that* Suzie.'

'Obviously I'll give you a couple of bob for food,' put in Arthur helpfully.

'I want . . . three hundred,' said Margaret slowly.

Scotch Harry looked disappointed. 'That's what you call blackmail? Is that all I'm worth?'

'What are you worth then?'

Scotch Harry got up, hobbled to his wife and grabbed her hand. 'Don't you be intimidated by these people . . .'

Terry moved to the door and said to Arthur: 'It's your problem.'

'They're threatening me,' he protested.

'No, they're not.'

'See – he's bottling out,' remarked Scotch Harry.

Terry stood by the door. 'No, he ain't. I'm just going. It's not my problem – that's all.'

'And I'm coming with you,' said Arthur.

But Scotch Harry was not having that. 'No, you're not. I'm out of pocket. For all I know I may be disfigured.'

'And he used to be a handsome man, y'know,' said Margaret, suddenly partisan.

'Not in a million years,' countered Arthur. 'Do you realise that *I* personally rescued you from Mister Plod?'

'Yeah? Did you?' asked Terry.

Arthur ignored him. 'I've brought you back to the wife you deserted eight years ago – not forgetting your married daughter – don't I get some gratitude? If it was 'This Is Your Life' they'd be cheering, crying and giving you a red book –'

Scotch Harry prodded a bandaged finger at Arthur.

'Never mind that. I did the bizzo on that safe . . .'

'But you *didn't* do the bizzo! That's why we're in this mess. Look, missis, I'll give you enough dough to get all the porridge and mince and totties that he eats.'

'All you cockney fly-men are the same,' said Scotch Harry miserably.

'I've gotta shoot now.' Arthur hurriedly followed Terry through the doorway into the corridor whilst the domestic brawl continued.

'Are you going to let him get away with it?' Margaret shouted.

Scotch Harry limped out of the room. 'I'm a bit shaky on my pins, y'know . . .'

'Get on with it!'

Outside on the council estate the bizarre chase began, with Arthur and Terry walking hurriedly along, trying to pretend Scotch Harry was not waving and shouting behind them.

'Where's my dough?'

Arthur turned round and hissed at Harry: 'Shooosh! the neighbours.'

'I want my grand –'

'Behave yourself.'

'I'll blow the whistle!'

Arthur stopped and glanced at Terry who smiled and waved goodbye. Now Arthur knew with a sinking heart that he was on his own.

'I'm not kidding, Arthur,' said Scotch Harry, catching up with him.

'What's all that stuff about the code of the underworld?'

'That was just for her. It's no' true, anyway. Not any more. I mean, Billy and Benny – they'd grass me in a minute. Wouldn't they?'

'I've heard they're loyal men . . .'

'Come on, Arthur? – eh? A couple of drinks and I'd do anything. But I'm dead sober now. I nearly had ten heart attacks in the hospital what with Chisholm

43

sniffing around. I mean, he knows me – and I said nothing – just daft sounds. You take off these bandages and I've aged in twenty-four hours.' He paused and sighed. 'My time in life . . . I couldn't handle another bit of porridge. Yeah – I wouldn't blow the whistle. But Christ, I need that money.'

For once Arthur was embarrassed, even touched. It was a very new state of mind for him to be in. 'Yeah, but a grand . . .'

'You always have a good wedge on you. Just to show her that I've got a bit of respect, eh? Come on – you're a big man.'

'I've got five hundred – that's all.' He pulled out a wad of money. 'Then we're quits, right?'

'You're a great man, Arthur.' Scotch Harry smiled. 'You'll feel better after that.'

'Wanna bet?' Arthur was already regretting his sudden generosity.

Back in the flat, Scotch Harry counted out the notes in front of his eager wife. 'I showed him, eh? I did the bizzo there. No flies on me.'

'You'd better give me half of that. Then in two days you're offski, pal.'

'Don't you love me any more?'

'I didn't even fancy you before,' she said with a grim note of finality in her voice.

Arthur parked the Jaguar beside the lock-up. He felt exhausted, jaded and smoulderingly angry. As he and Terry walked to the door, he stopped and said meditatively: 'You know what I think – I think that little Scotchman turned me over.'

'That was the most decent thing you've done for a long time,' replied Terry in a moralising tone.

'You would think that, wouldn't you?' snapped Arthur.

Arthur didn't realise how close the fates were drawing

in. Just across the courtyard, in another lock-up, Chisholm and Jones were uncomfortably concealed.

'No sign of the invisible man, eh?' asked Jones.

'They've spirited him away.'

'No proof though, have we?'

Chisholm gave him a weary smile. 'We have to find some – or even manufacture some. A patient disappears from a well-known hospital. We can't tolerate that. What next? It might be kidnapping – or body snatching. We had Burke and Hare, now we've got Daley and McCann.'

'I read somewhere that there's a thriving business in spare parts for surgeons. Makes you think, don't it?'

'Anything that makes you think, Jones, must be good for you.'

A few moments later a van arrived in the yard and Solly and Angie got out. They walked quickly over to Arthur's lock-up and Chisholm and Jones exchanged delighted glances.

'Well, well . . .'

'What d'you reckon, guv?' asked Jones.

'They're at it – obvious – they're in cahoots.' He was almost ecstatic.

'But what about the girl?'

'Don't make waves, Jones,' replied Chisholm bleakly.

In Arthur's lock-up a dispute was in progress about a sewing machine. Solly and Angie were trying to remove it and Arthur was determined to prevent them.

'Solly,' he said indignantly, 'these are no longer your property.'

'Did you give me cash?'

'You had my bond.'

'But did you give me cash?'

'That is immaterial. Cash is only a token.'

'I didn't even have a token. You took care of them for a night. And what a night? I've lost money, peace of mind –'

'Don't talk about money. I'm well out. I had to give –'
Arthur came to a grinding full stop, realising that
Angie was there. Terry, leaning against the wall,
grinned.

'Let's forget it,' said Solly.

'And we need those sewing machines,' put in Angie.

'She was your enemy yesterday.'

'Twenty-four hours is a long time in tailoring. Now
we're partners.'

'Brothers,' asserted Angie.

'So brother and sister. She got a good kopf. D'you
know you get money from the government? Enterprise, they say.'

'They'll do anything to stop you join a dole queue.
And Mister Salmon is putting up his own money as
well.'

'Where'd you get that from?' asked Terry in a
surprised voice.

'Seventeen grand – my life savings.' He gave a
cynical smile. 'Maybe I owe it to the girls, eh:'

'I think you owe some other people as well,' said
Arthur censoriously.

'All in good time, Arthur. We gotta get on our feet.
New premises, a modernised factory, fresh thinking.'

'Like a collective,' said Angie firmly.

'You know – a co-op,' explained Solly.

'A collective – a co-op! Solly, that's communism!'
Arthur was shocked.

'I've tried everything else. So maybe I'll get some gelt
out of it,' pronounced Solly.

'Come on,' said Terry, picking up the sewing
machine, 'let's take this to the party.' As he walked
outside he ran into Chisholm and Jones standing like
sentinels in the yard. 'Evening all.' He put the machine
in the van whilst Arthur and Angie followed with
another. Solly appeared to be supervising.

'Look at 'em – suspicious, eh?' whispered Chisholm.

'I've been thinking, guv . . .'

Chisholm's face clouded over. 'Not again.'

But Jones was persistent. 'Look, what's in it for us, eh? No money stolen, no circumstantial or forensic evidence, the prime witness has disappeared and the victim seems very friendly with the suspect. Lots of paperwork and even if we nick someone then what? GBH to a safe. What I'm saying, guv, is who cares?'

Chisolm stared at him for a moment and then continued to watch Terry and Arthur who smiled cheerfully back at him. Chisholm turned slowly back to Jones with a thoughtful, troubled look. 'Sod 'em,' he said quietly.

PART TWO

After his brush with Chisholm and Jones, Arthur felt a curious elation – and Terry noticed that he had extra bounce, a new confidence that was bound to spell trouble for both of them. So when Arthur opened his executive-style briefcase and Terry saw that it was full of notes, trepidation seized him. But there was nothing much he could do as they were standing in the queue at the bank.

'I didn't know you had that kind of dough. I could've mugged you.'

'And with your background I could believe it,' said Arthur magisterially. 'You're a very lucky man – not many employers would give you a second chance.'

'But some of them might pay my wages. You owe me eighty sovs.'

'You sure?'

Terry nodded, looking at the bundles of banknotes.

'I owe most of this,' said Arthur hurriedly.

'Some of it to me.'

'Don't get the idea that I'm a rich man. I graft, don't I? The sweat of my brow. Two weeks of hard work –'

'I've seen you every day during the last two weeks. I didn't see you work . . .'

'I get up in the morning. The world is a market and we all have our little stall. The man who shouts louder gets listened –' Arthur handed over the notes and the paying-in book to the clerk. 'Four thousand – you don't have to check 'em.'

The young female clerk was slightly intimidated by Arthur.

'Just routine, sir.'

'Well, what's wrong with my stall?' said Terry.

'You're not selling anything, are you? You've got no aspirations, have you? A quiet life – that's all you want, innit?'

'No chance of that with you bawling in my earhole.'

'I don't wanna see you on the scrapheap of life – mixing with bad company . . .'

'I can't. I haven't got the money. Bad company want

to see the colour of your dough. They like to spend a pound or two.'

'Excuse me, sir,' interrupted the clerk hesitantly. 'You're one hundred and twenty pounds light, sir.'

'Never.'

'I'm afraid so, Mister Harney.'

Terry started, wondering how Arthur would react to the mix-up on names. But he looked entirely unembarrassed.

'Happens to us all, eh?'

'Yes, Mister Harney.'

'Mister who?' whispered Terry.

'Nothing to do with you,' snapped back Arthur, *sotto voce*.

'A moody name!'

'For a man who hasn't even got a bank account – what's it to you?'

'Give me my eighty sovs and I can start one.'

The Bank Manager passed behind the counter and nodded at Arthur. 'Morning, Mister Daley.'

'Morning.'

The clerk glanced up, confused by the name and Arthur gave her a reassuring smile.

'He knows you,' said Terry.

'I'm well known in the manor.'

'Then what's the point of having an alias?'

'They all have 'em, don't they?'

'Who?'

'The top men. Corrupted coppers, the czars of the underworld, city wizards – it's not all under the floorboards, y'know. How d'you think they get their dough out to Marbella? Not in a plastic bag. They transfer it from bank to bank . . .'

Terry stared at him as if he had gone crazy. The sudden megalomania appalled him. 'You're pathetic.'

Arthur looked hurt. 'Am I?'

'Mister Harney . . .' began the clerk.

But Arthur wasn't listening. He turned angrily to

52

Terry. 'Why're you having a go at me? What is it –
envy? Just because I've got a couple of bob . . .'

The clerk tapped on the partition. 'Mister Harney?
Excuse me – Mister Daley –'

'Yeah,' said Arthur impatiently.

'This one's light as well – hundred and forty.'

'Can't believe it, young lady.'

'I'll check again, Mister Daley.'

'What did you call me?' said Arthur sharply.

'Mister Daley . . . Mister Harney.'

'That's better.'

'I've realised it for years,' whispered Terry. 'You
don't know who you are!'

Arthur was not amused. 'Don't you worry about me –
I get by. You accompany *me* to the jug. Not the other
way round.'

'Well, in that case you don't need me to take you
back.'

'You're a free agent,' said Arthur frostily.

'Fair enough. See you.'

'And you.'

Terry walked towards the door. He glanced back and
then stepped out into the street.

'I've altered the pay-in slip, Mister Daley,' said the
clerk dutifully.

'Yeah – you would, wouldn't you?' replied Arthur
acidly. 'And incidentally the name is Harney.'

'I'll remember Harney – Mister Daley.'

Arthur grabbed at the paying-in book. 'Thank you.
Where'd they get you from?' He walked away, leaving
the clerk wondering if he was dangerously – or just
quietly – mad.

Still wounded by Terry's remarks, Arthur carried his
executive-style briefcase towards his car in a nearby
car-park. But as he unlocked the door an unbelievable
figure appeared behind him. He seemed young and was
wearing a balaclava helmet and gloves and was
brandishing a toy revolver.

'This is an attempted robbery,' he said.

'Oh my Gawd. This is all I need!' Arthur didn't know whether to laugh or cry.

'It's loaded. Gimme the case –'

'I was paying in, not taking out. I haven't got a damn thing.'

The youth tried to grab the briefcase but Arthur hung on to it protectively.

'This is an executive briefcase –'

Arthur stumbled, still holding the case, and fell backwards into the car, ending up behind the steering wheel.

'I'm a desperate man,' panted his assailant.

'What about me?' spluttered Arthur. 'If you shoot me you'll have a guilty conscience for the rest of your life.'

'No, I won't –'

The briefcase had ended up on the passenger seat and they both began to tussle for it. The revolver waved unpleasantly in front of Arthur's face.

'Not the eyes –'

'Give us it –'

Finally Arthur handed over the briefcase and the youth ran off down the street. For a few moments Arthur sat shaking behind the wheel. Then he got out and saw his friendly neighbourhood policemen Chisholm and Jones.

'Mister Chisholm –' Excitedly he ran across the street. 'Did you see that – in broad daylight?'

'What?'

'Robbery – and I was the victim. Didn't you see the bloke?'

Chisholm gave him a jaundiced smile. 'No, I didn't.'

'You must have!' yelled Arthur indignantly.

Chisholm looked around him. 'I see no mayhem in the streets. I hear no sound of gunfire, breaking glass, the squeal of motor tyres, the voices of "Stop, thief!" No. I saw nothing. Did you, Jones?'

'Not a dicky bird, guv.'

Arthur was furious. 'This very second – up on his

heels with my briefcase and waving a shooter.'

Chisholm turned away from him, glad of the opportunity for such sweet revenge. 'Sheer fantasy,' he commented.

'That's great – the only time you need 'em and they don't see it. Just come out of jug and –'

'Oh, you bank in there, do you? Note that down, Jones. I like to see where the local scoundrels stash their ill-gotten gains. What is it? False name? Inland Revenue know about that?'

'I can't believe this.' Arthur was on the highest of his horses. 'A well-known ratepayer reports a serious incident and he's being cross-examined for his financial arrangements.'

'Yeah – but who's robbing who? Okay – you're reporting the incident. Very public spirited of you. I'll put it in the book.'

'Don't you want the details?'

'D'you know him?'

'Course not. I wouldn't be talking to you if I knew him. He'd be hanging from Blackfriars Bridge by the afternoon.'

'Was he black?'

'How do I know? He was wearing a wooly hat and gloves.'

'Good description, eh? What did he get away with?'

'Well – er – my executive briefcase.'

'I mean – the contents?'

Arthur was starting to get ever so slightly embarrassed. 'A gas bill and a letter from Readers Digest.'

'And?'

'Er – that's it.'

Chisholm gave him a strange, obsessive look. 'You winding me up?'

'Not for a million years.'

'We're busy men, you know. Undermanned, underpaid, overworked, unappreciated. And you come up with your irrelevant complaint . . . I could nick you . . .'

'For what?'

'Wasting my time, Mister. It's not actually the great silver bullion heist, is it?'

'I'm talking about the principle. The quantity is unimportant. If he'd got hold of me five minutes before he'd have had a result, wouldn't he? Is it only the rich man who can enter the gates of the Met. and get a bit of justice . . . ?'

Jones was impressed. 'We had a preacher in our chapel many years ago – a similar stamp of man . . .'

'Don't encourage him,' censored Chisholm.

'You want it cut and dry, bang to rights – without all them grasses you'd never arrest anybody.'

Chisholm turned to Jones. 'Are we gonna have a cuppa tea and a pie or not?'

'We've earned it, haven't we?' said Jones.

But Arthur was immediately indignant. 'Hang about – I haven't finished yet. You may not be interested in the robbery but what about the violence? A dangerous gunman is on the loose. I had a shooter up me nostrils.'

'Bad shot, eh? We'll have to have a whip round for his shooting lessons.'

'Thank *you*, Mister Chisholm. No wonder we've got a law and order crisis in the country –' But he was talking to air for Chisholm and Jones were walking away.

'Old ladies get symptoms like yours,' said Chisholm over his shoulder. 'Always being interfered with – meeting armed robbers, masked rapists. You don't need Old Bill, you need a doctor.'

'My medical records are impeccable.'

'I wouldn't say that about your police records,' muttered Chisholm.

By now Chisholm and Jones were across the street. From the opposite pavement Arthur shouted at them: 'I heard that. I pay my rates for the likes of you.'

Chisholm glared at him across the street. 'You're disturbing the peace. Go home!'

'I remember the old-time coppers – guardians of the

law,' said Arthur to himself. Then he shouted at the briskly retreating backs of Chisholm and Jones: 'Crime on the streets and all you want is a cup of tea and a pie. What's happened to the guardians of our law?'

People were looking round now, whispering to each other. Was this shouting man in the heavy overcoat a raving lunatic? It wasn't long before Arthur got the message of their wondering looks and hurried angrily away.

Terry strolled towards the lock-up, still curious about Arthur's behaviour. Was he cracking up at last with his delusions of grandeur?

'Are you Mister Daley?'

Terry started and then turned round to see an attractive woman in her late twenties, sprucely dressed, confident and charming. Definitely the right side of Sloane Square, thought Terry.

'Not me, lady.'

'Is *this* his office?' She looked askance at the lock-up.

'It depends . . . Are you from the Inland Revenue?'

'No –' She smiled.

'Excise and Customs?'

'No.'

'DHSS?'

'Wrong again,' she said, obviously enjoying the conversation.

'Well, you can't be all bad, can you?'

As Terry opened the door he suddenly had a thought. 'Not the lady from meals on wheels?'

'Is he that old?'

'Well. I'll tell you. If you ask him, he'll tell you that he's the same age as Paul Newman.'

Terry walked into the lock-up and held open the door for his new acquaintance to enter. She took in the usual array of track-suits, coats, portable TV sets, videos, fridges, Hoovers and other merchandise with some interest.

'Who is he – exactly?'

57

Terry was instantly suspicious. 'Well, who are you – exactly?'

She took a card from her handbag and gave it to Terry.

'Blimey! Caroline Selby – private investigator? You don't look like Mike Hammer.'

'They always say that.'

'They're usually retired coppers, aren't they?'

'So they say. But not me. And you?'

'A friend of Arthur's – sometimes a colleague. What's he done?'

'You're very suspicious.'

'That's what happens if you hang around with Arthur. So what's he done?'

Caroline inspected some track-suits on a rack. 'Nothing. Looking around here he probably has dozens of things. No, I'm interested in some information. He's rather well known in this area, isn't he?'

'So he thinks.'

'The godfather of the – er – the "manor". Is that the expression?' she said, trying the length of the track-suit trousers.

'D'you want to try them on?'

Caroline gave him a very cool smile. 'No fitting room?'

'That can be arranged. No, he ain't the godfather of the manor – but he does know people. What about changing behind those fridges?'

Caroline gave him a frosty smile. 'You do like helping the customers, don't you?'

'All part of the service.'

'Just a little bit slummy,' she asked gently, 'don't you think?'

'I'll give you that it ain't Lillywhites. But you being a tough private eye an' all – I know you won't be bothered.' There was a long pause, then Terry added: 'Okay, Caroline. Let's start again.'

'Well . . .' She was hesitant.

'You don't want a track-suit. Does Arthur want to see you?'

'Maybe. I'm trying to get hold of a man called Mister Goddard. Know him?'

'Old Albert, the penny stamp?'

Caroline looked bewildered.

'The tramp – a wino, a dosser – or a drop-out, if you like.'

'Does Arthur know him?'

'They're not exactly great pals. Why?'

'I'm working for a company of solicitors. They're trying to contact Mister Albert Goddard. What did you call him? A penny stamp? Apparently he's got great expectations . . .'

'You mean he's won the pools?'

'You could say that.'

'I see,' said Terry slowly. 'Well, I think you can take it that Arthur will be very interested.'

Scooter sat at the bar of the Winchester Club. He was forty-five, had a face that was as sharp as an axe and wore an ancient raincoat buttoned up to the neck. He had a watch on each wrist which he checked continuously, giving him a kind of Alice-in Wonderland aura.

'He's usually punctual,' said Scooter to Dave, sipping his drink.

'He's a busy man. You've got a meet, have you?'

'Course I have. I mean, we're all busy, in't we? I've gotta scoot, inna minute.' He checked one of his watches again.

'They got the same time?'

'Course. It's an 'abit. Time is of the essence. Incidentally, I'll have some Rolex watches in a couple of weeks. You in the market?'

Dave showed him his own watch. 'Arthur got me that. Cartier, isn't it?'

Scooter held Dave's wrist tightly. 'A lot of them

about, aren't there?' Scooter took out his jeweller's eye-piece and inspected Dave's watch. 'That's a ringer.'

'Eh?'

'Good 'un – mind you.'

'You can't tell anything from that.'

'Course you can. The face is everything. You have to be an expert. How much d'you give for that? Two hundred?'

Dave seemed embarrassed. 'Bit more'n that.'

Scooter was visibly impressed. 'He's a lad, inne – old Arthur? Keeps good time, does it?'

'Perfect.'

'Then you're all right, eh?'

Dave wasn't so sure. He looked at his watch again. 'Seems all right to me.'

'If you're happy – fine.'

Scooter glanced round and saw Arthur coming in. He seemed very agitated and gave them both a scowl.

'I was giving you up, Arthur,' said Scooter. 'I mean, I've gotta –'

'Yeah, I know. You gotta scoot, Scooter. I've had a traumatic experience . . .' He turned to Dave. 'A large vodka and slimline, and one for Scooter. Do I look different?'

'Good as gold.'

'Yeah? Well, I'm surprised. I'm a victim of armed robbery.'

'Never?'

'A masked robber.'

'Was he black?'

'How do I know? He was masked, wasn't he?'

'What did they get away with?'

'Well . . . I'd just deposited a sum of money. They took my executive briefcase.'

'They took nothing?'

'In a sense. Yeah, nothing.'

Dave appeared behind Arthur with the drinks. He gave Arthur a cynical glance. 'That'll be par for the course.'

'Eh?'

'They have to get up early in the morning to take money off you. That's three pounds twenty.' He gave him a hard smile. 'Cash.'

Arthur seemed mystified by Dave's attitude. He took something from his pocket – which Scooter tried and failed to see – and gave it to Dave.

'Cheers, Arthur,' said Scooter, raising his glass. 'I've got the stuff,' he whispered, tapping his raincoat. 'Are you ready? I've gotta scoot inna minute.'

'Arthur, these are luncheon vouchers,' interrupted Dave.

'They're cash – legal tender.'

'Not here. Restaurants, sandwich bars, pubs – but not here. I'm surprised at you – that's not true . . .'

'They're not counterfeit, you know. If the worker is worthy of his hire and needs sustenance – whether it be a lamb chop and two veg, or liquid calories –'

'Not here,' replied Dave sharply. 'And nobody works here – not in the real sense. I've got the membership list: a few shepherds, three deep-sea divers and twelve brain surgeons –' he placed his elbows on the counter – 'but no workers, Arthur.'

'What's the matter with you? A luncheon voucher is –'

'No. You've gone too far . . .'

It was an eyeball to eyeball confrontation and should have sapped Arthur's confidence. But it didn't.

'Well, in that case – put it on the slate.' Arthur turned and gave his full attention to Scooter. Glumly, Dave knew he had lost again.

'I worry about him sometimes,' said Arthur to Scooter. 'What have we got?' he added after a pause.

Scooter looked round warily. 'You'll love it. But in the back, eh?'

'Oh,' said Arthur, following Scooter to the door of the gents.

Scooter fastened the lock behind him and they stood, cramped together, in the small, tawdry lavatory. 'Wait

61

till you see this, Arthur.' He began to unbutton his raincoat and Arthur nearly fell into the pan trying to get away from him. But all Scooter put on view was a length of gents suiting cloth that was wrapped round his body. 'Beautiful, eh?' he said proudly. 'Twenty-four ounce, finest worsted.' Scooter began to unwind the cloth.

Arthur was both dismayed and relieved. 'It's blue,' he said at last.

'Lovely innit?'

'I wanted grey.'

Scooter stopped unwrapping the cloth. 'Blue's beautiful.'

'Scooter – I ordered grey . . .'

'It's the same, innit?'

'No it ain't. Blue and grey – cousins they may be but *not* the same. I don't want it.'

Scooter was astonished. 'You can't do that. I've grafted on this. Look, you go to your tailor and he'll tell you that this is first-class gents suiting –'

'I'm sure Georgie the Cypriot will recognise it as A1, top-notch English gear.'

'Yeah, he will – an' all.'

'And he will also recognise the difference between blue and – *What* did you say?'

'Well, I didn't know you go to Georgie . . .'

'Not only are you colour blind but you steal from one of our own . . .' said Arthur severely.

'It's dog eat dog in my game. All the chaps are wearing blue, y'know. Ronnie wore blue for his wedding in Broadmoor . . .'

'Yeah? Well, Michael Heseltine always wears grey and Elton John wears a big hat. We're not discussing high fashion. It's not as if you gotta large selection.'

'I'd have to have a bigger raincoat.' He fingered the cloth lovingly. 'I can't take it back, can I?'

The door began to rattle urgently.

'Any chance of having a Jimmy in there?' asked a desperate voice.

'This is a private meeting,' said Arthur reprimandingly. 'Kindly use the Ladies.'

'Charming. I've had four pints of Guinness,' the voice muttered.

'I was counting on you, Arthur,' said Scooter, quite unconcerned.

'Well, the customer's always right. You of all people should know that.'

Scooter wrapped the material round his body again and buttoned up his raincoat. 'I've got to scoot anyway . . .'

'And what about the sofa?'

'It's in the pipeline.' He touched the cloth lovingly again. 'Why don't you see this in the daylight?'

'Scooter – no. You've got to scoot, haven't you?'

'As it happens – yeah.'

Scooter unlocked the door – and scooted.

When Arthur returned from his meeting he found Terry carrying two glasses of lager from the bar to a corner table where Caroline was sitting. Terry sat down, raised his glass to her and said: 'There's your man.'

Arthur returned to the bar with weary dignity, picked up his drink and scowled at Terry, pointing an accusing finger at him.

'You deserted me,' he said in tones of injured innocence.

'Eh?'

Arthur turned to Dave and the other punters in the Winchester. He began a rhetorical speech. 'That man – a so-called friend, a colleague, never mind a comrade-in-arms, he's on the firm, he's on bloody wages – and what happened?'

'You gonna tell us, Arthur?' said Dave patiently.

Arthur walked dramatically towards Terry. 'That lager should stick in your craw . . .'

'Sorry about this,' said Terry to the surprised Caroline. 'It sometimes takes him like this, you know.'

'You're supposed to take care of me. That is your function in life . . .'

'What have I done?'

'Nothing. That's the whole point.' He turned back to the punters. 'He scarpas off, I walk out of the jug on me Jack Jones and then what? *Mugged!*'

'Was he black?' asked Terry, suppressing a smile.

'How do I know? He had a balaclava, didn't he?'

'But you didn't have any money.'

'So what? It's the principle that counts.'

'No bruises or cuts?'

'Would that be better? The point is – *you* were not there.' He favoured Caroline with a gracious, saddened smile. 'Is this your current paramour? Well, young lady, you must appreciate you can't depend on this swashbuckler.'

'This young lady wants to meet you.' His tone hardened. 'And incidentally, I don't like being slagged-off in public – particularly when I wasn't even there.'

But Arthur was still on his high horse. 'It was your *duty* to be there. That's your job . . .'

'What job? I haven't got a job.'

'Yes, you have.'

'I resigned – remember? In the bank.' He stood up. 'And I hope you get mugged again.' Terry nodded to Caroline and walked to the door.

Arthur stared at him as he stormed out. 'There's plenty of them around,' he said truculently. Then he gave Caroline an ingratiating smile. 'Well, young lady, how can I help you?'

Terry slammed the door of the Winchester and got into his car. For some moments he sat there in a blind rage, unthinking. Then, slowly, he began to mull over the traumatic years of his relationship with Arthur. It was not an edifying process. 'Sod 'im,' he muttered eventually and drove off.

Back at the Winchester Arthur and Caroline were sitting together. Her visit had not been in vain for

Arthur knew about Albert.

'As it happens, young lady, you've come to the right man. Although – I don't usually mix with the flotsam and jetsam of our society. And old Albert has got a trickle, has he?'

'Who knows? A solicitor wants to get hold of him. It usually is a legacy or whatever. And they give you what they call a finder's fee.'

Arthur was very interested. 'Didn't you go to the Old Bill?' Caroline gave him a puzzled stare. 'I mean, the rozzers? The filth – the bogeys – the police?'

'They couldn't help us – no address. He's never applied for social security benefits or registered with a G.P. He's a non-person.'

'I'll find him,' said Arthur confidently.

'Terry knows *of* him.'

Arthur sniffed deprecatingly. 'You can't trust him – you saw that yourself.'

'But he says he saw him the other day.'

There was an agonising pause. 'Albert is a local character,' said Arthur firmly. 'Don't worry about it, my dear. I'll find him. As for Terry, we have these little tiffs. He'll be crawling back by the evening.' Arthur gave an optimistic smile and raised his glass. Caroline was not so sure.

In fact it was not long before Arthur bumped into Terry. He was driving his Jag near the Scrubs when he saw Terry, head down in a track-suit. Hurriedly Arthur parked, puffed his way over the grass and yelled: 'Terry!' Breaking into a run he yelled again: 'Hang about!'

Terry waited unwillingly whilst Arthur approached him, smoking a cigar and breathing hard.

'When you get the hump you always go jogging. I suppose it's guilt,' panted Arthur admonishingly.

'Me?' said Terry, astonished.

'However, I forgive you.' He was magnanimous now. 'I don't believe you.'

Arthur flowed on, unconcerned. 'I'm a more mature man. I understand. You left me in the lurch – well, let's forget it, eh?'

Terry looked bemused. He shook his head and started jogging again. 'You're gonna forgive *me*?' he asked.

Arthur pursued him, puffing even harder, his cigar waving in one hand. 'That's the kind of person I am. Oh, incidentally . . . I owe you some money . . .'

'Yeah – eighty sovs. Due to me.'

'Obviously I haven't got it with me . . .'

Terry stopped, turned and took the cigar out of Arthur's mouth.

'I'll never carry dough again. What with the mugging and everything.'

'Oh. That the reason?'

'Very upset about that,' he panted. 'Can we stop for a minute?' He took the cigar from Terry and began to cough. 'Incidentally, d'you know where old Albert hangs out?'

'Ah,' said Terry thoughtfully. Now he knew the reason for Arthur's attempt at reconciliation.

'Well?' asked Arthur impatiently, but all he got from Terry was a blank stare. 'Terence, we are old friends. Why are you being like this? Other people know his address . . .'

'A dot on the card.'

'Well, then . . .' He tried another tack. 'Would you be interested in a length of material? Worsted – make a lovely suit.'

'Yeah.' Terry didn't sound impressed.

'It's blue – your colour.'

'Who said?'

'You've always fancied blue . . .'

'I don't like suits. I like money – particularly when it's owed to me.'

'Of course you'll get it. Unfortunately all that dough in the bank's spoken for. It's not exactly mine.'

Terry was cynical. 'Really?'

Arthur treated him to a big smile. 'I know what you'd like. Cop this . . .' Arthur took a watch case from his pocket. 'Cartier,' he said with simple modesty. 'Only the best kettle in the world. He invented it. Raich Cartier.'

'The inside forward –'

'Probably the same family. That's the business, innit?'

Terry tried it on. 'Same one that Dave's got?'

'Yes . . . I believe it is.' He sounded devious.

'Well, it is the same one, innit?' Terry insisted. 'You sold it to him.'

'Oh, *that* one. Yes, oh yes . . . no complaints from him . . .'

Terry inspected the handsome watch. 'Heard they're ringers.'

'These Cartiers?'

'Yeah.'

'More a figment. Who told you that?'

'Scooter – in a boozer the other day.'

'Never trust Scooter. He's well known,' said Arthur quickly. He looked annoyed. 'Anyway, so what? Those Cartiers are the best imitations in the world. They're all the same anyhow.' He paused and then said irritably: 'You'll get your dough tomorrow. In the meantime, I've gotta get hold of Albert.'

Terry gave him a resigned look. 'All right.'

'Well,' asked Arthur impatiently. 'What you gonna do?'

'Lead you to him,' said Terry.

Terry led Arthur to some undergrowth near the railway sidings. It was a particularly unpleasant place with discarded prams and mattresses as much a part of the tatty landscape as the stunted trees and bushes. Terry led the way and Arthur stumbled behind him.

'Hang about,' said Arthur.

Terry took his arm and guided him on.

'What was he in – the SAS?'

Suddenly a voice hissed: 'Freeze.'

'Gawd help us – he was in the SAS!'

Behind some bushes they could see Albert, levelling a shotgun. Albert was a surprisingly healthy-looking, bewhiskered sixty-year-old with a husky voice.

'Albert,' said Terry. 'We're friends.'

'Yeah?' He didn't sound convinced.

'Is that loaded?' squeaked Arthur.

'Yeah. You have to be careful around here, Arthur. See – I got mugged a few weeks ago . . .'

'Me too.'

'Yeah? Was he black?'

'He was wearing one of them balaclavas.'

'Same bloke – probably.'

'Any chance of putting down the artillery?' asked Terry gently, and Albert lowered the shotgun.

'Wouldn't want to upset you. Come to see me?'

'Yeah, well some guy . . .'

'This is my department,' cut in Arthur curtly. 'Thank you.' He smiled at Albert. 'You're a bit of a mystery man –'

'Well, I'm delighted about that. I ask nothing, and I give nothing.'

'Is this your abode?' Arthur indicated a collapsed-looking shack nearby.

'Come in,' said Albert in a welcoming voice.

Albert's shack was Heath Robinson with a suggestion of early seventies hippyness. Tools were littered on a table as well as weird contraptions, abstract sculptures, scraps of paper, drawings, and several bottles of cider and pale ale. On the wall there were astrology charts, maps of the cosmos and a bookcase was lined with dozens of scientific and philosophy volumes.

'Very comfy, eh?' said Arthur in his most deviously complimentary voice. 'And a bit of a reader? It's almost a haven from the hurly and burly of our teeming society.'

'*I* think so,' said Albert suspiciously. 'Now what do you want?'

'Think of me as a friend, Albert,' said Arthur. 'You don't usually get involved with solicitors, do you?'

Albert frowned. 'No?'

'Don't get too worried.'

Terry glanced at Arthur. What the hell was he up to?

'A solicitor is trying to contact you. Well, right away I thought to myself old Albert needs some advice . . .'

'I don't know any solicitors.'

'That's what I mean. It could be nothing. On the other hand – well anything. Insurance, your lease on this desirable property –'

Terry interrupted brusquely. 'It's nothing like that.'

'Probably not. More likely relatives, a distant cousin, somebody trying to get a hold of you –'

'More likely copyright,' said Albert.

'Eh?' asked Arthur surprised.

'My inventions.'

'Like what?'

'I do all kinds of things. Sit down – I'll show you.'

Arthur sat down, exchanging glances with Terry who was also mystified.

'See this?' Albert placed a tablet of soap on the table.

'Piece of soap,' commented Arthur.

'Yeah – but not an ordinary piece of soap.'

Arthur picked it up.

'It's radioactive,' said Albert.

Arthur dropped it at once. 'That's dangerous, innit? Like a bomb?'

'It ain't gonna explode.'

'Take it away.'

'You think of the power of the bomb. Well, this is a tiny, teeny particle of that power. That'll scour dirt, grime, grease –'

'It'll scour any bloody thing. Where d'you get the materials?'

'That's the secret.'

'Do the Russians know?'

'I wouldn't tell them.'

'What else d'you do?' asked Terry, looking around, studying the astrological charts.

'I want to market some of these things. My orthopaedic aids . . . You got bad toes, Arthur?'

'Yeah well, I don't want radioactive corn-plasters.'

'These are trainers. For people who have overlapped toes. There must be millions of 'em.' He showed them the toe-pads and Arthur studied them very seriously.

'And they work, eh?'

'Course they do. Painless remedial. It's a break-through, and it's British.'

Arthur was impressed. ''Er indoors suffers from her toes.'

'Let her try these. Look at my toes . . .' Albert starts to unlace his boots.

'I don't want to see your feet,' interjected Arthur quickly.

'I designed these for meself. I should patent them.'

'You should,' said Terry. He gave Arthur an appraising glance, seeing the greed in his eyes. 'There's some wicked people around.' He pointed at the astrological charts. 'What are these for?'

'I dabble with astrology –'

'You don't believe in all that?' said Arthur scoffingly.

'Yes I do. You're a crab, incha?'

'You what?'

'Your sign – Cancer. July maybe?'

Arthur was astonished. 'How d'you know that?'

'I just *know*, don't I?'

'How?' asked Terry.

'Look at him –' Albert shrugged. 'It's obvious.' He turned back to Arthur. 'What's your ascendant? Date, time, place?'

'I don't believe in that mumbo-jumbo. Twelfth of July, Fulham, half past four . . . p.m. It was a Wednesday.'

Albert looked carefully at his charts. 'Bit careful with your money –'

'Spot on, Albert,' said Terry sadly.

'Being a crab you retreat into your shell sometimes. You need affection,' continued Albert.

'I do, as it happens.'

'But your hunger for money gets in the way.'

'I'll vouch for that.' Terry was by now very amused.

Arthur was getting annoyed. 'He's just guessing, inne?'

'It's in the stars, my old son,' replied Terry with relish.

'This ain't science.'

'The planet Jupiter was passing by,' said Albert.

'I bet he didn't even get a tip.' Terry turned to Albert. 'Does it say he's obsessed about eighty sovs?'

'All the signs suggest –'

'I don't need all this. He's just winding me up.'

'No, he ain't,' said Terry, delighted. 'The man has studied the subject. He even got your birthday –'

'He's got an *aura* –see,' Albert stated.

'That's bad, innit?'

'Yeah,' replied Albert.

Suddenly Arthur could take no more. He jumped up, threw aside the toe-pads and went outside. Terry followed him, surprised at his unaccustomed sensitivity, and found Arthur lighting a cigar.

'No call for that, you know,' pronounced Arthur in a wounded voice.

Terry was amused at Arthur's touchiness. 'You're being a bit touchy, incha?'

'Even the Wizard of Oz said I needed affection.'

Terry grinned. 'But you don't believe in it.'

'That is not the point. He doesn't know me. All right, I'm a hard man. But if they prick me don't I bleed?'

'Come on, Arthur –'

'No, no . . . I don't want any sympathy. The matter is finished. I don't harbour grudges. But when I'm talking to him don't push your oar in . . .'

Albert appeared in the doorway, 'All right, Arthur?' he asked.

Terry watched a strange metamorphosis come over Arthur. Gone was the unpredictably sensitive plant and back was the old Arthur with an ingratiating smile. 'In the pink, Albert. D'you have any family? Distant relatives or whatever?'

'Suppose so. Not around here, though. Sydney.'

'Sydney who?'

'Australia – the place. Titled people they are.'

'Who?'

But Albert walked slowly back into the shack. Hurriedly Arthur followed him, intrigued. Terry brought up the rear, still wondering at Arthur's schizophrenia. Once inside, Albert poured some cider for himself. He didn't offer any around.

'You've got titled relatives?' asked Arthur eagerly.

'Why not? They emigrated – seventy years ago. The whole family, penniless they were. My old mum told me about it.'

'Have you been in touch with them?'

'Why should I?'

'Christmas?'

'I don't even know 'em.' He was becoming suspicious under Arthur's relentless questioning. 'What's it to do with you, anyway?'

'If a solicitor wants to get hold of you – it may be good news, eh?'

'Who knows? I don't trust 'em.'

'I know what you mean. But you trust me, don't you?' He was now at his most unctuous and Terry had the sudden urge to throw up on the spot.

Albert stared at Arthur suspiciously. 'Yeah . . .' he muttered. 'I don't like officials –'

'Well, in that case I can help you. I know these people. Should I suss it out? Find out what they're up to?'

'Yeah . . . why not –'

Albert was obviously suspicious and Terry knew he had good reason to be.

They returned to the lock-up where Arthur began his plan of action by, as usual, getting Terry to take the initiative.

He put down the phone. 'She's out.'

'How come she's out?' said Arthur irritably.

'I don't know. She's gotta eat. Even private eyes have to have a dinner. Two fingers of bourbon or whatever.'

'What d'you mean?' Arthur was mystified.

'Forget it,' said Terry abruptly, looking out of the window. He saw a green Harrods van draw up outside and to his amazement watched the driver get out. It was Scooter.

'Look at this, Arthur. What a turn-up!'

Abstractedly Arthur went to the window. 'Blimey,' he said and then hurried outside.

Scooter was wearing a white coat with a Harrods badge.

'Where'd you get that from?' asked Arthur, walking towards him and flapping his hands at the van.

'It was the only way I could get the sofa . . .' He opened the rear doors. 'You'll love this,' he said proudly.

Inside sat a grey three-seater sofa. But if Scooter thought Arthur was going to be pleased he was wrong.

'That ain't Pale Arctic Blue . . .'

'Ain't it?'

'Not in a million years.'

'That's what you told me.'

'No, I didn't. Scooter . . . I gave you the order number.'

Scooter produced a piece of paper. 'Got it, got it. That's the one you wanted.'

Arthur studied the order form. 'Right – pale arctic blue. 'Er indoors saw it in the window.'

'It's the same – or similar . . . It's called – er – Icelandic Grey?'

73

'I'll give you that it's grey.'

'That's the one they're after now. In fact, they don't do Pale Arctic Blue any more.'

'Don't you give me all them little porkies,' said Arthur threateningly.

'Stand on me, Arthur. They've had a lot of complaints about the whatchamacallit – pale arctic blue.' He continued in a hopeful voice: 'And polar bear white, an' all. You'll be well pleased with Icelandic Grey.'

'I can't go home with a sofa in Icelandic Grey. No matter how popular it is. 'Er indoors has certain views on interior decoration and accoutrements and with your Icelandic Grey you're gonna bugger up the whole gaff.'

'It's a special order, Arthur . . .'

'If you're in business, you're in business.'

'Leave it out. Harrods is a wonderful place but they ain't gonna take it back.'

'Why not? You got it out – you've even got the van.'

'It's a snip, innit? Half price. It's even got a price tag.'

'Doesn't matter. It's the principle, innit?' Arthur was adamant.

'I can have this on my hands for months.'

'You go into the big league – that's what happens. You have a cavalier attitude to colour schemes anyway . . .' He smiled. 'Remember the blue worsted suit length?'

'Yeah, and I told you that was the coming colour. I shifted that – no problem, see.'

'Then you'll shift this . . .' Arthur turned away.

'I was counting on you,' wailed Scooter, slamming the van's rear doors. 'You're a hard man.' Just as Arthur was about to go back to the lock-up, Scooter asked: 'What's your sign?'

Arthur stopped dead in his tracks. 'What's it to you?' he said, with a flash of temper in his eyes.

'There are some signs I don't want to do business with.'

'How d'you know my sign then?'

'I don't – but whatever it is that's the sign I don't want to do business with.'

Arthur turned on his heel. 'Kindly don't talk about what you don't understand,' he said furiously.

In another part of London, Detective Inspector Chisholm was being measured for a suit by Georgie the Cypriot in his tailor's fitting room.

'The suit is the man,' said Georgie grandly. 'I always recognise one of my suits – in the street, a restaurant, a club –'

'Or in the Crown Court?'

'It's possible,' allowed Georgie cheerfully. 'A natural shoulder line, Mister Chisholm?'

'Please.'

'I don't like to ask this – but will you be carrying?'

'Carrying what?' asked Chisholm puzzled.

'I mean –' he gave a wild gesture –' under the shoulder, hip, waist? A PPK Walther ... or a Browning – it spoils the line. You don't mind me asking? Some of them *are* carrying.'

'Like who?'

'Clients – and they're not all policemen.'

'I don't want to know about this,' Chisholm said sternly. Then, after a pause, 'What do you suggest?'

'Single breast, I think. The gangsters like a double breast – like the early Edward G. Robinson or Lloyd Nolan – you remember him? Warner Brothers, nineteen forties, a touch of the Jimmy Cagneys. I never saw him wearing a single breast.' Georgie smiled reflectively. 'The good guys wear a single breast so they can get their shooters out quicker.'

Chisholm gave him a wry grimace. 'Fascinating sartorial styles for villains, eh? And what kind of customers order these suits?'

'Different people,' he replied airily.

'Like who?' pressed Chisholm.

But Georgie was not going to play ball. In fact he

seemed to be deeply affronted. 'Mister Chisholm, d'you want me to be a grass?'

'It's your public duty.'

'I'm a tailor. We've got a code of honour – like doctors. Four buttons on the cuff?'

'Is it legal?'

'Perfect, Mister Chisholm. Now – material?'

'You'll like this . . .'

He opened his holdall and took out a suit length. It was a blue worsted material and Chisholm waited, anxious for approval, as Georgie felt the cloth.

'Nice material – first-class worsted. I've used the same cloth . . . I see he's cut off the manufacturer's stamp –'

'Who?'

Georgie glanced over the shelves. 'Whoever. Was this a present, Mister Chisholm?'

'Sort of.'

'Bankrupt stock?'

'Probably.'

'From a genuine supplier?' asked Georgie, pressing the point.

Chisholm shifted uncomfortably. 'I would think so.' He gave Georgie a wide smile, but Georgie suddenly exhibited a burst of Mediterrnean fury.

'The bastard nicked it!'

Chisholm looked completely baffled as Georgie pointed to a shelf by the window. 'It was up there. Look . . . Bleeding tea-leaves everywhere.'

'I trust you're not suggesting –'

'Bloody right I am,' he shouted. 'I recognise my own material . . .'

'One bit of blue worsted is much the same as another,' said Chisholm defensively.

'No it's not. I know what's mine.' He went over to the desk. 'I'll have to get the police.'

'I *am* the police,' said Chisholm quietly and very calmly.

Georgie stared at him. 'You're right.'

'They deliberately did this,' Chisholm muttered to himself, a manic gleam in his eye. 'It's a set-up . . .'

'Who?' asked the worried Georgie. But Chisholm wasn't listening.

'I'll get him. Don't you worry about that. D'you know the Winchester Club?'

'Vaguely. My only customer from there is Arthur Daley and he wouldn't –'

'Why not? He's behind every tawdry crime in this manor . . .'

'But he's such a nice man,' said Georgie hopefully.

Terry was driving the Jag through the streets of London's Temple whilst Arthur was reading the 'Your Stars' section of a tabloid. He was soon quick to comment.

'See . . . he doesn't do all that stuff about the planets ascending and passing by. Listen –' He began to read in a rather sonorous voice: "It's a time to gamble socially and in business. A loved one appears to change their mind" – that'll be 'Er indoors about the sofa. "Don't worry about financial problems." Nothing wrong about that.'

'You don't believe in it anyway.'

'I might – occasionally.'

'There she is,' said Terry suddenly.

'Your lady friend,' said Arthur reprovingly.

'And your Lady Bountiful.' Terry pulled the Jag over to the kerb. Hurriedly they both got out, leaving the Jag on a double yellow line.

'Where's Mister Goddard?' Caroline plunged straight in without formality.

'Well, he's a strange character. Doesn't like to meet people.'

'Then you don't get your cheque,' she snapped.

'All in good time. I am his proxy,' said Arthur pompously.

'*What* are you?' asked Terry incredulously.

'Proxy is the word. And I think I should see this solicitor – alone.'

'If you wish. Next building, first floor.' But she didn't sound impressed.

'Thank you. My man will take care of you for a few moments.'

Terry smiled as Arthur brushed past him. Caroline, however, paused. 'D'you trust your friend?'

'Why? Don't you?' asked Terry.

'He's a bit pushy, isn't he?'

'Yeah.'

'A cheat?'

'Yeah – you're right. And that's the good side of his character!' Terry shrugged as Caroline walked thoughtfully away.

Arthur was perhaps over confident when he arrived in the office of the middle-aged and urbane lawyer whose name was Prosser. Clearly he was not at all impressed as Arthur paraded round his office like a distinguished Q.C.

'My client feels he needs more information . . .'

'He's not your client, Daley. All we want is his address – very simple. Do you have to walk around like that?'

'He is my client, Mr Prosser, and in my care. You don't want him walking the streets on his tod. Violence is rife in the inner city and he could be mugged – as indeed I was the other day . . .'

'Really?' said Prosser in a totally disinterested voice.

'Yes indeed. He was black, of course. Thus, our client is tucked up nicely in one of my properties and he's briefed me to suss out your predicament.'

'I think I've sussed you out as well,' muttered Prosser. Then he said in a louder voice: 'Mister Goddard may be the beneficiary of a legacy –'

'Like how much?'

'Not your business. There may be other candidates.'

78

'How many runners?'

'Look, Daley,' said Prosser angrily, 'this may go to the courts. There is a question of identity . . .'

'No worries about that. My man's previous is pristine.'

'Eh?'

'He even got away with loitering with intent a few years ago.'

'Just bring him here.' Prosser was not prepared to continue with the dialogue.

'All in good time.'

'Have you abducted Mister Goddard? That is a grave violation of the law, you know.'

'Stand on me, Mister Prosser. I'm for fair dos – and a little result for Albert.'

'And one for you as well?' asked Prosser sarcastically.

Arthur smiled rather sadly. 'I'll ignore that, Mr Prosser – although of course I could take action against you for slander.'

'Yes,' said Prosser. 'I'm sure you could.'

The boot of the Jag was half open as Terry drove it slowly down a residential street. Inside reposed many of Albert's possessions and, indeed, there was more stuff on the back seat where Albert sat. In the front, Arthur turned to give him an encouraging smile.

'You'll like this,' he said, as Terry parked the Jag in front of a particularly seedy-looking Victorian terraced home.

Albert looked apprehensive as they all got out. 'Never fancied houses,' he said dubiously.

'This is a real modernised conversion,' said Arthur sharply. 'Central heating, a bath, kitchen units, a fridge, and a chiming bell. You'll love it, Albert.'

'I'm an open-air man.'

'It's got plants – creeping things – I picked them out meself.'

'My place is detached.'

79

'You'll have neighbours – air hostesses.'

'Since when?' asked Terry, but Arthur ignored him.

'Terry would like to live here,' he said to Albert, 'but the rents are too high . . .'

'I hate aeroplanes,' confided Albert.

'They don't park 'em outside. Now get your gear.' Arthur had had enough and he signalled Terry to pick up as much of Albert's gear as he could carry. Thus encumbered, Terry staggered up the front steps of the house, whilst Arthur was followed unwillingly by Albert.

Once inside Arthur unlocked a door in the hall. As he did so, a burly Irishman, wearing a donkey jacket and boots, walked down the stairs towards the front door.

'Who are you?' asked Arthur indignantly.

'I live here,' said the Irishman.

'You're supposed to be a fourth girl sharing a flat with three happy-go-lucky air hostesses.'

'They went. Now you've got three happy-go-lucky McAlpine's brickies.'

'You can't do that.'

'Who says? Our Giros are as good as theirs.' He hurried away.

'Who'd want to be a landlord, eh?' asked Arthur in an aggrieved tone.

Showing Albert round the flat Arthur pointed to a single plant. 'I've put in foliage – see.' He took Albert to the bathroom and stood over him whilst he stared dubiously down at the fittings. 'Good – eh? Hot . . . cold . . . And this – soap.'

'I do wash, you know,' said Albert. 'I actually wash.' He walked back into the living room and walked round, staring suspiciously at the bleak, sparsely furnished flat. 'Don't like it,' he said.

Arthur was upset. 'People would give their right arm to stay here. Just for a few days . . . and Terry is going to take care of you.'

'No he ain't,' said Terry firmly.

'He'll guard you.'

'No.' Terry was determined.

'Course you will,' said Arthur in a jolly voice.

'Who's threatening him?' asked Terry.

'Who knows? He's a valuable commodity. And we've got to discover who he is.'

'I know who I am.'

'Really?' said Arthur cagily, opening a cupboard and finding some beer. 'How do we know that? You got a birth certificate?'

Albert shook his head.

'See. And what does that mean anyway?' He gave an expansive gesture. 'After all,' continued Arthur, 'who is the real Terry McCann?'

'See it in the mirror.'

'Not enough. They need proof.'

'Me dabs, me records.'

Arthur turned to Albert. 'This is why you're staying here. *They* don't know who you are. We could manufacture an Albert Goddard. And so could they. Philosophers have pondered the riddle of identity since Socrates.'

'The bubble?' asked Terry.

'The bubble?' Arthur gave him a pained look. 'You can't describe Socrates as a bubble. He was an ancient Greek . . .'

'That's what I mean.'

'Nick, who runs the dry cleaners down the road – he's a bubble. But your ancient Greek was a different breed. Olympians, a classic profile. They looked more like English people. Look at their statues; they don't even look like bubbles. Can you imagine Socrates running a take-away kebab gaff?'

Terry thought for a second. 'Yeah – they reckon Athens was the cradle of civilisation.'

'And so it was.'

'Like the Parthenon Social Club in Tufnell Park.'

'I don't know if they had darts . . .'

Albert suddenly took a more aggressive part in the conversation. 'I ain't Greek, y'know.'

'Course you're not. But hundreds of Albert Goddards could suddenly appear – that's the point. A little sniff of wealth and they'd be crawling out of the woodwork.'

They all sat down as comfortably as possible on the scanty furnishings Arthur had provided whilst Terry passed round the beer.

'You're not exactly a pillar of the community,' said Arthur censoriously. 'Now do you understand?' He paused. 'They always have distinguishing features.'

'Who?'

'The mysterious inheritor.'

'Yeah, you're right,' said Terry enthusiastically. 'They always have a birthmark. But only one person knows about it . . .' He looked at Albert hopefully.

'I ain't got one.' He paused. 'Except a little mole – behind me knee.'

'And it's always the old nanny who knows about it.' Terry was very matter-of-fact.

'How do you know that?' asked Arthur surprised.

'Read it,' said Terry.

'I never had a nanny,' pleaded Albert.

'Yeah, but you had a Mum, didn't you?'

'And?'

'Well, I want you to write down your life story. Family, where you lived, friends, school, your first job, your first doctor . . . And then explain how you got into this terrible mess . . .'

Albert was not best pleased. 'Because I like it. That's why.'

'All right. We'll put it all down. Facts . . . facts . . . They like facts.'

'What's in it for you, Arthur?' asked Albert bluntly.

'Me?' Arthur's innocence was hard to take. 'I'm like the Good Samaritan – a helping hand – a simple philatelist.'

'Don't you mean philanthropist?' suggested Arthur, amazed.

'Oh . . . do I?' Arthur was clearly surprised.

Terry was becoming embarrassed in face of Arthur's gathering fantasy.

'See – I can advise you. If you offer me a simple gratuity – I may accept it.'

'And Terry?' asked Albert.

Terry gave him a warning glance. 'I'm not involved.'

'Terry always supports me,' said Arthur hopefully.

'Not this time,' he said as he got up and went to the door.

'He's a strange lad, inne?' commented Arthur.

Arthur would not have been so confident if he had known what was going on down the local nick, where Detective Inspector Chisholm was deep in conversation with Mr Prosser, the solicitor.

'He's hardly a missing person, sir,' Chisholm was saying doubtfully. 'And as you don't even know his address I can't feed it into the Yard's computer . . .'

'You've got his name,' protested Prosser.

'He's not like a nine-to-five punter, is he? Albert is a social dissident, a knight of the road. You don't know where he'll appear . . .'

'But I have good reason to believe that he has been held against his will . . .'

'Some old inoffensive tramp – what kind of monster would do that?' asked Chisholm wonderingly.

'Do you know a chap called Arthur Daley?'

For a moment Chisholm was stunned. '*He's* a monster.'

Arthur was standing at the bar of the Winchester Club, waiting for his usual drink to be marked up on the slate. But Dave was not feeling generous.

'That'll be cash – I mean, no luncheon vouchers.'

Arthur treated him to a winning smile. 'You're getting very fractious these days . . .'

'It's the atmosphere here. You don't know where you are . . .' He turned to the till and as he did so Arthur noticed that he was limping.

'Dodgy foot?' Arthur was sympathetic.

'As it happens – toe. Seems to be twisted. I've had it for years.'

'Seen your chiropodist?'

'They can't do anything about it –'

'Oh really? That was yesterday. Medical science is remarkable. They've cracked that problem – the overlapping toe. And as it happens, I'm about to market a revolutionary remedial device –' Arthur produced the toe-pad from his pocket.

Dave reacted immediately. 'No thanks.'

'You haven't even seen it.'

'That's what happens to seventeen years of friendship. I don't trust you any more!'

Arthur was shocked. 'What?'

Dave waved his watch in Arthur's face. 'Cartier!' he said scornfully.

'The very best.' Then he whispered: 'Who told you?'

'Scooter.'

Arthur gave him a tired and resigned smile. 'Innit marvellous? Scooter is suddenly an expert – a man who can't even pick out the right colour in Harrods.' He descended into a conspiratorial whisper. 'That *is* a Cartier. That was the first one – the come-on for the others. If Dave buys one, it's got to be kosher gear – get it?' He paused for effect, seeing that Dave was beginning to be convinced. 'My dear friend, you actually thought I'd turned you over?'

'Yes I did. But . . .' He hesitated uncertainly.

'Thank God I told you,' said Arthur in a voice of profound relief.

Dave was now won over and seemed deeply grateful. He squeezed Arthur's arm. 'I'll tell you what, Arthur, I'm gonna bar that horrible Scooter –' He turned to the next customer whilst Arthur took a great draught of vodka. It had been a near-run thing.

Albert sat at the table in his bleak flat. Terry arrived,

carrying stocks of booze, and found him writing something. He was so deeply engrossed that he didn't even look up when Terry came in so Terry tactfully didn't interrupt him. He opened a bottle, poured out a drink for Albert and placed the glass on the table. It was only then that Albert decided to sit up and take some notice.

'Good exercise this,' he said reflectively. 'Remembering things.'

'Got the facts?'

'Too many. Trying to think when I first decided to sleep rough. I suppose I just drifted into it. Nothing dramatic – just lots of little crises. Like jobs . . . You could get jobs at that time so I was waiting for a decent job – more-or-less settled. But I had a gap of a month, see. Now, all my family was killed in the Blitz – some old auntie in Hull but I'd never met her.' He paused, trying to remember the details. 'I had enough money for food but not enough for rent. Beautiful night, it was. Couple of drinks – I wasn't much of a drinker – stretched out, smiling at the stars, and I thought "this is a doddle". Funnily enough, it didn't rain for eleven nights – but by that time I'd got into sleeping out.'

'You could have got some help, couldn't you?'

'After six years in the army, being told what to do . . . What should I have done – gone into one of those hostels or somethin'?'

'Yeah,' said Terry laconically. 'Why not?'

'Because I'm an independent man.' Albert smiled philosophically. 'An awkward sod. I'd never been on the dole, you know. I got the job – but I didn't even go. I was living on the land. I've been everywhere in this country. That's when I started studying the stars.'

'The way you tell it – it sounds good.'

'It ain't romantic, y'know.'

'Living on the land? Did you have a spotted handkerchief with a stick?'

'It was all right for *me*, see? I've met other blokes who've done it out of desperation. It only needs a bit of bad luck. I met a bloke in Sheffield and he was an accountant,' he said in a voice of awe. 'An accountant,' he repeated. 'Have you ever met an accountant?'

'Course I have.'

'Yeah?'

'Yeah.'

'Under the railway arches, a bottle of British sherry and studying a P45? He was always writing to the Inland Revenue asking for a rebate.'

'And what happened?'

'I dunno. He was always moving on, didn't have an address . . . so he never got the replies. Mind you, I think he was a nutter.'

'Don't you want to settle down?'

'I can't settle down any more, can I? What can I do with that dough – assuming that I get it, eh?'

Terry gave a wry smile. 'I think Arthur's got a few ideas.'

'Yeah,' said Arthur thoughtfully. 'He's a busy man, inne?' He paused. 'A very busy man.'

Arthur strolled out of the Winchester and walked slowly up to his Jag. He didn't see Chisholm's car drawing to a halt a little further down the street. Nor did he see Chisholm himself until it was too late.

'You!' said Chisholm in tones of icy fury.

Arthur started, staring up at Chisholm with a look of injured innocence.

'Stay where you are!'

'Why?' said Arthur, puzzled.

'I want you, Daley. And I've got you.'

'If it's about the Road Tax, it's in the post.'

'Don't be smart with me,' said Chisholm, hardly able to contain his anger. 'I was going to get a warrant, but the Magistrate couldn't believe it.'

'Believe what?'

'You may well ask. What are you? A Sicilian bandit? A German urban terrorist? The mind boggles. At what point do you stop?'

'I've no idea what you're . . .'

'Yes, you do,' yelled Chisholm, losing all control.

Arthur was, for once, intimidated. 'Do I?'

'Kidnap. Unusual in this country – not an Anglo-Saxon crime, you know. More like a Latin country or even the Yanks. Where's Albert?'

Arthur seemed relieved. 'He's staying at a flat of mine – self-contained, central heating, well-fitted kitchen and luxurious bathroom and handy for the West End. One, incidentally, that I was going to rent to a visiting American academic.'

Just then, Arthur noticed that Scooter's Harrods van had drawn up nearby.

'So you say. But I want to see the body,' said Chisholm, showing no signs of cooling off.

'Why not, Mister Chisholm? I often help the casualties of our diverse society. A bit of charity, Mister Chisholm.' Arthur began to get on to one of his soap boxes but he was interrupted by Scooter.

'Hello, Arthur, I've got the sofa. Pale Arctic Blue, just like you said . . .'

'Not now, Scooter,' snapped Arthur.

Too late, Scooter realised who Arthur was talking to. 'Later then . . .' said Scooter, retreating. But Chisholm had already turned on him.

'I want you!'

Scooter jumped into the van. 'I gotta scoot,' he said predictably, slamming the door.

Chisholm stared reflectively at the disappearing van. 'Where did he get that vehicle?' he asked with steely patience.

Arthur opened the door to the flat and ushered Chisholm in. The place seemed strangely quiet.

'Albert . . . Terry?' bellowed Arthur.

Terry suddenly emerged from the sofa.

'Are we disturbing you?'

'Not now – thank you.'

'Where's Albert?'

'He's gone to meet a solicitor,' said Caroline, also emerging from the depths of the sofa. 'Two hundred thousand – apparently.'

'He doesn't know what he's gonna do with it.' He paused. 'It *is* his dough!'

For a long while Arthur said nothing while Chisholm ran a practised eye round the flat. But he didn't know what he was looking for.

'You traitor!' Arthur bitterly addressed Terry. 'I was going to help him.'

'He's a grown-up man.'

'Yeah – and what about you?' He turned scornfully on his heel and walked out.

'Well . . . afternoon . . . all,' said Chisholm in a rather embarrassed voice, following Arthur out and closing the door abruptly.

'He's not very happy,' said Caroline.

Terry gave her a resigned smile. 'It was going to end some time or other.'

'Upset?'

'We're pals. If it was a marriage, I would have walked out ten years ago. Let's forget it.'

'Do you want a job?'

'Like what?'

'Our company . . .'

'I ain't no private eye.'

'No . . . I mean . . . I should think you could call it security. Guarding places, escorts, bodyguards, bouncer at a charity ball . . . minding the family jewels.'

Terry gave her a long hard look. 'What are you trying to do? Am I supposed to join the right side?'

'Nicer people.'

'Yeah – who says?' said Terry with profound cynicism.

Terry walked into the lock-up to find a disgruntled and testy Arthur poring over his account books. Terry handed him an envelope and Arthur looked up in angry suspicion.

'That's your cheque. The finder's fee.'

Arthur tore open the envelope. 'Forty-five sovs? I don't even set my alarm clock for that.'

'That's the rate.'

'Yeah . . . well, if that's respectable employment I'll walk on the wild side.'

'Well, I'll see you,' said Terry, a little hesitantly.

'And just as well. You're very strange these days. I should've sussed it out – the mugging.'

'What could I do?'

'You should have been *there*,' said Arthur unreasonably.

'Yeah . . . okay.' He walked away. 'See you.'

'And you.' But when Terry had gone, Arthur began to think. 'He's bloody hopeless anyway,' Arthur muttered. 'There's plenty of pebbles on the Fulham Road, y'know,' he said more loudly, as if to reassure himself. Suddenly he jumped up and dashed to the door. 'Terrance, hang on – Terry.'

Terry was walking out of the yard as Arthur rushed out of the lock-up. He stopped but didn't turn round. 'What do you want?'

Arthur waved the cheque at him. 'I suppose you want half of this?'

Terry walked on.

'Well?'

Terry turned round and shrugged.

PART THREE

Locked once again into his uneasy relationship with Arthur, Terry wondered for the hundredth time why he had allowed himself to be persuaded back. He could only answer that he was very weak-willed. At the same time, a future without Arthur's presence seemed curiously incomplete. These thoughts were very much on Terry's mind as he wrote a betting slip. It was a serious business, for he would only be free to stand on his own feet in the style that he needed if he won a fortune. And winning a fortune was a fantasy indeed.

It was early afternoon. There were few punters in the shop – and all of these were studying their copies of the *Sporting Life*. The second race at Newbury had just ended and the 'blower' voice was intoning the starting prices. It was an old-fashioned shop – one of the independents. It still had a boardman, chalking up the runners and prices and the results, instead of the bank of TV monitor sets on the wall.

Dolly, who was taking the bets, was an attractive blonde – thirty-sixish, well groomed, with expensive jewellery and a world weary attitude. Terry was surprised and interested. Dolly seemed a class above the usual betting shop assistant.

'What d'you reckon – any chance?' asked Terry as he gave her his betting slip.

'Not a lot.' She stared at the slip and then looked up at him.

'They're my lucky numbers – one and two.'

'Can't you count after those?'

'After three I get stuck.' He was beginning to like her more and more.

A settler came up and gave a slip to Dolly. 'This guy's had a result on the first two winners – and he's on a 12 to 1 shot for the treble,' said the settler.

'Get on the bell and spread that around . . .' Dolly looked up at the TV screen. 'Anyway, the favourite's a dot on the card.' She gave some change to Terry.

'You're a keen student of form, are you?' said Terry. He was impressed.

Dolly gave him a very cynical grin. 'It's not difficult, darling,' she said. 'All numbers – mathematics. Didn't you get an "O" level . . .?'

'You kidding? I didn't even get one for woodwork . . .'

'Well, don't polish the woodwork here, darling. You're preventing the punters from giving me their bets . . .'

'Sorry,' said Terry, but he only moved away a couple of steps and it was obvious that Dolly didn't want him to go far as she kept glancing up at him while she was taking the betting slips. Then, as the last punter trotted away, Terry returned to the counter. 'You new here?' he said, somewhat lamely.

'Quick, aren't you?'

'Not really – but I'm a trier.' He smiled. 'Now you'd look better behind a roulette table in Curzon Street.'

'I thought you'd say Tesco's. You work there?' she asked sweetly.

'I'll tell you what – you can hear my life story after you finish.'

'No thanks.'

'Not even a runner?'

'Not even under starter's orders. I was Charlie's wife.'

Terry was very surprised. 'You? Old Charlie's wife? I mean – I'm very sorry . . .' His voice trailed away and Dolly busied herself with the betting slips. 'That's okay. Anyway, it's five months now.'

'Don't matter. I was definitely out of order.' He was considerably mortified now.

'Why? A lot of people are surprised.' She smiled. 'He was a bit older than me – good man though.'

After a respectful pause, Terry said: 'Nice guy.'

'Thanks.'

'So – you're going to manage the shop, eh?'

'Why not? Been around with bookmakers all my life. Charlie – God rest him – my dad was a bookie and his brother. I didn't have nursery tales as a kid – just the

94

runners and riders for Kempton Park and the Timeform black book.'

'I've been looking for you since I was about 14 years old,' said Terry wistfully.

'You work for Arthur Daley . . .'

'*With* not *for*,' said Terry quickly. 'And we can still have a drink after you close the shop.'

Dolly thought about it. She stared at Terry hard, as if she was weighing up his personality. 'Okay. Just for a drink,' she said at last.

'Great. Meet you at the boozer on the corner. And bring your Timeform book – *and* bring my winnings, an' all.' He walked out, leaving Dolly staring pensively after him. Suddenly she looked extremely vulnerable.

As Terry came slowly out of the betting shop, Arthur came hurrying up, looking flurried.

'Where've you been?' he asked in the old domineering way and Terry sighed. Clearly nothing had changed. 'I've been in that boozer for fifteen minutes . . .'

'Somebody didn't give you a drink?'

'There is always a flock of respected people to buy me drinks. And you – spending your wages on some horse . . .'

'Dogs. Hackney.'

They walked back towards the pub. 'No class, you,' said Arthur. 'I mean – Ascot, Epsom, glorious Goodwood . . . and what do you do – Hackney?'

'Reversed forecasts doubles – right across the card. Traps one and two.'

'One and two! Science . . . You don't need a computer to add up one and two.'

'I don't care. I'm in love. Ever met old Charlie's widow?'

'Very handsome woman. And a few bob in the bank, as well. And I don't want to know about your flirtations. Serious business is afoot . . .'

95

They strolled into the pub where Terry found that the drinks, predictably enough, were on him. Arthur deliberated for a moment and then turned on Terry with a grave expression.

'Barry's been murdered.'

Terry was stunned. 'I don't believe it!'

'Murdered.'

'Shot? Strangled? What?'

'I don't mean "murdered". I mean he's been murdered by the horses.'

'Oh, *that* kind of murder.' He was immediately relieved.

'Precisely. Take heed, my old son, if a bookie like Barry can't win – who can?'

'Well, he lays the odds to a lot of nasty people . . .'

'Not nasty – just people who can't have accounts with kosher turf accountants. And people who don't like paying tax.'

'Who does?'

'Anyway, he needs you. He's going to pay out today.'

'What am I supposed to do?'

'Company – that's all. Go to the bank with him.'

'Okay,' said Terry, but he showed no sign of moving.

'Go on, then,' said Arthur impatiently.

'This minute?'

'Now.'

Terry regretfully emptied his glass. 'You coming, then?' he asked.

'I've seen a bank,' said Arthur. 'And I've also got to see a feller about some fireplaces.'

'What?'

'Old fireplaces. Victorian. They're knocking down some old houses and I can sell the fireplaces to decent middleclass people who want to gentrify their houses after they've evicted the sitting tenants who've put in their high speed gas fires.'

'Say that again?'

'Fashion full circle. Don't you ever read House and

Garden?' asked Arthur with withering scorn.

Arthur stepped carefully over the rubble of the demolition site. The tippers, cranes and bulldozers were making vast inroads on a delapidated terrace of old houses and there was a general atmosphere of dust and devastation. With a cigar clenched between his teeth and his shining black toe-caps now dirtied, Arthur looked an alien in a rough and macho world. The Irish foreman, wearing a hard hat and a donkey jacket, looked at him askance.

'You want all of them?'

'Whatever you've got. They're just rubbish, aren't they? No intrinsic value.'

The foreman looked at him suspiciously. 'Well, in that case why do you want them?'

Arthur gave him a manipulative smile. 'I'm a collector, Pat . . .'

'The name's Dermot.'

'Dermot?' Arthur sounded rather surprised. 'All right, Pat, I'll call you Dermot. A tenner for each piece. Intact though – I don't want to know about damaged goods.'

The foreman prodded at a mantelpiece that was lying on the ground. 'I seen an article on them the other day. Quite fashionable these things. House and Gardens . . .'

'Never,' said Arthur, too quickly. 'These – would you like one in your house? Course not.'

'I've got under-floor heating.'

'There you go – You know, the Romans invented that?'

'Yeah? Funnily enough I got the stuff from two Greeks.'

'Greeks, Romans – it's all part of our Western culture. Pat . . . innit, Dermot? Now how about our little deal?'

*　*　*

The keen young uniformed policeman standing on the street corner was becoming increasingly suspicious of Terry as he waited outside the bank. Terry was all too well aware of his presence – and his growing interest. Desperately he tried to look unconcerned as the policeman scrutinised him, but looking unconcerned can be very difficult. Leaning casually – too casually – against a parked Rover, Terry examined his shoes, stared at the sky, smiled hopefully at some passing girls, examined his shoes – and looked at the sky again. But when he stole a glance at the young policeman, Terry saw he was talking into his two-way radio. Had he really been acting so suspiciously? Finally, to Terry's intense relief, Barry came out of the bank. He was in his mid-forties, confident, brash and well groomed with a small leather case. Barry could have been a successful accountant, a sales executive or an advertising man – as it happened he was an illegal bookmaker.

Terry caught his arm and pushed him towards the Rover. 'Let's move, Barry.'

'What's up?' said Barry, alarmed.

'Just get in the motor. In about two minutes I'm going to be nicked.'

'What have you done?'

'Loitering, sus – you name it . . .' He glanced back at the policeman. 'Young Old Bill. I mean, what am I doing outside a bank, eh?'

They got into the Rover with Barry behind the wheel, and as the car filtered into the traffic the young policeman jotted down the licence number. Just to be on the safe side, he obviously thought.

'When are you going to pay out?' asked Terry.

'Later,' said Barry quietly. 'But don't leave me alone. I get very nervous when I'm carrying cash.'

'How much have you got in that case, then?'

'Twenty-three K,' said Barry after a pause.

'That's a heavy load, innit. Bad week, eh?'

'Week? That was a day. It's a high-risk business, mine.'

'So it seems,' said Terry doubtfully.

Barry grunted as he negotiated the streets. 'Most times it's a good living. But I'm not like Ladbrokes. You know, the margin is dicey. And the people I associate with – they don't like to hang around for their winnings.'

'Yeah, but I've got a meet tonight . . .'

'You'll be through by nine.'

'Two minutes then. Left, second right, left again.' As Terry gave the directions, he began to wonder, yet again, what he had let himself in for. A picture of Arthur floated into his mind. Mentally Terry threw a dart at it.

Once inside the betting shop, Terry hurried towards the counter – and Dolly. He gave her a discreet wave and a few seconds later she joined him.

'You know that little meet we were having . . .'

'Yeah?'

'Well, something's come up.'

'Yeah.' She gave him one of her cynical looks.

'But I'll be through by nine . . .'

'Yeah.'

'We could have a little Chinese meal. By the way, what happened to my bet?'

'You lost.'

'Oh, great. But anyway, d'you know Mr Wong's?'

'Yeah?' She still wasn't giving much away.

'Well, I thought we could meet there. Have a nice bit of sweet and sour and – You don't seem all that thrilled –'

'We were just going to have a drink.'

'Well, we're going to have a meal instead.'

'Just remember – there's no yo-yo on the end of this string, Terry.'

Terry looked affronted. 'Leave it out. It's a meal – that's all.'

'Okay,' she said after a longish pause.

'I'm well known at Mr Wong's. I've gotta shoot – see you.'

Dolly smiled to herself as Terry rushed out.

Once again, Terry was waiting for Barry, sitting in the wake of his salubrious life style. Barry's executive case was on the seat beside him and the car was parked outside a shop proclaiming the legend *Sauna and Massage*. Eventually Barry sauntered out, Terry opened the car door and Barry got in. He passed the case to Terry.

'Nice massage?'

Barry smiled. 'Just had to chat to the feller. He's a regular customer . . . I mean, he usually loses.' Looking satisfied, Barry drove off.

At Arthur's familiar haunt, his home-from-home, the Winchester, all was warmth and light. A far cry, he thought, from 'Er indoors, sweeping all before her with the hoover. Arthur was in his usual corner by the bar, chatting to Dave.

'Could there be anything nicer – in these chilly nights – than a cheery fire, eh, Dave?' said Arthur, putting his thoughts into words.

'I dunno . . .'

"Just listen to me, Dave. Just say, for instance, in a place like this. The decoration is in impeccable taste . . .'

'She chose the wallpaper.'

'Oh yes – no problem with the wallpaper. Sort of Regency motif? I may tell a lie – Victorian, I think.'

'Is it? She just saw it in the book.'

'She's got an eye for interior decoration. But as I was saying – a roaring fire, a warm hearth, a beautiful mantelpiece . . . it's more sort of welcoming, don't you reckon?'

'Oh yeah – nice. I like a fire meself.'

Arthur gave him a quick smile. 'Now just for example – could you picture a lovely fire, say, there –' He pointed to a space on the wall.

'Not there, Arthur. That's only a hardboard wall, that.'

Arthur sighed. 'Over there, perhaps?' he asked hopefully.

'No chimney – party wall.'

But Arthur was not non-plussed. 'Them architects can do anything these days. We ain't talking about building Rome, Dave. A simple chimney. As it happens, I *know* the district surveyor – personal friend.'

But Dave was distracted by the arrival of a new customer. 'Members only, pal.'

'Just a visitor, Mister.'

Arthur turned round to see the Irish foreman from the building site. He was still wearing his working clothes and looked extremely dusty.

Arthur burst into speech. 'Hello, Pat. Howe're you going, Dermot? What'll you have – a Guiness?'

'Just a dry Martini with a dash of lemonade – and lots of ice, please. About them fireplaces . . .'

Dave gave Arthur a wry glance but Arthur was still unperturbed. He turned to Dave.

'This is my contact in the civil engineering business, Dave.'

Dave looked singularly unimpressed.

A few miles away, Terry was still waiting for Barry – this time outside a fish and chip shop. Once again, when Barry emerged, Terry opened the car door for him and this time Barry offered him a paper bag.

'Chip?'

'Didn't he give you some cod as well?'

'Later, Terry. I'll get it back . . .' He slid into the driver's seat.

'You're confident, aren't you?'

Barry began to drive carefully through the streets. 'Because he's a mug punter. Are you a betting man?'

'I like a punt. Nothing big, mind you.'

'And do you win?'

'I'm about even, I suppose.'

'They all say that, Terry,' said Barry, smiling. 'Occasionally they get lucky – and suddenly they think they're winners. You can't beat the book. The clients? I call them mugs. I despise them.'

'Why don't you do something else?'

'Stockbroker – insurance? That's a game – the odds on a man's life? Fifty cigarettes a day and a bottle of whisky a day and he'll die before sixty?' He smiled again. 'Well, I'd like to get a piece of those odds – it's all in the book.' He abruptly changed the subject. 'Have a look at the rear window. Anybody following us?'

Terry glanced out of the window. The road was completely empty.

'Nothing. D'you expect somebody?'

'I told you – most of my clientele are villains, thieves, con men – you name them. I'm lazy, Terry. I'm a scavenger. When the big cats get their kill I'll mop up the remains.'

Terry stared at him wonderingly.

'I'm not proud, why should I be?'

'How much did you lose?' There was a long, stony pause.

'Twenty-three K.'

'Well, as the man said, it's only money.'

Barry grunted and drove on his careful way.

Eventually Barry and Terry arrived at a huge barn of a country pub on the outskirts of London. A vast car park adjoined it, but it contained only a few cars and the general impression was one of utter bleakness. Once they had driven in, Terry noticed that Barry's mood had changed. He seemed tense now – even nervous.

'Great place,' said Terry, staring round him at the vast, empty space.

Barry moistened his lips. 'They love these places. No prying eyes and all that.' He fidgeted with his leather case and Terry noticed that it had a combination lock. He gave Terry a quick smile. 'Sometimes I forget the combination . . .' He twiddled the lock, but as he did so a large car drove in, flooding the car park with its lights.

'That's him – the big saloon.'

The car drew in about thirty yards away and Barry, having achieved the opening of the combination, drew out an envelope from his case.

'Only be a minute,' he said rather apprehensively. 'Sixteen K . . . eh?'

'Should I go with you?'

'No,' said Barry hurriedly. 'No problem.'

He opened the door and Terry watched him walk across the car park. As he approached the car, the headlights were switched off and a man wound down the window.

'There you go, Ray,' said Barry, passing over the envelope. Then he took a closer look and panicked. 'You aren't Ray! Hey . . . just a minute . . .' he shouted. 'Terry – Terry!'

Terry's reactions were fast and he began to run towards the saloon as its driver gunned the engine. Terry grabbed at the door handle. The car accelerated and swerved as Terry tried to hang on to the driver. But he was a second too late. The man spun the steering wheel and the edge of the door caught Terry in the shoulder. The tyres squealed and Terry fell to the ground unconscious as the car sped away in a cloud of dust.

'Terry . . .' said Barry, helplessly standing over him. 'Somebody help me, please.' He began to babble. 'I'm sorry . . . honestly, Terry.'

Terry showed no sign of movement. Suddenly bright headlights again raked the car park and Barry squinted into them warily. A similar car to the one that had knocked Terry down ground to a halt in front of them. The driver was fiftyish, burly, prosperous, tweedy and bearded. Barry knew him all too well.

'Ray – it's you at last.' He seemed terrified now. 'Help me. A guy robbed me. Get me to the hospital . . . Terry – he could die . . .'

'What're you talking about? Robbed?'

'He took my dough. Just help me, Ray. Get him into the car. For God's sakes!'

'Your dough,' said Ray slowly, with growing menace. 'That's *my* dough.'

He looked at the prostrate Terry with resentment.

Dolly walked into Mr Wong's restaurant got up to the nines.

'How are you, Mrs Warner?' greeted Mr Wong.

'Not so bad . . .'

'Mr McCann has booked – in the corner. I had a bad day – no favourites. The three o'clock at Newbury – twenty to one and it lun like a locket.'

'Sorry about that,' said Dolly heading for her table.

But Terry was on another kind of table – a surgical table. He winced as the doctor finished off the task of stitching up the wound on his shoulder.

'I think you should stay here for the night,' said the doctor in a concerned voice.

'No chance,' said Terry firmly.

'Have three days off work.'

'What work?'

'I beg your pardon?'

'Nothing. It doesn't matter.'

'Well, just take it easy.'

'In my job,' said Terry wistfully, 'that's not easy.'

In Mr Wong's restaurant Dolly was not only impatient but also embittered as she toyed with her wine glass. She glanced at her expensive watch as Mr Wong came up to the table.

'Another drink, Mrs Warner?'

'I don't think so,' she said, pushing away her chair. 'If you meet Mr McCann,' she added, 'will you tell him he's just lost another bet . . .'

The impatient knocking on Terry's front door came to him as if in a dream. Or was it a nightmare? Abruptly he woke up, calling: 'Just a minute.' He got up and winced as he flexed his shoulder. Then he stumbled towards the door, only wearing his underpants. He opened the door, turned away from Arthur as he entered the flat and went straight back towards his bed.

'Chop, chop,' said Arthur briskly. 'I need help. Never mind about getting back to kip. You know you've got some stuff on your back . . .'

'I know,' said Terry in a pained voice, poised by the side of his bed.

Arthur, however, was not interested. 'I've got to get some fireplaces back to my drum.'

'I'm ill, inni?' He flopped on to the bed.

'Flu? Ill?'

'Poorly. I've got a bad back. I don't want to know about humping fireplaces.'

Arthur gazed at him blankly so Terry had to slowly spell it out. 'Look, Arthur, I've got eight stitches in my back. The doc said to take it easy for a few days . . .'

'What do they know, these doctors? Did you slip or something?'

'Yeah! Slipped – just as a guy was about to decapitate me.'

'Bit of bother?'

'You've got it at last.'

'Well, there you are. In your game it's an industrial injury. It's a hazard of the profession.'

'Thanks for the sympathy. Your pal – Barry the

Book – what do you reckon about him?'

'Eighteen carat. One of our own.'

'That's what I mean,' replied Terry dryly.

'Eh?' Arthur sat down heavily on the bed. 'Make a cup of tea,' he demanded.

'I'm supposed to be the invalid.'

'You could surely put some boiling water on a tea bag, couldn't you?'

'No.' He pulled on his shirt painfully.

'Sometimes, Terry, you can be truly selfish,' Arthur admonished.

'Well, I've got that from you,' he said, pulling on his trousers. He began to mimic Arthur. 'Chop, chop . . . we've got work . . .'

Arthur gave him a superior smile.

Dolly was about to open the door of the betting shop when Terry hurriedly got out of Arthur's car.

'Dolly . . .'

She glanced at him casually and then ignored him.

'I know what you're thinking . . .' He grabbed at the door before she could open it.

'That's right.'

'Look – I couldn't phone you. I was at the hospital.'

'Measles?'

'Yeah – okay. I'm sorry. Honest . . .'

'Why did you go to the hospital?' asked Dolly after a pause.

'It doesn't matter. But . . . I'll tell you what. Have you got an hour at lunchtime?'

'Where?'

'Anywhere. The boozer?'

'I've got to get back before the first race at Catterick. Half past twelve then . . .'

'Okay. And I'm sorry – really sorry.'

'Well, don't blow me out again,' she said, relenting slightly.

Terry grinned. 'Would I do that? Be fair, Dolly.'

'See you,' she said, already regretting her weakness.

Arthur gave Terry a leering smile as he got back into the car. He was about to break into raucous speech when Terry said: 'And don't *you* start.' He slammed the car door firmly.

The drawing room in Barry's flat was grandiose indeed. It contained top quality antique furniture, paintings on the wall and an ornate gilt mirror. But none of these appeased him as he sipped coffee from a delicate china cup and listened to a Bartok quartet. Thoroughly depressed, he took a cigarette from a silver box on a side table and fitted it into an ebony cigarette holder.

The door bell rang and Barry went to the record player, turned down the volume and walked gloomily to the door. He seemed relieved when he discovered his visitors were Arthur and Terry.

'Hallo, Barry. What a terrible thing last night. Are you okay?' asked Arthur, now conversant with the problem.

'Yeah. I'm fine – fine. Terry . . .'

'I was just saying to Terry about you –'

But a grim Terry interrupted him. 'I'll ask him.'

'You'd better come in,' said Barry quickly. As they crossed the threshold he said in a worried voice? 'How're things? I mean, the back? Really sorry about that. I mean –'

'You set it up . . .'

'Me?'

'Don't give me all that,' he continued angrily. 'You set it up.'

'You've got it all wrong.'

'Now, now,' said Arthur in a conciliatory tone. 'My Terry gets a bit impetuous sometimes. I've told him, in my book you are eighteen carat . . .'

But suddenly Arthur was conscious that Barry

wasn't listening and his flow of attempted reassurance trailed away.

'I apologise,' said Barry quietly. He looked guilty and ashamed.

'You what? Apologise? What are you saying, Barry? You're owning up? Is that what you're saying?' Terry was amazed.

'It all went wrong – see . . .'

But he didn't have a further chance to explain as Terry threw him up against the wall. 'You bastard . . .'

Arthur grabbed at Terry as Barry cowered away from him.

'Don't hit me – please.'

' "Don't hit me!" ' scoffed Terry. 'I'll break your arm.'

But still Arthur hung diplomatically on to Terry's arm. 'Now, Terry, be reasonable.'

'Me?'

'The man may have a decent excuse.'

'I'd like to hear it.' His fist about six inches from Barry's face.

'Calm down,' admonished Arthur. 'And look what you've done. You've knocked a picture off the wall.'

'Maybe I'll put him up there instead.'

'Obviously you're a bit distraught, Tel . . .'

'That's right.'

'I'll explain,' began Barry a little more calmly. 'Can we go into the drawing room?'

Reluctantly Terry released him. Barry picked up the painting and hung it back on the wall and they walked into the palatial drawing room. Seeing that Terry's aggression had not lessened, Barry hurried into an explanation.

'It was going to be simple. You were just there as a witness. So when Ray Newell drove into the car park, you'd substantiate my story – a guy robbed me. But you were too quick, Terry. I swear to you that the guy was going to drive off, that's all. But when you grabbed the car door, the man panicked. He didn't know what to do. You were too brave, Terry.'

108

'A fool to himself. There you are, Terry – you're too brave.'

'Yeah, eight stitches in my shoulder. So you did a moody – no money in the envelope?'

Barry nodded silently.

'And you reckon that Ray Newall would swallow that? You must be kidding.'

Barry sat down. 'What else could I do? I'm skint.'

'I beg your pardon?'

'I'm skint . . .'

'Yeah, I heard you,' Arthur repeated. 'It just takes a few seconds to sink in. You haven't weighed in for Terry's performance last night . . .'

'I've got that,' he said quickly, pulling out a money clip and giving seven twenty-pounds notes to Arthur. Terry watched the transaction with interest and then looked up at Arthur questioningly.

'You'll be all right.' Arthur gave him a mirthless smile. 'Don't worry.'

'Oh great,' Terry replied bitterly.

'What am I going to do?' asked Barry hopelessly.

Arthur shrugged, fastened his jacket and prepared to leave. 'An early holiday?' he suggested helpfully, but Barry was taking it badly – very badly. He looked away and began to sob but Arthur was clearly unmoved. Compassion had never been his strong suit and he began to make urgent signals at Terry to leave. Terry, however, was indecisive. He wanted to go, but he felt desperately embarrassed by Barry's weeping. He looked away, staring out of the window.

'What will he do?' asked Barry between sobs. 'I mean, Ray –' he paused hopefully – 'he isn't going to kill me, is he?'

Terry's gaze hardened. 'I dunno,' he said. 'You can ask him – in a minute.'

Barry and Arthur wheeled round on him.

'What the hell do you mean by that?' asked Arthur in a voice of rising concern.

* * *

Ray got out of his car. With him was Cyril – sixty, wearing a sloppy suit and what looked like a permanent cigarette with very long ash. His half moon spectacles were perched on the end of his nose. As a complete contrast, the third member of the trio was Ram. He was young, big and black, a flash dude who only temporarily knew his place. Behind them was a Ford transit van. Two men sat in the cabin. The ill-assorted threesome crossed the road, walked towards the entrance to Barry's mansion block flat and, ignoring the lift, purposefully climbed the stairs.

'You mean they're coming up here?' Arthur's voice was shrill with anxiety.

'If you listen, you'll hear them walking up the stairs,' said Terry maliciously, playing on Arthur's fears. 'They've probably got a machete apiece.'

'My God – it'll be a bloodbath,' said Barry. He was no longer sobbing and his eyes were alight with adrenalin.

Arthur however was in a terrible state, crouched on one knee with his ear pressed against the keyhole. 'I hear footsteps,' he said tremulously.

'The footstep on the stair,' hissed Terry dramatically.

'Do something,' whispered Arthur. 'Get out there an' confront 'em.' The knocking on the door was so sudden, so loud and insistent that Arthur fell on to the floor. Sprawled there, he said: 'Get to it, Terry. Bung a chair under the handle. Be decisive!'

But Barry was already going to the door. Stepping over the spreadeagled Arthur, he opened it.

'We're done for,' muttered Arthur.

Ray, Cyril and Ram came into the room with a rush. Ray advanced into the centre, Barry backed off, Arthur moved away on all fours and Cyril and Ram blocked the doorway. Terry leant on the mantelpiece, smiling brightly, waiting for the action.

Barry began to stutter into speech but Ray angrily interrupted him.

'I don't want to know about your problems. All I'm worried about is my dough.' He sat down while Arthur scrambled to his feet, gazing at the human barrier of Cyril and Ram with great trepidation.

'But you see . . . Well, you were there . . .' He was almostly entirely inarticulate and Ray began to get really aggressive.

'I don't *care*. You lost your money. So? I've just told you – it's your problem. Are we going to fight about it? I don't fight anymore. And Cyril – he doesn't fight. And Ram, he doesn't want to fight – in case he ruins his clothes . . . Although, mind you, he's a bit handy with that kick box and the martial arts.' Ray turned to Arthur. 'Do you want to fight, Arthur?'

'As it happens, we were about to go,' said Arthur quickly.

'How's your back?' Ray asked Terry.

'All right,' he said unevenly.

'Nasty wound. Now, where's the money?'

'I need time.'

'You're terrific. Have a look at this guy. I give him bets every week – thousands over the months. And now I get a little tickle and he can't pay. I don't believe it, eh?'

'Well, as I was about to say . . . it's nothing to do with us.' He tried to be brisk, matter of fact, but only succeeded in sounding scared out of his mind.

'But I want you to stay and see that there's fair play.'

'Fine. But I've got some business to do and I can't really afford the time.' He began to walk towards the door but stopped halfway there.

'Haven't I? The restaurant . . .'

'Funnily enough, I had lunch there the other day,' said Arthur uncertainly.

'Good.'

'And the second-hand furniture shop?'

'The what? Antiques, Arthur. An antique emporium –'

111

'That's what I meant.'

Ray turned to Barry. 'Your car keys,' he rapped out.

'Why?' asked Barry fearfully.

'Why? Because you owe me sixteen grand. Keys.'

Barry handed over the keys.

'What I'm doing, Barry, is distraining your goods and chattels. Rover, four years old— three thousand and five hundred. Fair?'

'Well, I don't know about that . . .'

'It isn't a seller's market, Barry. Get the log book.'

Barry went to the desk and found the log book whilst Ray took out his pocket calculator and punched '3.500'.

'Ram,' said Ray, 'find his dough.'

Ram nodded and went into Barry's bedroom whilst the others waited uneasily, saying nothing. Arthur kept clearing his throat.

In the bedroom Ram was doing a professional job — one that he had clearly done before. He felt the pillows, he stripped the bedclothes, took a quick look at the mattress and opened the wardrobe. He flicked the suits — weighing them as if they contained money — and felt inside the shoes. But so far he was unable to find anything.

Outside, conversation was resumed.

'What're reckon, Cyril?'

'Well . . .' He flicked ash carelessly and lit another cigarette from his stub. 'The secretaire is nice.' He looked at the piece with avarice.

'Regency — mahogany. Say — four hundred pounds.'

'Four hundred,' Barry echoed hollowly. But Cyril didn't hear him and ran on like a television antique pundit. 'People say "Regency" and they think they've got a gold mine. Put it in an auction — you won't get any more.'

Ray punched at his calculator. 'Four hundred.'

Cyril, blowing ash everywhere, took his bulk on a browse through the rest of the room. Arthur watched him respectfully; Barry watched him in pain — and Terry just watched.

'Eighteenth century mahogany topped occasional table – good tripod – one hundred and forty pounds.'

'One hundred and forty,' said Ray, punching again at his calculator.

Cyril looked up at the mantelpiece and Barry winced.

'The carriage clock is pretty.' He studied it for a moment. 'Movement by Bolviller of Paris. Four hundred and fifty.'

'The chair?' suggested Ray.

'Would you mind getting up?' said Cyril politely.

'Eh?' Arthur was bewildered.

'Get up,' said Ray.

Arthur rose very rapidly.

'Sorry, sir. Very good repro.'

'This is a Charles the Second chair,' said Barry in shocked tones.

'You've been done, Barry. Just look at it. It's *too* perfect. See – walnut. Good wood, as well. But the carving and these holes – they should be bevelled by time. We're talking about a piece that was made more or less three hundred years . . .' He tipped up the chair. 'On second thoughts, on scrutinising it more closely, I reckon this was done just before the First World War. A handsome chair, I'll agreee, but it's not a Charles the Second piece. Sorry.' He turned to Ray. 'Two hundred.'

With ponderous academic dignity, Cyril walked on to another piece. Meanwhile Arthur, still very impressed, whispered to Terry: 'This guy's mustard, inne? He's better than the bloke on the television.'

Cyril was now looking at a mirror. 'Where did you get the mirror, Barry?'

But by this time Barry was becoming disillusioned with his possessions. 'I don't know. Got it in a junk shop.'

'Really? Mm . . . Don't say that I'm not honest . . .' He took out a tape measure. 'We're talking about eight hundred pounds, Ray. George the First, gilt wood . . . circa seventeen thirty.'

Ray punched the calculator. 'It's your lucky day, Barry,' he said drily.

'I tell you,' Arthur hissed at Terry enthusiastically, 'he's a real winner, inne?'

'Why don't you just shut up?' was all Terry could reply.

Ram had now moved methodically into the kitchen and was indulging in a minute examination of the kitchen units and any of their moveable contents. Carefully, systematically, he examined tins, saucepans, tureens, casserole dishes – indeed nothing escaped Ram's eagle eye. Then he turned his attention to the double-doored fridge and its contents. He opened all the yoghurt cartons and plunged in his finger, tasting each one with relish. He tore open the kipper bags and anything else that was in a carton or wrapped in cellophane. Then Ram went through the freezer compartment and began to turn over packets of frozen peas, fish fingers and cod steaks. Suddenly he found what he was looking for, buried under a pile of frozen chips – a frosty wad of pound notes. He smiled the smile of a satisfied craftsman. Back in the drawing room, the inventory was continuing at a cracking pace and some of the items had been stacked in the centre of the room. Cyril was intoning with a liturgical air:

'Music Canterbury with brass dividing poles – circa eighteen forty. Say – one hundred and forty-five. German silver mounted clear glass claret jug. A very fine piece. Late nineteenth century – two hundred and fifty pounds.'

Barry continued to watch gloomily while Arthur whispered: 'It's the fall of the House of Usher.' Terry ignored him.

'Four landscape water-colours – simple stuff. Say, fifty pounds a piece . . .'

Arthur interrupted. 'I'll take one of them. If that's okay?'

'Why not? Cash?' said Ray.

'Course. 'Er indoors likes a nice water-colour.'

114

Barry looked at him in amazement and Terry couldn't believe it either.

'Whose side are you on, Arthur?' asked Terry abrasively.

Arthur appealed to Barry. 'You don't mind, do you?'

Barry shook his head, smiling. After rummaging about Arthur gave five ten-pound notes to Ray whilst Cyril lit another cigarette and stubbed the discarded one into an ashtray. Instinctively he scrutinised the ashtray.

'EPS Edwardian cigarette ashtray – a tenner.'

Ram jubilantly entered the room as Ray clocked up the tenner on his calculator. He dumped the frozen wad of money in front of Ray.

'See what I've got. Birds-Eye dough.'

Ray gave Barry a pained glance. 'How much is this – after it thaws?' he asked.

'Two K,' Barry mumbled.

'Eh?'

'Two thousand,' said Barry in a slightly louder voice.

'Have you got anything else in your airing cup-board?' asked Ray pleasantly.

Barry shook his head dolefully and Ray punched '2.000' on the calculator.

'Ram – start taking this stuff downstairs.'

'Me? You know I don't do manual work, man.'

'Oh, sorry . . . Sorry about that.' Ray sighed as Ram flicked some dust from his sleeve.

'Well, get the other fellers. And just a minute – what d'you reckon about the record player?'

Ram looked at the player and amplifier and loud speakers. 'Second hand sounds? Nobody wants them. Two hundred maybe.'

Ray turned to Barry. 'Fair?'

But Barry had given up. 'Yes,' he muttered, looking lovingly at the chairs. He would have liked to sit down but the chairs didn't belong to him now.

Ram glided off into the hall while Ray punched the total button on his calculator.

'Would you like to check this, Barry? Nine thousand, eight hundred and seventy-six, okay?'

Barry didn't even look up. 'Yeah. Whatever you say.'

'Sixteen grand minus – well, we're talking about six thousand one hundred pounds. We can forget the twenty-four pounds. When?'

'I don't know.'

'Really? Let's say – three days.'

'I haven't got it . . .'

'I love this guy.' He turned to Arthur. 'Am I being reasonable, Arthur?'

Arthur gave him a quick smile but he didn't venture into speech.

'It's a debt of honour, Barry. I don't like violence. And I can't sue you. I can't ask the Ombudsman to write to you.'

'I need time . . .' said Barry desperately.

'No!' Ray suddenly became angry. 'If you can't give me the money you owe me then I'm going to hurt you.'

'What do you mean?' said Barry, terrified.

'I've told you – I'm not a violent man. But I've got to have some satisfaction. Don't you understand that? If you can get away with it – what will the others do? Eh? They'll all start to knock me. You do it and you're making me out as a right wally.' He turned to Arthur again. 'Tell him, Arthur.'

'Well, Barry,' Arthur began carefully. 'I think he's saying that you've gotta be fair.'

'That's right. What is an arm, or a leg? Six grand? I'd rather have the dough. But if I can't get the dough,' he added with emphasis, 'then it's got to be an arm or a leg.' He paused. 'I haven't done a thing like this for . . . Gawd knows. And Terry isn't going to protect you, are you, Terry?'

Terry gave him a cool, ambiguous glance.

'Maybe he is.' Ray gave Terry a hard smile. 'But it isn't going to help you, Barry. Do you get me?'

'Yes, I get you.' Barry's voice was barely distinguishable.

116

'Right,' said Ray briskly as Ram smoothed his way back into the room. 'Ram will need some more helpers. Cyril isn't built for lifting, and besides – he'll have a fag on.' Ray's gaze hovered over the room. 'Barry's in no fit state,' he muttered. Then he smiled. 'Arthur.'

'I can't do heavy lifting.'

'Why not?'

'The old ticker.' Arthur clasped at the opposite side of his body to the heart. 'It can play up.'

'Oh, I don't know,' said Ray. 'They tell me exercise strengthens the heart muscles – and your young friend could lend you a hand.'

'It'd kill me,' said Arthur.

'It's a risk we'll all have to take.' Ray glanced at Terry. 'Are you up to helping him?' he asked.

'I might be,' said Terry laconically.

Dolly walked into the pub and looked round for Terry. Then she went up to the bar, glancing at her watch. It couldn't be true, she thought. He couldn't be doing this to her. But he was.

Arthur staggered down the stairs of Barry's flat with the last piece of furniture – a desk – shared between him and Terry. Puffing, blowing, puce in the face, Arthur swayed to a halt by the transit van. The two men who had driven up in it – and who had grudgingly helped with the furntiure – took the desk and put it carefully in the back of the van.

'Gawd,' said Arthur, leaning up against a wall.

'The old ticker?' asked Ray, getting into his car.

'I'm ill,' said Arthur.

'Here,' said Ray, throwing him a fiver. 'Have a couple of vodkas on me.'

Arthur limped over to collect it.

'Back on your feet?' asked Terry pointedly.

Arthur looked at him with offended dignity. 'You'll be sorry when I drop dead,' he said as he picked up the fiver.

'Let's hope there's something worth having in your pockets when you do,' said Terry unsympathetically.

Back in Barry's drawing room, there was a near wake-like atmosphere. There were bare patches on the walls where paintings had once hung and the remainder of the once ornate chamber was chillingly empty. Arthur and Barry sat on the carpet and Terry leant against the door.

'You wouldn't like to make a pot of tea, would you?' Arthur asked Terry.

'No.' There was a long pause. 'Anyway, they took the cups.'

Arthur looked around at him at the bleak expanse with more than a hint of admiration. 'In and out – they're better than Pickfords. No mess – very efficient.'

'Does he mean it? Does Ray really mean it?'

'I think so,' said Terry quietly.

Barry looked at Arthur.

'Of course he means it,' he said sympathetically. 'Anyway, you've got three days,' he added as if this made all the difference in the world.

'Thanks,' said Barry.

Arthur pursued his theme. 'You can't blame the man, Barry. Can you fault his logic? No. He paid you – for months. But now you can't pay him. And now, he's got the hump – it seems reasonable to me.'

'But he isn't giving me a chance. A few weeks and I'll be okay. I don't suppose you could give me . . .'

'No, I can't,' said Arthur without hesitation. 'Sorry. A debtor nor a lender be, etcetera, etcetera, and so on.'

'Just a long shot, Arthur.'

'Not a chance. All that you can do now is to have a very early holiday.' Arthur tried to get up from the floor but failed. In the end he had to ask Terry to give him a hand. 'Time for my lunch,' said Arthur.

Terry grabbed his hand. Then he said: 'What time is it?'

'Nearly one.'

'Oh no . . .' He suddenly realised that he should have met Dolly. In his agony he let go of Arthur's hand and he sprawled back on the floor again.

'Terry!' he spluttered indignantly.

'Come on – I've got a meet,' said Terry, running for the door.

Arthur's car cornered fast and screeched to a halt outside the betting shop. Terry jumped out while Arthur and Barry remained in the car.

'I didn't know that Terry was a friend of Dolly Warner's,' said Barry curiously.

'Very close. He's a right bird bandit, is old Terry. I think he's in love . . .'

Barry nodded reflectively, his recent loss giving him the look of the chief mourner at a very high-class funeral.

'Don't take on so,' said Arthur with hollow sympathy. 'It'll be all right on the night.'

'It's all very well for you,' said Barry acidly. 'You haven't lost all your worldly possessions – and you're not about to lose your life.'

Arthur nodded sagely. 'I can see you're in a bit of a spot,' he said.

Terry dashed up to the counter as Dolly took a betting slip from a punter. 'Dolly . . . I . . .'

Dolly looked up with an icy smile. 'Shove off, pal.'

'I can explain everything – really I can.' Terry was desperate.

'So you keep saying –' She was adamantly cold, determined not to show the hurt in her eyes.

'Look, the thing was –'

'I don't want to hear.'

'But I've got good reasons.' The punters were beginning to notice now and a silence had fallen of which Terry at least seemed oblivious.

'I don't want to hear them.'

'Dolly –give me a chance.'

119

'You've had 'em – had 'em all.'

Now they were both the sole object of attention in the crowded betting shop.

'Meet me after work.'

'You won't be there.'

'Nothing can go wrong this time.'

But Dolly wasn't having any more. 'I told you to shove off – Now shove off!'

Terry, however, stood his ground. 'Dolly –'

'Look, what do I have to do? Get me a bounce.'

'You don't have to, lady. I'm right here.' The man was six foot four of hard muscle with arms and legs like tree trunks. His large black moustache only partially covered the scar that ran from nose to mouth and he had a head like a battering ram.

'He's leaving,' said Dolly.

'I'd like to help him,' said the burly punter. He was in his early forties, and as he bunched his fist Terry watched the muscles bulging in his arm.

'Please, Terry,' said Dolly, 'go.'

Terry weighed up his chances. They weren't good. 'I'll see you around, Dolly.'

'Not if she sees you first,' said the heavy.

Terry strode past him. As he did so, he planted two steely fingers in the man's massive stomach. He collapsed with a little whimper onto the floor, scattering punters. 'Got to push off now,' said Terry, leaving with dignity.

The Jag drew up beside the demolition site, and as Terry and Arthur got out, Arthur continued the moralising conversation he had been laying on Terry for the entire journey.

'What we're talking about, Tel, is a moral dilemma.'

'I thought we were talking about breaking a leg?'

'Precisely. A leg *or* six grand. Is there a fine distinction?'

'Yeah . . . there is,' said Terry, very definitely.

'The man knocked Ray. If people like us can't trust

ourselves, who *can* we trust? I'd rather have the Inland Revenue give us the option. Six grand for a leg. Be nice, wouldn't it?'

'You'd be walking about with no legs – or arms.'

They were walking towards the foreman's hut, Arthur picking his way gingerly through the rubble.

'It's a dog eat dog world, my son. In a couple of minutes I'm going to stitch up a simple Irishman . . . What's wrong with that, eh?'

They passed a demolished house and paused to survey the ruins.

'I think your simple Irishman might suss you out,' said Terry hopefully.

'No chance.'

'And if he does, you could be rubble.'

Arthur gave Terry a withering look. 'He wouldn't be capable,' he said confidently.

Inside the foreman's hut, about twenty fireplaces were stacked neatly beside the wall.

'Really nice, Pat – Dermot. Any more?' Arthur was at his most patronising.

'A few. But here is something else,' he said proudly.

He walked over to a covered fireplace beside the opposite wall and whisked off the dust sheet.

'What about that?'

'A fireplace,' replied Arthur woodenly.

'Do you know what it is? An original Adam fireplace.'

'I know that,' said Arthur quickly. 'Obvious, innit.'

'Did you see the little Georgian cottage at the end of the street? Well, I got that from there. And I know – an Adam fireplace has got to be valuable.'

'Not particularly.' Arthur was playing for time and to Terry's cynical amusement he pretended to inspect the fireplace, with much bogus expertise. 'What d'you reckon?' he asked Terry briskly.

'Me?' Terry was surprised to be consulted.

Arthur smiled confidentially at the foreman. 'One of my staff. He's a bit of a connoisseur.'

'Oh yeah,' said Terry, trying to rise to the occasion. 'That's the old Adam. Definitely.'

'The real McCoy,' said the foreman appreciatively.

'Yeah . . . probably Adam McCoy,' said Terry over-enthusiastically.

Arthur gave him a pained smile and hurried into speech again. 'I realise, Pat, that you're a simple artisan, Dermot . . . but what do you expect for this item?' He was horribly patronising but the foreman didn't seem to react.

'Four hundred,' he said stolidly.

'Four what? Have you gone completely bananas?'

'Four hundred.'

Arthur was quiet for a while. 'Let's not quibble, Pat,' he said in his most bogusly reasonable voice. 'I'm a very fair man, Dermot. I'll give you a ton.'

'*No* sir.'

'Well Adam Whatsisname is well known in the fireplace world . . .'

'Well respected,' put in Terry.

'You're a hard man, so I'm going to up the offer.' Arthur pulled out a wad of notes and counted out fifteen twenty-pound notes. Then he appeared to dither. Terry winced – this was one of Arthur's oldest tricks. 'No – no. I can't do it.' He made a ploy of being about to stuff the wad back into his pocket and the foreman looked dismayed.

He can't be falling for this, Terry thought. But he was.

'I'll tell you what,' Arthur said. 'Three hundred and we'll touch hands now.' Arthur brandished the notes and it was clear the foreman was going through tantalising agony. Arthur smiled innocently and the foreman finally swallowed the bait.

'Done,' he said.

You burke, thought Terry.

The fireplace was now esconsed in the lock-up and being lovingly dusted by Arthur.

'A thing of beauty,' he told Terry. 'Knew it straightaway.' As he dusted, Arthur was reading an antique handbook at the same time. 'Robert Adam . . . the guvnor, they reckon. He'd be well pleased to see the pleasure that punters still have after all those years.'

Terry looked over his shoulder at the book. 'I bet the Irishman's well pleased, an' all. Five grand?'

Arthur studied the book again. 'More . . . possibly. I knew it. I could feel it in my water. That's why I'm an entrepreneur – not a simple trader.'

'Yeah, I can see it– Arthur Daley takes over Harrods.'

'A cheap gibe, Terrence. But it might happen – and you'd be very happy to be part of the firm. However, right now, drive round to Des's garage and borrow a van tonight and get them other fireplaces . . .'

'Not tonight. I've got Dolly.'

'I thought you had a ruck.'

'You know me – I'm a smooth talker. You've got the dough – I've got the charm. That's what keeps the home fires burning . . .'

'Eh?' Arthur was not listening as he caressed the fireplace. Terry sighed and departed. He couldn't afford to wait.

Barry lay on his bed, deep in gloom and fearful of every noise in the house. Time was running out and the nightmare of the step on the stair would soon become a reality. He thought of Ram's sleek strength and shuddered, already hearing the crunching of his own limbs. But perhaps it wouldn't be Ram. Maybe Cyril would plunge cigarette butts up his nostrils. He could already smell the stench of burning flesh.

The telephone rang and he started up in sudden terror. It was them – him – what did they want? For some time he let it ring – which it did, persistently. Eventually Barry could bear it no longer. He climbed out of bed and staggered into the dark emptiness of the

123

drawing room. Barry switched on the light and picked up one of the three telephones on the floor.

'Yeah?' he said in a voice of dread. Then he became brighter. 'Hello, Peter.' He listened carefully. 'Of course I'm still in business. What do you mean? Where did you get that idea? No . . .' He listened again. 'Yeah, Kempton – the three o'clock. Bandy Lad . . . a monkey to win. Fine. Have you got a whisper? I hate to do this, Peter, but I need the cash. I'm with a new firm y'know. No tax – of course not. Okay . . . I'll see you in the club. Cheers!'

Barry smiled as the sudden relief flooded him. He looked round the empty room, knowing his problems were unexpectedly over. He was back in business.

Meanwhile, in Mr Wong's restaurant, a waiter was carrying a tray with two large glasses of brandy. He placed them on the table between Terry and Dolly.

'Compliments of Mr Wong, sir.'

'Thanks . . .' He grinned at Dolly. 'I told you – I'm well known here.'

'Why?'

'Nothing – really.' He lifted his glass. 'He had a bit of bother about fourteen months ago.'

'Like what?' said Dolly.

'Just bother. Nothing special. A couple of hounds – terrifying the punters . . .'

'So you sorted it out?'

Terry gave a self-effacing shrug.

'Have you ever thought of taking a job?' asked Dolly. She had forgiven him now.

'Eh?'

'Yeah – job. Y'know – employment? Career? A pay packet at the end of the week. Promotion? Full pay holidays?'

'And a pension?'

'You think that's funny, don't you?'

'Yeah. I think you're having a pop at me.'

'I'm not . . .' She sounded hurt.

'I mean, why do people always want me to get a nice job?'

'Because you haven't got a job. Arthur Daley – that's no job. He's just a small time gangster.'

Terry laughed uproariously. 'Gangster! Don't make me laugh. He couldn't sleep for weeks after he saw The Godfather!'

'Do you like him?'

Terry toyed with his glass, thinking about it for a few moments. Then he said, quite seriously: 'Yeah.' He shrugged. 'We're pals. He's dishonest – he's a bit tight – he's a liar – not really – a bit of a rogue.' He grinned ruefully. 'And that's the good side of his character!'

'I give up.'

'So did I – years ago.' He took her hand across the table. 'But don't let's waste time talking about Arthur.'

Whilst Terry dined Dolly, Arthur was consulting an expert in the lock-up.

'You're going to love this, Cyril,' said Arthur, switching on the light. 'As you know, I'm something of an antique expert myself . . .'

Arthur steered Cyril's vast bulk towards the shrouded Adam fireplace. He lit a fresh cigarette from the stub and stamped the discarded cigarette end into the floor.

'You're a walking fire hazard, Cyril,' murmured Arthur.

'Sorry,' said Cyril.

But Arthur was immediately placating. 'No – no. But I do try to keep the place tidy. What with all the expensive merchandise in the gaff.'

Cyril raised his eyebrows slightly as he gazed round at the motley items in the lock-up.

'Voilà – as they say,' said Arthur, revealing the fireplace. 'Nice, eh?'

'Ah,' replied Cyril.

Arthur smiled uneasily as he wondered what the 'Ah' could mean.

'Needs a clean up.'

'I suppose it should – what with all those years. Robert Adam.' He turned to Cyril confidentially. 'As you well know.'

'But there's Adam and Adam.'

'We all know that, Cyril . . .'

Cyril examined the back of the fireplace closely. 'Yes, I thought so,' he said and Arthur's mood changed from confidence to acute anxiety.

'What?'

'Yes – that's Adam.'

'Knew it straight away.' Some of his anxiety lightened.

'Ah – but not from his factory. That's the rub, Arthur.'

'I got this from a Georgian house . . .'

'They were all at it in those days. Just as nice – but not from the master's workshop. A good one from him and we'd be talking about five grand – plus.'

'That's what I thought.' Arthur's face was puckered and a little pulse beat under his eye.

'I'd mark this down as, say, seventeen ninety.'

'That's old, y'know.'

'It is. But it's only worth six hundred pounds,' said Cyril flicking ash over the mantelpiece.

'You're quite sure?'

'Sorry. How much did you pay for it?'

'Enough, Cyril,' said Arthur dolefully. 'More or less what you said.'

'You should always come to an expert,' replied Cyril in an admonishing voice.

'Yeah. I suppose you couldn't erm . . .'

'I'll tell you what. Seven hundred – and I'm being silly . . .'

Arthur brightened up. 'Well, it's better than nothing, eh?' As usual, Arthur was the eternal optimist.

Terry's car was parked outside a suburban villa with a

small driveway. Still sitting in the car Terry stared at the house hopefully. 'It looks better than my place,' he said to Dolly.

'One of these days you might see inside,' she replied tantalisingly.

'I've got the message,' said Terry with a sad smile. 'I mean, I thought you might give me a cup of coffee.'

'I don't think you're the coffee type.'

'Well, okay, why don't you just ask me to . . .'

'I don't want to hear what you're about to say,' Dolly interjected with a grin.

'Yeah. Well, thank you for a lovely night.'

'I bet.' She was cynical.

'Honest. On my landlord's life.'

'Thanks.' Dolly kissed him on the cheek affectionately. She paused and then leant forward and kissed him passionately. As Dolly's passions soared she grasped at his wounded shoulder.

'Bleeding hell!'

'What's the matter?' said Dolly, concerned.

'Nothing, nothing – I've got a few stitches on my back. But don't let that stop you . . .'

'I thought it was passion.' Dolly was amused.

'It was getting on that way –'

The moment had gone and Dolly began to collect up her bag and coat from the back of the car.

'It was a very happy marriage,' she said by way of explanation.

'Yeah.' Terry was morose, staring straight ahead out into the darkened street.

'Hey . . . As you don't work in the day –' Her hand was on the door.

'Are you going to open that, or aren't you?'

'No. I was going to say – would you like to go racing tomorrow? I've got to meet some people at Kempton. Fancy it?'

He turned to look at her. 'Yeah.' He grinned.

'Okay. Pick me up here at about twelve.' She kissed him on the cheek quickly and finally got out of the car.

As she opened her front door she waved.

Terry winked back at her. Maybe, he thought, it might get going at last – after all the jinxes.

'How come I'm not invited?' asked Arthur, in a very peeved voice. He was sitting on the couch in Terry's flat and examining a pair of binoculars whilst Terry was knotting his tie, patting his hair and splashing aftershave lotion on his face. 'You're well tarted up,' he continued maliciously.

'Because you're not – that's why.'

'What am I – a leper?'

'Only in the social sense.' Terry put on the jacket of his best suit and picked up a clothes brush. Whilst he dusted himself down Arthur continued to moan.

'Charming, innit? I loan my bins. You're having a day off and what am I doing? Humping fireplaces.'

'It's a hard life as a watchamacallit – entre-preneur . . .' Terry took the binoculars and a leather case from Arthur's curious clutches and strode purposefully towards the door.

'Anyway, it's only Kempton. We're not talking about Royal Ascot.'

'Yeah . . . but it beats humping fireplaces – tarra.'

Arthur, left on his own in the flat, soundly cursed him. For a moment he thought about going home to bed. But then he remembered 'Er indoors with the hoover – it would be going strong now – and he thought again.

Dolly poured the drinks. She was wearing an attractive costume, ready for the date with Terry, as she turned to her visitor and gave him a brimming glass.

'The problem with you, Barry, is that you've got no credibility. People just don't trust you . . .'

'Me? Come on, Dolly,' he pleaded smoothly. 'I've just had a bad spell. Some of the bookies that I've worked for, they were being greedy. They wanted to cut my commission . . .' He paused for dramatic effect. There

128

wasn't any reaction so he continued rather desperately. 'And the big firms won't entertain me. That's why I'm asking you to take a small bet.'

'What's "small"?'

'A monkey, and it's not even the favourite. The punter will be happy to have starting prices. So you can shave a few points by laying out the opening prices.'

'Simple, eh?'

'Well, it is simple.'

'Cash.'

Barry took a wad of notes from his pocket.

'Bandy Lad at Kempton – the three o'clock.'

'Well, as it happens I'm going to Kempton so I'll lay it on the course.'

'Even better. I'm very grateful, Dolly. See . . . I'm really helping a pal. He's in real trouble.'

'Like what?' she asked cynically.

'Like . . . well, *real* trouble. He might lose his legs . . .'

'Nice people you mix with.'

'Friends. You can't disown friends. He's an old pal – old Terry.'

'Terry who?'

'Oh, you wouldn't know him,' said Barry cunningly. 'A guy called Terry McCann.'

'You say he's in trouble?' she asked in a very surprised voice.

'I didn't know you knew . . .'

'What's wrong with him?'

'Nothing. I shouldn't have told you.' He was all false dismay.

'What's happened?' For the first time in months Dolly's voice held real alarm and Barry knew how much she cared.

'I'm sorry. But if you know Terry – well, you know what he's like . . .'

'No, I don't.' Dolly's voice was very agitated by now.

'Always getting into scrapes. I mean, I put it down to

129

that Arthur. But he won't listen. Just between you and me – there's a real tasty mob after him. He owes them six K . . .'

'Oh no,' said Dolly in distress.

'They're after crippling him.' He glanced at Dolly quickly, calculating the effect. 'I mean, I haven't got that kind of dough. And he hasn't . . .'

Dolly was aghast. 'They're going to cripple him?'

'Yeah . . . A good-looking guy as well.'

'I can't let it happen,' she muttered. 'I just can't let it happen.'

Terry was in a very good mood as he arrived outside Dolly's house. He was looking forward to spending a terrific day in the company of a woman he both admired and was very drawn to. He liked her directness, her maturity, her looks. Who knows what might happen at the end of such a great day. Why, he might even get into Dolly's house – he never knew his luck.

Terry was just about to turn his car into Dolly's drive when, to his amazement, he saw Barry leaving the house. They recognised each other at roughly the same moment. Terry called out to him but Barry seemed anxious to avoid him. He crossed the road and almost ran towards the corner. Terry yelled after him, but it was clear that Barry just wasn't going to stop. Getting out of the car, Terry slammed the door and hurried up the garden path. He wondered why the hell Barry, of all people, had been calling on Dolly.

Meanwhile, Barry scurried down the road, looking back in case Terry was chasing him. Seeing there was no pursuit, he hailed a taxi and sat back on its hard upholstery, breathing heavily. What a life, he thought. It was like a continuous game of hide and seek.

Inside Dolly's home, Terry was taking a careful look at a framed painting of the famous racehorse Nijinsky.

130

'Derby winner – nineteen seventy. Nice, innit?' Terry was standing in front of the painting and Dolly was sitting on the sofa.

'Yeah . . . Nijinsky,' she said in a dull voice. There was not even a hint of her usual effervescence. 'Won the Two Thousand Guineas, the King George VI and Queen Elizabeth Diamond Stakes – and the St Leger as well.'

'Some form, eh?'

'It's called breeding, Terry.'

Terry glanced at her, realising that something was wrong. 'You don't seem all that happy about our little excursion.'

'Of course I am.' She gave him a fleeting, artificial smile.

'Have I got the wrong suit, or something?'

'It's smashing. Let's go.'

Terry took her hand. 'What was Barry Duncan doing here?'

'Nothing – just business. That's no crime – is it.'

'You never now – with Barry,' said Terry drily. 'Good friends, are you?'

'Friends? Yeah, he put me in hospital – the shoulder, y'know – he stopped me meeting you the other night . . . Apart from that, we're terrific pals!'

Dolly gave him a very searching glance as she suddenly got up and went to the door. 'I know all about it, Terry,' she said acidly.

'What?'

'You know.'

'What're you talking about?' Terry asked, totally mystified. 'What *are* you going on about?' he repeated, following her towards the front door.

Parked on the drive outside was Dolly's new Audi GT five-cylinder saturn-coloured coupé.

'Don't kid me,' said Dolly as she walked slowly towards it.

'What're you talking about?' he said again, beginning to feel annoyed.

'You don't care, do you? Cool as a cucumber. All relaxed, sitting down . . .'

'I'm standing up.'

'You know what I mean?'

'Did he ask you for money?'

'It doesn't matter . . .'

'How much?'

'Get in the car . . .'

'How much?' Now he was really furious.

'Enough to buy you a wheelchair,' she said enigmatically while Terry stared at her in bewilderment.

Suddenly Terry snapped. 'Dolly!' he yelled. 'You're really great – what a stupid cow!'

He ran towards his car, leaving her watching him hopelessly.

Ray and Cyril were talking to a well-to-do female customer in Cyril's large and expensive antique shop as Terry's car screeched to a halt outside.

Ray gave him a casual smile as he came running into the shop, but he waved him aside before he could say a word.

'It is an authentic Adam piece,' said Ray to his customer and Terry noticed the fireplace was very prominently displayed.

'From the master's own workshop, madam.' Cyril was at his oiliest.

'We can vouch for that,' said Ray.

'And you're asking five thousand five hundred?' reaffirmed the lady in a strangled, albeit somewhat amazed, voice.

'I'm afraid so.' Ray was soothing.

'Very rare piece,' put in Cyril, very much the expert.

Ray took another look at Terry. 'Excuse me for a moment,' he said ingratiatingly.

Ray steered Terry to the rear office. Before he could close the door Terry said: 'Have you seen Barry?'

'Fifteen minutes ago. He came up with trumps.

132

Surprised, eh? You never know in this world . . .'

Terry interrupted him angrily. 'He nicked it . . . from a friend of mine.'

'It's in the bank, son.' Ray was quite unruffled.

'He thieved it,' said Terry indignantly.

'A lot of people do. Look, he owed me. Now he's owing a friend of yours.'

Terry stared at Ray, knowing it was stalemate.

'Yeah, but . . .'

'I don't care where he got it. Finito! He's a wrong 'un.' Ray was brisk now. 'I mean, we all duck and dive . . . But that's Barry – he's disrupting the whole alternative economy. Cheat a bit, rob a bit – that's business. But gambling debts – that's indecent.'

'Yeah . . .' Terry turned away.

'Hey, Terry . . . what're you gonna do?' He was slightly alarmed at Terry's lack of aggression.

There was a long pause then Terry said: 'The same as you.'

He hurried away whilst Ray murmured? 'He'll be home. I mean, where can he go?'

Terry ran up the stairs to Barry's flat two at a time. He did not look a reassuring sight. In fact anyone passing might have mistaken him for a tribal warrior sent on a revenge-seeking mission. His face was contorted with anger, his fists were clenched and when he arrived at the door he pushed at the bell and kicked at the same time. There was no immediate response so he began a tatoo of kicks.

'Open this bloody door or I'll beat it in,' Terry shouted. Still nothing so he shouldered the door and kicked it in again. The door opened and Barry stood there, a sad smile of resignation playing on his lips.

'Have you got the dough?' asked Terry, giving him one slender chance.

Barry shook his head and the inevitably happened.

133

Terry hit him and Barry staggered back, thudding to the floor. He lay there, dazed, with a trickle of blood staining his mouth.

'Come on – get up.' Terry was beside himself with a blind fury he hadn't known in years.

Barry stared at him as if he was crazy. 'Why? You're only going to hit me again.'

'Get up!'

But Barry continued to lie on the floor. 'Ray was going to break my legs. Are you?'

Terry wasn't sure. What he did know was that he wanted to hit something. Now.

'I've owed people who're tougher than you, Terry,' said Barry, by way of comment.

'You don't even care . . .' Terry gave vent to his pent-up anger by hitting the door. It hurt him and he licked his fist. 'Why couldn't you rob a bank?' he asked Barry hopelessly, his angry energy spent.

'You get nicked for that,' said Barry reasonably. He sat up against the wall.

'Why Dolly – anyway?' demanded Terry.

Barry pondered for a while. 'I like long shots.' There was a long pause. 'She'll get it – eventually.'

'Yeah? When?'

Barry gave a shrug of futility. 'I don't know. The thing is – I'm a very dishonest man.'

'You can say that again,' said Terry with great depth of feeling.

Arthur lit a panatella and studied a newspaper crossword as he sat in his parked Jag outside the betting shop. He wasn't in the happiest of moods and there was a vague feeling of impending doom in the very small part of Arthur's mind that he reserved for the future. But it was also a part of his mind that he could very easily close off – as a security measure. This ability made Arthur what he was – a survivor. To prove it, a smile lit his face as he relit his panatella and began to whistle tunelessly.

In the back office of the betting shop, tension reigned between Dolly and Terry. She sat behind her desk, pretending to busy herself with papers whilst Terry prowled angrily about her minute office.

'I mean . . . of all epople – Barry!'

'He can be very persuasive.'

'That's his game.'

'I was just helping you.'

'I don't need helping. And anyway, it wasn't me who needed helping – it was Barry . . .'

'I didn't know that, did I?' she said angrily.

'Yeah, but . . . Sorry.' His anger left him and she realised that he was touched. 'Dolly – I'm sorry. I'm really grateful. I mean, honestly. I don't usually have people giving me favours.'

'I won't do it again.'

'Well, I don't know. I quite like it. Not six grand, but somebody in my corner for once. And I promise you, I'll get it back . . .'

'Forget it. You can buy me a drink – some night.'

'Tonight.'

'Some other night.'

'I thought we'd have a few nights?'

Dolly gave him a very sad smile. 'No.' She paused. 'You're trouble, aren't you?'

'Me? You kidding?'

'It's true, Terry. Nice bloke – but you're trouble, and you always will –'

'You don't know me really.'

Dolly gave a resigned nod. 'Yeah? I've only met you three days. I've been stood up three times. You've been in hospital once and you've had two fights. You're always chasing people. If you're not hitting people, you're humping fireplaces. You mix with rotten people – you're bad news, Terry.'

Terry looked very deflated. 'Triffic.'

135

'You know it, don't you?'

'It's been a bad week.'

Dolly's cynicism returned. 'I don't want to know about the good weeks. I'm supposed to be a very shrewd business woman. Next time, I'll have to be more careful. So . . . you and me, Terry . . . we're going to be good friends – and that's it.'

Terry shrugged. 'Yeah . . . good friends. Okay.'

But as he turned towards the door she said with a smile: 'Mind you, I'll still take your bets. One and two, Hackney reversed.'

'I'll pay the tax. And if I see Barry –'

'Forget it. I'll get the money.'

Terry opened the door and walked slowly out, leaving Dolly to wonder whether she had over-played her hand. But the more she thought the more she came to the same irrevocable conclusion. Terry was trouble – and always would be.

As Terry passed into the main betting shop he did an absolute double take, for who should be chalking the board but Barry. He glanced at Terry just before he wrote down the results of the last race and they exchanged the look of two people who understand each other all too well.

Terry approached Arthur's Jag and clambered in. Arthur looked at him and smirked. 'Hello, the bird bandit seems a bit downcast,' he said as he switched on the ignition.

'Don't you start.'

But Arthur was anxious to press home his advantage. 'Oh, you've had a blank . . .'

Terry gave him a threatening scowl. 'Shurrup, Arthur.'

Knowing Terry in this mood, Arthur was not prepared to quarrel. He stole a covert glance at Terry who was looking straight ahead. There was a long silence. After a while Terry said:

'How did you get on with old Adam?'

'A reasonable deal. A lot more than I gave to the Irishman.'

'Well, *he* wouldn't understand – a rare piece like that.'

'Rare? I had it valued, authenticated – the whole thing.'

'But not five grand?'

'Eh?' Suddenly he was discomforted but Terry wasn't saying a word. 'Well, come on. How do you know anyway?' There was a note of agitation in his voice now which gave Terry a great deal of pleasure.

'Oh – just browsing in an antique shop. Cyril and Ray were there.'

'Five grand? You're winding me up.'

'Want to bet?' asked Terry and began to laugh.

PART FOUR

'Who's the old faggot?'

'None of your business.'

Arthur wandered across the yard in front of the lock-up, his hands behind his back, the inevitable cigar clenched in the centre of his mouth.

'She's a respected septuagenarian – come to pay her respects to a charitably-minded businessman.'

'You!' Terry was stacking hundreds of boxes of garishly yellow teddy bears – another line of Arthur's that looked like spending the rest of its shelf life in the lock-up.

'You may not care for the old, Terence, but I do.' Arthur ruminated. 'We're the only country in the world with a terrible record of looking after those in their twilight years – at the eventide of life.'

'Been reading the Guardian?'

Arthur ignored him. 'And if I can do my little bit to bring some light into their autumn days – then I'll be humbly thankful.' His voice rose rhetorically. 'I'm doing my little bit – and you, Terence, are going to share it with me.'

Terry stacked his last bear and sat down heavily on a packing case. 'What's in it for you, Arthur?' he said bluntly.

Arthur looked at him sadly. 'In one so young, I find your callousness quite horrifying. Don't you have an elderly grandparent?'

'Yeah. She's just married again and she's up the bingo every night. Nothing twilight about her.'

But Arthur was not to be put off his stride. 'A very fortunate old lady –'

'And what about you?'

'Eh?'

'How are you looking after your oldies?'

'Mine passed on some years ago.'

'I bet they did! What'd you do? Sell 'em a line in cardboard coffins?'

'You're in bad taste, Terence. As usual. 'Er indoors has a mother I'm devoted to.'

141

'Where is she?'

'In an eventide home. We visit her regularly.'

'I haven't seen you doin' that.' Terry sounded doubtful.

'You don't know everything about me.'

'Mystery man, eh?'

'No, Terry,' said Arthur in a firm, gentle voice, 'I just have certain parts of my life that I don't normally talk about.'

'I bet you do.'

'Parts reserved for visiting the sick, the needy – and the old. Good works that modesty forbids me discussing.'

'So who was the old girl?' Terry insisted.

'If you must know, she resides at Sunnybanks.'

'The old people's home?'

'None other.'

'And you *visit* her?' Terry was incredulous.

'Regularly.'

'I just don't believe it.' Terry got up off his packing case and began to stride about. 'It's completely out of character.'

'I beg your pardon?'

'*You* – to do a generous act. Never. Has she got any money?'

'None,' said Arthur triumphantly. 'Now, Terence,' his voice took on a brisker note, 'here is your chance to join me in the field of worthy endeavour.'

'Eh?'

'Surely you can spare a few hours for the old folks at home?'

'You gone off your rocker?'

'I've organised a mystery tour –'

'A *what?*'

'An outing for the sunset people – for the residents of Sunnybanks.'

'Where do I come in?'

'I want you to drive the coach.'

'Where we going?'

142

'I told you – a mystery tour.'

'Do *you* know where we're going?'

'Of course.' Arthur looked at his watch. 'I must be off.'

'Where are you going?'

'I'm going into a part of my life that I don't talk about.'

'Your good works.'

'And when I get back I'd like those gollywogs stacked.'

'You'll never get rid of those, Arthur. They're against the race relations act.'

'There's a place for all God's children –'

'Not if they're done up like the Black and White Minstrel Show.'

Arthur frowned. 'Don't bother me now, Terence. My mind's on higher things.'

'Your good works.'

'I'd rather not –'

'– talk about it. Yeah, I know. But someone should warn those poor old things at Sunnybanks.'

Arthur hurried away across the yard to his Jag. 'You've no soul,' was his parting shot.

'Well, this is most kind of you, Mr Daley. I don't know how to thank you.' The matron of Sunnybanks was young, in her late twenties, yet despite her youth she had an air of authority.

'It's the least I can do.'

'And is this the result of a consortium?'

'No – I haven't had one of those.'

Anne Maybury looked mystified. 'Sorry?'

But Arthur rattled on, oblivious. 'As you know, I am a respected businessman in these parts. Well liked, trusted, you could say.'

She nodded dutifully.

'I've had my ups and downs. Runs of good and bad luck. I mean – don't we all?'

Again she nodded.

'But now I'm in middle years, I've had time to reflect. I've made my money – and I'm looking back.' He paused.

'Looking back?' she prompted.

'At my old mum – God rest her soul. And how she ended her days.'

'Peacefully?'

'I wasn't a wealthy man, then. But I did my best for her.' He looked around him. 'She ended her days very pleasantly – in similar circumstances to this.' Arthur cleared his throat emotionally and Anne looked away. Was he going to cry? she wondered. 'Ever since then,' Arthur continued with a catch in his voice, 'I've wanted to repay those who cared for her.'

'Was she here?' Anne's voice was startled.

'No –' Arthur sounded regretful. 'She was in Dunroamin – at Clacton.'

'Oh.'

'Most pleasant.'

'Then –'

'I just want to repay the system. The system that cared.'

'So what exactly did you have in mind, Mr Daley?'

'A delightful surprise – or a series of them. A mystery tour.'

'How – how interesting.'

'Next Wednesday, perhaps.'

'The coach –'

'Don't give that a second thought. I have interests in that area – many interests.'

'What about a driver?'

'Oh, I have my own man. My chauffeur. He is also a qualified coach driver.'

'And do you have in mind ending up somewhere?'

'Another contact. A catering establishment run by an associate of mine.'

'Thank you, Mr Daley.'

'And now, if I might slip along and see Mrs Croxton?'

'Please do.'

144

Arthur bowed his way out of the office and walked along the corridor to Mrs Croxton's room. He knocked. 'Ada?'

'Yeah.' Her voice was gravelly.

'It's Arthur.'

'Come in.'

Arthur entered the small over-furnished room and looked around for somewhere to sit.

'On the bed,' she snapped and he sat down gingerly in the sea of crumpled tabloids that covered the counterpane. Mrs Croxton was in her late seventies, her veined, lined face rigid with hostility.

'Now – you set it up?'

'Yes – and it's gonna be a beezer.'

'It'd better be. One slip and –'

'Yes,' said Arthur hastily. 'There won't be any.'

But she continued. 'And Lennie will 'ave yer.'

'Come, come –'

'He'll break your legs.'

'It is entirely unnecessary to –'

'I know you, Arthur Daley – and your mother before you. The Daleys always were twisters.'

'Remember I'm doin' you a favour.'

'You're on fifteen per cent – and that's it. No fiddlin'.'

Arthur smiled sadly.

'Terry drivin'?'

'Yeah.'

'Then I want Lennie on board too.'

Arthur looked horrified. 'No.'

'On board.'

'He's not the right type,' Arthur protested feebly.

'Bugger that. He's comin'.'

'But what can I pass him off as?' Arthur was desperate.

'Courier.'

'What?'

'I said – courier.' Her voice became even more gravelly and she clenched her fists. 'You do what you're bleedin' well told, Arthur Daley.'

'Now –'

'I said – do what your bleedin' well told!'

'Yes, Ada,' said Arthur humbly. 'Anything else you want?'

'Yeah – put a crate of booze on the coach.'

'That won't be allowed.'

'Put it in the boot.'

'It'll cost yer.'

'I'll pay – although I'd have thought you could've been generous to a few lonely old people.'

'Generous?' asked Arthur. 'Me?'

'What the hell's this?'

Arthur and Terry were standing in the middle of what appeared to be a graveyard of motor coaches. Most were rusted almost beyond recognition. One – battered, rusty and desolate – stood before them. Leaning on the dented bodywork was Mick and a sign above him read MICK'S TRANSPORT – LUXURY MOTOR COACHES FOR HIRE.

'This the vehicle you want, Arthur?' Mick was old too, in fact he looked almost as old as Mrs Croxton.

'It's the only one you got, innit?'

'In working order. At the moment.' Mick was forced to concede.

'That?' asked Terry wonderingly. 'In working order?'

'This is a charitable enterprise,' Arthur reminded him. 'I don't have the capital for the spit and polish jobs.'

'It won't get them there.'

'She's dead reliable,' said Mick defensively. 'Been abroad, she has.'

'Ought to have stayed there,' objected Terry. 'I can't drive that.'

'You'll have to,' said Arthur. 'Where's your initiative?'

But Terry shook his head. 'It's not roadworthy.' Mick spluttered something but Arthur interrupted him.

'There's a few sovs in it for you, Tel.'

146

'What the hell are you up to, Arthur?'

Arthur swallowed and drew him aside. 'Listen – it's like I said. A charitable venture.'

'And what else?'

'A little bit of business too.'

'What business?'

'Mrs Croxton's business.' Arthur lowered his voice until it was practically inaudible. 'She's gonna drop off.'

'Kick the bucket?'

Arthur frowned. 'Drop off from the coach and pick somethin' up.'

'Why can't you take her in the car?'

Arthur cleared his throat uncomfortably. 'They're watching her.'

'They?'

'The Baggart twins.'

'Them– they croaked long ago.'

'Did they?' Arthur looked smug. 'Did they, hell?'

'But they must be geriatrics.'

'Not quite.'

'Where are they?'

'At Sunnybanks.'

'Blimey – how long they been there?'

'Moved in last week.'

'Why?'

'Croxton – Mrs Croxton.'

'Croxton.' Terry paused reflectively. Then he stared unbelievingly at Arthur. 'Not Billy Croxton's widow.'

'The same.'

'But –' Terry shook his head. 'When was it?'

'Thirty years.'

'The Kemp Street job.'

'Half a million.' Arthur actually licked his lips. 'Never found. Stashed away by Billy. And the Baggarts been searching all that time.' Arthur grinned.

'Charity begins at home, Arthur?'

'It's a percentage. A small one for helping a helpless old lady.'

'Helpless?'

'It's an act of mercy.'

'Look, Arthur,' hissed Terry while Mick stood impatiently in the background. 'You out of your mind?'

'I'm on to a good thing, Tel. And I'm taking you with me.'

'Why not go and get it? If the old girl knows where it is. The Baggarts are senile. Must be.'

'Their lads aren't. Jim and Joe.'

Terry thought.

'They watch her every move – like their Dads do. She's stitched up everywhere. Unless it's public. Very public.'

'Then –'

'The outing! The matron – I'm inviting the vicar. They can't do nothing in front of that lot.'

'I wouldn't be so sure,' said Terry. 'I know them lads. Had the odd encounter.'

'Yeah,' said Arthur without interest.

'Can't we even get a decent coach?' pleaded Terry.

'Terrence,' admonished Arthur. 'When you're on a tight charitable budget, *any* economy is essential.' Arthur turned back to Mick. 'Don't worry about fixing that spare tyre – we'll take a risk on that.'

'They seem very happy.'

'Oh, they are. We have our ups and down,' said Anne Maybury to the new visiting vicar. 'But basically they're content.'

They were standing by the canteen hatch, watching the Baggart brothers and Mrs Croxton drinking tea together.

'And the local community? Does it involve itself in any way with the residents?'

'Well, it's not renowned for doing so. But more recently a Mr Daley has come forward and organised a coach outing.'

'How kind.'

'He's some kind of businessman. Anyway, he

148

particularly asked if you would be able to come along.'

'How kind,' the vicar repeated.

'It's on Wednesday. A mystery tour.'

'How exciting.'

'Yes – even I don't know the destination. So that's a treat on the horizon.'

'And this Daley chap – you say he's a local businessman?'

'Yes – commerce of some kind. He has a lot of contacts. The coach – he's supplying that. And taking us to a restaurant where he knows the owner. It's all free.'

'Well, I must say I do look forward to meeting the benevolent Mr Daley,' said the vicar, once again watching the corner table where Mrs Croxton was passing one of the Baggart brothers a rock cake. 'Yes,' he added, 'they do look so content.'

'And I hope it bleedin' chokes you.'

'All right. Watch it, Ada. The vicar's looking this way.' Arnie Baggart raised a hand in cheery greeting and the vicar waved and smiled benignly.

Meanwhile his brother Sam poured out more tea. 'Ada,' he said, 'we'll get there in the end, you know.'

'I don't know what you're talking about.'

'Sure you do. You know where he stashed it – and you're waiting your chance to get your hands on it.'

'Why should I know after all these years? How d'you know I ain't had it before?'

'Because we've spent years watchin' you. And we know you haven't. And the grapevine says you got the tip-off when Porringer popped off. You was at his bedside.'

'So were you.'

'Yeah,' put in Arnie, 'but he didn't choose to confide in us.'

'He didn't tell me nothin',' gravelled Ada firmly.

'I've known you for seventy years, Ada Croxton,' said

Arnie, 'and I know when you've got the light of greed in your eye.' He picked up another rock cake. 'And you've got it now.'

'Sod off,' she said, just as the vicar wandered across. He was a youngish man with a bulging adam's apple and a high-pitched, enthusiastic, jollying sort of voice.

'And how are we today?'

Not knowing to whom he was speaking, all three smiled ingratiatingly, giving him a fine display of toothless gums.

'Very well, thank you, vicar,' said Arnie. 'Can't complain.'

'Sunnybanks is a sunny place, then, is it?' chortled the vicar.

Ada gave him a withering look. 'Only place I could get into. My bastard kid's got no money.'

'Real old Cockney through and through,' Arnie confided in the confused vicar.

'Born within sound of Bow bells,' put in Sam. 'And calls a spade a bloody shovel.'

The vicar laughed doubtfully. 'The salt of the earth, they say,' he volunteered.

'Born with a heart of gold,' added Arnie and the vicar laughed more heartily.

'Drop off,' replied Ada.

'Why don't we look for it – save the hassle?' asked Terry, stacking gollywogs in the lock-up. But Arthur wasn't horning in.

' 'Cause I don't know where it is – exactly,' he admitted.

'So how's she gonna show us – on a mystery tour?'

'Ada'll give me the nod.'

'With the vicar on board?'

'And the matron,' Arthur added firmly.

'And Lennie Croxton, the Baggarts, their lads – Jim and Joe. Arthur, you've half London's underworld travelling on that coach with you. You barmy?'

'Terence,' said Arthur reprovingly, 'you don't seem

150

to understand. I'm looking after the interests of a very old lady. It's the least I can do for her.'

'At fifteen per cent?'

'I have incurred expenses.'

'You'll incur a bloody sight more than that with Lennie and the Baggart boys around.'

'I'm not worried,' said Arthur.

'You should be.'

'Why should I? I've got you on board.'

Terry gave Arthur a strained smile. 'And if I decide not to come?'

'You'll come. I told you – I'm cutting you in.'

'What's my share?'

'Two and a half per cent?' Arthur was hopeful.

'Of a million?' Terry couldn't do sums. 'How do you know there's a million there?'

'She swore on her mother's life.'

'Ada? Her mum's been six foot down for years.'

'I trust her.'

'You what?'

'She's still spry,' said Arthur defensively.

'You bet she is.' Terry paused to think. 'Okay, I'll come,' he said eventually. 'On one condition.'

'What's that?' Arthur was immediately suspicious.

'I get to meet the old boot.'

'Why?' said Arthur, his suspicions increasing.

'Because I want to suss her out.'

Arthur sighed. 'We can't go there – the Baggarts –' He left the sentence suitably unfinished.

'I know,' said Terry. 'Does she play?'

'Play?' Arthur was bewildered.

'Bingo.'

'Oh yeah – down at the Capitol.'

'Fix a meet there, then.'

'It's risky,' said Arthur unwillingly.

'But necessary,' replied Terry.

The Capitol had been a glorious nineteenth-century music hall, but its fortunes had declined since the forties and its life as a cinema and now a down-at-heel bingo hall had considerably tarnished the gilt, chipped the stucco and cracked the colonnades. Clad now in peeling red paint, the whole place had an air of decay. Inside it was no better, and even the carpet in the auditorium was so worn that it had holes in it. A sea of refuse lay under the seats and the bingo caller spoke in a nasal, flat voice.

Esconsed on the springless seats either side of Ada Croxton, Arthur and Terry watched their cards gloomily.

'Legs eleven,' intoned the caller.

'Come on, Arthur – it's your card.'

Arthur vaguely looked down – his thoughts were elsewhere. 'Yeah.'

'Key of the door – twenty-one,' came the dirge.

'You got that too,' said Terry.

'Sod off,' said Ada furiously. 'You're ruinin' me concentration.'

At last the session drew to a close and Arthur, casting a furtive glance around him, drew Terry and Ada into a grubby coffee bar.

'My man wanted to meet you,' he said.

'Eh?' Both Terry and Ada looked at him uncomprehendingly.

'My man – my driver. Terry.'

'Oh yeah?' Ada didn't seem interested.

'He'll drive the coach,' insisted Arthur. 'And he's a – a friend.'

'What d'yer mean by that?'

Arthur turned commandingly to Terry. 'Get us a cuppa.'

'Now?'

'Yeah.'

'Haven't got a bob on me.'

Reluctantly Arthur dug into his trouser pockets and gave Terry some change. When he had gone, Arthur said: 'He wants in.'

Ada gave him a sour look. 'Why?' she rasped.

'It's on my percentage.'

She shook her head, clearly not satisfied, and Arthur tried again.

'He won't drive unless.'

'Ah.'

'He's a trustworthy young man.'

'Ah.' Ada looked at him out of rheumy eyes. 'You wouldn't be trying anything, Arthur?'

'Now why should I do that?'

'You would if you could.' Ada delved into a huge, cracked black leather handbag and pulled out a dusty bottle of lavender water. She dabbed some of it behind her ear as Terry returned with some severely slopped cups of tea.

Arthur took his and sipped at it. Then he screwed up his nose. 'This is bats' piss,' he said.

'Lucky it's as harmless as that,' said Terry.

'You want the in?' rasped Ada. 'Why?'

'Because you've got a coachload of heavies – and only little me. I'm not in the risk business to that extent.'

'The Baggarts?' she scoffed.

'Their kids – and yours.'

'My Lennie?'

'He's trouble.'

'So you're on Arthur's take?'

'But that's not all,' said Terry firmly, ignoring Arthur's anxious gestures.

'What else?'

'How do you know it's there?'

'I had it on the best authority – and the amount.'

'Yeah?'

'I'm sure Terry –' began Arthur but Ada cut across him.

'You look a nice boy,' she said grudgingly. 'Handy, are you?'

'For what?'

'Trouble.'

'You expecting some?'

'No.'

153

'Right, then.' He lowered his voice. 'Where is it?'

But she grinned and cackled at him, sipping at her brackish tea like some ancient bird. 'You think I'm a mug?'

'I could get it for you – no bother.'

'I don't trust you.'

'He's a very –' But Ada cut Arthur short again.

'Shut up, you. We do it my way – or not at all.'

'How do I know when to stop?' protested Terry.

'I'll tell you.'

'Then there'll be a ruck.'

'Ruck?' She laughed raucously again. 'I'm not stupid. They won't know what's going on. I've got plans, you know. Got a fag?'

'Don't smoke.'

'I'll try one of your panatellas,' she said to Arthur. He reluctantly gave her one and she stuck it in the corner of her mouth. 'Light?'

Arthur lit it.

'That's elegant,' commented Terry.

'Sod off,' she said.

'Tell me one more thing, Ada –'

'What?' she asked suspiciously, eyeing him through the smoke.

'All this loot. What are you gonna do with your share? Settle it on Lennie?'

Ada looked at Terry as if he were mad. 'That Lennie?'

'Yeah.'

'Not bleedin' likely.'

'Then what?'

'On me,' she snorted.

'What are *you* gonna spend it on then?' asked Arthur patronisingly.

'Number one,' she said. 'Who else?'

'And what would you be doin' with all that money?'

'Spendin' it. I'm going to Monte Carlo.'

'Eh?' Arthur was shocked. Terry grinned. He was beginning to like the old girl.

154

'I'm not gonna die at Sunnybanks,' she said.

'Where are you gonna die?' asked Terry.

'Pissed as a newt in a casino,' she replied with a smile at Terry.

'So Daley's in on the act,' said Jim Baggart. The brothers were in their early thirties and both were built like bulls, with big shoulders and bulging biceps. But there wasn't much in their heads. They were sitting over pints in a big, garish pub.

'So they say. He's been poking around at Sunny-banks.'

'What the hell's he up to?'

'What d'yer think?'

'So – you reckon she knows.'

'She was at the deathbed.'

'Porringer didn't tell nobody nothin'.' Joe sounded bleak.

'He may have told the old girl – they were close.'

'That close?'

'They say they was knocking it off.'

'So what do we do? Put a tail on Daley?'

'No need – I got a hot-line to God.'

'Wassat?'

The vicar walked gently into the pub. He was wearing a dog-collar, a black sweater and jeans.

'Talk of the devil,' muttered Joe. 'How'd you get hold of that?'

'I was in St Barnabas – eating me sandwiches, taking a look-see.'

'Anything worth taking?'

'Lead on the roof. Bit of plate. And he came up all friendly like. So I invited him up here for a drink.'

'What the 'ell for?'

'Because he's going into Sunnybanks regular like. Thought he might know somethin' we don't.'

The vicar spotted them, waved enthusiastically and came bouncing over to them. 'Hail fellows,' he said gratingly. 'Is the ale good here?'

'Sit down, vicar, and I'll get you a pint,' said Jim, already on his feet.

The vicar sat down, his hands on his knees.

'How you findin' your new parish?' asked Joe politely.

'Super, really super – it's all so genuine, isn't it?'

'Eh?'

'Real working class roots. I was in Surrey before.'

'Yeah?'

'Godalming. Rural town. Delightful spot. Nothing like this, though.'

'No –' Joe was feeling at a loss and was relieved to see Jim returning with the drinks.

'Saw you coming out of Sunnybanks, Vicar,' said Jim, coming straight to the point.

'A most pleasant rest home,' he said, sipping at his pint.

'Lively place by all accounts,' said Jim.

'Yes, we're all off on a coach outing soon.'

'Oh yeah.'

'Local benefactor.'

'Who's that?' asked Jim. 'Or is he anonymous?'

'Oh no. His name's – er – I never remember names. Dial, Dolly, Daley. That's it – a Mr Arthur Daley.'

The vicar was quite astonished to see what an effect he had made; Joe and Jim sat there with mouths open and eyes dilated.

'You know our benefactor?' he asked, taking another sip of beer.

'Yes,' said Jim. 'He's an old mate.'

'Well, isn't that a coincidence.'

'It certainly is, Vicar.' Joe nodded enthusiastically. 'When is all this taking place?'

'Wednesday.' He laughed. 'We're praying for good weather.'

They laughed with him for a while. 'What a smashing bloke Arthur Daley is,' Jim said eventually. 'Of course he's always been full of – good works.'

'I'm sure,' said the vicar. He began to laugh again but Jim hastily interrupted him.

'Vicar, I've got a request. And I'm sure I speak for my brother too.'

Joe smiled winningly.

'A request?'

'Yes, Vicar. Would it be possible for me and my brother to perform some small voluntary service on the day in question.'

The vicar beamed. 'I'm sure it would. The more the merrier.'

'If we came on the coach,' suggested Joe, 'we could help the senior citizens on and off.'

'And provide any other useful function,' put in Jim.

The vicar's grin widened. 'This is most thoughtful,' he said, looking round him at the desolate pub. 'What a splendid sense of involvement there is in our genuine working class communities.'

'Eh?'

'Such warmth, mutual help – a veritable –'

But Jim interrupted him slightly impatiently. 'You've lost me there, vicar. Can we come on the coach or not?'

The vicar clapped his hands. 'Of course you can,' he said.

'That's all right then,' commented Joe.

The coach rattled and growled as it crawled up the hill towards Sunnybanks. 'This is a wild one,' muttered Terry to Arthur, who sat rigidly in the seat behind him. 'Right mystery tour this is gonna be. Mystery is – how do you drive the bleeding bus?'

'You're driving it very well, Terry,' said Arthur with encouraging patronage. 'Could put your foot down a bit more though?'

'It won't *go* any faster, Arthur.'

'It's steady then.'

'And it's belching black smoke.'

'Dirty fuel,' said Arthur knowledgeably as the bus

finally pulled up outside Sunnybanks. He looked out and said: 'Oh my Gawd.'

'What's up?' asked Terry through gritted teeth as the steering wheel juddered violently in his hand.

'You see what I see?'

Terry looked – and saw a motley crowd waiting on the pavement. The two ancient Baggarts were flanked by their sons, Jim and Joe, whilst standing beside old Mrs Croxton was her son Lennie. And Lennie was quite something. He was a squat, heavily bearded Hells Angel with arms and legs like tree trunks. The vicar stood a few feet away, wearing an off-white linen suit, and the old people were scattered around him. Most of the men wore faded sun hats whilst the women wore floral prints. There was a fair scattering of crutches and frames. Chatting to one of her guests was the matron, Anne Maybury, and it was she who caught Terry's attention.

'What a cracker!'

'Eh?'

'The blonde.'

'That's matron,' said Arthur in a sacred tone.

'Nice bit.'

'She has a calling.'

'Yeah.'

Arthur's mind returned abruptly to the current problem. 'There're some of the worst crooks in South London lined up out there.'

'And there's you.'

'Terry – please be serious.'

Terry ran his eye over the Baggarts – and Lennie. 'Nice to see them doing a bit of voluntary work.'

'Terence,' wailed Arthur. 'This could be nasty.'

'Don't say I didn't warn you,' was all that Terry would contribute.

It took half an hour, with much merry banter from the vicar, to load the ancient coach with its ill-assorted cargo. As Mrs Croxton came on board, she hissed at Arthur:

'Got the booze?'

'All the arrangements have been made,' he said blandly.

She paused in her measured progress down the aisle and poked her wizened face close to Arthur's. 'I *said* – have you got the bleedin' booze?'

'It's in the back.'

'It had better be. And remember, Arthur, we want plenty of stops on your mystery tour. Old people get caught short easy.'

Arthur nodded irritably and whispered 'There's one stop that's up to you, Ada.'

She cackled again. 'Don't get your knickers in a twist, Arthur. I'll take care of that.'

'Ladies and gentlemen – the young in heart.' Lennie snarled up at Arthur as he stood in the aisle, making his speech, whilst the two generations of Baggarts yawned. Many of the old people had already dozed off and Anne was whispering to Terry at the front of the coach so there was not much of an audience for Arthur. Nevertheless, he pursued his theme relentlessly.

'By courtesy of Daley Charitable Enterprises, we are about to embark on a grand mystery tour.' The vicar began to clap and an old lady gave a particularly rending snore. 'It is my pleasure,' continued Arthur, 'our pleasure – me and my associate at the wheel – to bring a little variety into the lives of a group of citizens – senior citizens – who are now coming to the end of life's great highway – to the rich pastures of the eventide fields.'

'Git on with it,' gravelled Mrs Croxton.

'And now, without further ado –' Arthur paused with a sudden realisation. he didn't have the slightest idea in which direction they were meant to be heading. With a little cough he said: 'Before we depart I will come

159

amongst you, ensuring all are comfortably seated.'
Majestically Arthur paraded down the aisle whilst the
vicar began enthusiastically clapping again. Under
cover of this steady tattoo, he paused by Mrs Croxton's
seat.

'Where are we going?' he hissed.

'Eh?'

'Where we *goin'*?'

'Which *direction?*'

'It's your mystery –'

'Go to Brighton,' she said. 'And bloody step on it.'

Arthur straightened up with a beatific smile, only to
find the Baggarts, senior and junior as well as Lennie,
were straining forward in their seats, trying to
overhear his conversation.

'Strewth,' muttered Arthur, as he rejoined Terry at
the front. 'That was a close one.'

'Eh?' Terry looked up at him blankly and Anne said:

'This really is extraordinarily good of you, Mr Daley.'

'Drive on,' said Arthur, wiping his brow with a silk
hanky.

'Where to?'

'Brighton,' snapped Arthur. 'Go to Brighton.'

'Some mystery tour,' grinned Terry.

The coach crawled down the road out of London to
Brighton, belching black smoke and holding the traffic
up. Terry bad-temperedly wrestled with the wheel,
Arthur produced more smoke inside with his cigar and
Anne Maybury moved amongst the residents, some of
whom were singing and others who slept noisily. The
Baggarts, junior and senior, all sat in a group, whilst
Hells Angel Lennie sat a few seats in front of his
mother, his lips moving silently to the minute din of his
personal stereo.

'Where's the booze?' asked Mrs Croxton of Anne
whose reaction was slightly tight-lipped.

'Oh dear – I don't think there is any.'

'Arthur Daley said 'e'd provide it. If 'e 'asn't I'll skin 'im alive.'

'I see.' Anne Maybury looked even more tight-lipped. 'I'll go and see him.' She made her way to the front, a social smile hovering on her lips. Inside she groaned – she might have known there would be a drawback.

'Mr Daley –'

Arthur was jerked out of his cigar-puffing reverie.

'At your service, my dear.'

'Mrs Croxton is talking about drink.'

'All taken care of.'

'Oh –'

'Stout and port in the luggage locker under the coach.'

'I see.'

'A little tonic –'

'Gin?' she asked with rising horror.

'I'm using a metaphorical word,' said Arthur. 'By which I mean an uplift.'

'Ah . . .' She relaxed. 'It's just that –'

'Yes?'

'They're very difficult to handle when they've had a few drinks.'

'Aren't we all?' said Terry, still fighting the wheel.

'They in particular,' she stated bleakly.

'Don't worry your head,' said Arthur. 'I quite understand that at their mature age the digestinal tract is not what it was – and the urinary functions –'

'You're a medical man as well?' asked Anne in surprise.

'He's a quack,' said Terry. But Arthur ignored him.

'I'm a man of parts – with some experience of the problems of old people. I nursed my old mother through her last days and –'

Terry began to give a verbal imitation of a violin whilst Anne tried hard not to smile. Arthur was not in the least non-plussed and was about to carry on when Anne said:

'That must have been quite a task, Mr Daley.'

'Arthur – please.' He beamed at her.

'Once they've had a few, they're impossible – Arthur.' She lowered her voice, despite the roaring of the coach's engine. 'And Mrs Croxton's the worst. Becomes quite abusive.'

'Leave it to me,' said Arthur magnanimously, grabbing at the vicar's sleeves. 'I'm sure the vicar will agree with me.'

Terry groaned aloud.

'Yes, Mr Daley?' The vicar, who was talking to an old man in the seat behind him, looked up smiling.

'I'm sure you'll agree that abstemity is very much to be desired.'

'Well, of course.'

'And particularly in the older person.'

'In everyone.'

'Of course. Now I've supplied – absolutely free – a limited amount of alcoholic beverage for the old people to while away the hours of the trip. But our Miss Maybury is a little concerned about its effect . . .'

'Ah yes.'

'In immoderate quantities. So I was wondering if you, as a man of the cloth, would reassure her by addressing the old folks on the subject.'

'Me?' For once the cheeriness left the vicar's eyes.

'You could put it so much better than I can.'

'But . . . I don't understand.' The vicar seemed at a loss.

'A homily – on the value of moderation.'

'*Now?*'

'Yes,' said Arthur baldly.

The vicar reluctantly stood up in the centre aisle, breaking off a ragged chorus of 'We'll Gather Lilacs'. He could not, however, do much about the more gutteral snoring.

'Friends.'

There was a muttered reaction.

'Mr Arthur Daley – our benefactor – has provided

some refreshment for our mystery tour.'

'We're goin' to Brighton,' someone said.

'To help us on our way.' There was a ragged cheer. 'Alcoholic refreshment.' A louder cheer. 'And when we get into the country I propose to ask our driver to stop so that I can allocate it.'

'Allocate!' shouted Mrs Croxton. 'What do you bleedin' mean?'

The vicar smiled at the old lady uncertainly. 'I shall hand it out – and I know we'll all be abstemious,' he said encouragingly.

'We wanna get pissed,' said Mrs Croxton, getting up and shouldering the vicar aside. She went straight up to an apprehensive Arthur. 'This your doin'?'

'No –'

'Try to save a bob or two?'

'Hardly. I'm a charitable –'

'You wally, Arthur,' she hissed at him out of the side of her mouth, 'I want them all pissed. Don't you see, it's all part of the plan.'

Arthur gave his widest, most placating smile. 'I'll tell you what, vicar.'

'Yes?'

'I'll do the dishing out. Save you the responsibility.'

'But I thought –'

'You can rely on me to be abstemious,' Arthur said. 'Can't he, Terry?'

'Oh yes,' said Terry. 'You signed the pledge years ago, didn't you, Arthur?'

Arthur ignored him, turning to Mrs Croxton. 'That suit you, Ada?'

'You know what I wants,' she said darkly, as she returned to her seat.

'I've got a drop.'

'Gin?' Mrs Croxton's voice rasped as they stood under the awning of a tin shack, the rain lashing down viciously on their huddled figures.

'Just a drop.' Old Mrs Manser had always been aloof,

163

genteel – not on Mrs Croxton's level. Now she was on chatting terms. Gin-offering terms. It was all a mystery, but Mrs Croxton, her mind slightly dulled by two bottles of brown ale (dished out by Arthur) and some port (purloined from the luggage compartment of the coach) justified it blearily to herself. 'We're on a mystery tour, after all,' she muttered as she followed old Mrs Manser round the back of the shed and into a young wood. There, surrounded by saplings and crouched under an umbrella, the two old ladies shared a bottle.

Elsewhere, the remainder of the party were crowded into the steamy atmosphere of a very tatty transport cafe owned by an acquaintance of Arthur's known as Greaseball. It was an unfortunate name for a chef. He was in his late fifties, entirely bald and had the skin texture of lard. Somewhat grudgingly he had bestowed grey tea in chipped china mugs to the coach party while he argued none too discreetly with Arthur about money.

'I'm not a rich man, Arthur.'

'No,' said Arthur, staring gloomily at the décor.

'And I hadn't counted on such a large party.'

'This is a charitable trip,' reproved Arthur.

'Not for me it ain't.'

'You said refreshments on the house – and a smiling welcome.'

'Yeah – that was before I took delivery of that dishwasher of yours.'

'What's wrong with it?'

'It spits plates, Arthur. Spits 'em.'

'Where?'

'Out.'

'You must be loading it wrong.'

'I followed the manual. I want you to take it back, Arthur.'

'Now?'

'Now – and I want it returned as good as new.'

'I can't take it on the coach!' said Arthur indignantly.

164

'Why not?'

'It wouldn't be seemly.'

'Seemly!' Greaseball exploded, and some of the old people looked round enquiringly.

Feverishly Arthur put a finger to his lips. 'Be discreet,' he implored.

'Listen,' said Greaseball, leaning over the counter, 'either you take away my dishwasher and get it fixed – or I charge double for the Mary Lee.'

Arthur looked down at his cup analytically. 'You call this tea?'

'I'm warning you!'

'All right,' said Arthur. 'All right. You know my motto.'

'Eh?'

'The customer's always right.'

'All right, Ada. Where is it.'

She swung round to find herself facing two generations of Baggarts standing under umbrellas in the pouring rain.

'What the hell do you want?' she asked sweetly.

'The money.'

'Eh?'

'Come on,' said Jim, steeping forward menacingly, 'let's get this over. Where is it?'

Ada turned slowly back to Mrs Manser. 'You old bitch,' she hissed. 'You set me up.'

Mrs Manser's acquiline nose twitched as if she had smelt something extremely unpleasant. 'I don't know what you mean.'

'How much you getting?' she asked.

'I'm sorry?' Mrs Manser's tones were now even more superior.

'Don't you look down your hooter at me – they paid you to set me up.'

'I really feel I have to terminate this –'

'Exterminate, you mean,' yelled Mrs Croxton, swinging up her capacious handbag to contact Mrs

Manser smartly on the nose. 'Cop this!'

As Mrs Manser staggered back, Mrs Croxton bellowed:

'Lennie – your old girl's in trouble.'

Meanwhile the Baggarts moved in.

'What's it like then?'

'What?'

'Looking after this lot.'

Terry and Anne were sitting at a corner table, drinking the scummy tea and eating stale doughnuts.

'It's not too bad. I've got quite fond of them.'

'Even Ada?'

'Yes – even Ada. The Baggarts are a bit sad, though.'

'Sad?' Terry wouldn't have described them that way.

'Yes, they strike me as old men who've lost their power. I bet they were on the wrong side of the law.'

'They still are,' muttered Terry, but as Anne looked up at him sharply he abruptly changed the subject. 'So what did you do before you was a matron?'

She smiled. 'You may not believe this, but I was a –' She paused.

'A model?'

'No – a policewoman.'

'Blimey!' Terry stared at her open-mouthed and she laughed.

'Can't you see me as a copper?'

'Frankly – no. You weren't on this manor?'

'No – I was in Sheffield. Why?'

'You would have known Arthur Daley – that's all.'

'Is he a crook?'

'No,' said Terry quickly but she was laughing again. 'Why did you come out of the force?

'I've always been a bit soft, I s'pose, and I didn't find nicking people that constructive. I went and looked after some kids for a while – and then this job came up. I like it.'

Terry nodded, looking out at the rain and then round

166

the tawdry interior of the cafe. 'Some mystery tour.'

'I think Mr Daley means well.'

'He *never* means well,' said Terry disloyally.

'Anyway, they're just pleased to come out,' said Anne. 'Whatever happens.'

Terry glanced round the cafe again and then he struck the rickety table with his fist.

'What's up?' asked Anne, amongst the slopped tea.

'Something's happening,' said Terry, 'that won't make 'em so pleased.' He left the table in a hurry and ran up to Arthur, who was lecturing the vicar.

'Arthur –'

'Terry, I'm in the middle of –'

'The Baggarts aren't here.'

'They've probably gone for a leak.'

'Lennie isn't here.'

'Gone for a –'

'Old Mrs Croxton's not here.'

At last Arthur was alarmed. His eyes narrowed and his cigar trembled in his mouth.

'Desertion of the troops?' asked the vicar.

'Desertion of bloody sense,' said Arthur, hurrying after Terry.

The vicar, temporarily thrown, turned to Greaseball. 'Thank you for the cup that cheers,' he said.

When the vicar eventually wandered out into the subsiding rain to find the missing members of the party, he came across a strange little scene in the woods. Mrs Manser was nursing a bloody nose, Mrs Croxton was bawling obscenities, Terry had Lennie in a half nelson and Arthur was backed up against a tree, surrounded on all sides by Baggarts.

'What's this then?' asked the vicar in the bright voice he usually reserved for children. 'A game of some sort?'

Arthur looked up at him in relief. 'They're young at heart,' he improvised desperately, laughing mirthlessly. 'Old? They're ready for anything.'

* * *

The singing was louder and more raucous as the coach chugged into Brighton.

'They won't touch a bleedin' drop – them Baggarts,' slurred Mrs Croxton to Arthur. 'I had in mind getting 'em so pissed they'd get off my back.'

'Where we goin'?' whispered Arthur.

'I'll tell you.'

'When?'

'Later.'

Arthur swore and then walked grandly up the aisle. He paused halfway. 'Ladies and Gentlemen, boys and girls, we've arrived at our mystery destination.'

'We could see the road signs,' said an old man, and the Baggarts sniggered. Lennie scowled. His arm still hurt from Terry's ministrations and he was determined to get back at him. Arthur, oblivious of them all, ploughed on. 'Now we shall sample the air –'

'And the pubs,' said Mrs Croxton indistinctly.

'Perambulate the promenade and even have a little paddle. Then a packed lunch, compliments of my own organisation in the luggage compartment, and we shall rendezous at five for the journey back to the smoke.'

Arthur paused, waiting for the applause that did not come. The vicar leapt boldly into the breach.

'And many thanks to Mr Daley for helping us to arrive at our mystery city.' His sally was greeted with tepid laughter.

'We've got to get rid of them Baggarts,' hissed Mrs Croxton as she and Arthur stood in a bus shelter on Brighton sea front. 'Any ideas?'

Arthur shook his head mournfully. 'Where are they now?' he asked.

'In the next shelter,' she said, 'watchin us.'

'And Lennie?'

'Sitting in the coach watching them.'

'Oh my Gawd!' He looked around for Terry and saw him, also in the coach, talking to Anne. The rest of the old people had scattered.

'Got it,' said Arthur suddenly.

'Well?' She looked at him suspiciously.

'A false trail,' said Arthur in excitement.

'How?'

'You tell me where it is – where the money is. I'll go there and collect it.'

'Yeah?'

'But in the meantime you go somewhere else – and let the Baggarts follow you.'

'Very nice, Arthur.'

'It's good, innit?'

'Just two problems.' Her voice was at its most gravelly now.

'I'm sure we can solve 'em.'

'Yes, Arthur – I'm sure you can. Well – the Baggarts may kill me – that's the first. The second is I don't trust you. And the answer is no.'

Arthur looked deflated. 'Got any better ideas? Or do we sit here all day?'

'What exactly is your boss up to?' Anne looked curiously at Arthur and Mrs Croxton sitting in the shelter.

'He's not my boss.'

'What is he then?'

'A mate.'

'I see.' She stared at Arthur and Mrs Croxton again. 'Well, what's your mate up to?'

Terry cast a jaundiced look outside. 'Gawd knows. Hey you free after this – this little frivolity?'

'I've got to settle them back.'

'How long does that take?'

'Hours if they're drunk. But I'm off shift at nine.'

'What about a meal somewhere?'

She grinned. 'Why not?'

'Tell you what – I'll pick up the money and you lay the false trail.'

'No – that's not the bargain, Ada. And you know it.'

She grinned toothlessly. 'Don't you trust me, Arthur?'

'No.'

'Then how about this? We both lay a false trail –'

'And we both collect the money?' asked Arthur.

'Provided we're minded.'

'You by Lennie –'

'And you by Terry.'

'You've got yourself a deal, Ada. And to see fair play – we should take the vicar.'

'They're shaking hands,' said Anne in tones of amazement. 'I wonder why?'

'No good will come of any bargains struck by these two,' he muttered. 'Watch out – they're coming over.'

'Terry – if I may interrupt.' Arthur was slightly out of breath as he mounted the coach steps. 'Ada and I would like to treat you to a drink at the Metropole – and you, my dear,' he added magnanimously. 'Where's the vicar?'

'Outside. Chatting to the Baggarts.'

'I should like to include him in our spree.'

Anne hurried off in search of him and when she had gone Terry said:

'What's up, Arthur?'

'A ruse – a diversion.'

'Oh yeah –'

'A clever trick that should work,' Arthur was suddenly decisive.

'What should I do?'

'Be on your guard,' said Arthur melodramatically. Then his voice took on a more familiar wheedling tone. 'Lend me a few bob, Tel.'

'Why?'

'Drinks come pricey at big hotels.'

The oddly assorted group made their way to the main cocktail bar of the hotel. It was lunchtime and busy.

'What'll you have?' asked Arthur generously, jingling Terry's change in his pocket. Terry under strict instructions, had a lager, Anne the same, Lennie a tomato juice, the vicar a lemonade. Only Arthur and Ada hit the hard stuff.

'Why look who's here,' said Terry as the four Baggarts entered the bar.

'Nobs paradise,' said Arnie and his son Jim asked,

'Another part of your mystery tour, Arthur?'

'For some,' came the sour reply.

'The more the merrier,' whinnied the vicar, whilst Joe contented himself with asking,

'How's the arm, Lennie?'

Lennie scowled. So far, Terry hadn't heard him speak.

'Who's in the chair?' asked Arnie.

'Your call,' chimed in Arthur.

'I've got another call – the call of nature,' cackled Ada and gathered up her handbag. She seemed slightly less drunk now – despite the double vodka and lime she had just consumed. As she began to walk to the door, she was followed by Arthur, Terry, Lennie and the Baggarts, leaving only the vicar and Anne propping up the bar.

'It must be catching,' laughed the vicar.

'Where the hell are we going?' hissed Arthur as Ada led the procession down the corridor in the direction of the ladies lavatory.

'Trust me, Arthur.'

'I don't.'

'Then stick it.'

For an old lady she was going at a considerable pace and the elderly Baggarts had difficulty in keeping up. Suddenly the lift opened and she darted for it, followed by Arthur.

'Tell your mate to fend 'em off – except Lennie. I want 'im in 'ere.'

'Terry,' said Arthur commandingly. 'Stop 'em.'

Terry, who was right behind him, swung round,

blocking the access to the lift and Arthur pulled Ada's hand away from the stop button. Lennie surged forward but Terry put the flat of his hand into his face and sent him hurtling back into the others. The lift doors closed, the lift began to rise and Arthur and Ada were alone.

'You conning bastard,' said Ada furiously, swinging her handbag at him.

'Ada – calm down,' Arthur replied, trying to dodge the blows in the tiny, enclosed space. 'Ada!'

But in her fury she continued to hit him with her handbag. Then, suddenly, the lift stopped between floors and Ada subsided, panting. There was complete silence and sweat began to pour down Arthur's forehead.

'What's up?'

'Dunno – I think I suffer from claustrophobia.'

'You *think*.'

'I *do*.' Arthur began to beat at the doors and punch at the alarm button. 'Let me out!'

' 'Ang on, Arthur.'

'Let me out,' bellowed Arthur, still pounding at the doors. 'Lemme out.' ·

'Try some of this.'

'What?' He looked down and saw she was pulling half a bottle of gin out of her handbag. No wonder it had hurt so much, he thought.

'That's not gonna help.'

'Isn't it? Try some.'

Dutifully Arthur did as he was told.

'The lift's broke,' said Jim Baggart to the hotel manager.

The manager ran his eyes suspiciously over the motley, rather dishevelled throng standing round the lift. 'What exactly –'

Terry took over. 'We're an old folks' outing – at least – some of us –' he added as the manager's eye took in Lennie, himself and the younger Baggarts. 'We're

172

volunteers. Anyway, we got two of 'em stuck between floors in the lift.'

'Two of them?'

'A – a volunteer and an old lady. Listen – there goes the alarm bell again.'

The manager gave a world-weary sigh. 'Most unfortunate – that lift has only just been serviced.'

'They made a good job of it then, didn't they?'

The manager frowned. 'Technical faults develop – I'll have to phone the engineers.'

'How long?' asked Lennie, rubbing at his nose. It was the first time he had spoken all day.

'We shall move with all speed,' said the manager, hurrying away. Terry got the impression that he didn't think much of his customers. When he glanced round at them again he could see why.

'What on earth is happening?' asked the vicar, looking at his watch. 'They've been away at least half an hour.'

'Shall we go and see?'

'There's safety in numbers,' said Anne.

They walked out of the bar, down the corridor and found the little group standing silently by the lift. From the lift shaft they heard a faint banging. Then a voice was distantly raised in song – a female voice.

'Arthur and Ada are stuck in the lift,' Terry told the vicar bleakly.

Suddenly another voice joined, and a faint chorus of My Old Dutch began to vibrate down the shaft.

'Well, said the vicar, 'at least those good people are keeping their spirits up.'

Terry looked at his watch. It was 2.30 and the occupants of the lift remained stuck fast. As the coach was due to leave at five it seemed that time was running out fast. Meanwhile, the engineers were working in a desultory fashion, watched by the silent group who had maintained their determined vigil throughout.

'Can't you winch 'em down?' asked Terry.

'No way.' The engineer was happily pessimistic. 'Something happened to the cable.'

Terry suddenly had an idea and drew the engineer aside. 'Look, one of 'em suffers from claustrophobia.'

'Haven't heard no shouting.'

'No – you wouldn't. He's probably flat on the deck, grovelling about giving the old lady trouble. Can't I get up there and talk to him?'

'You insured?'

'For climbing up lift shafts? It's not in the usual run of the day's business.'

'Then you can't go.'

'Look – I don't need insurance. This is a mercy mission.'

'Yeah.' The engineer looked dubious and Terry pressed home his advantage.

'I've got to get to him. For the old girl's sake.'

'But I don't hear nothin'.'

'Listen –' Terry looked over his shoulder and saw the Baggarts and Lennie watching him with growing suspicion. 'You know what people with claustrophobia can do?'

'No.'

'They can attack. They're dangerous.'

'I don't hear –'

'He may have done it already.'

'Better call the police.'

'And have an innocent party nicked?' There was an edge to Terry's voice.

The engineer hesitated and Terry rushed on. 'Look – is it possible for me to communicate with 'em? Isn't there an inspection ladder or something?'

'No.' He looked shamefaced. 'It's broke.'

'Broke?'

'It was our next job to replace it.'

'So what is there?'

'A broken ladder.'

'Blimey – is it climbable?'

The engineer shook his head. 'Dodgy.'

'I'll take the risk,' said Terry firmly and added even more firmly, 'It's *my* risk.'

'On your own head . . .'

'Sure, but if I climb it – can I speak to 'em? Will they hear me?'

'You'll get up to the floor of the lift. *If* you get that far, they'll hear you. But if it breaks free, you'll be a gonner.'

'I don't want to think about that,' said Terry, striding towards the lift cage doors and opening them. Jim Baggart moved forward but Terry said, 'Stand back, Jim.'

'What you doing?'

'I'm going to bring some comfort to those folks up there.'

'Well done,' cried the vicar. 'A real errand of mercy.'

Now it was Anne Maybury's turn to move forward. She grabbed Terry's arm. 'Don't you go. Can't we call the fire brigade – or the police or something. Can't *they* do it?'

'That's what I said.' The engineer's voice whined as he muttered to his mate.

'No,' said Terry, squeezing Anne's fingers gently. 'I'll be fine.'

Climbing the first few rungs of the inspection ladder was not an essentially difficult task, but when Terry was just short of the base of the lift several of the rungs were completely missing. Bracing himself, Terry grabbed upwards, swayed and grabbed the next rung of the ladder. With a heave he wrapped his arms round it – leaving his legs dangling in space – and then hauled himself up with a gigantic effort. For a moment he clung to the wood and metal contraption, sweating profusely. Then he climbed on upwards until he was under the floor of the lift.

'Arthur.'

There was no response.

175

'Arthur – it's Terry.'

Still nothing.

'*Arthur!*' he bellowed, and a kind of snuffling sound was heard.

'Wake up!'

Nothing.

'Wake *up!*'

There was another snuffling sound and then he heard the mumbling of Ada's voice.

'Ada,' said Terry sternly. 'Is that you?'

'Life is sad,' she said.

Terry groaned aloud.

'Life is no longer beautiful,' she continued in a heavily slurred voice. 'Not beautiful at all.'

This is all I need, thought Terry. 'Ada, sober up.'

'Eh?'

'Sober up – you old bat.'

Perhaps insults would help, he thought.

'What was that?' Her voice was not so slurred now.

'I said sober up, you old boot.'

'Who's that?'

'Terry McCann.'

'Then I'll thank you, young man, to remember your manners. I'm as sober as a judge.' She belched loudly.

'Where's Arthur?'

'Where else could he be?'

'All right. What sort of condition is he in?'

'He's fine.'

'Eh?'

'Having a kip.'

'Gawd. Listen, love. Time's runnin' out.'

'What time?'

'The coach is due to leave at five.' He looked at his watch. 'It's now three. We've got two hours.'

She cursed. 'The pubs'll be shut.'

'Listen, Ada –' Terry lowered his voice – 'there's another little job we got down 'ere. Remember?'

She was silent.

'Ada –'

'I know. But we're stuck in this bleedin' lift.'

'Tell me where it is.'

'No chance.'

'Trust me – and I'll get it.'

'Ain't they gettin' this bleedin' lift down?'

'They're working on it. I said – the sands of time are runnin' out.'

Again she was silent.

'Ada –' Terry hissed desperately.

'All right – I'm thinkin'.'

'You can trust me.'

'As far as I can throw you.'

'I'll get it and come straight back.'

'What about the Baggarts?'

'I can handle 'em.'

'Yeah? You take Lennie.'

'No.'

'Why not?' She was becoming aggressive.

'Because the Baggarts will follow, bound to.'

'So –'

'I'll take the vicar,' said Terry. 'Discreetly.'

'A discreet vicar,' she mumbled.

'Now trust me.'

'Well –'

'Come *on!*'

'All right.' She suddenly gave in. 'But if you let me down –'

'I won't.'

There was more snoring from Arthur and his voice suddenly burst into drunken song. 'Only a rose – I love you . . .'

'Shut up, Arthur,' said Terry.

'Wassat?'

'Keep him quiet, Ada.'

'Shut up, Arthur.'

But Arthur was recovering consciousness. 'Don't I hear Terry's voice – or is it all a dream?'

'Arthur,' hissed Terry, his arms aching desperately. 'Please.'

'I can't see you.'

'I'm below you.'

'Have I ascended into heaven?'

'You're stuck in a lift. Now shut up – if you wanna see your percentage today.'

The magic words worked and Arthur was silent.

'Now Ada –'

'I don't know if –'

Terry cursed Ada. 'Look, I can't hang on here much longer.'

'Listen,' she relented. 'I'll 'ave to trust you. But you take that vicar with you. With him around, the Baggarts can't do much – and you can't do much either.'

'He's an inhibiting influence,' hiccoughed Arthur.

'Where do we go?'

'Turn right out of here – and go down to the Pavilion Amusement Arcade. Ask for Barney.'

'Barney who?'

'Barney'll do.'

'S'pose he's not there?'

'He's always there.'

'Okay.'

'And come back, mind.'

'I'll be back.'

'Cos if you don't – my Lennie'll chase you to the ends of the earth.'

'Yes, Ada,' said Terry, beginning to climb down. Then a peremptory voice intoned.

'Terence.'

'Arthur?'

'How much longer we gonna be up here?'

'They're working on it.'

'How long?' His voice was insistent.

'I don't know, Arthur,' grated Terry. 'I've told you – they're workin' on it.'

'I tell you – I can't take much more of this.'

'I'd've thought you'd taken enough already.'

★ ★ ★

When Terry rejoined the crowd downstairs, Lennie spoke – slowly as if he was not used to it.

'How's Mum?'

'Bearing up very well.' Terry turned to the vicar. 'Er –' Suddenly all his loquacity deserted him as he looked into the suspicious and menacing eyes of all the Baggarts. 'The old lady wants a word with you. She's in need of comfort.'

'She don't like priests,' said Lennie.

'Needs must,' replied Terry, pushing the vicar into the lift shaft.

'Shh!'

'I beg –'

'Whisper.'

'Of course,' said the vicar, puzzled but willing.

'Don't try to go up any higher – the ladder's broken.'

'I see.' The vicar hugged the wooden supports, staring up at the creaking lift. 'I don't think I can communicate from here.'

'I don't want you to.'

'Then –'

'Look, I need your help.'

'Here?'

'Outside. For the old lady's sake.'

'Why are we talking about it here?' The vicar's voice was suddenly high and querulous. He had had enough.

'Because she's in danger.'

'Danger?'

'Them Baggarts.' Terry suddenly had a brainwave. 'They want to humiliate her.'

'Oh?'

'Yes. Years ago she had an affair – whilst she was married – with this bloke who ran an amusement arcade.'

'Oh dear.'

'And the Baggarts found out. Now they're trying to blackmail her.'

'How very wicked.'

'Well – that's why they're hanging around her all the time.'

'She has a loyal and loving son.'

'Sure. But he can't do much, can he?'

'And you?'

'Well – luckily, her . . . her lover –'

The vicar winced.

'Well – he has agreed to give her back all her letters – before them Baggarts can get 'em – hang on to 'em. Then she'll be able to burn the lot – and not have to put up with all this hassle.'

'And where do I come in?'

'I want you to escort me down to the hand-over.'

'In what capacity?'

'As a man of the cloth – to see fair play.'

'I see.'

'Will you do it, vicar? For an old lady who's sinned?'

'I don't –'

'She only has a few years to go. Surely she ought to be allowed to live them out with peace of mind?'

'Very well.' The vicar made a sudden decision. 'I'll assist.'

'Good – but we must get away without getting the Baggarts on the trail.'

'Of course.'

'I mean, it wouldn't be good if those letters got into their hands.'

'No.'

'Because that's what they want.'

'Quite.' The vicar was definitely partisan now. 'Her wild oats are very much a thing of the past.'

'In her twilight years . . .' Terry suddenly realised how much like Arthur he sounded and he pulled himself together abruptly. 'Now listen – you go and have a pee.'

'I beg your –'

'You go to the toilet – and then walk quickly out the back of the hotel and go round to the car park. You'll see the sign.'

'And then –'
'I'll meet you there.'
'Mr McCann.'
'Yeah?'
'Are you certain this is all quite legal?'
'Absolutely, vicar. I wouldn't involve you if there was anything dodgy. It's the old girl – lady – I'm concerned for.'
'And you're right, Mr McCann.'
'Do call me Terry.'
'Terry. And now –'
'Yeah?'
'Do you think we could get down? I'm dizzy.'

'What's goin' on down there, Ada?' asked Arthur, staggering to his feet.
'What yer mean?'
'I heard voices. I thought I heard the vicar.'
'Where do you think you are? At your own bleedin' funeral?'
Arthur ignored her. He had a blinding headache and there was a nasty sour taste in his mouth. The empty gin bottle lay discarded on the floor.
'So you finally put your trust in my man.'
'Against my judgement.'
'He'll see you through.'
'He'd better.'
'Perhaps a raising of the percentage for the trouble caused.'
'Not a chance.'
'You're a hard woman, Ada,' said Arthur, sitting down on the floor again.

Terry and the vicar made their escape from the hotel safely – the vicar from the loo and Terry from a conveniently placed open window. As they hurried down the promenade the vicar said, 'I feel quite clandestine.'
'Eh?'

'Never mind.' Suddenly the vicar seemed exhausted. 'Dear me – it's been such a busy day.' He looked at his watch. 'And it's not over yet,' he said hollowly. 'Are we expecting pursuit?' he added nervously, noticing that Terry kept looking over his shoulder.

'Maybe. Any good at legging it, vicar?'

'Well, I was in the penthathlon –'

'What?'

'At theological college,' the vicar added proudly. 'But that was a few years ago now. Still, as you say –' he gave a little laugh – 'I think I can still leg it.'

'Here we are.'

The Pavilion Amusement Arcade was crowded with space invader and fruit machine players. As Terry and the vicar entered, the noise volume increased.

'Okay,' said Terry. 'Let's head for the admin.'

They hurried towards a small sign marked OFFICE and knocked on the door.

'Yeah?' A pimply girl opened it.

'Barney here?'

'Barney who?'

'It's Barney I want.'

'There's no Barney here.'

Terry's heart sank. 'There must be – friend of Ada Croxton.'

She turned to someone else in the dim space. 'You ever heard of a Barney?' she asked.

'Barney who?'

Terry turned to the vicar. 'We've been done,' he said.

The vicar stared back at him uncomprehendingly. 'I don't understand,' he said.

'I do,' said Terry. 'Ada's buying time.'

'Oh!' The vicar blinked as they walked out into the watery sunlight.

'Blimey,' said Terry. Three of the Baggarts stood, massive arms folded, at the entrance to the amusement arcade. On the opposite pavement, leaning against a lamp post, was Lennie.

'Gentlemen,' said the vicar, 'I feel I must –'

'Wait,' said Terry. 'We could have trouble.'

'Trouble?'

'You got it,' said Jim Baggart. 'Hand it over.'

'There was no Barney,' said the vicar.

'There'll be plenty of barney,' said Joe Baggart.

Lennie crossed the road to join them. 'Hand it over,' he said to Terry.

'Piss off!' commented Jim.

Lennie turned to him. 'Don't you tell me to piss off.'

'Gentlemen,' said the vicar, 'I really deplore –'

'Piss off,' Lennie told him, advancing on Terry.

'Hang on!'

'Eh?'

'I *said* hang on.' Terry was looking around him. 'Where's Arnie?'

'He didn't come with us. Wanted to keep an eye on Ada.'

'You mean she's out of the lift?'

'Yeah – they got her down.'

'Where's she gone?'

'That's the point. She went toddling off to the ladies. So Arnie followed her.'

'Into the ladies?' asked the vicar, horrified. He was ignored.

'Wait a minute,' said Terry. 'Just wait a minute.'

'What's up?' asked Lennie suspiciously.

'We've been done. We've all been done.'

The party ran back to the hotel, the elderly Baggart assisted by the two younger ones and the vicar showing a graceful athleticism. When they arrived, they were greeted on the steps by a doleful Arthur.

'We've been done.' He looked terrible.

'Where are they?' asked Terry.

'Gone away – and I'd be very surprised if they ever come back.'

'They was in it together,' said Jim. 'In it bloody together.'

Just then a taxi swept up to the hotel and slowed down momentarily. Ada's head emerged from the window and inside they could see Arnie Baggart. Ada waved a bundle of fivers at them.

'Dad,' howled Jim. 'Dad – what are yer doin'?'

But he didn't reply and only Ada remained at the window.

'Ada –' howled Arthur. 'Where you going?'

'To Gatwick,' she said.

'Gatwick?' Arthur was almost apopletic.

'And on to Monte Carlo!'

'How wonderful,' said the vicar in total bewilderment. 'A real spree.'

'Mum!' yelled Lennie. 'Take me with you.'

'Take a wash,' was all she said. 'And a shave. I'll see you when the money runs out.'

'But Ada –' Arthur's voice was strangled – 'where was it?'

'In a safe place.' She cackled with laughter, knocked on the partition – and the taxi drove away.

'As bold as brass,' muttered Arthur. 'As bold as bleedin' brass.'

'Never mind,' said the vicar. 'We'll all have a good old sing-song on the way home.'

A top secret SBS mission during the Falklands
War soars into explosive action . . .

SPECIAL DELIVERANCE

ALEXANDER FULLERTON

In the war-torn, storm-swept South Atlantic, a small band of
highly-trained SBS experts embark on a vital secret mission: to
sabotage Argentina's stock of deadly Exocet missiles.

The dangers are unthinkable: the coastline is exposed and treacherous,
the missile base is surrounded by vast tracts of open land, they must
infiltrate and destroy without ever being detected. Some say it's
impossible . . . but no one underestimates the SBS's lethal capacity.

And one man, Andy MacEwan, an Anglo-Argentine civilian recruited to
the team as guide and interpreter, has more than the success of the
mission on his mind. His brother is a commander in the Argentine Navy
Air Force and there is no love lost between them . . .

*'Good rollicking stuff – full of tension and highly authentic on SBS
technique'*
TODAY

'The action passages are superb. He is in a class of his own'
OBSERVER

0 7221 3719 2   ADVENTURE THRILLER   £2.99

SAM LLEWELLYN

DEAD RECKONING

Picturesque Pulteney, a charming fishing village and a yachting haven for the wealthy on the south coast, is home to whizz-kid boat designer Charlie Agutter. But beneath the gleaming hulls lurks deadly treachery. For someone is out to get Charlie. Someone who doesn't care who else gets hurt in the process. Charlie's brother is dead – and everyone is blaming Charlie, designer of the revolutionary new yacht that killed him. Charlie knew it had to be sabotage.

It looks like a personal vendetta. But with the Captain's Cup approaching fast, and serious money at stake, something more sinister is bringing the surf to the boil. Charlie will have to move swiftly if he is going to save his career and still win the race . . .

'The Dick Francis of ocean racing' *Sunday Express*

0 7474 0086 5   ADVENTURE THRILLER   £2.99

ROUGH CUT

GORDON McGILL

The perfect script for blackmail and revenge . . .

John Brodie's agent just loves his new filmscript. His bank manager loves the six-figure fee. Film star Henry Harper loves his new leading role. Brodie's beginning to hate the whole thing . . .

There's his mysterious backer – Vietnamese millionaire Han Lo Phu. There's Han's new screen goddess, Marie – the 'successful model' no-one's ever seen. And then there's the question of Harper's past, and the secret that haunted his old Vietnam buddy.

Caught up in a web of blackmail and violence, Brodie finds himself acting out a plot that's crazier than anything he's ever written. Crazier – and deadlier . . .

0 7221 5880 7   ADVENTURE THRILLER   £2.99

SPECIAL DYNAMIC
Alexander Fullerton

ON THE RUN FROM THE SOVIETS
IN A DEADLY ARCTIC WILDERNESS . . .

Former SBS Captain Ollie Lyle is assigned to a
civilian expedition into Norwegian Lapland.
A nationalist movement has sprung up among the
Lapps, and their actions have seemingly escalated
into terrorism and murder.

As Lyle and his expedition penetrate further into
the icy interior, they discover the terrible truth
behind the killings: a vicious Russian undercover
operation serving as a prelude to a full-scale
invasion of Lapland.

What began as a peaceful, fact-finding mission is
now a deadly struggle against two implacable
enemies: the brutal, highly-trained Soviet guerilla
force, and the pitiless Arctic winter. Hampered by
his inexperienced companions, Lyle must use all his
combat and survival skills to stand any chance of
coming out alive . . .

0 7474 0087 3   WAR/FICTION   £3.50

RICHARD HUGO

FAREWELL TO★RUSSIA

Running desperately. Shouting breathlessly. His voice screaming itself to soundlessness for want of air: 'Get away from here! Get away from the water!'

The unthinkable has happened at the Soviet nuclear plant at Sokolskoye. An accident of such catastrophic ecological and political consequence that a curtain of silence is drawn ominously over the incident. Major Pyotr Kirov of the KGB is appointed to extract the truth from the treacherous minefield of misinformation and intrigue and to obtain from the West the technology essential to prevent further damage. But the vital equipment is under strict trade embargo . . .

And in London, George Twist, head of a company which manufactures the technology, is on the verge of bankruptcy and desperate to win the illegal contract. Can he deliver on time? Will he survive a frantic smuggling operation across the frozen wastes of Finland? Can he wrongfoot the authorities . . . and his own conscience?

'Immensely well-researched . . . growls with suspense . . . even without the recent memories of Chernobyl the novel has an authentic ring'
Independent

'Diverse loyalties are suspensefully stretched and nerve ends twanged'
Guardian

0 7474 0061 X   THRILLER   £3.50

A selection of bestsellers from SPHERE

FICTION

KALEIDOSCOPE	Danielle Steel	£3.50 ☐
AMTRAK WARS VOL. 4	Patrick Tilley	£3.50 ☐
TO SAIL BEYOND THE SUNSET	Robert A. Heinlein	£3.50 ☐
JUBILEE: THE POPPY CHRONICLES 1	Claire Rayner	£3.50 ☐
DAUGHTERS	Suzanne Goodwin	£3.50 ☐

FILM AND TV TIE-IN

WILLOW	Wayland Drew	£2.99 ☐
BUSTER	Colin Shindler	£2.99 ☐
COMING TOGETHER	Alexandra Hine	£2.99 ☐
RUN FOR YOUR LIFE	Stuart Collins	£2.99 ☐
BLACK FOREST CLINIC	Peter Heim	£2.99 ☐

NON-FICTION

MONTY: THE MAN BEHIND THE LEGEND	Nigel Hamilton	£3.99 ☐
BURTON: MY BROTHER	Graham Jenkins	£3.50 ☐
BARE-FACED MESSIAH	Russell Miller	£3.99 ☐
THE COCHIN CONNECTION	Alison and Brian Milgate	£3.50 ☐
HOWARD & MASCHLER ON FOOD	Elizabeth Jane Howard and Fay Maschler	£3.99 ☐

All Sphere books are available at your local bookshop or newsagent, or can be ordered direct from the publisher. Just tick the titles you want and fill in the form below.

Name _____

Address _____

_____

Write to Sphere Books, Cash Sales Department, P.O. Box 11, Falmouth, Cornwall TR10 9EN

Please enclose a cheque or postal order to the value of the cover price plus:

UK: 60p for the first book, 25p for the second book and 15p for each additional book ordered to a maximum charge of £1.90.

OVERSEAS & EIRE: £1.25 for the first book, 75p for the second book and 28p for each subsequent title ordered.

BFPO: 60p for the first book, 25p for the second book plus 15p per copy for the next 7 books, thereafter 9p per book.

Sphere Books reserve the right to show new retail prices on covers which may differ from those previously advertised in the text elsewhere, and to increase postal rates in accordance with the P.O.